Diogo's Chronicle
Siam in crisis, from Ayutthaya to Thonburi to Bangkok

Diogo's Chronicle
Siam in crisis, from Ayutthaya
to Thonburi to Bangkok

Edward Van Roy

The contents, views and opinions expressed
in this book are those of Edward Van Roy.

First published and distributed in 2025 by
River Books Press Co., Ltd
396/1 Maharaj Road, Phraborommaharajawang,
Bangkok 10200 Thailand
Tel: (66) 2 225-0139, 2 225-9574
Email: order@riverbooksbk.com
www.riverbooksbk.com

 Riverbooksbk riverbooksbk @riverbooks

Copyright collective work © River Books, 2025
Copyright Text, maps and photographs © Edward Van Roy 2025
except where otherwise indicated.

ภาพประกอบในหน้า 115 และ 233 มาจากหนังสือ
"สมเด็จพระเจ้าตากสินมหาราช ฉบับเยาวชน" หน้า 6 และหน้า 58 ตามลำดับ
เป็นผลงานของ นายวิริยะ ชอบกตัญญ ตำแหน่งจิตรกรปฏิบัติการ สำนักช่างสิบหมู่ กรมศิลปากร
สำนักพิมพ์ริเวอร์ บุ๊คส์ นำมาทำซ้ำโดยได้รับอนุญาตจากกรมศิลปากร

All rights reserved. No part of this book may be reproduced or
transmitted in any form or by any means, electronic or
including photocopy, recording or any other information
storage and retrieval system, without prior permission
in writing from the publisher.

Editor: Narisa Chakrabongse
Production supervision: Suparat Sudcharoen
Design: River Books

ISBN 978 616 451 104 0

Publisher: River Books Press Ltd., Bangkok, Thailand
EU Authorised Representative: Easy Access System Europe Oü,
16879218 - Mustamäe tee 50, 10621 Tallinn, Estonia,
gpsr.requests@easproject.com

Printed and bound in Thailand by Parbpim Co., Ltd

Contents

Editor's Preface	7
Translators' Prologue	9
Provenance / Translation / Reunion	
Diogo's Testament	29
Ayutthaya / Macau / Santa Cruz / Rosario / Sampheng	
The Diogo Chronicle	53
1. Death of a Dynasty	59
Treachery / Abdication / Deliverance / Catastrophe	
2. Burmese Ramayana	85
Invasion / Siege / Defeat / Captivity	
3. Upstart Regime	111
Comrades / Elites / Reconstruction / Reintegration	
4. Royal Scoundrels	139
Pretensions / Conspiracies / Exile / Requital	
5. Warlords of the South Seas	167
Conquest / Détente / Asylum / Retribution	
6. Turning Point	189
Subterfuge / Invasion / Gauntlet / Breakout	
7. Reign Change	215
Distractions / Disorder / Coup / Countercoup	
Translators' Epilogue	249
Postscript / Coda	
Endnotes	261
Bibliography	279
List of Maps and Tables	285
Acknowledgements	286

So very difficult a matter it is to trace and find out the truth of anything in history, when, on the one hand, those who afterwards write it find long periods of time intercepting their view, and, on the other hand, the contemporary records of any actions and lives, partly through envy and ill-will, partly through favor and flattery, pervert and distort truth.

Plutarch (c.110 A.D.)

He that undertaketh the story of a time, especially at any length, cannot but meet with many blanks and spaces which he must be forced to fill up out of his own wit and conjecture.

Francis Bacon (1605)

History is that certainty produced at the point where the imperfections of memory meet the inadequacies of documentation.

Julian Barnes (2011)

Preface

Every so often a long-lost manuscript is retrieved from the dusty shelves of some obscure archive to challenge our collective memory of former times, far-off places, exotic peoples. Such a find, a controversial chronicle that brings to life a pivotal moment in Siam's tumultuous history, forms the centerpiece of this book. It presents an apocryphal account penned by a Portuguese scribe, Diogo d'Almeida, serving at the court of Siam during a time of turmoil, that describes in classic terms the kingdom's tortious eighteenth-century metamorphosis from Ayutthaya to Thonburi to Bangkok. Accompanying his chronicle of rapid reshaping under a succession of dynasties, Diogo penned a brief autobiographical account elaborating on his personal observations as an obscure eyewitness to events at the court of Siam. His intent was to recount for future generations the causes and consequences of his troubled time as precisely as his trained mind would permit. The telling constitutes a tale within a tale within a tale.

The Translators' Prologue and Epilogue stand as a pair of bookmarks framing Diogo's historical narrative. The Prologue introduces Claude Williams and Cláudio da Ceira, the paired discoverers and translators of Diogo's long-lost reign chronicle and accompanying biographical testament. Their tale centers on their international search for those rumored eighteenth-century manuscripts and then, having discovered them in Lisbon, their struggle toward the transformation of Diogo's arcane Portuguese writings into an English rendering readily accessible to the modern reader. The Epilogue presents the translators' brief postscript to the events narrated in Diogo's Chronicle, plus an editorial coda referring to their tragically aborted holiday to Lisbon in celebration of the completion of their quest.

Diogo's Testament provides a short autobiography of the Chronicle's author, Diogo d'Almeida. It relates the main phases of his life, from his difficult childhood in Ayutthaya's Portuguese community to the buoyant years of his education in Macau, his joyous return to Thonburi and appointment as a court scribe, followed by his internal exile under suspicion of disloyalty, his new career as a Chinese trader's comprador, and subsequent events that drove him to write his dissident Chronicle. Diogo wrote his Testament on his deathbed as a brief dénouement, explaining why he had come to write his iconoclastic annals of the times. Although prepared near the very end of his life, Diogo's Testament forms a useful overture to the Chronicle that he had only recently completed and is therefore presented here as an introduction to the Chronicle itself.

Diogo's Chronicle charts the course of the half-century of turmoil that dominated Siam's transition from the decline and fall of its ancient capital, Ayutthaya, through the rise of Thonburi, to the emergence of Bangkok as the kingdom's new metropole. Its seven chapters narrate, in a sequence of dramatic episodes, the political discord that culminated in the collapse of Ayutthaya's last dynasty, the events of the catastrophic Burmese conquest of 1767, the kingdom's meteoric revival at Thonburi, the machinations and ruination of a dissident prince, the conquest of a rival maritime power, the struggle to withstand a renewed Burmese invasion, and finally the factional strife that led to Thonburi's transition to Bangkok in 1782. Diogo's stirring contemporary account of those times and their main protagonists humanizes this extended drama. It fills in many gaps in the conventional record, while it contests a number of commonly held opinions and beliefs about that pivotal moment in Siamese history.

As honorary editor of this book, unexpectedly and perhaps injudiciously appointed to that role by the discoverers and translators of Diogo's long-lost writings, permit me to enter a few preliminary words concerning that duo of remarkable literary conservators. Claude Williams and Cláudio da Ceira dedicated a decade of their lives to unearthing Diogo d'Almeida's centuries-old Chronicle and Testament and then translating those abstruse manuscripts into a fluid modern narrative. Having completed their task, they embarked on a celebratory holiday to Portugal. There, on September 19, 2019, they died in a tragic fall from the fabled clifftop Moorish castle overlooking Sintra while on an excursion to that scenic seaside city. Their funeral took place there a week later, and their remains were interred in a quiet church cemetery, attended by their grieving Lisbon friends João Ferreiro and Leticia Carvalho de Fomoso, and myself.

Claude and Cláudio were delightful companions, genial hosts, marvelous raconteurs, trusted confidantes, and generous benefactors. Bangkok was their beloved home, and they became a vibrant part of the local community in return. Their passion for Thai history piqued my own, and over the years we met frequently to discuss the progress of their research, their remarkable discovery of the Diogo manuscripts, and their efforts to transform those archaic Portuguese writings into a readable English text. I assisted them in preparing the footnotes and was privileged to be allowed to compose an introductory section for each of the Chronicle's seven chapters. We celebrated together the completion of their epic project only weeks before their untimely deaths.

It was with consternation that I learned that their last will and testament, which they had prepared years before, bequeathed to me their entire library, including their written work. That final evidence of their affection has fortified my determination to see their remarkable, years-long project through to its successful conclusion. My posthumous contribution to the final product, beyond a bit of straightforward copy-editing, have been limited to the addition of various chapter introductions, maps, tables, figures, and footnotes that help illuminate the complex tale.

Translators' Prologue

Let us be candid. As the translators of the ancient writings that comprise the bulk of this book, our role has been peripheral. The work that stands before you was written by another – Diogo d'Almeida, a proud member of Siam's small Portuguese community and first-hand observer of the half-century of unprecedented dynastic discord, recurrent warfare, and repeated insurrection that saw the end of the Ayutthaya era and the rise of another that set the course of Thai history to the present. At great personal peril, Diogo set himself the task of recording a candid account of the events of those decades with no purpose but to set the fragmented record straight. For fear of reprisal, he hid his writings. They have remained missing for more than two centuries. Simple curiosity, progressing over time to outright compulsion, has driven our yearslong quest to raise Diogo's long-forgotten texts from their anonymous crypt for presentation to a modern audience. As one must start somewhere, let us explain briefly, in this prologue, the course of our journey.

Provenance
Bangkok

We two, the partnered translators of this book, bear the improbably paired names of Claude and Cláudio. That curious coincidence fated our meeting over four decades ago in an "introductory Thai conversation" class at Bangkok's venerable AUA Language Institute, a school devoted mainly to teaching Thai students passable English but also providing a wonderful opportunity for a small coterie of Western newcomers to this Land of Smiles to gain a firm footing in Thai language and culture. It was Cláudio's patient guidance in helping me master the intricacies of the Thai language that touched off our lasting bond as we struggled through those thrice-weekly classroom/coffee-break encounters. Now, years later, in his typically self-effacing manner of leading from behind, Cláudio has insisted that I write this introduction on our joint behalf, though the main product, translated from his native Portuguese, is primarily his doing.

My youth had been shaped long before in a far-away world, a victim of mid-America's narrow-minded smalltown provincialism, followed by escape into a prosaic college education, several fumblingly illicit affairs, and dim prospects. The unremitting melancholy of those early years came to an abrupt end with army induction. Most of my two-year service was spent dodging death in Vietnam, interrupted only by several scintillating Saigon and Bangkok R&R (rest and recuperation) interludes. That tempestuous military experience opened my eyes to the realities of the wider world, and not long after returning to my claustrophobic roots, I fled my past's unwelcome resumption in desperation for the promise of the Orient's more tolerant lifestyle. My impulsive acquisition of the necessary visa, smallpox/cholera/yellow fever shots, and 'round-the-world Pan Am ticket (return leg undated) were paid out of my paltry military savings bolstered by the resale proceeds from my treasured Mustang coupe, leaving me a virtual pauper. Shouldering my old army duffel bag, I departed amid a flurry of bewildered goodbyes in utter disregard of the fervent protestations of family and friends. Not a day has passed since that cathartic moment without self-congratulatory reflection on my life-changing decision.

Arriving at Bangkok with barely a penny in my pocket, I managed to find ready employment at one of the city's several schools advertising the teaching of English as a second language. Despite my weak credentials, the school took me on in an era when few Americans were ready to abandon the comforts of home for the wilds of the Far East. I was hired initially on an adjunct basis under the headmaster's personal coaching and then, once I had managed to obtain my TOEFL certificate, was awarded full-time teaching status. The offer of a living wage and a manageable teaching schedule was accompanied by a work visa, while the bonus of an afterschool Thai-language course filled much of the remainder of my weekday life. A convenient rental apartment provided for my personal needs and left me free to complement many of my prosaic daily classroom rounds with late-night wanderings among the city's louche watering holes. Through the ensuing years a steady stream of adolescents struggled through their curriculum under my pedestrian tutelage. Their parents treated me with unexpected gratitude for guiding their offspring through puberty and even offered me a modicum of respect for weaning them through those unpromising years toward an independent future. It was a gratifying sequel to my dismal past.

Cláudio arrived at Bangkok several years after I did, as a junior officer in the Portuguese foreign service. The pampered youngest son of a pedigreed landowning family, he had sailed through school and university as a stellar student but found his conservative social life increasingly oppressive. Appointment to the Ministry of Foreign Affairs was his salvation, and further good fortune found him an early opening in Thailand. The Portuguese foreign service was unusual in its resistance to the modern convention that overseas postings rotate among different assignments every few years. Thailand beckoned as a possible lifetime tour of duty, and for Cláudio that was a godsend. At his Bangkok Embassy post his polyglot talents came under constant demand; the addition of Thai language facility became a professional essential. Leading me by the hand as he effortlessly navigated our AUA (American Alumni Association) Thai-language curriculum, he added Thai to his already impressive linguistic résumé with panache while I puttered through by the skin of my teeth. With our Bangkok tenure assured, we agreed to pair up. The deal was sealed with our shared rental and reconditioning of a vintage canalside house, which we furnished in style, dividing our chores between his cooking and my gardening. The additions of a housekeeper and a secondhand towncar set us up in posh postcolonial style. That comfortable arrangement set the stage for further shared adventures, particularly the exploration of Bangkok's endless byways and then, with increasing frequency, points beyond.

After more than three idyllic decades of that shared expat lifestyle, tucked away along a quiet back lane amid the rising cacophony of Bangkok's frenzied modernization, we approached retirement age. Our combined pensions plus accumulated savings allowed us to adjust and enjoy a more relaxed pace of life while we searched for renewed purpose to our affairs. A welcome opportunity emerged with the runup to the 500th anniversary of the Portuguese presence in Siam. Cláudio was requested to represent the Embassy in discussions at the Thai Foreign Ministry on the planning for the commemorative festivities, and I was dragged along as a contributing "expert." The result was the preparation of an elaborate agenda of VIP invitations, flamboyant local celebrations, plus an international conference on the centuries-old Thai-Portuguese relationship. As adjunct members of the organizing committee we participated in the hosting responsibilities of guiding the crowd of visiting attendees through the maze of receptions, dinners, seminars, and excursions. Cláudio's natural affinity with the bevy of Portuguese-speaking guests gained him a new circle of friends with whom we spent much time in animated conversation. Though I could not follow much of the talk, I learned later that many of those guests shared with him their sense of bewilderment over the remarkable proliferation of random, often-conflicting facts and opinions on Thailand's historical Portuguese associations. Clearly, limitless blanks remained in our knowledge of the local past. We were glad to discover that we were not alone in that impression.

During one of those rambling cocktail-hour conversations, one of our conference intimates, Alvaro Montoya, from the University of Macau, recalled in passing having been told of a manuscript thought to have been composed in Siam around the start of the nineteenth century. It had apparently been part of a hoard of artifacts recovered from the recently excavated crypts under the ruins of Macao's former St. Paul's Cathedral and had presumably been transferred to the Macau Archives along with the rest of that storied trove. Our interest was piqued, and we followed up with him. He explained that he had heard nothing further of that find but cordially invited us to visit him in Macau and search it out. The invitation offered us a fine excuse for a carefree overseas vacation. Furthermore, the thought that such a find might form a real contribution to the collected lore on Thai-Portuguese relations excited our imagination. We wrote Alvaro, received his enthusiastic response, and a month later set off on a junket to that venerable Portuguese trading post turned modern gambling mecca. Our two-and-a-half-hour flight was spent in meandering dialogue imagining that our commuter run would several centuries ago have required a month-long perilous sea passage, contingent on heavy weather, pirate encounters, and frequent port layovers, and with the return voyage being necessarily delayed for many months pending the turn of the monsoon, allowing only one round-trip per year. Yet, with the remarkable advances of the intervening centuries, our plane could complete several comfortable round-trip flights per day. Siam's old Portuguese community had certainly been a very isolated cultural outpost in former days.

Macau

Alvaro welcomed us to Macau with open arms. Without his guidance through the local bureaucratic maze, we would surely have failed in our quest, and we expressed our gratitude with deep sincerity. As a first step, he escorted us to the Museum of Macau, built in 1995 in the parkland behind the still-standing hilltop façade of the destroyed St. Paul's Cathedral, overlooking the city center's Santo Antonio neighborhood. Bypassing all the formalities, we were informed by a superintending official that archeological excavations in the fort area behind the cathedral grounds a decade earlier had uncovered a number of old crypts, perhaps the cellars of former clerical residences set atop the breezy hill. The collapsed underground chambers had been found to contain rich stores of church vestments and liturgical paraphernalia, tableware and kitchenware, wine casks and beer kegs, religious images and related artwork, written materials ranging from bibles, hymnals, and collected sermons, to accounting daybooks, portfolios of miscellaneous correspondence, and more. The museum had been built directly over the excavation site, and most of the finds had been conserved either among its display or on storeroom shelves. We scanned the many display cases and found nothing of particular interest beyond the musty aura of antiquity. A young curator allowed us to examine some unexceptional porcelains and statuary shards in the museum's crammed stockrooms. Their catalogue numbers identified them as having been dug up at the St. Paul's site prior to the museum's construction; so something actually had been stumbled on. But what of the literary finds? The museum had no detailed record. The curator suggested that they had likely been moved to the Archives of Macau.

The iconic façade marking the site of St. Paul's Cathedral, Macau. (Wikipedia Commons)

After several days of delay negotiating introductions and arranging appointments, we traipsed over to the Archives' director's office, only to find him absent "on urgent business" and represented by two senior assistants ready to fill the gap. Once the awkward introductions had been concluded, all went smoothly, lubricated by Macau's genteel Iberian etiquette. Yet, all the small talk over the standard offerings of Macanese tea and biscuits got us nowhere. Our inquiries were met with steely smiles covering toothy denials of knowledge of any manuscripts that may have been retrieved from the recent excavation site. Cláudio, with his diplomat's training and experience, later remarked to me that for all their professional gamesmanship those archival guardians could not have been more transparent. That they knew something was beyond doubt. But what they knew, they were not prepared to share with us. We could only guess. Undeterred, we pressed on with our inquiries at another museum affiliate, Macau's Cultural Institute, downtown. There, offered strong coffee instead of tea, we received from an architect attached to the Department of Cultural Heritage the honest information that a sizable cache of documents and charts had been unearthed at the St. Paul's excavation site but that, to the best of her knowledge, no official inventory of the collection had been compiled. She had been informed that the materials were so thoroughly waterlogged and rotted by a century's groundwater

The Macau Historical Archives, along a restored downtown Macau street-front. (Google Images)

immersion as to be entirely illegible. The entire lot had been listed in the archeological report as unsalvageable and had presumably been disposed of. The sum of our inquiries left us with the understanding that the excavations had uncovered a substantial manuscript collection that had never reached the government repositories. Could it be, as is all too common in the world of Oriental antiquities, that they had vanished into the local vintage art market and, ultimately, into the vaults of private collectors? The sum of our inquiries left us with a firm suspicion that that was the case.

Intrigued, we embarked on a further search for the ghost manuscript. Through questions posed on a visit to the genial director of Macau's Ricci Institute – a Jesuit-sponsored and -staffed research institute focusing on Macau issues – we were introduced to a scholar with a thorough understanding of the local antiquarian art market. Through him we learned that rare books and incunabula formed a very thin, secretive slice of the local market, which was said to be more firmly situated in nearby Hong Kong. The high unit value of goods passing through that market made for very profitable opportunities, which also fed the industry's reputation for contraband dealings and explained its notoriety for price gouging, forgery, fakery, and inscrutability. Our informant agreed to assist us in gaining access to the market

Translators' Prologue 13

through correspondence with a Hong Kong arts and antiquities dealer of good standing. Once we had managed to establish our bona fides as prospective buyers, we arranged the two hours' jet-ferry crossing of Pearl River Estuary to his office in Hong Kong's seedy Mong Kok neighborhood. Inside his well-guarded upper-floor inner sanctum, we presented a detailed explanation of what we were searching for, and why. He proclaimed total ignorance of all that we had referred to. More to get rid of us than to enlighten us, it seemed, he suggested that we should contact an antiquarian expert in Lisbon who he claimed would likely know something of such matters and offered us a slip of paper containing that possible informant's name and fax contact number. With that scrap of information, he wished us well in our quest and bade us a breezy farewell. Thus did our Macau-Hong Kong inquiries come to a desultory end. It all made for a flimsy conclusion to a tortuous mission. But it had provided us with a glorious opportunity to see something of Macau and catch a glimpse of Hong Kong beyond the usual tourist haunts, and an enjoyable couple of evenings at the Lisboa Casino to enrich our stay.

Lisbon

The particulars we had received were those of a Lisbon-based specialist in Portuguese empire memorabilia named João Ferreiro, a tradesman said to be of fine reputation but a most reclusive, cantankerous fellow. Indeed, our repeated efforts to open a dialogue with Ferreiro by fax, the only contact information we had received, proved fruitless. Now preoccupied with the challenge of the chase, and with no other option left open, we decided to meet the issue head-on by stretching our vacation budget and casino winnings to book direct passage to Lisbon, a city familiar to Cláudio from his student days, and which he was eager to introduce to me. Through Alvaro's unremitting assistance we were put in touch with a former student of his, Leticia Carvalho de Fomoso, a linguistics instructor at the University of Lisbon's Faculty of Arts and Letters. She agreed to meet us on arrival. Our introductory discussion with her, directly upon disembarkation at Lisbon's Portelo Airport, proved her to be a person of sharp intellect, unaffected vivacity, and voluptuous proportions. We soon learned that her university's wretched pay scale had left her no option but to accept our modest proposal for her services as our assistant in seeking an interview with Ferreiro and working with us on further research possibilities. She quickly grasped the nature of our quest and the demands it might impose on her time but insisted, if she were to join us, that her title be raised from "assistant" to "associate," along with a commensurate adjustment to her wage scale. We agreed, and her professional abilities, it turned out, fully justified those conditions. She became an indispensable colleague in our quest.

Cláudio had reserved for us a comfortable stay at his well-heeled family's currently vacant Chiado District pied-à-terre. Having left Leticia with her first assignment, we set out with her early the next morning, with guarded expectations, on our Lisbon quest. Leticia led the way on a cross-town tram bound for the Alfama District. Nestled in a nook of alleyways within the neighborhood's labyrinth of cobbled, steep-stepped hillside lanes, Ferreiro's lair proved to be a well-worn but respectable four-story inner-city townhouse. Repeated tugs on the doorbell roused an aged, broad-beamed charwoman who, after a protracted exchange with Leticia in the local patois, ushered us grudgingly into Ferreiro's presence. We entered a large, windowless study lined with disorderly shelves of stacked tomes and incunabula, rolled charts and painted canvasses, and bulging portfolios of manuscripts and illustrated matter, with every spare centimeter of the remaining floorspace littered with a profusion of cabinets, tables, and stands crowded with vintage artifacts. In the midst of that confusion an odd figure, gangly, sallow, unshaven, straggle-haired, dressed in an oversized red-velvet robe entirely inappropriate to the overheated room's tobacco haze, sat hunched on a raised swivel stool peering down through an antique magnifying glass that slid slowly across what appeared to be a creased, faded palimpsest spread across his cluttered desk.

View of the Tagus River from Lisbon's Chiado hills, painted by Carlos Botelho, 1935. (Museu de Chiado, Lisbon)

João Ferreiro's Alfama neighborhood, Lisbon. (Editor's photo)

Airing his resentment at having been so abruptly interrupted in his studies, he sullenly identified himself and asked our business. We introduced ourselves as vintage book dealers recommended to him by our Hong Kong contact. To our reminder of our previous unanswered fax messages he offered no response. Ignoring his opening discourtesies, we carried on as best we could with a stilted description of our interest in acquiring a rumored Portuguese manuscript describing late eighteenth-century Siam. His sneaking suspicion that we were not quite what we claimed was confirmed the instant he saw our startled reaction to his mention of the exorbitant price that such incunabula would carry. Shocked into realization of our awkward position, we relented, with Cláudio apologetically backtracking with the explanation that as mere amateur historians our primary purpose in visiting him was simply to confirm or put to rest the street-talk of his knowledge of a mysterious Ayutthaya-era chronicle. If the rumor proved true, we hoped to be allowed to examine the text for its content. Actual purchase was a secondary consideration that could be discussed once authenticity had been established.

Through all that, we noticed Ferreiro's shy glances at Leticia, waiting for a chance to seek some explanation of her connection with these strangers' inquiries. When the question was finally raised, she explained our association in her charming way, which seemed to satisfy him. With that delicate point settled, he deliberated for several moments and then, on our sworn promise of utmost discretion, admitted that he possessed, as part of a larger consignment of goods that had never been thoroughly vetted, an item that might be the one we were seeking. A further hour of bantering, with Leticia at center-stage as a skilled interlocutor, managed to broach his reserve. He finally deigned to separate himself from his work and descend from his stool in search of the phantom manuscript.

As he uncoiled his stooped frame to upright stance, he revealed himself to be a man of far more appealing mien than our initial impression had made out – a lanky, goateed figure of no more than 50 years of age who belied his crotchety temperament, secluded lifestyle, and shady profession with noble Iberian bearing. His brisk return ten minutes later bearing a weighty canvas-covered packet showing the scars of time offered a first glimpse of our hard-sought prize. Taking great care and much time in unwrapping the bundle, he allowed us a supervised viewing of its contents, the suspect document, on several firm conditions: that we have no physical contact with it while he turned the pages himself with gloved hands, that we take no photographs, that we limit our inspection to an hour, and that we consider our viewing strictly confidential. (The cascade of subsequent events has surely freed us from that last stricture.) He refused adamantly to reveal his supplier – a case of honor among thieves? – with the justification that all his transactions were conducted through anonymous mailing addresses and numbered bank accounts.

As neither Cláudio nor I have any expertise in the forensics of antique manuscripts, we can only report in hindsight that the bundle was bound in a pliable oilskin wrapping tied with hempen cord bearing at the knot a red wax seal stamped with an unintelligible signet impress, long broken. Unwrapped, the more than 30-centimeters-thick pack consisted of several hundreds of large parchment-like sheets, each inscribed in India ink in a cramped Portuguese hand. Leticia remarked that the pages displayed what was certainly a centuries-old calligraphy. Ferreiro offered no comment, though he certainly had his own views. If this was indeed the church crypts' rumored documentary lode, the Macau officials' assertions that they had been ruined by generations of waterlogging had been proven a blatant falsehood. Assuming they were authentic, an alternative explanation for their survival was called for. We avoided discussing that issue with our truculent host for fear of being thrown out on our ear.

Closer inspection showed that the pack contained two manuscripts, not one. They were untitled, but Ferreiro leafed through the page with expert fingers to permit Leticia to decipher that the author, identifying himself as Diogo d'Almeida, consistently referred to the larger, multi-fascicle document as a "chronicle" and to its accompanying brief autobiographical sketch as his "testament." We have retained those self-styled titles here. Our second surprise was that the Chronicle dealt not simply with the experience of Siam's Portuguese community at the time of the fall of Ayutthaya – though evidently written by a member of that community – but with a much broader history stretching from late Ayutthaya to early Bangkok. Our mission had suddenly been vindicated, and transformed. We explained the implications of the find to Ferreiro as best we cautiously could, and to his credit (no pun intended) he concurred that he had already recognized its larger scope and potential market value.

On the spur of that portentous moment, with Leticia's smiling assent, Cláudio proposed that we undertake a thorough study of the two documents, at least to clarify their authenticity. I foolishly added that it might be a considerable professional coup for Ferreiro to announce the discovery of this pair of historic documents. He bridled at that, reminding me that ours was a private arrangement, sworn to secrecy. I had evidently trampled on a very sensitive nerve. After further, more relaxed conversation, we opened the door to the possibility that a modern Portuguese typescript of the two documents might greatly enhance their market value. That suggestion caught his attention.

With our visit's stipulated one-hour limit long expired, our rambling conversation gravitated progressively from the excitement of our find to Ferreiro's debt to humanity, to the public's right to know versus the collector's right to privacy, to the personal satisfaction to be derived from a fuller appreciation of his rare possession, and finally to the financial rewards to be reaped from a clear verification of provenance and modern-language clarification of the text. Only during that final phase of our conversation could we discern a glint in his eye.

Further lively conversation led to an understanding that Leticia would be asked to transcribe the entire text into modern Portuguese disentangled from the disintegrating pages, florid calligraphy, and archaisms of the original. To that she voiced no objection so long as she were paid a reasonable fee and permitted to work evenings, leaving her daytime hours free for her teaching and other pursuits. We readily agreed to those particulars, reaching agreement that Leticia and the two of us would spend each weekday evening, 6:00 to 10:00, at Ferreiro's office to deal with the transcription, subject to his supervisory control of the two manuscripts. It was estimated that the entire process would require about eight weeks, the first week for the Testament and the following seven for the Chronicle. Our own commitments would require us to return to Bangkok after the first two weeks, after which Leticia would continue the work with Ferreiro alone. The manuscripts would not leave the office; they would be handled solely by Ferreiro; and photography and photocopying would be prohibited. Each of us would be provided a copy of the final transcripts for further use – for the two of us and Leticia as the basis for further scholarly research, and for Ferreiro as an aid to his personal marketing activities (though we continued to plead for preferred consideration as prospective buyers, while he continued to caution that the cost might well be beyond our means).

The rendering of Diogo's scribbled Testament into a typed facsimile and then a modern Portuguese equivalent took much longer than anticipated, as Leticia ran into many issues along the way requiring, in the first instance, close study of the author's faded handwriting and then, in reworking the typed version, clarification of the idiosyncrasies of eighteenth-century Portuguese vocabulary, colloquialism, and syntax, as well as interpretation of numerous obscure Thai referents. Ferreiro found an unexpected facility in deciphering obsolete Portuguese and took obvious pleasure in assisting Leticia's struggles with modernization, while Cláudio and I contributed our own views wherever Thai terms intruded, setting aside deeper problems for consideration upon our return to Bangkok. After having laboriously completed the transcription of the shorter Testament, Leticia turned to the far more challenging Chronicle. As the work progressed, the questions grew less distracting, and her progress on the latter of the two manuscripts accelerated as a result.

We had planned for a two-week Lisbon stay, with each of our ten weekday evenings set aside as Leticia's chaperones in Ferreiro's stuffy office. Each evening we arrived to the surly reception of his elderly housekeeper and were ushered wordlessly into his sanctuary. At the end of each four-hour stint, we departed for a much-needed meal, let out by Ferreiro himself, who locked up behind us to set the night alarm in protection of his precious stock. During our successive evening sessions, we were not once interrupted by another visitor. Evidently, Ferreiro had no social life; all his business with his secret suppliers and anonymous clients, he told us, was conducted at odd hours via anonymous channels across distant time zones. His only physical contact with the outside world so far as we could make out was the occasional visit of the courier service that transported his merchandise, a daytime intrusion that was never witnessed by us night owls.

Our working arrangement circled Ferreiro's desk. He occupied the stool-shaped throne behind his desk while our chairs faced him obliquely across the littered surface. Leticia was seated at the right-hand corner with enough desk space cleared to suit her typing needs, while the two of us were off to the left, our view neatly obstructed by the backsides of Ferreiro's oversized computer monitor, tower, and printer. Directly across from Ferreiro, separating us from Leticia, stood an ornate plinth supporting a bulky bust of Portugal's renowned eighteenth-century prime minister, the Marqui2s de Pombal; Ferreiro claimed it had originally graced the residence of Goa's governor-general. By our second evening's visit the Pombal bust had been replaced by a more massive marble Ching Dynasty nude stepping out of her robe, a fine Victorian-era example of soft-porn kitsch that Ferreiro insisted had formerly embellished a Macau merchant's mansion. More likely, it had a century ago ignited pipe dreams inside a Cantonese opium den, or the more lurid dreams within a high-class Macau bordello. That awkward change of statuary, it can safely be inferred in hindsight, was intended specifically to isolate the two of us from Ferreiro's interaction with the lovely Leticia.

To each evening's tremor of Leticia's furious typing under that working arrangement, we engaged in casual talk with Ferreiro. Leticia did not mind the distraction; indeed, she asserted that she welcomed it as a balm on her labors to "civilize" Diogo's exposition. Each night we brought along a satchel of good Oportos, always selected with an eye to high alcohol content for shortening the hours while lengthening the conversation. Watching Ferreiro, and ourselves too, slowly unwind as the evening's refreshment took effect was a revelatory experience. Gradually, we came to learn more of one another: my escape from a claustrophobic upbringing, and Cláudio's rather similar experience. Ferreiro's chronic inertia, brought on not only by his father's dominance in directing his upbringing as heir to the family firm but, more tellingly, by fear of the unknowns that escape from his self-imposed imprisonment would call forth. And Leticia's struggles to lift herself above the genteel poverty of her upbringing, followed by her disappointing academic life. So, under the influence of the grape, we grew increasingly convivial.

Alcoholic excess liberated me sufficiently one evening to comment quite rudely on Ferreiro's dusty, smoke-filled, untidy workspace. Wouldn't he find it more comfortable to spend his office hours in a more orderly, cleaner setting? Why hadn't he scolded his irascible housemaid into setting things aright, as was surely within the purview of her duties? He sat for some moments with his mouth agape and then burst into peals of laughter, nearly falling off his stool. It took him minutes to recover his composure. Then he exclaimed, between lingering wine-tinged chuckles, that his "housemaid" was his mother, and that she had never been known to take kindly to a scolding. In response to my red-faced, stuttered attempts at an apology he proved most obliging, sympathizing with my discomfort with a grin and a wink. I need have no concern, he said, as he had dealt his whole life with the harridan who stayed on with him, occupying her own upper story of the townhouse, only because she had been unable to find any better offer. We learned that Ferreiro's father, long departed, had barely put up with her and had willed his entire estate, including the family firm, to his only child as some small recompense for her years of neglectful abuse. Indeed, over the two weeks of our daily visits we never saw her except on arrival, never received a good word from her, nor were we offered so much as a cup of tea in her home. Leticia, in her allusive way, referred to her as a "type." The old lady's unmotherly presence survives in our memory as an added hardship in Ferreiro's cloistered life.

On another of those inebriated evenings Ferreiro told us that he had been poring over Leticia's typescript of Diogo's Testament with great interest as each page rolled off the carriage but had never found the stamina to more than leaf through the Chronicle's complex typescript. Initially we put his disinterest in the Chronicle down to his ignorance of Siamese history and the tedium of Diogo's recondite Portuguese. But why his fascination with the Testament? Only belatedly, after we had ourselves read Diogo's miniature memoir and discovered that he had been burdened with a lifelong disability, did it dawn on us that Ferreiro's reading preferences were intimately personal, providing a rare opportunity for sober reflection on his own failure to end the constraints of his own cloistered upbringing with a courageous leap into the larger world. The historical celebrities portrayed in the Chronicle had left him cold. The remarkable lifelong struggle against adversity described in the Testament, on the other hand, had evidently aroused in him a profound recognition of his own inadequacies. Ferreiro must have been deeply affected by Diogo's success in transcending his resentments – an existential effort at which Ferreiro had failed. Every life has its moment of moral clarity, a pivot upon which hangs the worth of the whole. For most the spark is quickly quenched, but for an exceptional few it lights a consuming fire. Ferreiro must have felt the inspiration of Diogo's example and lamented that he had lacked the strength of soul to take up the challenge. It must have left him with an ache of self-realization.

To balance the intense energy of our evening workhours in the cramped, cigarette-stained confines of Ferreiro's office, we spent our daytime hours in touristic indolence, roaming the serpentine sidestreets of Lisbon's old neighborhoods, descending to the Tagus River and then climbing back through the steep-stepped ways toward Alfama's ancient citadel, peering blankly into shop-windows and open doorways, glancing back at the young studs staring derisively at this passing pair of elderly flâneurs, gazing from a park bench atop the Alfama Mount at the sparrows wheeling across the cloudless sky, sharing midday siestas at our spartan living quarters while the city dozed, until the late afternoon hour when we would meet Leticia for coffee and a discussion of the coming evening's work before heading off to Ferreiro's workshop. During those aimless wanderings we discovered a neighborhood bookshop that stocked, by good fortune, a first edition of José Saramago's *History of the Siege of Lisbon* as well as an English-language paperback translation. Saramago's narrative kept us both awake far into the night, especially the pages that provided a bookish insider's street guide to Alfama and its ancient Moorish citadel of "Lissabona" that

Panoramic montage of Alfama peak, Lisbon, merging different historical images. (A Lisbon postcard)

had failed to withstand the Galician reconquest of 1147 CE. The novel's bemusing tale of a proofreader who in a trifling, subversive moment inserted a single word to reverse the reader's understanding of that epochal event in Portuguese history enthralled us with its vertiginous interplay between the doubt of certainty and the certainty of doubt.

I have referred more than once to Ferreiro's infatuation with Leticia. We had suspected from our first visit that our requests to view his manuscripts and undertake a modern transcription had been entertained by him due as much to Leticia's allure as to the prospect of financial gain. A cluster of subliminal cues – a certain diffidence in his manner, shadowed by furtive glances directed her way, a husky tone in his mention of her name, as well as his curiously, perhaps Freudian display of the Ching Dynasty nude – became increasingly apparent over the course of his many evenings of suppressed cross-table flirtation. To all those subtle signals she feigned a blithe insensibility. It made us realize that we had much more to thank Leticia for than her research assistance. We spent many an idle moment ruminating over that bit of good luck. When it came time for our departure for Bangkok, we cautioned her concerning the difficulties that might crop up in further, unchaperoned work at Ferreiro's office. She assured us that she felt fully capable of handling the situation; Ferreiro's self-loathing, she observed with her usual intuition, would prevent his risking rejection. However, as she later wrote us with some embarrassment, she had managed to ward off as gently as possible his timorous advances – his allusive words of endearment, his little gifts, his offers of late-night refreshment, and finally his trembling reach

Translators' Prologue

for her hand. Somehow, she had succeeded in avoiding irreparable hurt. Upon the completion of her work, they had parted amicably, he obviously distressed at the leave-taking despite promises of future reunions – adding yet another torment to his fragile, self-absorbed psyche.

The strictly enforced terms of our economy-class bookings barred us from extending our two-week Lisbon sojourn, so we bade fond farewells to our new-found companions João and Leticia and returned to Bangkok accompanied by our precious transcript of Diego's Testament. Back home, we searched our mail daily in eager anticipation of the companion Chronicle. Finally, the thick parcel arrived. After a quick preliminary read-through of Leticia's Portuguese text, Cláudio suggested it would be useful for me to undertake some preliminary research into the Thai royal chronicles tradition while he prepared an initial English translation of both manuscripts for our further joint editing. Also, we decided to seek Leticia's assistance on an additional assignment – a search through Lisbon's historical repositories for documentation on Diogo d'Almeida, the manuscripts' professed author. With our guarantee of an additional lump-sum fee, she readily accepted that extra job. Her archival search eventually produced an impressive piece of detective work.[1] She found much more than we had anticipated, and what she discovered corroborated in almost all respects what Diogo had stated in his autobiographical Testament. Provenance had been traced to the source.

Translation
The translators
With Leticia's two neatly typed transcripts of Diogo's Chronicle and Testament safely in custody, Cláudio and I agreed to dedicate the next year of our lives to the preparation of a competent English-language translation of both. That agenda, as is invariably the case with even the best-laid plans of mice and men, went far astray, and only after a near-decade's delay are we now nearing the end of our task.

While Cláudio set off on a preliminary modern English rendering of Leticia's Portuguese transcript of the Testament, I sought clarification of the Thai tradition of royal chronicles (*phra racha phongsawadan*) into which Diogo's narrative apparently fit.[2] The result was a deep dig through the murky waters of Thai academia – involving months of far-flung reading, library searches, and interviews with local scholars on ever more esoteric aspects of Thai history and linguistic exegesis. A vast conglomeration of latter-day reprints of the Thai royal chronicles – not to mention corresponding collections of Burmese, Lao, Cambodian, and Vietnamese annals – was uncovered in the course of those inquiries. Among that disorderly assemblage of musty volumes, I was able to locate several nearly identical versions of the redacted *Thonburi Chronicle* to which Diogo had referred in his Testament as the impetus behind the writing of his "true record of the time" (Diogo's words).[3]

My search exposed me to the arcane discipline of Thai historiography – the study of the inbred literary genres applied over the course of the kingdom's history by royal and ecclesiastical scribes to record the passage of events for their privileged audiences, rarely exposed to public view.[4] Within that literature, the royal chronicles tradition served as the ruling elite's collective memory of its righteous place in the realm that they had created through their virtuous effort. Its style centers on the condensed reportage of memorable royal-related events and achievements. Its recounting of each reign's royal progress consists of a relentless cadence of crisp declarative statements rushing by without a moment's reflection; truly a series of "chronicles" – journals or daybooks. (Diogo's rendition departs from that strict protocol primarily in its fuller, Western-inspired narrative form, its emphasis on causality, its personality sketches of a number of leading characters, its stress on the role played by the nobility, and its many passing references to issues of the day extending well beyond the royal gaze.)

As the old manuscripts rotted away, those emblematic regnal documents were subjected to periodic scribal replication to allow for the preservation and dissemination of the written record. That practice enabled their refinement – or, more trenchantly, editing, revision, alteration, and expurgation – with successive rewritings, known in Thai as "cleansing" (*chamra*, or *kanchamra-lang*). Successive rewritings were thereby amended, as one scholar has put it with tactful phrasing, "heeding the king's sensibilities on certain delicate episodes."[5] In short, *chamra* provided a convenient means of rewriting history to suit the preferences of the victors. The complexity of that process infuses the surviving Thai chronicles with an enigmatic character, with the annals of the Thonburi period standing out as a particularly perplexing case. My many discussions with local scholars and readings of learned treatises on that obscure topic allowed me to absorb no more than the general gist of it all. For our immediate purposes, however, the successive "cleansings" of the record help explain Diogo's exasperation with the expurgated version of the *Thonburi Chronicle* that had been penned to replace the definitive original that he had helped produce years before. Diogo sought with his rewriting to right what he considered a corrupted text – a severely redacted record creating a historical mythology favorable to successor regimes.

Having mastered as much of that abstruse field of Thai disputation as I could endure, I joined Cláudio in his translation project. We battled with the fundamental problem of expressing eighteenth century Portuguese declamation in terms of twenty-first century English narrative. To communicate the intent of Diogo's rhetoric efficiently we resorted to terminology embodying conceptual nuances far removed from the mindset of Diogo's day – allowing us to accommodate such modern metaphors as feudalism, social class, ethnic group, and galactic polity. We found it impossible to avoid reference to such modern mental constructs if our purpose – to convey the substance of Diogo's centuries-old Chronicle to a modern audience – was to be achieved. Diogo's Testament, with its more personal subject matter, was somewhat less difficult. Our approach was intended to avoid the unappealing, modern style of Thai historical literature, which insists on treading so close to the archaic Thai terminology and syntax as to lose the reader in translation. (Though future debate over that editorial strategy is inevitable, it will fortunately be consigned largely to obscure scholarly journals.)

Amid all that, Cláudio represented the two of us in convincing a local bank to extend a credit line for our hoped-for acquisition of the original pair of manuscripts. Despite our success on that front, repeated contact with Ferreiro failed to convince him to sell them to us. In each response to many communications, he found one politely phrased excuse after another to reject our bid. After a year of such fruitless overtures, we turned to our trusted interlocutor Leticia to represent us with some of her gentle persuasion. Our endeavor finally came to a dead end with the arrival of a lengthy message informing us that Ferreiro had decided to sell the two manuscripts to a nameless buyer for an undisclosed sum, said to be substantially higher than any offer we could possibly afford. With the door thus firmly shut, we were left to speculate that he had fabricated the secretive sale as no more than a pretext to be rid of us. Most likely, we mused, both the Testament and Chronicle remain in his possession; he loves his antiquarian treasures too much to have so blithely parted with them.

And then a sequence of unpredictable obstacles intervened to extend our translation work into years of spasmodic struggle. What had been anticipated as a year or so of leisurely preoccupation soon showed itself to be far more complex than initially envisioned. An unexpected interruption arose several months after the start of our work with the death of Cláudio's widowed mother. After her funeral, his estranged siblings decided to drag him into a lawsuit over his rightful share of the family estate. In defense of his inheritance, he was required to extend his funerary sojourn at his Portuguese upcountry hometown near Coimbra to see the legal dispute through to his vindication. To fill the empty days between court proceedings, he took to searching the local university libraries for a Portuguese translation of the ancient Plutarch writings that Diogo had likely relied on for his many citations.[6] Then, during Cláudio's lengthy absence, I was diagnosed with a case of thyroid cancer – possibly a Vietnam War souvenir – its debilitating treatment extending months beyond his rushed return. Through lengthy recovery – despite doctors' assurances that it was a relatively "mild" case – resumption of our collaborative efforts strengthened our personal bond, and that in turn fortified our resolve to see the daunting project through to the end.

Cláudio's inheritance was eventually confirmed. The endowment created from the sale of his family vineyards left our combined pensions in the shade. From our unhappy youths, the struggles of our four-decades-long shared lives were suddenly transformed into the promise of golden years. Strange karma! Our good fortune was celebrated with a high Mass at the Santa Cruz Church in commemoration of Diogo's exemplary life, followed by a joyous merit-making excursion to Wat Intharam, resting place of Diogo's patron, King Taksin the Great (coinciding roughly with the 250th anniversary of Taksin's coronation). With our newfound financial freedom and my gradual return to health, we have finally been able to proceed unencumbered toward completion of our long-suffering translation project.

Diogo

Over the course of our lengthy quest, Diogo – separated from us by more than two centuries but still very much alive in our thoughts – came to assume an evermore compelling presence. As our work progressed we spent many idle hours musing on what we had learned of him: his Portuguese Catholic upbringing in Buddhist Siam, his childhood struggle to accept his lifelong handicap, his Jesuit education at Macau, his employment as a multilingual scribe at the court of Thonburi, his resilience in framing a new life in exile at Rosario and Sampheng, and finally his resolve in composing his controversial Chronicle. The discomfort, boredom, and loneliness of my lengthy convalescence during Cláudio's absence gave me endless opportunity for meditation on that tempestuous life, based on Diogo's own introspections as expressed with fervor in his Testament and implied at various points in his Chronicle. Cláudio's return allowed us to devote the later months of my convalescence to ever deeper contemplation on the compulsions that had driven our hero to compose his dissident treatise.

It can easily be guessed why, wedged between contrasting cultures, estranged from his father and his peers by the curse of his deformed body, and caught in the vise of historical events, precocious Diogo adopted the persona of an angry young man, a nonconformist, a freethinker. That helps explain why his narrative is a dissident history in both content and style. He had an axe to grind. His stated intent was to contest the redacted *Thonburi Chronicle* of 1795.[7] More subtly, he sought to refine the Siamese chronicles tradition along Plutarchian lines by emphasizing the influence of individual personalities and interpersonal relations on the course of events. His Chronicle's iconoclastic interpretation of many critical events of the day, its uninhibited characterization of the main protagonists, its dramatization of the ambitions and stratagems pursued by the leading contenders for power, its insights into the shifting alliances that energized the aristocracy and nobility, its recurring reference to the discontent of the commons over their unremitting exploitation – all show a radical turn. Its episodic presentation diverges from the strictly chronological Thai narrative form and monotonous recitation of royal ceremonies, religious rituals, and auspicious events that fill the pages of the standard treatises, while tracing a half-century's political turbulence from a variety of human perspectives. In all that, Diogo's Chronicle constitutes a revisionist history in the most profound sense of the term. He risked his life in challenging so forthrightly the official history of the times.

Stretching eastward across Portugal's Asian empire (and westward into the Americas), the Iberian culture of Diogo's day transmitted a burst of enthusiasm for classical humanism that Diogo adopted as his moral linchpin. Plutarch's *Parallel Lives*, a work dedicated to tracing the influence of human character on the course of historical events, inspired him. He used his profound knowledge of Plutarch in two overlapping ways. One applied Plutarch's humanistic values to the events he was describing. That intellectual debt is apparent in his persistent stress on the moral precept of virtue, the essence of personal integrity that he believed rises above the vicissitudes of life to apply in all historical contexts. The other, more unusual borrowing reimagined the events of his own day as if they were being reported by Plutarch himself, sometimes even ascribing Plutarch's ancient dialogues to his protagonists.[8]

In his literary style, Diogo follows Plutarch in structuring his work as a series of contrasting character studies (though here they are the intersecting lives of contemporaries rather than Plutarch's parallels between Greeks and Romans often of different centuries). Like Plutarch, Diogo emphasizes the manner in which his subjects' personal imperfections, especially the vice of hubris, shaped the course of events. He highlights martial affairs – coups, battles, expeditions, defeat and revival – as vehicles for the display of character. As in Plutarch's Greco-Roman world, he treats as commonplace the frailties of life in a society far more brutal than our own. He splices Plutarch's civic ethics with Machiavellian pragmatism to portray a distinctly Thai political ambivalence. However, unlike Plutarch, who scarcely mentions the suffering, downtrodden commons, and unlike the royal chronicles tradition, which ignore them entirely, Diogo repeatedly voices consideration for their plight. Straddling the intellectual chasm between Plutarch's classical West and eighteenth-century Siam, it is as though Diogo were intent on exposing the universality of the human drama of personal honor, social order, state making, and heroic warfare that links the two cultural universes. We found that tale well worth our retelling in modern translation. Through all that, Diogo himself deserves credit for having lived his life in accord with his own ethics.

Reunion
Leticia
A decade has passed since our eventful visit to Macau and our providential meetings with Leticia Carvalho de Fomoso and João Ferreiro at Lisbon. After our return to Bangkok and Leticia's further investigation into Diogo's biographical details and her completion of the full transcription of the Diogo manuscripts, followed by her assistance in our unsuccessful effort to persuade Ferreiro to part with the originals, years passed with little further contact with those two old friends. That absence ended a month ago with the arrival of an extraordinary letter from the long-silent Leticia, composed in her graceful hand. It carried the surprising announcement of her forthcoming marriage.

Her letter introduced us to her prospective husband, Guido Azevedo, an official with the commercial crimes branch of Portugal's judicial constabulary. She reported that their romance had been sparked as a fortuitous outcome of our earlier Diogo quest, so she had much to thank us for. They had met, incongruously, at her interrogation during the course of police inquiries into the international trafficking of contraband antiquities. Mounting evidence of a smuggling racket centering on the transfer of art treasures from Portugal's former overseas empire to the Lisbon market had brought the local constabulary to Ferreiro's door, and she had been mistaken for his collaborator, only to be fully exonerated. We thus served jointly as the Cupid who had brought her to the threshold of marriage. Her letter included an invitation for us to attend the wedding. Guido must surely be a member of Lisbon's upper crust, as the invitation assured us that our travel expenses and accommodation at one of Lisbon's finest hotels would be fully covered.

She accompanied that news with the even more remarkable disclosure that her betrothed had generously endowed her, as a nuptial gift, with Ferreiro's townhouse and all its antiquarian fittings. How that real estate transfer was negotiated and why Ferreiro would have acquiesced to it were left unexplained. Surely, no civil service salary could have borne such a weight. Only the persuasions of a senior police officer could have played such a decisive role. It had evidently been an offer that Ferreiro could not refuse. Leticia confessed to us with a thrill of excitement her intention to continue the antiquarian business at Ferreiro's former premises under her own name, with the existing inventory as her starting point. (We are left to infer that her serendipitous marriage into Lisbon's criminal justice establishment will protect her from any future dangers of official harassment in that newfound profession.) And Ferreiro? We are told that he had walked away from the affair with satisfaction. He had been provided with immunity from prosecution and an attractive property settlement that will ensure him and his irascible mother a comfortable retirement.

That astounding news was surpassed by the final portion of Leticia's letter, which stated that she and her betrothed had started several weeks ago a listing of the entire inventory cluttering their newly acquired antiquary's office and storage vaults. During their stocktaking they had discovered among the riot of merchandise cramming the firm's storage space an old hobnailed, tin-lined teakwood seaman's chest. A brass nameplate on the face of its lid, above the padlock hinge, was engraved "*Companhia Marítima Menam*," the name that Diogo had devised for the Bangkok-based trading firm that had employed him as its comprador. This trunk must surely have been his. Leticia explained with excited words that the chest contained more than thirty separate manuscripts, each bound in ancient Siamese accordion fashion and written in what she took to be archaic Thai script. The exact number of separate documents represented by this wealth of miniature manuscripts is not certain because some of them may form detached segments of single items. It is possible that this cache of parchments was intended to accompany Diogo's Chronicle as corroborating evidence, which would suggest that the chest had formerly contained both his manuscripts; Ferrairo had offered no clue to that possibility. She lamented that it was all far beyond her competence. To cap off that astonishing news, she asked whether we would be interested in staying on as her guests for some days after the wedding to examine this collection of newfound antiquities. Perhaps we could consider them for translation, just as we had done earlier. Her lawyers had instructed her in their typically stuffy way to explain that the nature of those materials and the related legal issues would prohibit their photocopying or scanning for personal use or dissemination, even on the strictest conditions of confidentiality. So, our only access to them would have to be in person.

Ferreiro

Then Ferreiro telephoned, the first contact he had ever initiated with us. His palpable agitation spoke even more clearly for his overwrought emotional state than did his words. He had recently learned through the local tabloids of Leticia's forthcoming wedding, and he voiced great resentment at having received neither forewarning nor invitation. That shock, he explained in anger, had compounded his deep distress over the recent coerced sale of his firm and residence, under threat of criminal prosecution, by the very man Leticia was about to marry. Further, as a condition of the sale of his property and immunity from prosecution, he had been forced to sign away his right to ever again engage in the antiquarian trade. He considered Leticia's coming marriage, especially to such a man, a personal betrayal, and he detested her for it. In his eyes she had lost her innocence, her sincerity, her honor. We suggested to him that Leticia had perhaps been unaware of the full particulars of his ouster from house and home. In his rage, he would accept no such rationalization. A spasm of vindictiveness drove him to blurt out that he might write an exposé on Lisbon's police corruption, a subject on which he said he had plenty of juicy information. We urged him to rethink such a rash move.

Ferreiro's melodramatic rant fizzled with the lament that his world had collapsed; he was seeking an epiphany – or at least, on a more mundane level, our advice on how he should best proceed with his life. We explained to him as gently as we could that we had been invited to attend the Lisbon wedding and assured him that we would use that occasion to get together with him for a reunion of our own. In the meantime, as an immediate commentary meant as a dose of lighthearted shock therapy, we offered several off-the-cuff suggestions: First, that he should end his angry isolation from the world: try yoga lessons, go on a European junket, write his memoirs, join the Foreign Legion. Second, that he might consider an alternative livelihood to keep himself occupied in his new life: bookbinding, philately, vintnery, perhaps a museum affiliation building on his antiquarian expertise. Finally, that he should negotiate an affectionate armistice with his insufferable mother. Thankfully, several of those risqué suggestions elicited muffled snorts and chuckles. We ended with the murmured suggestion that we looked forward to many pleasant evenings with him accompanied by an appropriate sampling of well-aged Oportos, with an accompanying flask of Aguardente de Medronho to soften his mother to our return. After a tense moment of silence, he responded, phlegmatic as always: "Agreed. Thanks. Let's talk when you get here."

Diogo's Testament

My design has been not simply to write histories, but lives. The most glorious exploits do not always furnish us with the clearest discoveries of virtue or vice in men; sometimes a matter of less moment, an expression or a jest, informs us better of their characters and inclinations than the most famous sieges, the greatest armaments, or the bloodiest battles whatsoever.[1]

So stated my literary mentor, Lucius Mestrius Plutarch, many centuries ago. His ancient counsel has weathered well in guiding my chronicling of Siam's recent history coupled with this brief codicil recounting my personal experience through those turbulent times. At many moments during the course of this writing, my hand has been guided across the page by a mysterious, unfathomable inner force acting independently of my own volition to shape entire sentences and paragraphs of the narrative. The more superstitious among us would consider it the intervention of a guardian angel, but I prefer to believe it the abiding spirit of Plutarch. What you have before you, therefore, are my thoughts given shape under the guidance of that venerable scholar.

Ayutthaya childhood

It was my freakish fate to find myself a misfit born far from my ancestral land, a Portuguese outsider in the remote kingdom of Siam, a Christian in the midst of a Buddhist populace, stumbling through my troubled life betwixt two incommensurable cultures. On the twelfth day of the twelfth month of 1745 by the Gregorian calendar, the year 2388 by Buddhist reckoning, I was baptized as a newborn at the Church of Santo Domingo, bordering the River Menam in the great city of Ayutthaya, as Diogo Luis Gomes d'Almeida, son of Rodrigo Romero d'Almeida, Captain in the Portuguese Artillery Corps in Siamese service, and Maria de Fonseca Gomes. As a British wit has recently gibed, "I wish either my father or my mother, or indeed both of them, as they were in duty both equally bound to it, had minded what they were about when they begat me...."[2] For, from the very moment of my birth I was disfavored by an unsightly infirmity – my withered left leg – believed by many of Ayutthaya's Portuguese churchgoers to be akin to a sacred stigmata, and considered by my equally devout Buddhist contemporaries to be an ill-fated memento of an unmeritorious previous existence. Whatever the case, I was rendered from the start a pitiable creature within our household and a virtual outcast among my age peers. Only the nurturing love of my mother and my two elder sisters ensured my frail childhood's survival in Ayutthaya's Ban Portuket, as the capital's Portuguese village was known.[3]

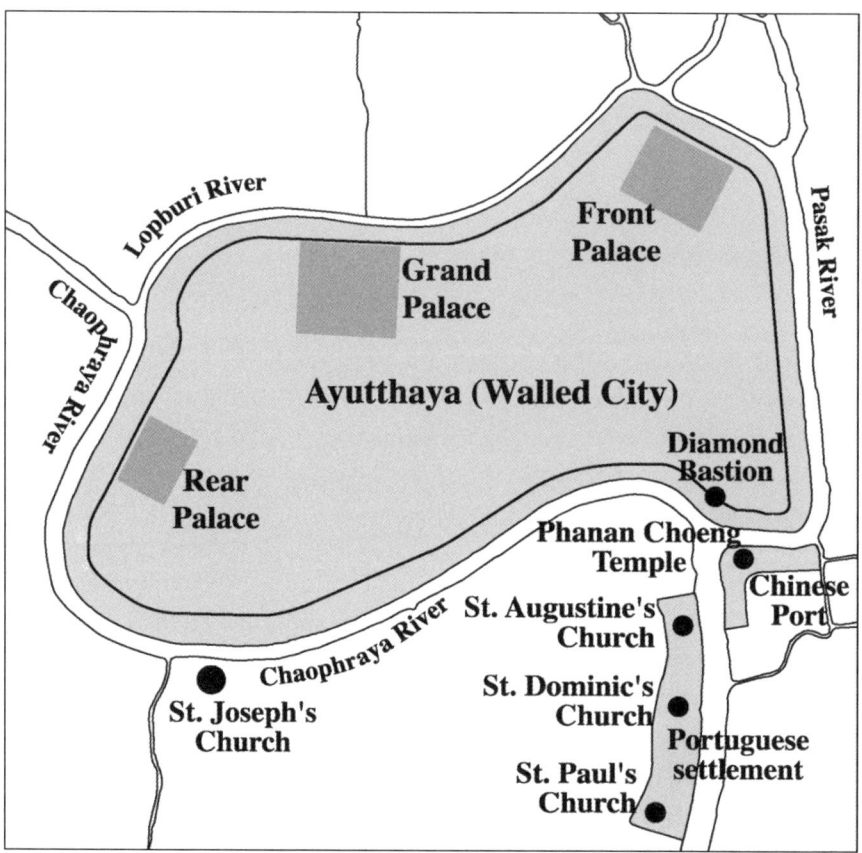

Ayutthaya's Portuguese settlement and its environs, late Ayutthaya.

To my physical affliction was added an inborn acumen that isolated me doubly from my age-mates. My blighted childhood introduced me to my staunchest companions, my crutch and my books – precious possessions gifted by our compassionate parish priest – which eased my confinement while confirming my estrangement from the revelry of the village scene. Although I was spurned for my physical defect by my father and my two elder brothers, who were devoted to naught but their military careers, my mother and sisters showered me with their kind-hearted nurture. It was they who introduced me to the rudiments of the curiously curlicue Thai script. Recognizing my aptitude, my mother pleaded with our community's church leaders to secure my early acceptance as a day-pupil at the Jesuit-run St. Paul's Church, near our riverside home.[4] In that courageous representation she had notable success. Under the sympathetic instruction of Fr. Tomás Xavier, I readily mastered the catechism and received my first formal Portuguese and Latin tutelage, but his patient religious instruction did not have the desired effect. I found myself, in cloistered contemplation, to be an inveterate freethinker, though I did not until years later become acquainted with that perfidious term or its far-reaching philosophical underpinnings. Childhood convictions tend to stick, and that one certainly did, though I was clever enough to realize from the start that I had best keep all such heretical views to myself.

Macau education

Upon approaching the manly age of 13, my life was transformed through the intervention of my mentor, Fr. Tomás, who entered a petition on my behalf for a scholarship to pursue higher studies at the great Portuguese emporium of Macau. My mother was persuaded through his referral to Fr. Martim Villanueva, an inspirational preacher and eminent linguist well remembered in Ayutthaya's Portuguese community for his eloquent protests against Siamese injustices, which had led to his untimely recall in 1754 to the Jesuit Vicarage at Macau. A half year's wait was rewarded with the receipt of a positive response; and then the wait for a Macau-bound sloop willing to accommodate a crippled lad. Fr. Tomás's letter of introduction was safeguarded against my breast throughout the interminable sea voyage leading to our arrival at the Kwangtung's Pearl River estuary and my joyous disembarkation at the magnificent port of Macau. There, Fr. Martim received me with a warm embrace. My precious introductory letter, supported by my final Ayutthaya schoolyear's private tutelage under Fr. Tomás, prepared my smooth sail through the formalities of examination before a committee of learned clerics, followed by acceptance as a lay seminarian at Macau's premier center of learning, St. Paul's College, attached to the great cathedral of that name.[5]

The remains of St. Paul's Cathedral after the great fire of 1835, 41with St. Paul's College alongside. Sketch attributed to George Chinnery. (Google Images)

Diogo's Testament 31

Diogo Luis Gomes d'Almeida, biographical resumé, 1745-1808

1745
birthdate

Unrecorded. However, baptism registered as son of Rodrigo and Olivia Gaspar d' Almeida, December 22, 1745.
Documentary source: Register of vital statistics, St. Dominic's Parish, Ayutthaya, 1738-1765 (contained in "Overseas Missionary Records of the Dominican Order (transferred from St. Paul's Cathedral, 1926), cached in the Torre do Tombo National Archives collection, Lisbon.

1759
age 13

To Macau for seminary education. Matriculated at St. Paul's College as a charity student, September 14, 1759.
Documentary source: Vicar's daybook, St. Paul's College, Macau, 1759 (cached in the Estado Português da India archives, Lisbon).

1771
age 25

Return to Siam (Santa Cruz, Thonburi).
Documentary source: Date interpolated from surrounding events in Diogo's Testament and the history of Santa Cruz.

1772
age 26

Marriage of "Diogo Almeida" to Maria Ribiero Gonçalves at Santa Cruz Church, Thonburi, March 2, 1772.
Documentary source: Marriage register, Santa Cruz Parish, Thonburi, 1770-1779 (cached in the historical archives of the Societé des Missions Étrangères de Paris, Paris).

1782
age 36

Forced into retirement from government service and prohibited from consorting with members of the aristocracy and entering the walled city precincts.
Documentary source: Referred to in "History of the Holy Rosary Parish, 1820(?)," contained in "Overseas Missionary Records of the Dominican Order ...," (see above).

1782
age 36

Residence relocated to the Portuguese settlement of Rosario, a kilometer downriver and crossriver from Santa Cruz.
Documentary source: Date identified from Diogo's Testament.

1783(?)
age 37

Recruited into employment as a Sampheng-based Chinese trading firm's comprador and eventually earned his way up to a partnership role.
Documentary source: References to a "Menam" trading venture, listing the name of "D. L. d'Almeida" as one of its partners, in a file entitled "Commercial projects" (entries from 1783 to 1807), (microfiche copy of Macau historical archives file contained in the Estado Português da India archives, Lisbon).

1786
age 40

Upon the government's formal recognition of the Rosario settlement, Diogo joined in sponsoring construction of the Church of the Holy Rosary.
Documentary source: "History of the Holy Rosary Parish, 1820(?)," contained in the "Overseas Missionary Records of the Dominican Order . . . ," (see above).

1808
age 62

Date of death unrecorded.
Documentary source: References to the Menam Company and Diogo's participation in the import-export trade contained in the abovementioned "Commercial projects" file, which does not extend beyond 1807. However, Diogo's Testament refers to "the recent death of Prince Chak" and "his forthcoming cremation," both of which events occurred in 1808.

prepared by _____ (signed) _____

Leticia Carvalho de Fomoso
October 15, 2017

Affidavit of Diogo' biodata, prepared by Leticia Carvalho de Fomoso, Instructor, Faculty of Arts and Letters, University of Lisbon. (English translation of the Portuguese-language original.)

Many lonely years followed, distant from home, though living happily among well-meaning savants who thought nothing of my provincial background or infirmity in their single-minded devotion to abstract learning. I accepted their schooling without demure, despite my secret skepticism of their spiritual premises, as scholastic attainment was my only recourse to anchoring a vocational future. A few did not take an entirely benign view of my situation. In well-meaning but misconceived counsel, several of my tutors gently advised that it would be to my long-term advantage to amputate my wasted leg, which flapped like a broken chicken-wing, impeding locomotion. My mother had convinced me long ago that my affliction was none of my own doing, nor an act of Providence, but stemmed simply from the mindless ministrations of the midwife who had attended my birth throes. In her loving way, she had stoutly defended my offending limb, fantasizing it perhaps the very seat of my fluttering soul. Furthermore, having often witnessed the drunken ineptitude of Macau's supposedly brilliant surgeons, I resolutely resisted all suggestions for their intervention. My mentors accepted my remonstrations in their usual stoic manner, and plodded on.

Within Macau's larger Portuguese establishment, however, I was treated with less tolerance. Disdain was showered on me in so-called "polite" company not only as a cripple but, surprising to this innocent country lad, as a mestizo in view of my rustic speech and the admixture of Thai in my mother's bloodstream that darkened my complexion. Through all that, my affliction force-fed me a steady diet of pain, bitterness, and disappointment – my personal, lifelong Calvary. Proscribed from both a military and clerical future – as my father and less so my mother would surely have preferred – it became clear to me that I had been relegated to the life of a scholar, by function an observer, never an actor. But that lesser vocation neither crushed my independent thought nor did it crush my will.

Macau at that time was much affected by the political machinations of Portugal's formidable Marquis de Pombal.[6] Among his imperial pursuits was the expulsion of the Jesuit missionary priesthood from all Portuguese territories – which posed a direct threat to my scholarly ambitions. To this day I cannot fathom how I managed to thread the needle of that sectarian purge. Despite Pombal's political equivocation in the Manichean struggle between dogma (the Dominicans), and discernment (the Jesuits), the struggle impinged but lightly on my career. Consequently, I managed to absorb at St. Paul's College the inspirational teachings of Aristotle, Marcus Aurelius, Plutarch, Aquinas, Dante, Montaigne, de Fonseca, Erasmus, and Descartes, and even such modern heretical thinkers as Montesquieu and Voltaire, without reproach. From my readings of Plutarch during those difficult days I took to heart the motto that has guided my work ever since: "a man's character appears more by his words than, as some think it does, by his looks."[7]

The four leading Catholic clerical orders at Macau, 18th century: (left to right) Franciscan, Jesuit, Dominican, Augustinian. (Basto da Silva, *Cronologia da Historiade Macau: Seculo XVIII.* Macau, 1997, p. 51)

Of those years I remember more clearly Macau and my friendships than I can recall my schooling, which in retrospect was a blur of concentrated study. My fellow seminarians, a polyglot crew of young scholars – predominantly Chinese but also Annamese, Filipino, Japanese, and others – formed my family, though I was the sole "Siamese" among them. In high-spirited debate we conversed over our daily rice porridge in our multifunctional Portuguese/Latinate patois, salted with a smattering of the local Cantonese street argot. In a more intimate setting, Fr. Martim and I often luxuriated at his vicarage quarters in genial wine-laced discussions conducted in our "native" Thai. The cosmopolitan port-city offered a surfeit of diverting attractions, drawing me into its belly more often than was good for me. The rough-cobbled streets and muddy lanes over hilly terrain were a daily challenge for my hobbled walk. In the most difficult circumstances, I resorted to transport by coolie-drawn barrow, uncomfortable and humiliating but convenient and cheap – litters and sedan-chairs were reserved for the moneyed. By such locomotion I often proceeded from our lower-city lodgings up the steep, slippery cobblestone slope to St. Paul's Praça, where our college stood, past the doorways and balconies of giggling, beckoning girls. My occasional visits to their quarters were met with kindness, even affection, ignoring my disfigurement with a delightful charm that lingers with me still. Upon completion of my three-year baccalaureate in theology and rhetoric, I was allowed to stay on at St. Paul's as a lay teacher under Fr. Martim's guidance, earning a meager stipend supplemented by room and board plus the wages I managed to earn from the tutoring of privileged youngsters and my occasional services as a Thai interpreter for local maritime trading firms.

Siam return: Santa Cruz

Toward the end of the southwest monsoon, in mid-1767, the first junks returning from the South Seas brought shocking rumors of a Burmese attack on Ayutthaya. Months passed before I finally received confirmation with terrible details of the fall of Ayutthaya to massive Burmese assault and the devastation left in its wake, accompanied by the flight of Ayutthaya's Portuguese survivors to Kampot, a Cambodian coastal province far removed from the Burmese threat. It took another year before the arrival of an anxiously awaited message from my mother, informing me of the deaths of my father and both my elder brothers in battle, her escape along with my sisters to Kampot, and their safe return to Siam after several years of unspeakable privation. Finding all destroyed, they had decided to settle with their fellow survivors far downriver from our former home, under the protection of a new king who had reestablished Siam's capital at the Thonburi stronghold. It was only after my return that I became fully aware of the magnitude of Ayutthaya's military debacle and the scale of the catastrophe that Siam had experienced during my dozen-year absence.[8]

My mother's passionate entreaties for my early return provoked in me an unprecedented surge of emotion. Now, suddenly, despite my infirmity, I was needed! Befitting the moral precept of filial piety that had been inculcated in me from infancy, I determined to rush to my family's aid. With the onset of the northeast monsoon, I booked passage on a Cantonese trading junk, made my farewells, and sailed off for Siam with my personal effects, Shantung silks for gifts, the coins and baubles I had managed to accumulate as savings, and a ration of sticky rice cakes and hardtack to sustain me through the voyage. The rolling waves that had borne untold generations of intrepid Chinese mariners across the South Seas scudded us perilously but swiftly, and ultimately safely, to the bar of Siam's great river and thence up that sluggish tropical waterway to our destination, my homeland.

At Thonburi I was rowed ashore to a blissful reunion with the ragged remnants of my family. I learned that they had spent their last savings to flee the sack of Ayutthaya with their Christian fellows by junk bound for the promised bounties of Cambodia but had returned to liberated Thonburi in penury when they found the hardships of their Khmer exile intolerable. Conditions at Thonburi upon my arrival proved somewhat better than I had been led to expect. Reunited with my mother and sisters, and fellow Ayutthaya refugees, I happily joined them in their new home to rebuild with them a diminished replica of my childhood village. With my Macau experience and scholar's status, I was welcomed to the community's newly founded Santa Cruz parish, nestled alongside the Hokkien riverport of Kudi Chin.[9] Fortunately, my scrivening abilities, complemented by my multilingual skills in Thai and Portuguese plus some Cantonese and Malay, not to mention my Macau baccalaureate – exceptional by Siamese standards – soon caught the attention of the fledgling government. A post was found for me in the understaffed Royal Secretariat, a unique office within the Grand Palace, situated a short boat ride upstream from our village.[10]

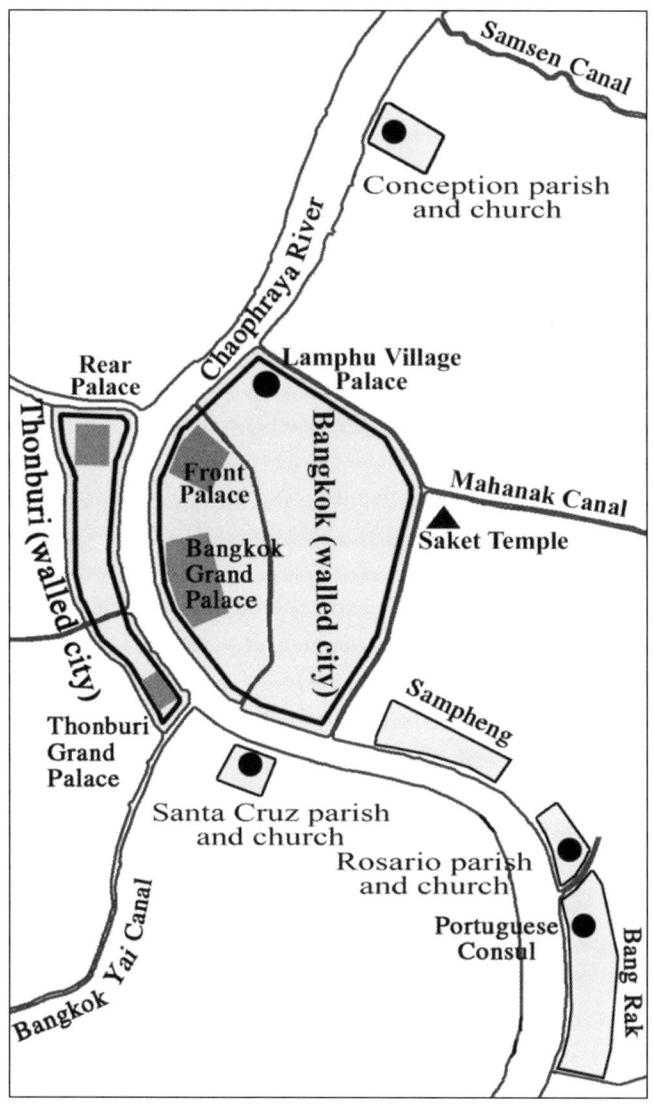

Santa Cruz and other Portuguese settlements, early Bangkok.

My appointment required that I pay formal homage to the king at a ceremony presided over by one of his most revered Buddha images and officiated by the Royal Secretariat's wizened director, Colonel Sunthon Wohan. In an avuncular moment, my new supervisor cautioned me in no uncertain terms to abide by the four precepts of royal service: practice decorum, pursue knowledge, perform assigned responsibilities, and adhere rigorously to righteousness. To both his profoundly non-Christian initiation rites and his sound advice I raised no objection, and with that guidance I managed to establish a respectable place for myself as a minor court functionary.

That illustrious appointment, plus a dribble of private tutorial commissions, provided sufficient compensation – a set of died silk garments for official wear to validate my financial stipend supplemented by monthly allotments of milled rice – to raise our household out of poverty.

The proud day of my appointment to the Royal Secretariat was followed in short order by the joyous festivities marking my marriage to Maria Ribeiro Gonçalves. My beloved wife had been orphaned during the siege of Ayutthaya and in the aftermath had been embraced by my mother as a surrogate daughter. She had then joined my mother and my two sisters in their odyssey to Kampot and then back to Santa Cruz. I had been enraptured by Maria from the day of our first meeting at my mother's Santa Cruz home. Without hesitation, disregarding my affliction, she accepted my marriage proposal. Our joy in wedlock lasted all too briefly, terminated by the death of our newborn child a year into our marriage. Notwithstanding our shared grief, we gradually rebalanced our lives; I immersed myself in my work, while she found solace in the Church. Not long thereafter, each of my sisters, in turn, married a hardworking man of good standing in our community. Since then, under Maria's tender care, and my mother's, I have lived a cloistered existence, with my crutch and my little library of Plutarch and his literary fellows remaining my closest companions.

Each morning I paddled with leisurely strokes upstream from Santa Cruz to the staff entrance of the Grand Palace, proceeding by crutch to my assigned post at the Royal Secretariat pavilion, alongside the Chapel Royal (better known as Wat Noi), to await the king's summons, or perform other duties. My sturdy sampan was one of my personal treasures, and my waterborne travels were a daily pleasure, no matter the weather, as I proved a worthy sailor with my withered leg tucked at my side while my arms did all the work.[11] Within the Royal Secretariat I joined a select group of scribes responsible for preparing the king's edicts, military directives, civic injunctions, diplomatic missives, and the like.[12] The transcription of official proceedings required my frequent presence at state functions, and so I was privileged to be in attendance in the Royal Audience Hall at many an ambassadorial reception, awards ceremony, religious rite, ministerial council, and more private policy deliberation presided over by the king himself. The king's charismatic presence invariably transformed those prosaic gatherings into unforgettable events, while I crouched with my scribe's stylus and black-rubbed palm-leaf accordion scroll in the shadows as an invisible observer, much like the gentle little geckos staring down silently from the roof beams.

The king was no scholar and like most of his kind had a gratifying regard for those who were. I was thus treated with kindness and accorded a modicum of respect. As he gained familiarity with my presence, I was drawn increasingly into his confidence. Perhaps the king's own painfully ulcerated leg, the result of an old sea mishap – an injury of which he never spoke, though it was common knowledge among his attendants – induced in him some affinity for my own afflicted life. Perhaps, in favoring me, he sought in my crippled survival to gain some solace from his private suffering.

Although never mentioned, it was evident that his old injury caused him incessant misery, and a need for light diversion. I provided him moments of innocent escape from the never-ending press of state issues. On the not infrequent occasions when the king sought my comment, my Portuguese-accented Thai amused him, as did my mix of Thai and Western mannerisms, my passing acquaintance with Chinese dialects, as well as my double familiarity with Buddhist and Catholic theology.[13] As if whispering to a wall, out of public earshot, he lamented to me over the loss of friends – through death in battle or from other causes, as well as through the inevitable isolation of his increasingly august persona and his distancing from former friends through unspoken disputes. During one such moment of relaxation the king asked me of my father. I explained that he had died by the sword as an artillery officer defending Ayutthaya's Phet Prakan Bastion against Burmese assault during the climactic battle of 1767.[14] The king replied in wistful candor that his father had not been afforded such a distinction, as many years earlier his junk had been lost at sea, in unknown waters. Such moments of intimate reflection greatly endeared the king to me. I came to realize that he struggled endlessly to repress his pent-up emotions and conquer his personal failings in his resolve to fight valiantly on behalf of all who chose to cling to his leadership. To ease his way, I took great care to earn his trust through diligent, unquestioning compliance with his every instruction.

Such loyalty was, I believe, recognized by him, and prized. My efforts to satisfy the king's demanding temperament proved successful. He took to referring to me, as the Chinese-Thai are wont to do, as *chiaw oe* or *koh*, Taechiu terms for "servant" or "helper," and called me affectionately "Ai (Mr.) Chiaw Oe," and sometimes "Koh Diogo," and even, once or twice, with a chuckle, "Achan (Professor) Diogo." Within two years I had risen in rank to senior scribe, carrying the title of Lieutenant Akson Phakdi. In that post I was one of the select few charged with maintaining a log of all royal audiences and related official events. In due course, I was honored with appointment to membership in an inner circle of palace officials entrusted with the task of compiling the reign chronicle, to be kept updated with annual installments in keeping with ancient protocol.[15] Selection for the post of helping compile the key document that would forever commemorate the reign's achievements was a singular honor. Our committee continued that duty to the end of 1781, when our efforts were brought to a halt by the cascade of calamities that culminated shortly thereafter in the reign's catastrophic end.

Watershed

All those events took place long before the sultry morning of April 6, 1782 – exactly fifteen years after the fall of Ayutthaya and a decade since my return from Macau – that saw the illustrious reign of King Taksin come to an abrupt end, heralding the immediate elevation of his Minister of War, General Chakri, to the throne.[16]

Ille dies fuit vitae meae momentum climacticum.
[That day was the most momentous of my life!]

Over the course of the previous months, I had witnessed from afar the developing disruption of King Taksin's reign with his declining health, but I had had no suspicion of what lay ahead. Trustworthy informants later whispered that he had been beheaded ignominiously by executioner's sword, considered beneath the dignified death by sandalwood club reserved for royals – a shameful act performed among the cannon lining the base of the Wichai Prasit Bastion.[17] It has been reported that, in a parting riposte, the king had rebuked his executioners: "'I had rather,' said he, 'perish by you than with you.'"[18] His corpse had been conveyed without ceremony for burial in the charnel ground at Wat Bang Yi Roea Tai, well removed from the Thonburi citadel.[19]

The foreboding portents of that early morning had left me entirely unaware that the king had been deposed and put to death. A ten-minute sampan paddle downriver from the execution site, at Ban Portuket, otherwise known by the name of its village church, Santa Cruz, I had just risen from my cot, still drowsy, entirely oblivious to those momentous events. My daybreak ablutions at our riverside jetty were disturbed by sounds of uncommon commotion emanating from the direction of the Grand Palace, but I paid them no attention, imagining that a naval patrol was engaged in one of its frequent morning exercises at the Bang Luang estuary, or that a unit of the palace guard was going through a boisterous change of sentries. Recollections of my innocent proximity to the unfolding tragedy continue to haunt me to this day.

Later that morning the river breeze carried to my ears the distant drumbeat and oarsmen's chant of a royal barge procession. I peered across the waters to glimpse a multitude of longboats setting off from the opposite shore. My little sampan drifted to midstream to allow a better view and there, holding my own against the rolling current, I observed far upstream a grand water-procession escorting a royal barge from the Wat Pho landing across the river to the Thonburi Grand Palace, conveying upon its midship throne, shrouded behind billowing canopies, a personage I believed to be King Taksin. My gaze was interrupted by the swift approach of a pair of patrol boats, which ushered me brusquely back to shore. What I had unsuspectingly witnessed was an epic event – the progress of General Chakri to his seizure of the Thonburi throne. Only in the aftermath did I come to appreciate the full significance of what I had glimpsed, not only for Siam's future but for my personal prospects.

Recent reports of the new king's investiture have emphasized the grandeur of that event, though the ceremonial trappings were concealed from all but his inner circle and hid a hard edge of political intrigue. I was informed that General Chakri had reached his final decision to assume the throne only after weeks, perhaps months, of troubled musings. He had spent the night before his dramatic river crossing – the event that I had momentarily happened to observe – at Wat Sakae, in the Bang Lamphu backwoods.[20] There, he had worked through the sleepless hours in non-stop planning of the final details of his takeover. To prepare him for his spiritual transfiguration, he was anointed in accordance with ancient Brahman ritual at sunrise on the day of reckoning – possibly at the very moment that the former king was facing execution.[21] Several hours later, at the moment determined by his astrologers as most propitious, he mounted his caparisoned war elephant surrounded by his bodyguard regiments and proceeded in regal splendor to Wat Pho, where he embarked for the river crossing to the Thonburi Palace's Royal Audience Hall. There, out of view to all but a privileged few, the solemnities progressed according to Brahmanic script. All culminated in his assumption of the throne, announced by a terrific crescendo of drums, trumpets, shrilling conch shells, trilling flutes, and chanting oarsmen, flanked along the river shore by a hushed crowd of cowering nobles and unarmed troops. That dynastic transition, as it turned out, augured the end of a generation's political turmoil.

Among the new king's first edicts, as I later learned, was his dismissal of all officials of the former regime from their administrative posts. Some of King Taksin's senior-most supporters were executed, though most were only briefly imprisoned and then reinstated upon swearing fealty to the new king. Evidently, I was among the many lesser officials considered so inconsequential as to be neither punished nor rehabilitated but simply cast aside. The results of my work in the Royal Secretariat, including my latest contribution to the Thonburi reign chronicle, were confiscated, and I was warned against further association with my former colleagues. With most other decommissioned retainers of the old regime – disenfranchised minions of a fallen master – I was banished from the Thonburi citadel. Initially, my housebound idleness, out of harm's way, was accompanied by nothing worse than fears of denunciation and detention. The surveillance network administered by the new king's viceroy, Prince Surasinghanat (his younger brother Bunma), kept us all on a tight leash. I learned through my mother's marketplace companions that several of my fellow functionaries had been imprisoned in shackles for nothing more than their loose tongues.

Within a month or two of the reign change I could see across the river from the Santa Cruz shoreline the beginnings of a new royal redoubt, which I was advised to refer to as Rattanakosin. First, the line of elegant riverside residences opposite the Thonburi Grand Palace was torn down, and then the crowded line of Taechiu wharves and warehouses stretching upstream past Wat Pho was dismantled, leaving a barren shoreline facing the Thonburi citadel. The vacated land was leveled by work gangs of captive Lao and Khmer conscripts who could be observed as ant-like ribbons of trudging slaves shouldering a limitless flow of mud-filled baskets from the dredged riverbank through the landward muck to fill the desolate terrain's many drains and ditches and raise its level above the flood mark. Completion of that task was followed by the excavation of a seemingly endless trench to receive the pilings and brick-work foundations of a great wall to encircle a new royal citadel. I heard that a moat was being dug across the inland reaches of the designated area but could see nothing of that work from my riverside venue. What I did see were recurrent convoys of

Mon-manned rafts carrying heaped loads of kiln-dried brick and slaked-lime powder for the construction of the great wall that gradually rose to front the new citadel. Taking shape behind, as could only be glimpsed from afar by those daring to paddle a half kilometer upstream, were the emerging lineaments of a new Grand Palace.

Rosario exile

After many months of home confinement following the reign change, my isolation was formalized with a police announcement listing the names of former Thonburi palace functionaries slated for banishment to the capital's outer fringes, where they would be allowed their freedom under condition that they stay in place and mind their business. Along with several other Santa Cruz natives, I moved our little household an easy half-hour's boat-ride downstream and across the river, to the sleepy Portuguese parish of Rosario, tucked away along a willowed, crocodile-infested shoreline, offering a new life under straitened circumstances.[22] Welcomed as a kinsman and scholar of some worldly repute by a congregation of barely 150 unschooled souls, I was called on to assist in upgrading the community's flimsy bamboo-walled, unfloored prayer-house to a full-blown church, along with assisting the village elders in their dispatch of a petition to Macau in hopes of acquiring the services of a resident pastor. Both those tasks were successfully accomplished – first with the arrival of Brother Francisco de Chagas, a Dominican friar, followed by the founding of our Holy Rosary Church.[23] My duties as warden of that fledgling sanctuary were supplemented by my tutoring of the village children, which paid for my subsistence, while my surreptitious friendships among the local scattering of similarly exiled Taksin partisans helped sustain my spirits through those transitional years. Life was made all the more bearable through the firm support that my loving

A highly stylized lithograph of the residence of the German missionary Karl Gutzlaff near Rosario, early-19th century. (Charles Gutzlaff, *Journal of Three Voyages Along the Coast of China*. London, 1834, frontispiece)

wife and mother offered in mobilizing the village women to support our struggling little church. At home, my mother helped Maria in caring for me to her last years, and then I cared for her to the end.

My isolated Rosario vantagepoint offered few amusements, so I decided one idle afternoon to paddle upstream past a long line of moored cargo vessels for a visit to the new Taechiu anchorage, a riverside junk traders' community of Taksin partisans that had been banished downriver by the new regime several years earlier from Thonburi's cleared out Taechiu port district.[24] The new port's main junk landing, backed by a Daoist shrine, proved to be a popular late-afternoon gathering place for the local seamen.[25] They were surprised at the abrupt arrival of a lame fellow in shabby Thai dress but of obvious Western profile speaking passable Cantonese. Following polite introductions and the cordial offer of a stool and a cup of tea, a guarded rapport was struck up, followed by stronger lubricants to grease the way. I paddled home that sunset in a state of inebriation that both my wife and my mother lamented, between hand-hidden titters.

On repeat visits I brought along a basket of my mother's egg-yolk pastries while the shrine habitués, seafaring merchants one and all, supplied abundant quantities of relaxing toddy (coconut palm wine), lingering in animated conversation until the evening's mosquito invasion drove us home to our net-enclosed bunks. As our friendship and mutual trust strengthened, our banter eased, leading to shared lamentations over the demise of King Taksin and grievances over the rough reprisals that had been meted out to his partisans by the new regime. In exchange for my reflections on the current state of affairs they willingly shared with me the latest gossip on the new royal citadel being raised on the very site from which they had recently been evicted. My companions recalled, in passing, King Taksin's former plan to upgrade Thonburi's port precinct into a formal extension of the royal city, a project that he had announced years earlier with the digging of an eastern moat and construction of a wall along the port district's inland bounds, installation of a regiment of Chinese marines in a cantonment to the rear of the port area, and construction of a palace for the king's eldest son, Prince Inthara Phithak, just upstream. Only an element of modesty, salted with an abundance of caution, prevented me from adding that, as a royal scribe under the former regime, I had myself recorded the minutes of several ministerial committee sessions at which those plans had been thrashed out.

In return for their hospitality, I invited my newfound Taechiu friends to visit Rosario. Half a dozen accepted that invitation and, to my delight, appeared one fine day at my jetty. We established our presence in the village churchyard, where our animated conversation and their proffered tea and toddy were joined by many a curious local, and I found myself serving as two-way interpreter for the remainder of the day. The unexpected result of that genial gathering was a lasting bond between the two communities. Unexpected business dealings emerged out of that budding relationship, providing steady work for Rosario's ropemakers, sailmakers, and blacksmiths. That business soon grew into the makings of a regular Rosario ship-chandlers' vocation for the outfitting of our Chinese neighbors' seagoing junks. Additionally, a regular flow of Rosario housewives' sampans materialized between Rosario and the Taechiu waterfront to vend Portuguese bread, cakes, and honeyed deserts in the Chinese marketplace, while Rosario home meals were increasingly enlivened with diets of Chinese dumplings and noodle dishes. Through that strengthened association a back-and-forth smattering of Taechiu terms and Portuguese-Thai idioms came to be shared between the two communities. Over the ensuing two decades, more than a dozen intercommunal marriages were arranged.

Sampheng comprador

Just as I had recently been expelled from my Santa Cruz home to downriver Rosario, Thonburi's Taechiu community had shortly before been evicted from its flourishing Thonburi port district to a waterlogged anchorage directly upstream from my new quarters. That pair of remote shoreline settlements had more in common than their juxtaposition. The Taechiu traders had been ousted for fear of their vested interests as financiers of the former regime. It was well known that Taksin's Taechiu patrimony and linguistic affinity had provided them with many advantages over their Hokkien rivals at Kudi Chin.[26] The Taechiu eviction from their Thonburi anchorage was recognized by one and all as a boon for the new regime's Hokkien partners. Expectations of a Taechiu decline, however, proved ill-founded. Just as our little band of Santa Cruz exiles had accommodated ourselves to the inhospitable downstream riverbend to which we had been relegated, the Taechiu traders had made the best of circumstances by proudly installing their communal shrine, dredging and filling the crocodile-infested riverside, and implanting rows of shoreline pilings to withstand the floodwaters. That reclamation project had enabled the construction of a line of docks overlooked by a collection of solid warehouses and a rapidly spreading cluster of sturdy merchants' dwellings backed by the hovels, vegetable plots, and piggeries of their immigrant workmen.

The rapid rise of the new Taechiu port was energized by its stalwart headman, Li-ang *sae* Tang, a Taksin intimate who had accompanied him in war and peace, serving him in successive ministerial capacities, most recently as chief of Siam's Taechiu community. It was thus a matter of public consternation when, within a year of King Taksin's overthrow and execution, not many months after Li-ang's exile to the new downriver settlement site, his macerated, crocodile-gnawed remains were discovered early one morning floating in the shallows alongside Wat Sampheng, having been carried by the rippling waters well downstream from his new riverside residence. To the best of my knowledge, no inquest into that deplorable incident was ever conducted; the mystery of Li-ang's untimely death lingers on. In keeping with Chinese funerary tradition, his remains were accorded a hero's farewell at the fledgling Taechiu port's shrine and then borne on his flagship junk to China, to his native village near the port of Chaosan, where they were interred with fitting ceremony at his family's ancestral gravesite. Bangkok's new Taechiu anchorage thrives today as his legacy. It is whispered that he followed his king in some premeditated manner to his unnatural death. To repeat the stirring words of Plutarch: "I cannot commend the death of either of these great men; the suddenness and strangeness of their ends gives me a feeling rather of pain and distress."[27]

Much hushed conversation circulated through Rosario in contemplation of Li-ang's sorrowful death. It reminded us daily of the perpetual peril in which our own lives stood as Taksin partisans. Our struggle to make sense of it turned increasingly to rumination over the strange parallels between the juxtaposition of our little waterside village and the neighboring Taechiu anchorage, on the one hand, and our former situation at Santa Cruz alongside Kudi Chin's Hokkien wharves, on the other. The barriers of contrasting language, religion, and lifestyle had restricted our contact with both those Chinese communities. Perhaps, in view of our common ostracism under the current regime, it was time for us to strengthen our bonds with our Taechiu neighbors. It thus came as a happy surprise that my innocent visit to their newly established waterfront settlement, referred to above, sparked a convivial association. Perhaps our neighbors had been having similar thoughts.

That budding intercommunal bond brought me great personal reward when Captain Liu Hia-buan, a leading Taechiu junk merchant, sent me an invitation to visit him at his waterfront business premises. His boatsmen poled me the short distance upstream from my Rosario cottage to his dock, where several seagoing junks were tethered awaiting lading. The even shorter trudge past his stout warehouses led me to his securely walled compound, built so recently that several of its interior structures were still only half completd. Hia-buan's self-possessed bearing struck me immediately as the personification of a well-seasoned seaman, reliable captain, competent merchant, and trustworthy friend. Our cordial greetings and formal introductions led seamlessly into an innocuous chat – conducted in our awkward mix of my limited Cantonese-Taechiu fluency and his equally limited Thai – eased by countless interruptions for tea and sweetmeats. We found that we had much in common, including our travels along the China coast, though neither of us had ever visited one another's neighboring bailiwicks of Macau and Canton, separated by no more than a day's sail through the Pearl River estuary.

I learned that Hia-buan had formerly worked as a junk trader based at Chanthabun and Trat, Taechiu ports along Siam's eastern seaboard, and had served as one of King Taksin's early financiers. In reward, he had been allotted a dockyard site not far downstream from Wat Pho, alongside the prestigious riverside residences of Li-ang (in his capacity as Colonel Rachasethi, head of Siam's Chinese community) and Thien-tu *sae* Mac (Colonel Rachasethi Yuan, head of Siam's Vietnamese community), both of whom had been his former acquaintances. (I did not mention to him that I had encountered both those dignitaries years ago at state functions in my capacity as a royal scribe.) Initially, Hia-buan's junks had shipped in cargoes of rice to help feed

Thonburi's starving populace. Later he had joined the annual royal trading convoys to Canton and other southern Chinese ports to supply the king's needs. He had participated in the Taechiu creditors' consortium that had financed and then repeatedly refinanced the Thonburi regime's acquisition of arms. Following the recent reign change, he had joined the evacuation of Taechiu mariners to their new downstream riverside settlement and with them had suffered the loss of his sizable loan balance to the Siamese state, though he had had managed to rebuild his trading firm and thus lay his grievances aside.

Hia-buan's extended conversation eventually turned to the subject at hand, an astonishing invitation to join his trading firm as its warehouse inventory comptroller – in effect, its port-based supercargo, equivalent to a Portuguese comprador. He explained that his advancing age and uncertain health required that he ease his workload with the delegation of key administrative duties to a reliable deputy. I had been referred to him by his Thai patron, Prince Chakra Chesada (La) – well known to me as a former colleague in the Royal Secretariat, though we had not met since his astounding elevation, several years earlier, from his humble civil service rank as Lieutenant Chinda to royal rank as a younger brother of the newly crowned sovereign of Rattanakosin.[28] I expressed my surprise, exclaiming that I had not met him for years, and protested that La's recommendation was extravagant, as I knew nothing of mercantile affairs. Hia-buan, who I eventually came to refer to by the avuncular sobriquet "Ah Buan," assured me that La's positive sentiments ensured that my proposed new calling would not prove unduly challenging under his tutelage, and I soon discovered that to be the case.

My duties centered on the firm's inventory accounts. Trade negotiations were a secondary task in which I served as Hia-buan's amanuensis and occasional interpreter. Workforce supervision was delegated to a sturdy Taechiu foreman who helped ease my way, often simply through his physical presence and commanding voice in the midst of coolie gangs. The rigors of record-keeping – keeping track of an unending flow of arriving and departing cargoes of a dizzying array of goods, both from upcountry and overseas – pulsated with the flow of the agricultural seasons and the oscillating monsoons. I was required to keep track of the fluctuating stocks and their storage locations, which gravitated from the cool season's arrival of ironware, chinaware, silks, tea, and a diversity of delicacies, to the hot season's exports of rice, black pepper, chili pepper, sugar, and hides. Each step of merchandise transfer between ship and shore presented opportunities for pilferage, which my work was dedicated to preventing. More serious cases of wholesale theft and port piracy lay beyond my personal ability, but my inventory journals provided a necessary preventive. Although I lacked experience in my new vocation, my intrusive presence on the docks and in the warehouses, peering into every nook and cranny as my crutch clomped across the planks, my logbook always at hand, my foreman often at my side, must have had a beneficial effect. Thus, I found a new vocation, and the means once again to escape poverty.

As my responsibilities grew along with my competence, I convinced Hia-buan to name his firm the Menam Navigation Company as a Western translation of its Chinese form. I also prevailed on him to hire my nephew, José Gonçalves, a reliable lad, to serve as supercargo on the 400-ton junk *Kim Hok Hin*, the flagship of the firm's seagoing fleet. José served well as my eyes and ears at sea, a task that my withered leg would not allow me to assume. His insights into the means by which our convoys might evade South Sea pirates and deal with swindlers at the Canton end of our venture's trading expeditions could fill a book. Through José and my contacts from St. Paul's days, the Menam Company managed to develop a lucrative Macau side-trade, and by that means I rekindled a correspondence with Fr. Martim, now quite elderly but still in place at the Vicarage as Emeritus at St. Paul's College. Each exchange of lengthy letters across the ocean-wide Bangkok-Macau trade route took a year or more through the monsoon seasons. José personally conveyed that annual correspondence on my behalf and supplied me in turn with Fr. Martim's annual packet of the latest literature from Lisbon, which I never failed to reciprocate with consignments of preserved fruits, spices, and medicaments from Siam.

Through those annual literary bequests, I was kept informed of the rapid succession of European wars inspired by French imperial pretensions, the cauldron of maritime conflict that followed, and Portugal's efforts to maintain neutrality in the midst of her faltering maritime might, until her humiliating alliance with the Napoleonic powers in 1801 under the Treaty of Badajoz placed her on the losing side of that epic struggle. The fulcrum of global power continues today to favor the British and French empires, while Portugal has fallen by the wayside, despite Pombal's former ambitions. Fortunately, that ferment has left both Macau and Siam unscathed at the distant periphery of European expansion. Imperial ambitions being what they are, however, that isolation may not continue for long.

Chronicle

For more than a decade after the fall of the Thonburi reign and my subsequent transformation from royal scribe to junk trader's comprador, I heard no more of the reign chronicle on which I had worked so diligently years before. Then, one morning in February 1795, minutes after I had risen from my bunk, a regal Garuda-prowed barge manned by 20 liveried oarsmen moored at my modest landing, unannounced, with a summons that I return with them to attend upon Prince Chakra Chesada (my former colleague La) at his Bang Lamphu palace.[29] During my former employment in the Royal Secretariat, La, then a mere lieutenant in royal service, had been known to me as a soft-spoken junior colleague devoid of pretension. As a younger half-brother of Siam's then-Ministers of War and Interior – today occupying the dual thrones of King and Viceroy – he had been elevated to royal rank with the reign change, and we had naturally lost touch. Great pleasure attended my surprise that, despite his promotion and the many years that had passed since our Royal Secretariat friendship, he had not forgotten me. It dawned on me, in hindsight, that it may well have been his intervention at the time of the reign change that had saved me from imprisonment and torture, and perhaps even death. As I have previously mentioned, he had been the covert inspiration behind my recruitment into Hia-buan's trading venture that has been my source of livelihood for the past decade, but I had had no personal contact with him then, nor since. Never before, certainly, had I received the honor of conveyance by state barge into a royal presence.

The mystery of Prince Chak's summons was eclipsed by my warm reception. Our conversation lingered on the subject of our former camaraderie, recalling past collaboration in the exacting work of compiling the Thonburi chronicle. That exchange, in turn, brought to light the surprising fact that the present king, his elder brother, had recently enjoined him to oversee the preparation of a severely redacted recension of that chronicle. Prince Chak sadly confessed that the odious task had been thrust on him as a sort of penance for his well-known devotion to the former king, but it had been a royal command he could not refuse. My views were sought on a number of issues that he had wrestled with in the rewriting – technical terms, source materials, the sequence of events, and modulations of narrative presentation. That absorbing conversation made clear the Prince's unhappiness with the revised chronicle.[30] I was dismayed to learn of wholesale alterations of our original text, especially the excision of much that King Taksin had accomplished during his reign, and the revised version's false portrayal of him as an incompetent, volatile, demented ruler.[31]

All that, it gradually became evident, was a polite overture to the purpose behind Prince Chak's invitation. Without a word to voice our shared disquiet, it became clear that I was being asked to prepare a righting – a refutation – of the offending redaction. In silent confirmation, the prince entrusted me with a number of documents that I later found to substantiate our concerns, as they stood in solid contradiction to key passages in the revised Thonburi chronicle.[32] I agreed to look further into the matter. Our leave-taking was subdued, with promises of continued friendship and future conversation. To arrange for further clandestine meetings, he suggested that as comprador for the Menam Company I deliver to his doorstep on a prearranged schedule cargoes of Chinese roofing tiles and artists' supplies for the refurbishment of Wat Sakae, which the king had ordered him to renovate. That arrangement later cloaked a series of furtive meetings at which I was introduced to several distinguished personalities of shared sentiment who related particulars on obscure aspects of the past several decades' transformative events. My efforts to prepare a reconstructed version of the original reign narrative received their warm endorsement. Prince Chak himself spent much time providing his personal perspective on the course of events and lent me further confidential documents to fill in remaining gaps in my understanding. Thus, I was lured into my life's great enterprise.

As an aside, permit me to note that the recent death of Prince Chak allows me to refer to his influential role in this project with no sense of betrayal. In any case, lingering rumors relating to his latent affinity for the Taksin cause, leading some years ago to his forced retirement from state office and banishment from state ceremonies, all tend to confirm that his sentiments had long been common knowledge within the royal household. The relegation of his forthcoming cremation at humble Wat Choenglen, outside the walled city, only a few months after his demise, represents a final humiliation for this decent man who was propelled through no ambitions of his own into the political vortex.[33]

Having been introduced by Prince Chak to the redacted Thonburi chronicle, I found its textual assault on King Taksin's character, the staining of his reputation, more than I could bear. After careful consideration of the grave implications of compiling a true record of the times, I resolved to take on the task myself. Fortunately, the Menam Company's import-export business had thrived, and many of the daily burdens of my work had devolved to others. With the firm's rising prominence, so had my household's prosperity, allowing us to hire a reliable Rosario local as our boatman and his wife as our housekeeper, to care for our everyday needs. An equally welcome development had been the current regime's waning surveillance as it gained self-confidence. No longer formally ostracized, I had regained the dignity of free association with old friends. By that means, and with the continuing support of Prince Chak, I was able to cultivate a small circle of confidantes who provided unique perspectives on the events of former days to flesh out my chronicle. My preparation an accurate chronicle of Siam's past half century could not have progressed to fruition without the contribution of those witnesses, who had found themselves caught up in the turmoil of the times and had lived to tell me their remarkable tales. I was honored to receive their trust, transcribe their recollections, and bequeath thereby their memories to future generations. I have already referred to the vital contributions of Fr. Martim Villaneuva, Junk Captain Hia-buan *sae* Liu, and Prince Chak. Here I record the names and personal particulars of several others, all of whom, sadly departed from this world, have been freed thereby from the risk of retribution for their association with these writings.[34]

The Venerable Phra Phrom Muni (Ngao) was ordained at Ayutthaya's magnificent Wat Phanan Choeng, facing the Phet Prakan Bastion across the Mae Bia Harbor not far from my childhood home, and in due course became that renowned temple's deputy abbot, a position that placed him in close contact with many members of the royal household. In the final days before the capital's fall, he and his abbot, the Venerable Phra Thamma Trailok (Si), were evacuated by one of the last junks to escape the Burmese siege and managed to reach Nakhon Si Thammarat safely.[35] When that city was reunited with Siam by King Taksin several years later, the two of them were invited to Thonburi, where Si was installed as abbot of Wat Bang Wa

Yai (later Wat Rakhang) while Ngao was appointed abbot of Wat Sakae (later Wat Saket). There, he gained renown as an ascetic meditation practitioner, medicinal herbalist, and physician to King Taksin. I was privileged to gain this senior prelate's confidence through an introduction from Prince Chak, who had been designated to oversee the temple's reconstruction. In that capacity he commissioned our trading firm to acquire from Canton roof tiles, paving stones, decorative statuary, and other furnishings for its renovation, as well as rare pigments and other artisans' supplies for a comprehensive restoration of the sanctuary's many splendid murals. Through Prince Chak's introduction we gained a trusting acquaintance that allowed me many enlightening interviews on his recollections of Ayutthaya's fall and Thonburi's resurgence.

Lady Songkandan (Thong-mon), close kin to the governor of Phetburi, was distantly related to King Taksin's mother, into whose entourage she eventually was absorbed. At a young age she had been married off to a son of Prince Chit, himself a son of King Phetracha. She and her six children survived the Ayutthaya catastrophe by joining her husband and father-in-law in escape to Phitsanulok. Both her husband and his father died there in the mayhem of 1768, and in the aftermath Thong-mon and her children (one of whom was later accepted as a consort of King Taksin and bore him a son) were invited to join the new royal household at Thonburi. There, she entered into close companionship with the king's mother and, after her death in 1776, succeeded her as superintendent of the Grand Palace Women's Quarter with the title of Lady Songkandan. In that powerful position she played an increasingly active managerial role in palace affairs as the king's health declined, while assisting in the alleviation of the agonies of his cruel injury. In recognition of her exceptional royal links and many good works, her life was spared in the days after the 1782 coup, but she was banished to Ban Tawai, a riverside settlement of Andaman refugees located a modest boat-ride downstream from my Rosario home.[36] There, I visited her often to learn the details of her remarkable life and the many events in which she had been entangled.

Army Captain Sisorarat (Ngoen), the eldest son of Colonel Ramanwong (Madot), the executed commander of King Taksin's Palace Guard and putative leader of the Mon community at Thonburi, had served as aide to his father during the Phitsanulok campaign of 1775-1776 and with his two younger brothers had been assigned during the subsequent years of the Thonburi reign to help direct the Mon military regiments guarding the kingdom's western frontiers. Recurrent jungle fevers had compelled him to return to Thonburi on sick leave during the capital's difficult months of rising fractiousness, coup, and countercoup, and he had thus been privy to many of the events propelling the Mon community's troubles leading to the 1782 reign change. After the coup, having proclaimed his innocence from all charges of rebellion against the new regime and passing through a rigorous oath swearing, he had been reassigned to his frontier duties, where he soon rose to senior military rank. Ngoen continued his duties as military liaison to the Mon principalities along the Siamese-Burmese borderlands and as head of the family household until his recent death from a sharp recurrence of his periodic fevers. In personal conversation reflecting on happier times, his recollections of the General Staff dispute that had disrupted the Phitsanulok campaign and the Mon factional quarrel that had influenced the outcome of the Thonburi coup and countercoup provided me an insider's understanding of his father's ill-fated role in the events that led to King Taksin's downfall.

Major António da Costa, as a cabin boy in the Portuguese navy out of Goa, had been seized by the Burmese in battle near the Irrawaddy delta port of Syriam around 1756. After decades in Burmese military servitude and then Siamese sanctuary, he is now fast approaching the end of his adventurous life at Rosario. After more than a decade of Burmese captivity he was assigned to forced duties at the Shwebo army base.[37] Years of military apprenticeship led to his promotion to infantry instructor with the rank of major, and he thus came to be assigned to active service first at the siege of Ayutthaya in 1766 and then in Burma's Phitsanulok campaign of 1775-1776. When the long-awaited opportunity finally arrived, he managed to defect from his Burmese masters on the eve of the Kraphuang Canal battle by galloping full tilt through the lines and throwing himself at the feet of a Siamese military officer. Vigorous interrogation could not shake his insistence on having had no effective part in the hostilities, and he was allowed to accompany Siam's Portuguese artillery squadron back to Thonburi. After the 1782 coup, he was pensioned off and, like myself, consigned to the Portuguese community at Rosario under parole, managing to supplement his meager allowance with a modest livelihood as ropemaker and shipwright. Over many a shared flagon of rum he has recounted to me scores of vivid reminiscences of Burma's Ayutthaya and Phitsanulok campaigns. From him I have learned much of Burmese military life and lore, of which I had previously been ignorant. António's detailed diary of Burma's 1775-1776 invasion of Siam has been particularly valuable in my chronicling of the events that sparked the Thonburi reign's turn to decline.

Each of the abovementioned confidantes has related to me their penetrating insights into the course of events, each has shared with me their haunting reflections on the former Thonburi reign. I have found each of them to be a person of deep insight and unquestionable integrity. Their witness to the crucial events of our lifetime has animated my recollections of the original, lost chronicle, composed nearly three decades ago, and has gone far toward amplifying the record with their personal recollections of the events and the protagonists. Thus, each evening, couched comfortably in the privacy of my riverside cottage after the day's work, my oil-wick lamp lighting my nightstand, and parchment, quill, and inkstand (all valued gifts from Macau) close at hand, I have proceeded with renewed vigor to write my account, elaborated by the information provided by my confidants, to right the historical record. My overriding objective has been to commemorate with impartiality the deeds of the major participants in Siam's recent dynastic upheavals and, through that exposition, to do justice to the king whom I had once been honored to serve. The result, for what it is worth, lies before you today.

As a safeguard against retribution by the present regime's vigilant surveillance network, as well as to facilitate accessibility by my Portuguese executors at Macau, I have composed both this testament and the accompanying chronicle of recent events not in Thai but in the language of my ancestors. That surfeit of caution entails a certain betrayal of my intent, as it distances the fruits of my work from the Siamese audience that I had most ardently wished to enlighten on the true course of recent history. However, I see no other expedient if my work – not to mention myself – is to survive. As a further precaution, I have entrusted these writings to my nephew, José, to carry with him to Macau for transfer into the custody of Fr. Martim, until such time as he sees fit to release them. Only through such desperate measures can I rest assured of their preservation, in the hope that they may someday help to set the record straight.

Dénouement

These personal reflections have skimmed lightly over the six decades of my life, a lifetime favored by the love showered on me by my sainted mother and then my wife, my passing friendships with a sequence of great men and small, and the happy consequences of repeated strokes of good fortune, to compensate for my enduring physical affliction. For my Siamese homeland as well as my beloved Portuguese community it has proved a time of unparalleled trial and profound transition, but with a brightening future in sight.

Now permanently withdrawn from both public office and private enterprise, in declining health, I have found – resorting yet again to Plutarch's evocative words – that "ease and quiet, and the study of pleasant and speculative learning, to an old man retired from command and office, is a most suitable and becoming solace."[38] In my advanced years, settled serenely with my faithful wife in our modest cottage nestled along an isolated shoreline of this tranquil River Menam, I recall the terrifying childhood tales of the awful destruction wrought by the great Lisbon earthquake of 1755 and that celebrated city's remarkable recovery under the Marquis de Pombal. That Portuguese catastrophe and the renaissance that followed shadowed my thoughts years later as I learned belatedly, and from afar, of the 1767 rape of Ayutthaya and the horrors it loosed, and as I then witnessed, following my return to Thonburi, the unfolding of Siam's resurgence. And in the wake of the 1782 coup and its remarkable consequences they continue to becloud my thoughts .... But I ramble.

Let me simply close with the words of a recent clairvoyant, François-Marie de Voltaire: "Ruthlessly trenchant fellow, wordy pedagogue, meddlesome theorist, you seek the limits of your mind. They are at the end of your nose."[39] Those perceptive thoughts have persuaded me abandon further didactics, recrimination, and speculation while I proceed to cultivate my garden, until I too shall sink silently into an anonymous grave.

And so, it is finished.[40]

The Diogo Chronicle
Preliminaries

Dramatis personae
Ayutthaya: Ban Phlu Luang Dynasty

Phon	King Boromakot, thirty-third king of Ayutthaya, and fourth of Ayutthaya's Ban Phlu Luang Dynasty.
Kung	Prince Sena Phithak, Boromakot's son and viceroy, who sought to improve state policy but was executed on charges of royal adultery.
Dok-madoea	King Uthumphon, Boromakot's son, viceroy, and successor, who abdicated in favor of his elder brother Ekathat and died in forced exile at Ava after the fall of Ayutthaya.
Ekathat	King Surayamarin, Dok-madoea's elder brother and successor as the last sovereign of the Ban Phlu Luang Dynasty, who died with the fall of Ayutthaya.
Mangkut, Rot, Pan	Three princes – Chit Sunthon (Mangkut), Sunthon Thep (Rot), and Sep Phakdi (Pan), all sons of King Boromakot – who plotted to install Dok-madoea on the throne and later plotted to overthrow his successor, King Ekathat, resulting in their execution.
Khaek (cont. below)	Prince Thep Phiphit, another Boromakot's son, who collaborated with Mangkut, Rot, and Pan in in their conspiracies and then betrayed them, resulting in his exile to the distant island kingdom of Kandy, in the island of Sri Lanka.

Burma: Konbaung Dynasty

Mang Rong	King Alaungpaya, the first king of Burma's Konbaung Dynasty, who led the assault on Siam in 1760 and died that year at the siege of Ayutthaya.
Mang Ra	King Hsinyabyushin, Mang Rong's son and successor, who orchestrated two invasions of Siam, the first resulting in the destruction of Ayutthaya in 1767 and the second the destruction of the northern capital of Phitsanulok in 1776.
"Thosakan"	General Sihabodi, who commanded Burma's northern invasion forces against Ayutthaya, 1765-1767, and presided over the capital's fall in April 1767.
"Hanuman"	General Maha Noratha, who commanded Burma's southern invasion forces against Ayutthaya, 1765-1766, and died under mysterious circumstances during the siege of the capital in late 1766.
Asae Wunki	Burma's Minister of War, who led the 1775-1776 invasion of Siam and the siege of Phitsanulok, February-March 1776.

Thonburi: Taksin's ascendance

Taksin (cont. below)
: Colonel Wachira Prakan, formerly chief of Tak and then putative governor of Kamphaeng Phet in the final days of Ayutthaya, who had commanded the Thai counterattack against Burmese invaders of the Siamese heartland in late 1767, was elevated to the position of king with the popular name of Taksin; he then presided over Thonburi's rise and Siam's resurgence.

Mut
: Colonel Siharat Decho, who was appointed Taksin's first Minister of War (1770) with the title of General Chakri Si Ongkharak after his leadership in the campaign against Nakhon, dying a year later from wounds sustained in battle.

Li-ang
: A leading junk trader of the South Sea, who was appointed Taksin's first Minister of Trade with the title of Colonel Phiphat Kosa. Upon Siam's conquest of Ha Tien in 1771 he was appointed governor of Siam's Eastern Seaboard provinces, with the title of Colonel Rachasethi.

Duang (cont. below)
: Colonel Aphai Ronarit, joint head of the Royal Guard (1768), who was promoted to Minister of the Capital in 1771 and soon thereafter was raised to Minister of War with the title of General Chakri. He led a number of military campaigns in pursuit of Siam's reintegration and expansion.

Bunma (cont. below)
: Colonel Anuchit Racha, who was appointed joint head of the Royal Guard in 1768, promoted to Minister of the Capital a year later, and then raised to General Surasi, Minister of Interior. He served with his brother Duang as commander of a succession of military campaigns contributing to the kingdom's restoration.

Khaek (cont.)
: Prince Thep Phiphit, having been exiled to Kandy, slipped back into Siam in 1762 and four years later attempted to establish a new kingdom at Phimai in opposition to Thonburi. His efforts were dashed with his defeat in 1768, and he was executed.

Sisang
: Prince Thip Phiphat, brother of Khaek, serving as ambassador to Cambodia during the late Ayutthaya reigns, reconnected with Khaek at Phimai in 1766 and there, with his brother, suffered defeat two years later. He fled to Ha Tien and died in 1769 leading a war fleet against Siam's Eastern Seaboard ports.

Tui
: Prince Chui, the disabled younger brother of Khaek and Sisang, accompanied Sisang in their exile wanderings and died in the Cambodian wilderness, abandoned by his troops en route to Sisang's assault on Siam's Eastern Seaboard ports.

Thien-tu	Self-styled Prince of Ha Tien, defied Taksin's reign at Thonburi and was subsequently defeated in a Thai maritime assault on Ha Tien in 1771. He fled into Vietnamese exile but was later reinstated by Taksin as governor of Ha Tien with the title of Colonel Rachasethi Yuan, subsequently fled to Thonburi in 1777 to escape Vietnam's Tay Son Rebellion, and died at Thonburi several years later under accusation of treason.

Thonburi: Taksin's decline and fall

Taksin (cont.)	As king of Thonburi, he withdrew from active military command after the Burmese crisis of 1776 due to incapacity from a long-festering wound. Rising insubordination and factional disputes under his diminished leadership eventually led to insurrection, culminating in a coup in March 1782 that brought him down and led to his execution on April 6, 1782.
Duang (cont.)	General Chakri, Minister of War, entered into dispute with Taksin, resulting in his assignment to command of unsupported defense of Phitsanulok against the Burmese assault of 1776, and the city's evacuation. Over the ensuing years he distanced himself from Thonburi, heading campaigns that pacified the North and subjugated Vientiane and Cambodia. In response to the March 1782 coup at Thonburi he orchestrated a counter-coup that led to his enthronement as King Rama I on April 6, 1782.
Bunma (cont.)	General Surasi, Minister of Interior, joined forces with his elder brother Duang in their distancing from Thonburi, leadership of military campaigns, and orchestration of the events that ended Taksin's reign. In the aftermath, under his brother's reign, he was elevated to Prince Surasinghanat, viceroy of Siam.
Bunrot	Colonel Thamma Trailok, Minister of the Palace, associated himself with Duang during the 1782 coup and thereby retained his ministerial position into the following reign.
Kawin	Colonel Sankhaburi, a former gunnery officer who rose to director of the Royal Arsenal, led a coup against Taksin, replaced him as head of a regency council, was overthrown in a countercoup within a few weeks of committing those audacious acts, and was soon thereafter executed.
Ramlak	Prince Anurak Songkhram, an Ayutthaya royal survivor who re-established himself at Thonburi as director of the Royal Guard, joined the coup group to replace Taksin, participated in the regency council, was overthrown with his co-conspirators, and was executed.

Madot	Colonel Ramanwong, director of the Palace Guard, joined the 1782 coup group to replace Taksin, participated in the regency council, was overthrown with his co-conspirators, and was executed.
Thong-in	Colonel Suriya Aphai, nephew and aide to Duang, was assigned to confront the coup group and succeeded in overthrowing them, setting the scene for his uncle's takeover as the new king. He was elevated to Prince Anurak Thewet at the start of the new reign and in due course rewarded with the post of deputy viceroy.
Choeng	Colonel Cheng, head of a Mon militia, supported Thong-in toward overthrowing Kawin's coup. As reward, the new king promoted him to Colonel Mahayotha, later raised to General.

Some technical notes

Diogo divided his meticulously drafted Chronicle and its accompanying Testament into two separate, untitled manuscripts. Furthermore, the Chronicle text was segmented into seven separate fascicles, equivalent to chapters. That structure has been retained in this English-language translation, with the addition of brief descriptive titles to the two manuscripts and each of the seven chapters, including further inserted brief section headings to punctuate the narrative breaks.

Each chapter contains an editorial introduction providing a modern perspective on the broader context within which the historical events occurred and within which the protagonists played out their lives, built their reputations, and met their fates. Those chapter introductions also pay passing attention to some of the deeper issues arising from Diogo's contemporary viewpoint and distinctive style of presentation.

We found several passages in the original Portuguese-language manuscript so abstruse in their archaic idiom as to be beyond possibility of precise translation. Several segments – none longer than a page or two of manuscript text – were so faded on the mildewed page that we were left with no option but to reconstruct them to fit the surrounding narrative to the best of our interpretive abilities. In each of those cases our necessary elisions and retellings have been noted.

To facilitate presentation of both the Testament and Chronicle, we gathered at appropriate points in the narrative a series of biographical sketches of the major protagonists collected from information on their backgrounds and personalities that Diogo had scattered through the text. Every effort has been exerted in our composition of those minor textual adjustments to ensure against any disruption of Diogo's narrative or distortion of the intent of his presentation.

Weights and measures have been converted to their metric equivalents, and dates have been entered in their modern (Gregorian) calendar equivalents. Similarly, to facilitate comprehension, modern place names have in most cases been substituted for the archaic terms appearing in the original manuscripts.

Ranks and titles have been translated from their archaic Thai forms to their approximate modern Western equivalents. Under that procedure, many terms have inevitably been converted imprecisely; for instance, royal ranks have been generalized to "princes" and "princesses," except for occasional references to "celestial princes" (*chao fa* – queens' sons), "lesser princes" (*phra ong chao* – concubines' sons), and "adjunct princes" (*mom chao* – royal grandsons), where appropriate.

Similarly, such modern Western executive titles as "Minister of War, "Minister of Interior," and "Minister of Trade" have been applied as loose shorthand for their functionally more diffuse traditional Siamese counterparts "*kalahom*," "*mahadthai*," and "*phra khlang,*" respectively.

Unlike modern Western norms, Siamese noble ranks carried both military and civil functions, though the military function generally took precedence. Applying those imprecise equivalents, the senior ranks of the Thai nobility and their approximate Western military/civil counterparts are as follows:[1]

Siamese rank	Western equivalent	
	Military	Civil
Chaophraya	General	Minister
Phraya	Colonel	Department Director/Provincial Governor
Phra	Major	Division Director/District Chief
Luang	Captain	Bureau Chief

The military strengths of that rank hierarchy in terms of their approximate Western equivalents may be decoded as follows:

Rank		Unit of command		Troop strength
Siamese	Western	Siamese	Western	
Chaophraya	General	*kong-thap*	army/division	10,000+
Phraya	Brigadier	*kong*	division/brigade	3,000-5,000
Phraya/Phra	Colonel	*kong* (small)	regiment/battalion	1,000
Phra/Luang	Major/Captain	*mu*	company	50-100
Khun	Lieutenant	*mu* (small)	platoon/squadron	25-50
Cha	Sergeant	*mu* (small)	squad/patrol	10-12

The Diogo Chronicle 57

For ease of recognition, we refer to the principal protagonists by their personal names, rather than by their titles (with personal names attached) as was standard practice until 1913, the year that a royal edict was enacted requiring all Siamese subjects to adopt surnames – thus, Kung, rather than Prince Thamma Thibet (Kung); Li-ang, rather than Colonel Phiphat Kosa (Li-ang); Kawin, rather than Colonel Sankhaburi (Kawin). Two important exceptions are Taksin (Colonel and then King Taksin), never referred to by his given name of Sin, and Duang (General Chakri, later King Rama I), whose full personal name Thongduang has here been reduced to its diminutive form. Besides convenience, reference to the book's chief protagonists by their personal names rather than titles has the advantage of removing much of the unnatural aura surrounding those historic personalities. No disrespect is intended by those editorial modifications.

With respect to Chinese names, we have opted to reverse the standard Chinese practice of placing the family name first, reverting to the alternative first-name convention favored by Thai speakers, inserting *sae* (the Chinese term for "lineage") preceding the surname – thus, Li-ang *sae* Tang instead of Tang Li-ang.

"Siam" is apparently a term of ancient Chinese origin ("Sayam" in its archaic Western spelling, "Thailand" only since 1939). Diogo generally referred to both the capital and the kingdom as "Ayutthaya" (itself a term open to various spellings). For clarity, we have reserved "Ayutthaya" in reference to the capital and "Siam" for the kingdom.

Neither "Thai" nor "Siamese" were terms in general use at the time of Diogo's writing. In his day, ethnicity itself was not a well-defined analytical construct, nor did a Thai equivalent of that the term exist. The Thai culture zone was not clearly identified within the broader, equally vague Tai culture map, nor was the distinctive commonality of Tai culture recognized. For convenience, the diversity of subject peoples inhabiting the kingdom of Siam are here referred to as "Siamese." That a large share – perhaps the preponderance – of Siam's population was not culturally Thai was surely recognized by Diogo but was nowhere addressed by him explicitly. That hidden topic is examined here in the respective chapters' editorial introductions.

On the issue of transliteration, we have followed Terwiel's "much simplified system . . . that indicates an approximate equivalence with spoken Thai,"[2] rather than the cumbersome, Sanskrit-based, politically charged, often unpronounceable formulations of the Royal Institute's "General System of Phonetic Transcription."

Chapter 1
Death of a Dynasty

Editor's introduction

Ayutthaya, the fabled capital of Siam since its founding in 1351, occupied an island of 7.8 square kilometers well situated at the confluence of the Chaophraya, Lopburi, and Pa Sak rivers about 90 kilometers upstream from the Gulf as the crow flies, though near twice that distance if measured by way of the winding river. The city's storied splendor and cosmopolitan vigor arose, essentially, from its locational advantage at the heart of a bountiful, densely populated rice plain that lay at the cultural margin between the hinterlands reaching north to the foothills of the Himalayan massif and maritime trade routes following the Gulf littoral to the south. Over the successive reigns of the Siamese monarchy, that initial advantage had been greatly magnified by the peopling of the plains with masses of captive peasant communities. By the year of its climactic fall in 1767, Ayutthaya had flourished over the course of four centuries of expansion from a minor river port into an entrepôt of regional and even worldwide renown.

The sparkling spires of the city's many magnificent monuments were enclosed within an 11-kilometer crenelated wall, studded with cannoned bastions and sturdy gates. Travel-weary elephant caravans plodded toward its shimmering mirage across the wet-rice plain while Western barques and Chinese junks plied their way upriver from the far-off sea by sail and oar. Scattered among the sprawling city's resplendent palaces and temples stood hundreds of high-walled patrician mansions surrounded by the humbler dwellings of their retainers, interspersed by scores of craft villages, shophouse lanes, and bustling marketplaces, all crisscrossed by brick-lined canals crowded with sampans and barges, and brick-paved roadways boisterous from dawn to dusk with the traffic of bullock and donkey carts, man-drawn barrows, hawkers shuffling under their laden shoulder-poles, and hordes of unshod pedestrians making way for the slave-borne litters, sedan chairs, and occasional liveried horses or howda-topped elephants of their masters filing through the scorching sunshine towards their secluded destinations.

In its heyday, Ayutthaya and its suburbs harbored upwards of half a million inhabitants, equivalent to contemporary Europe's greatest cities. By the eighteenth century it reigned over a kingdom that may have comprised a total population of some three million, with the outer dependencies and vassal principalities adding another million or more at the most buoyant of times. The kingdom's hierarchy of aristocracy, nobility, commons, and slaves, with its saffron-robed Buddhist clergy forming yet a fifth class, was rigidly stratified. Its small, caste-like ruling elite, concentrated at the capital, capped a wide-ranging world of provincial market towns and rustic villages. The anonymity of modern society was unknown. Among the elite everyone knew everyone; among the rest, villages functioned as extended families. Presiding over that kingdom, transforming the raw wealth wrung from its far-flung peasant population into the opulence of its privileged classes, the governing tier of gentry, bureaucrats, and aristocrats functioned under the leadership of a sequence of kings of chronically contested authority. A series of 33 sovereigns representing five consecutive dynasties ruled Siam from Ayutthaya's mid-fourteenth century founding to its mid-eighteenth-century fall. Under the kingdom's last ruling house, the Ban Phlu Luang Dynasty (1688-1767), the persistent rivalry for command of the peasant base, pitting the royal dominion against the nobility – and within the royal bloodline nurturing tensions between the successive kings and the many princes – reached degrees of intensity that weakened the integrity of the state to dangerous depths.

At its weakest, the Siamese state was less a unified kingdom than a federation of feudal principalities. It was a time and place of divided loyalties, comprising diverse ethnicities – Thai, Lao, Mon, Khmer, Malay, Cham, Indian, Chinese, and many other, lesser elements. That human mosaic comprised a harmony of cultural communities, many uprooted from their ancestral homelands by the endemic warfare between kingdoms contesting control over the populations that would secure their hegemony. A defining feature of that diverse social world was the rarely mentioned but ever-present chasm between the extremes of privilege and plenty on one hand, and subjugation and deprivation on the other, although Siam's natural fertility ensured that even the poorest generally managed to stave off starvation. With that disparate mix of peoples and extremes of wellbeing, Siam functioned as a riven state favored by faith, altruism, tolerance, and fertility while damaged by dogma, arrogance, coercion, and avarice.

Two metaphors – feudal state and galactic polity – serve as useful descriptors of Siam's political landscape under Ayutthaya's governance. Social and political ties were hierarchical rather than egalitarian; power was monopolized; and ties of patronage prevailed over broader associations of community and nation. It was a society in which all knew their place. The kingdom functioned as a pyramid of class distinctions, patron-client bonds, kinship clusters, village communities. The only person who sought no patron was the king. Just as each patron showered his clients with security and sustenance, so each client was expected to reciprocate through unstinting service, preserving the age-old balance between ambition and duty, command and subservience. In the presence of primitive production, transport, and arms technologies, that hierarchy of alliances left the peripheral regions under indirect rule, controlled from the epicenter largely through threat, perquisites, kinship, and a shared fear of the Other. Thus, within the galactic polity, the full panoply of feudal institutions – dispersed power, indirect rule, fiefdoms and vassalage, serfdom and slavery, chivalry under force of arms, agrarian modes of production, administered trade under tributary relations – was applied throughout the Siamese kingdom. Shadows of that ancient system continue to haunt modern Thailand today.

Under Siam's feudal polity, the centrifugal pull of local autonomy contended against the binding forces of the nascent central state, generating a persistent power oscillation between center and periphery. Periodic pulsations between political integration and fragmentation in concert with the fluctuating qualities of statesmanship and the shifting locus of manpower control were governed as much by the commons' perennial struggle to escape oppression as by the powerbrokers' incessant rivalry for dominion, but historians have uncovered so little documentation on the former that there is a widespread impression that only the latter mattered. Yet, periodically the commons rebelled, or at least proved intractable, out of a sense of betrayal as the terms of trade between submission and security moved against them. More often and more forcefully than others, Diogo d'Almeida in this initial chapter of his Chronicle of the times refers to the plight of the commons, but in the final analysis he fails to fully escape the elitist preoccupations that pervade Siam's chronicles tradition.

As historians have often asserted, the critical economic issue in traditional Siam was the chronic shortage of manpower resources required to cultivate the land, to provide the labor for public works, to enforce the domestic peace, to fend off foreign invasion. The central state and its provincial minions sought to remedy that scarcity with both promises of beneficence and threats of coercion to its recalcitrant peasantry, supplemented by periodic slave raids and imperial conquests across the frontiers. It could be argued that the intensity of human exploitation was a function of manpower scarcity, but there is no evidence that the degree of abuse eased as the labor supply increased. Every indication suggests that the elite's oppresive treatment of the commons persisted, primarily out of its short-sightedness, self-absorption, greed, and incompetence.

This initial chapter of Diogo's Chronicle examines the contest for ascendancy within the ranks of the Siamese aristocracy over the course of the Ban Phlu Luang Dynasty, particularly in the habitually tense relations between king and viceroy. The elaborate hierarchy of royal rank and its associated gradations of court protocol, privilege, and preference included clear-cut hereditary distinctions between "celestial" princes and princesses (*chao fa*, the offspring of queens), "lesser" princes and princesses (*phra ong chao*, the offspring of concubines), and "princelings" (*mom chao*, the grandchildren of kings, whether by queens or concubines). Within the nobility, rank was prescribed through appointments to office rather than through the bonds of ancestry, although hereditary connections certainly played a major role. Ranks in the nobility held dual military and civil connotations. At the highest level stood ministers assigned essential state functions and governors of major provinces, generally occupying the rank of army general (*chaophraya*). Below them stood directors-general of functional departments and governors of smaller provinces, most holding the rank of colonel (*phraya*). Third in line were division directors and provincial deputy-governors, commonly holding captaincies or lieutenancies (*phra*, *luang*, and *khun*). To Ayutthaya's power elite, schooled in rank-consciousness from birth, sensitivity to gradations of feudal status was as instinctual as breathing.

In dealing with the quest for power among the leading personalities of the Ban Phlu Luang Dynasty, Diogo's account deviates in many particulars from what he sometimes refers to as the "official" Ayutthaya chronicles. It dwells on the virulent exploitation of the peasantry and the implications of that practice for the integrity of the state, implying that the death of the dynasty and the downfall of the Siamese state were not simply a consequence of the moral shortcomings of its rulers or the product of foreign aggression but were the outcome of a mounting systemic failure. Could the kingdom have fallen, ultimately, as the result of an illicit romance? The suspicion cannot be escaped that the tragic romantic affair between King Boromokot's son and viceroy, Prince Kung, and his favored Queen Sangwan was not merely the fabricated plot of a political conspiracy but in a larger sense was the product of a feudal reaction against the impulses favoring a more centralized state. As related in Diogo's Chronicle (while downplayed in the "official" chronicles), that artfully orchestrated elimination of Kung from the royal succession proved to be a turning point in Ayutthaya's political history. It is evident from Diogo's revisionist history that the kingdom's political course would have taken a different turn had Kung been allowed to accede to the throne, implement his reformist manpower policy, consolidate state power and control, and lead the Siamese defense against the Burmese invasions of 1760 and 1765-1767. Tragically, Siam lost its way under the weakened leadership of the aging King Boromokot, struggled on through the brief reign of his unwilling successor King Uthumphon, and then collapsed under the maladministration of the ineffectual King Ekathat.

Reigns

As King Narai lay dying in his Lopburi palace in 1688 at the peak of his benevolent, cosmopolitan reign, his nemesis, the ruthless commander of Ayutthaya's elephant corps, orchestrated a military putsch, occupied the capital, imposed martial law, and usurped the throne. Known thenceforth as King Phetracha, that audacious general's prime claim to fame had formerly been his ferocious practice of spicing his elephants' feed with gunpowder and their drink with liquor to madden the great brutes to fighting rage, to the extent that they would sometimes turn on their own troops in battle. In a more carefully arranged use of those beasts' lethal power, he took delight in the execution of his adversaries under the feet of the elephants' massive bulk. He also gladdened in feeding miscreant courtiers to the tigers that he kept caged for that singular purpose near the capital's prison stockade. His dramatic seizure of power replaced a glorious epoch of Siamese history with the scandal-plagued demise of his dynasty, the last of the Ayutthaya era.

Fast on the heels of that dynastic overthrow, the new king demonstrated his reputation for callous willfulness by exposing his abused people to the exceptional burden of a redoubled military mobilization and steeply raised rice taxes, all in the misguided fear that the kingdom was subject to imminent risk of attack. The corvée – the periodic exaction of state service imposed on nearly all able-bodied commoners – was increased from three to six months, leaving the women, children, and elderly to shoulder alone much of the back-breaking toil of sowing, tending, and harvesting the rice crop. In addition, with the rise in the traditional rice-land tax from 200 to as much as 320 liters of paddy for a typical 10-rai family smallholding,[1] the agony of the people's deprivation swelled to bursting. Those insuperable conditions drove many to defy the state's exactions in passive resistance, lawlessness, or flight to the hills. Sporadic mutiny and the growing threat of peasant rebellion, combined with opposition from some royal quarters, only intensified the savagery of King Phetracha's martial regime. The king's concern for his personal safety under those conditions led him to lay out a fortified royal residence within the Grand Palace with the appropriation of a section of the women's quarter for a separately walled and moated compound centering on the Banyong Ratanat Throne Hall, approachable only across a sentried drawbridge.[2]

After a 15-year reign notable for little more than its implacable repression, King Phetracha's clever but widely detested son Luang Sorasak succeeded to the throne without opposition, as all potential contenders had already been mercilessly removed from the scene. Consecrated as King Suriyen Thibodi, he came to be known to posterity as the Tiger King in recognition of the unparalleled cruelty of his impositions on the common folk no less than for his notoriety as a depraved lecher. That harshest, most cunning of kings presided over the rise of Siam's privileged classes to new heights of opulence, resting on the backs of the rice-farming commons. His father's oppression of the peasantry as a military expedient was transformed into an enterprise for the elite's aggrandizement. Siam under his rule prospered through the coerced clearing

Table 1. The Ban Phlu Luang Dynasty (principal personae), 1688–1767

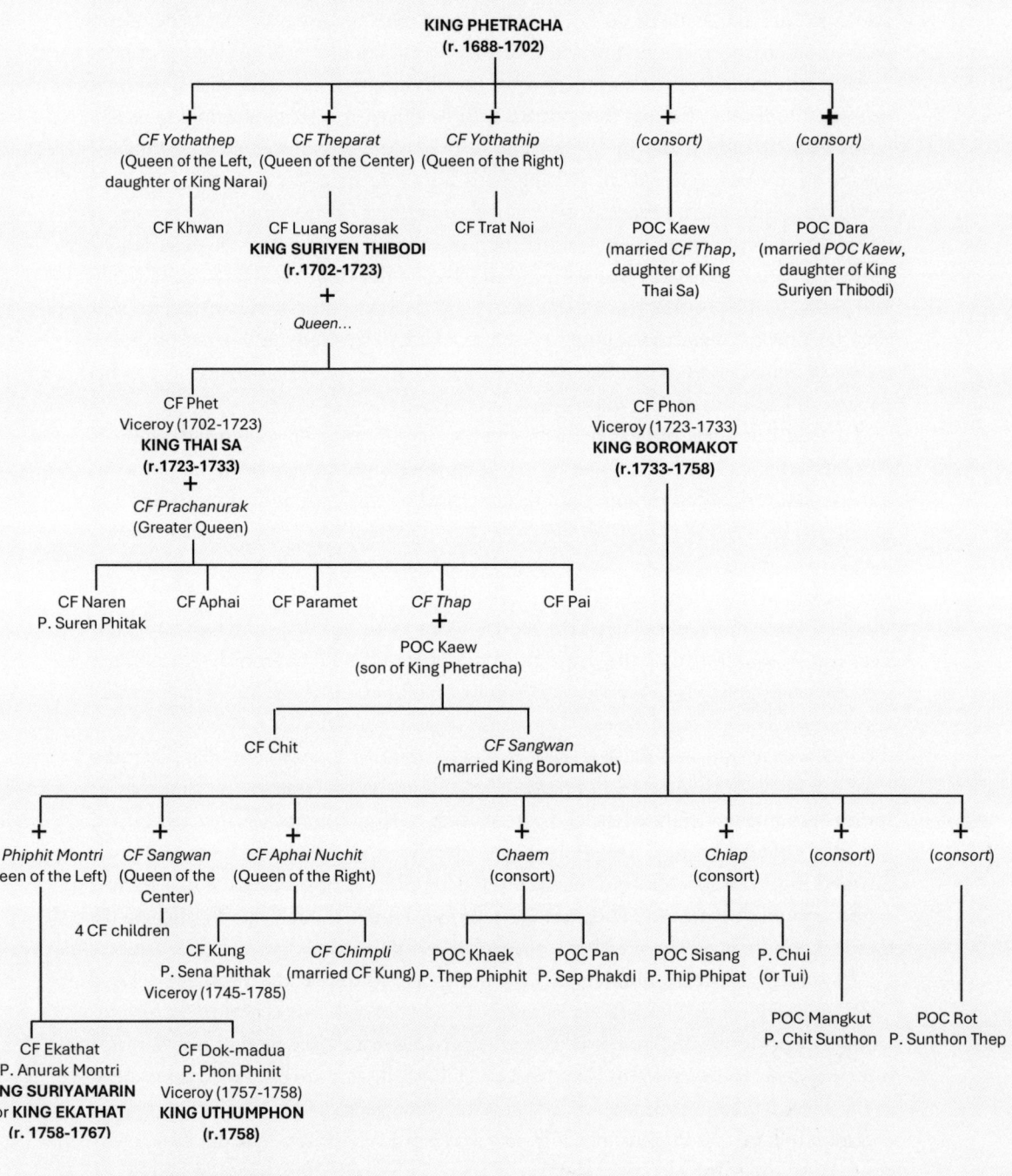

Map 1. The Ayutthaya Grand Palace and its royal environs, pre-1767

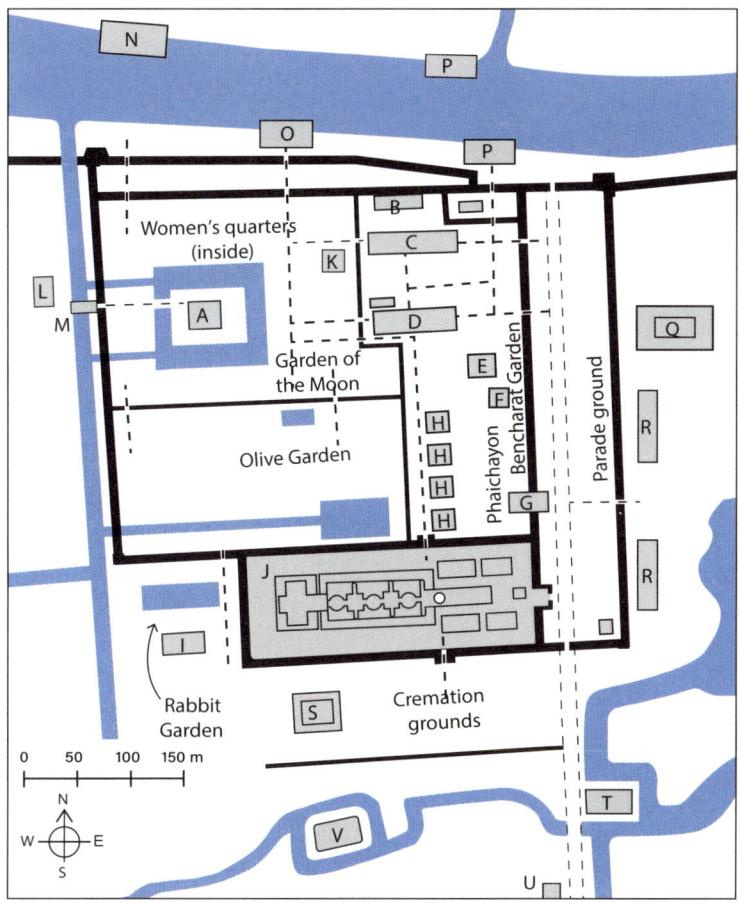

Based on Boran Rachathanin, 1969, fold-out map insert; and Baker and Pasuk, 2016, p. 56.

		Major Sites	
		Grand Palace	Palace periphery
	A	Banyong Ratanat Throne Hall	L Ministers' assembly pavilion
▬▬ Outer palace walls	B	Suriyat Amarin Throne Hall	M Drawbridge
— Inner palace walls	C	Sanphet Prasat Throne Hall	N Royal Guard naval landing
∷∷∷ Causeway	D	Wihan Somdet Throne Hall	O Wasukri Royal Landing
- - - Major palace walkways	E	Phra Monthien Tham Shrine	P Ministers' Landings
▨ Major structures	F	Phra Thep Bidon Shrine	Q Wat Thammikarat
	G	Chakraphat Phaicharon Throne Hall	R Cavalry barracks
	H	Storehouses	S Wat Phra Mongkhon Bophit
	I	Suan Kratai Royal Residence	T Wat Phra Ram
	J	Wat Phra Si Sanphet	U City pillar
	K	Water Tower	V Municipal prisoner

and irrigation of new agrarian tracts, exacted extraction of forest resources, and extortion of tribute, while its ruling classes descended into discord, decadence, and scandal under a regime of unrestrained avarice. Great personages, it has been said, are often marked by vices as vicious as their virtues are benign.³ The Tiger King's mercifully brief reign was followed in 1709 by the bloodless succession of his eldest son and viceroy, Prince Phet, as King Phumin Racha, better known as King Thai Sa. Lacking his father's brutality, King Thai Sa tolerated the

A crowned Buddha image in royal regalia, late Ayutthaya era. (Google Images)

provincial nobility's seduction of yeomen, serfs, and slaves from the royal manpower base with promises of eased conditions of servitude, sanctioning thereby a progressive dispersal of the crown's manpower resources to provincial control so long as he continued to receive his allotted tax, tribute, and trade revenues. Belatedly, he grew to recognize the dangers of that benign policy, but his sporadic attempts to reassert royal command over the kingdom's manpower base met stubborn resistance from covetous princes and provincial nobles and ultimately came to test their loyalty.[4] Sitting uneasy on the throne in the presence of his courtiers' unbridled venality, King Thai Sa departed from customary practice by appointing his seasoned brother Prince Phon as viceroy, in preference to his inexperienced senior son Prince Aphai, with the proviso that the throne should pass to Aphai in due course. Inevitably, upon the king's death in 1733, an armed struggle for the succession erupted between the supporters of Phon and Aphai, culminating in a furious elephant duel in the midst of the capital.[5] Victorious, Phon ascended the throne in 1733 as King Thammaracha Thirat II – or, as he was posthumously remembered, King Boromakot. To consolidate his position, the newly crowned King Boromakot ordered the immediate execution of Prince Aphai and scores of his supporters.

In contrast to the ferocity that had marked his ascent to the throne, King Boromakot over the course of his reign pursued a policy of harmonious relations with Siam's neighbors, while at home he maintained tranquility through the appeasement of contending court factions and the vigorous patronage of Buddhism. The royal treasury was filled to the brim with the proceeds of a thriving export trade in rice, spices, and forest produce. China's easing of overseas trade restrictions encouraged convoys of cargo junks in increasing numbers to ply the trade routes between Ayutthaya and the ports of southeast China.[6] Commerce with India, Lanka, and points west, through Siam's trade depots along the Andaman coast, also flourished. Preeminent among Boromakot's many meritorious projects funded by those trade profits was the reconstruction of many temples in the capital and surrounding provinces, as well as the refurbishment of the Grand Palace and numerous otherpalaces. Observers bedazzled by Ayutthaya's splendor came to speak of

Boromakot's reign as a cultural flowering, a Siamese Golden Age, although beneath the glitter the subjugation of the kingdom's peasantry continued undiminished.

Yet Boromakot, like his predecessors, was unable to quell the factional rivalries that continued to divide his court. Particularly troubling was the disaffection of the provincial nobility, who strove to benefit from the persistent flight of the much-abused royal-service labor force from the king's estates. The king sought to redress the rising power of the more irascible provincial governors by curbing their influence: reinforcing the apparatus for collection of tax on rice-land, creating new centrally directed state agencies to dilute local authority, introducing princely postings in royal oversight of key administrative offices, and outposting reliable junior officers to observe and report directly to him on provincial activities.[7] Those acts, however, had the perverse effect of nurturing clandestine alliances between malcontent royals and upstart nobles, further weakening the Siamese center as some of the more covetous princes took the opportunity to collaborate with the nobility in poaching royal-service peasants from the king's lands.

To counteract the persistent erosion of the royal manpower base, Boromakot in 1742 ordered a comprehensive registration of the kingdom's labor force requiring the tattooing of all adult male commoners to ensure their indelible identification. As with much other legislation aimed at strengthening royal command over the fragile, decentralized Siamese state, widespread evasion limited the effectiveness of that measure. Ancient wisdom cautions that a populace minds its rulers best when it is neither humored nor oppressed. Boromakot ignored that prescription by indulging his courtiers and ministers while reigning roughly over the provincial nobility. Consequently, while he sought to lead, the lesser, dispersed elites were loath to follow.

In his ongoing effort to tamp down dissension from various factions within the royal family backing alternative aspirants to the throne, Boromakot long delayed the appointment of his viceroy, but that deferral only fueled the smoldering ambitions of Ayutthaya's contending princes, sparking new factional conspiracies. Finally, in 1741, after years of delay, the king took the long-anticipated step of awarding that preeminent post to his eldest celestial son Kung, who received with it the eminent title of Prince Sena Phithak.[8] The appointment of Kung as viceroy exposed to the light of day the rankling resentments of an influential clique of lesser princes. Thinking that Kung's privileged position reflected adversely upon them, and envious of his elevation to greatness, they henceforth took every occasion, through private slanders, to render him obnoxious to the king.[9]

As King Boromakot declined into old age and failing health, Kung's vulnerable position as his viceregal factotum and heir presumptive in a sea of courtly intrigue was long safeguarded by the king's three ablest officers and most trusted advisors, nobles who had been rewarded with the ministerial portfolios for War, Interior, and Trade.[10] The deaths of all three of those stalwarts in the early 1750s saw an immediate return of the malicious bickering for royal favor that had been held in check under their deft management. The state administration fell into confusion. What had been a manageable contest for preferment and perquisites now blossomed into blatant political dissonance; what had been a gradual slippage of power from the sovereign center to the provincial periphery now intensified to troubling proportions. The king reigned, but he no longer ruled. Kung came into his own as the voice of royal authority in opposition to the rising tide of insolence among the lesser princes and truculence among the provincial nobility.

Alarmed by the Crown's eroding jurisdiction, which he expected soon to inherit as his patrimony, Kung devised a comprehensive strategy to reenergize the center's political dominion.[11] He evidently believed that the swift approval and execution of that plan while his father still reigned would smooth his way to the throne, but he never considered that this attempt to use the king, his father, as his cat's paw might cause a rift between them.[12] At a private audience with his aging father, Kung submitted his proposal to revitalize the monarchy. He fully expected the king's approval and active support toward its realization. Precisely what transpired during the course of that meeting is not known, but Kung came away from it dumbfounded. He subsequently revealed to his confidantes his dismay at the old man's befuddlement. In view of later events, the king's seeming confusion apparently served as a disguise for his displeasure. His insipid response was motivated not by an addled mind but by his suppressed rage at Kung's impudence in implying that the kingdom's governance had been mismanaged, his vexation at Kung's failure to appreciate his carefully calibrated balancing of the contending forces surrounding the throne, and his indignation at Kung's transparent pretensions for enhanced royal power.

Far worse than Kung's dismay in receiving what he saw as a noncommittal hearing was his consternation upon receiving his father's instruction that he present his proposal for consideration by the realm's princes and senior nobles gathered in formal assembly. That directive placed Kung in the untenable position of having to confront in open debate the very functionaries most certain to oppose him. Reluctantly, on the appointed day in February 1755, he presented his radical agenda for the kingdom's rejuvenation before the enthroned king and gathered aristocracy in the ministerial audience chamber of the Grand Palace. In the traditional formulaic terms used for supplicating the king, Kung cast his plan in moral tones. He recounted eloquently the plight of the peasantry and petitioned Boromakot, as an enlightened Buddhist monarch, to ease their suffering by invigorating the tradition of royal benevolence exemplified by the great kings of Buddhist lore, culminating in King Narai.[13] To achieve that end he offered a threefold strategy: a shortening of the annual corvée from six to three months; a reduction in the riceland tax by half; and a return of all absconded royal yeomen and serfs to the direct jurisdiction of the king. In pragmatic justification he emphasized that such a humane policy would enrich the kingdom by increasing agrarian productivity while deterring peasant recalcitrance and desertion.

Without offering his own opinion, the king invited the assembled ministers to voice their views freely, but no response was forthcoming. In astonishing contrast to the usual murmured commentary expressing polite approval or demurral, or the broaching of discreet questions seeking clarification or amplification, or the suggestion of possible lines of compromise, Kung's declamation was answered with deathly silence – a thunderous repudiation that spelled its fate. Kung had vastly underestimated the depths of opposition to his plan. The nobility and their princely collaborators had recognized instantly that an effective redeployment of the absconded royal yeomen and serfs back to the king's jurisdiction would sharply reduce their power and wealth. Even more seriously, it would reveal their established pattern of systematic underreporting of taxable proceeds, which would expose them to criminal prosecution and all its attendant horrors. Even in its rejection, Kung's proposal, with its revolutionary implications for the redistribution of Siam's wealth and power, unleashed a cascade of consequences that culminated, little more than a decade later, in the kingdom's destruction.

Treachery

Joyous celebrations attended the onset of King Boromakot's sixth cycle (seventy-second) birthday in May 1755. Behind the festivities, however, the king was dispirited by the recent deaths of several of his closest comrades-in-arms, his distancing from his ill-starred viceroy and heir presumptive, his vexation at the incessant bickering among his courtiers, and his suffering under the gathering indispositions of old age. His declining faculties had left him struggling against reliance on juniors younger by a generation or more. He had become piteously vulnerable to their machinations aimed at circumventing his temporal powers. Age, that stealthy thief, had stolen from him the strength of his manhood, leaving only the smoldering embers of reason and desire. Moreover, the inertia forced on him by his repugnant obesity and its associated ailments was a great impediment. Among his detractors – who expressed their views quietly under threat of dire consequences – it was whispered: "What use is this man, when all between throat and groin is taken up by belly?"[14] Beyond the inevitable ills of age, he had long suffered a shamefully disfiguring disease.[15] On public occasions he wore a high-necked garment to hide the suppurating lobes wobbling like a rooster's wattles from his throat.[16] The discomfort of that unsightly, unspoken stigma tormented him ceaselessly, as many of his courtiers considered such a blemish to bespeak a loss of spiritual merit.

Some 22 years earlier, upon his investiture as king, Boromakot had raised his two senior wives to the dual posts of Queen of the Right and Queen of the Left. A third, far younger princess, Sangwan, of impeccable royal pedigree, had later been added as Queen of the Center. Although daughter of no king, she was granddaughter of two through the marriage of a son of King Phetracha and daughter of King Thai Sa. Princess Sangwan's marriage to King Boromakot several years after his rise to the throne had been orchestrated to cement his royal credentials in hopes of uniting the contending court factions, but it had failed in that intent. Despite raising her to the highest position to which a woman could aspire in Ayutthaya's social hierarchy, her status as queen had inevitably drawn her into the web of factional envy and antagonism. While she was the youngest of the king's three queens, she was years older than most of his later consorts, many of whom were scarcely past puberty when bestowed on him in concubinage; they soon came to see her as their principal rival for his affections. Her sustained favor within the royal household was confirmed by the fact that, while many of the king's consorts remained childless, she bore him four children.[17]

Kung, the king's eldest celestial son, though wanting in political guile, was favored for his good looks, vivacity, and intellect, which had secured his popular standing and ultimately his appointment as viceroy and heir presumptive. Under Kung's residency as viceroy, the Front Palace became a center of artistic virtuosity and craftsmanship. Assisted by his circle of poets, Kung composed a corpus of celebrated boat songs, elegies, Buddhist reflections, and amorous verses.[18] His royal dance troupe, specializing in innovative interpretations of the *Ramayana* epic, was said to be the finest in the realm. Among the many royal construction projects that contributed to his renown was a comprehensive renovation of the Grand Palace Chapel Royal; along the outer wall of the gallery circling the chapel's three giant reliquary monuments his artists painted elaborate murals portraying scenes from the *Ramayana*.[19] With the participation of his scribes he produced a lavishly illustrated compilation of the ancient Thai texts on military strategy.[20] Under his command the Front Palace Pages Corps gained prominence for the excellent training of its aspiring junior officers.[21] For years Boromakot doted on this exceptional son as a fitting heir to the throne and bestowed upon him many extravagant rewards for his good works, until the king's growing susceptibility to malicious court rumors started to erode his confidence. As is often the fate of great men, Kung could escape neither the envy of his inferiors nor the naïve overconfidence nurtured by his own spirited nature.

Upon Kung's enthronement as viceroy, his full-sister Princess Chimpli, had been elevated to preside over the Front Palace as his wife in the expectation that she would someday reign over the Grand Palace as his senior queen. The marriage was a decidedly political arrangement rather than a love match; convention placed her, at more than 30 years of age, far past her prime as a bride, and she was no beauty. Nevertheless, Chimpli was exhilarated by the unexpected change in her status, as it transformed her prospects from those of an unmarriageable royal spinster into matron of the kingdom's second most prestigious court, with further honors in the offing. Moreover, Kung was evidently relieved to receive into his household such a trusted, competent, stabilizing companion and steward, leaving him untroubled in his other pursuits.[22]

Kung and his two celestial half-brothers Ekathat and Dok-madoea were subtly opposed by a cabal of three of their lesser half-brothers – Princes Chit Sunthon (Mangkut), Sunthon Thep (Rot), and Sep Phakdi (Pan) – lower in royal status as the sons of concubines rather than queens, though not lesser in age, acuity, or ambition. An anomaly in the mix was Prince Thep Phiphit (Khaek), elder full-brother of Pan, a confirmed opportunist who consistently equivocated between the opposing princely camps. That cluster of lesser princes had grown dissatisfied with their lot as appointments to higher office consistently bypassed their clique in favor of the celestial princes and their minions. Not daring to vent their frustrations directly to the king, Mangkut, Rot, and Pan plotted against Kung, the viceroy, while Khaek stood aside, uncommitted. Kung was initially accused by his detractors of *lèse majesté* for his failure to attend royal audiences for nearly three years. However, the king well knew that his son had contracted a debilitating disease and that it was his slow convalescence that had required him to miss attendance at court.[23] Failing in that attempt to drive a wedge between King Boromakot and his favored son, they devised an elaborate intrigue to oust Kung from his prominent position. In this they were abetted by a pack of provincial governors with whom they had previously collaborated in the diversion of royal manpower and revenues. Subsequent to the ministerial assembly at which Kung broached his subversive views on the manpower issue, that faction had good reason to dread the prospect of his imminent rise to the throne.

In October 1755 Rot, representing the conspirators, sought a private audience with his father the king. There, he hesitantly voiced his suspicions that Kung and Queen Sangwan, Boromakot's senior consort, had been conducting an adulterous affair.[24] Gossip, rumor, and scandal were favored currencies of court life. Ordinarily, experienced aristocrats paid little attention to such talk, but in this instance the suborned testimony of two of Sangwan's ladies-in-waiting, confirmed by several of her handmaids, corroborated the accusations. The gullible old king was astounded, then distraught, and finally outraged by the salacious charges leveled against his queen and his viceroy/son. Although well advanced in years, he allowed himself to be consumed by the passion of the moment as uncontrollably as any love-spurned youth; some such transport, it is thought, betrayed him into his fatal fury, which lost him the regard of many.[25] He ordered the immediate arrest of Kung and Sangwan to answer the charges.

That an illicit liaison between the king's senior son and favorite queen actually occurred is of course possible. The unattainable ever attracts temptation. If true, the accusations opened to public scrutiny a scandalous combination of romance, lust, and infidelity at the highest level. Alternatively, if the accusations were a

Amorous Couple. (Muang Boran archive)

Death of a Dynasty 71

fabrication, they revealed a uniquely perfidious instance of factional intrigue within the royal family. Inevitably, the question must be posed whether the charge, verdict, and penalty were justified. Would Kung have contemplated cuckolding his own father? As a mature man of 45, endowed with his own household as well as ready access to virtually any woman he might fancy, would he have found his royal stepmother an irresistible temptation? Would Sangwan, loved by the king and mother of four of his children, have willingly entered into such an ill-starred liaison? The weight of those considerations, substantiated by the absence of any evidence other than the coerced confessions of certain alleged accomplices, leans heavily in favor of the defendants.

Beyond the question of motive there lies the issue of opportunity. The means of orchestrating an amorous rendezvous between two ranking royals in the decidedly non-private, closely guarded confines of Ayutthaya's Grand Palace would have posed a daunting challenge. Unless called away by the king, Sangwan would have spent her nights with her young children and ladies-in-waiting. Intrusion into that scene, or her departure from it without companions, would have been unthinkable. Surrounded as both the viceroy and the queen constantly were by their separate coteries of servants and sycophants, and with the queen generally confined to the Inside (the royal women's quarter), arrangement of a tryst would have required the complicity of many attendants – not impossible, but highly improbable. It was asserted that Kung, disguised as a servant-woman, had entered the Grand Palace at dusk through the Din Gate, leading from a bustling riverside market behind the harem, and then after dark had climbed the inner wall to her personal quarters.[26] But Kung was a large man and well known; women dressed lightly and were closely scrutinized in their passage into and out of the harem, and the outer palace gates were well-manned and the walls high. In any case, all this is a moot point. It was the outcome and aftermath that require attention.

The twin tasks of verifying the allegations and designating the appropriate remedies were delegated to twin judicial panels – a court of inquiry and a tribunal to pass judgment and assign punishment – each headed by a select group of nobles most of whom were so senior as to be in their dotage. They were as convinced as the king by the testimony proffered by the queen's terrified servants. As heads of their own extended households, those dignitaries could readily sympathize with the anguish and indignation suffered by the allegedly cuckolded old man. As elder statesmen, they recognized full well the political implications of any suspected disruption to the royal line of descent. So, they proceeded down the conventional path of consigning the accused to trial by ordeal, under which they were subjected to the relatively gentle torture of repeated rounds of suffocation underwater until the truth burst forth from their throats.[27] The outcome was virtually preordained; both defendants were found guilty of adultery.

Under the criminal law, four types of wrongdoing warranted execution: treason, banditry, murder, and kidnapping; the prescribed forms of execution were 21 in number, ranging from slicing, chopping, spearing, and flaying to impaling, beating, burning, and boiling. There was no certitude that a prince's cuckolding of the king warranted capital punishment. Ayutthaya's palatine law specified execution as the standard remedy for treason, which was defined broadly as any offense, physical or

Caning as a royal punishment. (Editor's photos). These two details from the Ramakien murals lining Bangkok's Wat Phra Kaew cloister wall, dating from the First Reign, show the punishment of royal malefactors under judicial proceedings. Such flogging by bamboo cane, or alternatively by wooden cudgel, was calibrated in severity in conformity with the palatine law. These two images may well have served as elliptical references to the 1755 executions of Prince Kung and Queen Sangwan.

verbal, actual or threatened, against the person of the king, queens, or viceroy, but it did not go into specifics on that point. While the court felt that the gravity of the crime in the present instant warranted capital punishment, neither the palatine law nor the criminal code offered an unequivocal verdict on the matter. Thus, the judges prescribed the lesser penalty of caning – but, adding charge upon charge, caning to a degree of severity tantamount to a death sentence.[28]

After lengthy deliberations, it was decided that Kung should be allotted a total of 130 strokes while Sangwan should receive 30. The two wrongdoers were first divested of their royal ranks and entitlements and then placed in fetters and brought to the wasteland behind Wat Chai Wathanaram, situated across the Chaophraya River from the walled city. Standard procedure dictated that the offenders be stripped to the waist and made to sit on the ground bent forward facing a wooden stake, arms and legs forcibly extended with wooden splints. In that awkward posture, with their wrists and ankles tied to the post, their backs were beaten to a bloody pulp. The beating was inflicted on Kung in sets of 20 strokes per day, allowing him time between sets to recover his wits and strength, but that was of little avail, as he died in the stocks on the sixth day, after 108 strokes. Sangwan received her full punishment in one sitting; it is said that she died of a self-inflicted potion when the physicians deemed that her shattered ribs and lacerated spine would leave her forever an invalid. Both bodies were buried with minimal ceremony in the charnel ground adjoining the temple. With them were put to death (by less elaborate means) a number of their household staff

Death of a Dynasty

and servants who had been implicated as conspirators. Cremation and its attendant rituals were foregone, leaving their spirits to wander the world as ghosts or demons. So, justice for the aggrieved king was mercilessly exacted.

Once heads had cleared, informed opinion came to see the absurdity of the charges and the evil of the political motive behind them. Slowly it emerged that the betrayal had not been Kung's and Sangwan's but had been committed by the aforementioned cabal of lesser princes (Mangkut, Rot, and Pan) and their corrupt subordinates. They had been too readily believed in their scurrilous defamation. Eventually, even the king came to doubt the righteousness of the judgment, stating in a spasm of remorse that the evidence had been harshly misinterpreted and the penalty wrongly administered. Nor, he held, had the judges adhered to his guidance on the matter. He had not declared for capital punishment, he said, but only for a severe civil penalty, which should have required no more than a limited caning and a brief imprisonment.[29] In the aftermath, the king's health declined rapidly. Within three years he, too, passed from the scene.

Abdication

Beyond this personal tragedy, the death of Kung confronted King Boromakot and his councilors with a political predicament. Realizing that the king had not long to live, and that timely action was needed to forestall a succession dispute, it was proposed that Prince Dok-madoea be appointed as the new viceroy, bypassing his elder brother, Prince Ekathat, who was judged unfit for the position. The two brothers could scarcely have been more different in character. Ekathat was deficient in intelligence, diligence, discretion, and force of character. His worst vices centered on incognito nighttime revels among the back-lane brothels of the city's most disreputable precincts. Dok-madoea, in sharp contrast, was a reserved man of mild temperament and quiet integrity. To the dismay of the king and his advisors, however, Dok-madoea favored the monastic life over the unprincipled world of politics. He resisted the king's summons to the political fold, insisting that Ekathat, as his elder full brother, was the rightful claimant to the viceregal post. Nevertheless, his preference for obscurity was overruled, and he was formally enthroned as viceroy with the elevated title of Prince Phon Phinit in March 1758, as the 74-year-old king lay on his deathbed. One of his first acts in that new post was to beseech his elder brother to believe him when he pleaded to having played no willing role in that appointment. His humility convinced Ekathat, and they remained fraternal friends, although Ekathat's hurt at his father's decision was great: "to feel so woefully wounded at being refused such a distinction could only arise from an overweening appetite to have it."[30]

The ailing king took to his bed in the royal bedchamber attached to the secluded Banyong Ratanat Throne Hall. In keeping with court protocol, Dok-madoea as viceroy should have taken residence in the Front Palace at the far end of the city, an hour's palanquin procession to the fast-fading king's bedside. As a devoted son, he chose instead to remain close by the king at the Rabbit Garden Residence, a quiet retreat

Detail from an Ayutthaya-era gold-on-black-lacquer manuscript cabinet door panel depicting a military commander and his troops receiving orders from a king gazing down from his royal pavilion. (Editor's photo)

attached to the Grand Palace. Those lodgings, located directly behind the Chapel Royal, were remodeled to meet his needs, including the construction of a private entryway to the chapel for his daily devotions. Ekathat, not to be outdone, received his father's permission to occupy the residential quarters in the newly built Suriyat Amarin Throne Hall, an equally short distance from the king's bedchamber. The title of Prince Anurak Montri had been conferred on him, but since that title could be read to imply that he was now to serve in the subordinate role of protector and councilor to his younger brother he chose to refer to himself by the name of his royal quarters; the name Suriyamarin stayed with him through the rest of his life.

Much like Kung before him, Dok-madoea disdained arrogance in his everyday behavior. He had long studied meditative practice as a means toward the conquest of envy and anger. He professed that it is not sufficient for a man to be obliging to his friends but, rather, that he be ready to forgive those who have done him wrong, to let the world see that he did not value himself so much in excelling Ekathat in ability and conduct as he did in outdoing him in justice and clemency.[31] He was temperamentally incapable of committing the evils attendant to political command – the need to rely on intimidation, favor duplicity, turn a blind eye to corruption, manipulate subordinates, stomach sycophants, dole out awful punishments, plot bloody warfare, and the like.

Death of a Dynasty

His critics insisted, however, that a prince who professes goodness in everything is bound to come to ruin in a court brimming with those who are not good, and it is therefore necessary for him, if he seeks to survive, to learn how not to be good, and to use that ability as necessity may require.

Less than a month after Dok-madoea's designation as viceroy, King Boromakot died. As had been ordained by the dying king, the newly inducted viceroy was proclaimed his successor with the reign name of King Uthumphon.[32] He proved to be one of Siam's most popular kings; his early life as a younger brother had instilled in him all the arts of obedience, adding to his natural kingly qualities a strain of sympathy for the oppressed, which fitted him well for governance when it fell to his lot. Over the course of his all-too-brief incumbency as sovereign of Siam he was esteemed by the people, beloved by his friends, and admired by many as the best of men. "For he possessed a singularly gentle nature, an insensibility to the passions of anger or pleasure or covetousness, and an unswerving steadiness and inflexibility in his strivings for what he thought right and honest."[33]

The newly crowned King Uthumphon decided to continue his residence, for the time being, at the unpretentious Rabbit Garden Residence, adjoining the rear of the Chapel Royal, formally known as Wat Si Sanphet in honor of its presiding Buddha image. Ekathat, at war with himself in humiliation, avoided the reign change with a brief period of monastic ordination at Wat Na Phra Men, directly across the Lopburi River from the Grand Palace. He did not contest the throne by harsh word or armed might. Instead, he simply staked his claim silently with his refusal to vacate the Suriyat Amarin Throne Hall, confirming the ancient aphorism that it is safer to be hated than to be loved, as men have less hesitation about affronting one who makes himself accommodating than one who makes himself obdurate.[34]

While Ekathat sulked in his arrogated royal quarters, Uthumphon had the royal urn containing the remains of the former king, his father, placed with fitting reverence in the Banyong Ratanat Throne Hall, the moated redoubt that since the reign of King Phetracha had symbolized his dynasty's grasp of the reigns of authority. After appropriate obeisance before the great urn, he convened a gathering of all senior members of the royal family in the audience hall of his Rabbit Garden residence. At that grand event he announced with all the fervor that his newfound eminence would allow that he would not further abide the self-serving, divisive conduct of the contending factions at court. He spoke frankly that they should put an end to their scurrilous machinations. The plain words that he allowed himself on that occasion were unendurable to the cabal of lesser princes and provoked them into fomenting the conspiracy toward which they had long been drifting. Well aware of their discomfort, Uthumphon could not forbear from remarking to his advisors some days later that "this flock of sparrows would soon be scattered by a single stone and one loud shout."[35] It was not long before the prescience of that quip was realized.

A month later Uthumphon underwent formal investiture. On the eve of that event-the three dissident princes launched with their co-conspirators a coup aimed at replacing him with his more malleable brother Ekathat. There is no indication that Ekathat was party to their intrigue, though he could well have welcomed the fait accompli had they succeeded. Their rash action had been ill-planned, however, for they had failed to reckon with the capricious temperament of Khaek, their treacherous kinsman, who repudiated his association with the conspiracy by quietly warning King Uthumphon of the scheme. Unaware of Khaek's betrayal, the ringleaders, leading a hundred picked men, scaled a weakly guarded section of the Grand Palace wall and forced their way into the royal armory, where they confiscated a supply of muskets and other arms, commandeered a nearby palace gate, and awaited the anticipated arrival of a larger body of mercenaries from the military cantonment located beyond the Grand Palace Forecourt. The danger was defused when the reserve troops failed to materialize, for they had been confined to quarters under guard. The conspirators thus found themselves completely outmaneuvered, pinned down in a corner of the Grand Palace without the expected reinforcements. In a characteristic action, Uthumphon sent a party of senior monks to negotiate their surrender, promising lenient treatment to their families. The three princes were imprisoned in a heavily guarded palace storehouse, brought to trial, judged to be traitors, conveyed to the Wat Khok Phraya charnel ground located north of the walled city near the great Phukhao Thong Chedi and executed in the traditional manner for royal rebels.[36] Their band of stalwarts was disposed of with rougher treatment.

King Uthumphon was repelled by the requirement that he should personally be required to confirm the execution of the three princes and their collaborators. He finally gave in but refused to extend that sentence to cover the several provincial governors and lower-ranking officials who were judged to have been complicit in the conspiracy; after tortuous prison terms and a repentant swearing of allegiance, they were returned to their former posts. That dramatic instance of his leniency in the face of the cold-hearted temperament required of his royal duties confirmed in him his antipathy toward the office into which he had been propelled. It reinforced his conviction that Ekathat, his elder brother, was the rightful heir to the throne irrespective of his deficiencies. A half month after the three princes' debacle, following deep reflection, he invited Ekathat to a formal audience at which, to the consternation of all, he offered him the crown; and to the dismay of all, it was eagerly accepted. Uthumphon immediately departed the Grand Palace by royal barge for reordination into the Buddhist clergy at the ancient Wat Ayodhya, across the Pa Sak River from the walled city, and then took up monastic residence at the nearby Wat Pradu.[37]

Ekathat's investiture as king took place in June 1758, less than two months after Uthumphon's assumption of the throne. He took the official reign name of King Boromaracha III, although he was better known as King Suriyamarin, or more simply King Ekathat. On the throne, he quickly revealed his lack of the leadership skills needed to build trust and loyalty among his liegemen and came to rule, in effect, as little more than the puppet of his ministers. That met the interests of the nobility, who preferred a weak king, leaving them unchallenged in their quest for personal power and wealth, just as the ill-fated three princes had earlier foreseen. Ekathat's administration was marked not so much by what it achieved as what it failed to accomplish. Most crucial was his lethargic ineptitude in maintaining mastery over the subordinate ranks of the ruling elite. Lacking firm supervision, those lesser functionaries managed to lure great swaths of the peasantry into their individual feudal domains with promises of lenient servitude. Ekathat thus watched helplessly as the bulk of his royal-service peasantry evaporated into the entourages of various lesser princes and provincial nobles, or drifted off into the kingdom's ungoverned periphery. In that weakness, Ekathat's reign fulfilled Kung's worst fears.

Behind Ekathat's back, his critics called him the Leper King in recognition of a loathsome disease from which he suffered.[38] His ailment greatly affected his behavior, feeding his self-defensive arrogance, willfulness, and irritability. His rotted mouth contained not a regular row of upper teeth but a curved plate of blackened ivory with lines carved into it resembling dental divisions.[39] His recurrent bouts of venereal disease were treated by French priests at St. Joseph's Seminary, located on the outer Chaophraya riverbank along the southern perimeter of the walled capital.[40] The superstitious populace considered his ailments a form of cosmic retribution for his moral failings. Just as many had considered the former King Boromakot's ills to be a consequence of his usurpation of the throne, they believed that Ekathat's ailments were a result of his assumption of dominion against his father's wishes. In his struggle to cope with his afflictions, Ekathat sought solace in supernatural beliefs. Desperation turned him to a series of soothsayers, adepts in black magic, and purveyors of amulets and potions, one and all charlatans who gladly fed him the fraudulent auguries, incantations, and elixirs for which he hungered.

He disregarded the wise adage that above all the things against which a ruler must guard himself is being despised and hated, both of which are easily incited by libertine pursuits.[41] In his official duties he was often not seen at all. If he deigned to give audience, he was most often violent and overbearing. His vulnerability to the worst counsel of his false friends lured him into seductive vices. Many at court were revolted by the profligate lifestyle into which he sank. Being a loose, decadent, and effete prince, under the power of his pleasures and his women, he grew so besotted with his own gratifications that his busiest and most serious hours were spent in celebrating lubricious feasts in his palace.[42] In his absence, the great affairs of state were overseen by the Queen Mother, King Boromakot's former Queen of the Left. Even her caretaker governance was short-lived; the old lady died not long after her elder son's ascension to the throne.

Within a year of taking the throne, Ekathat had alienated most of the kingdom's aristocracy and high-ranking officials. Particularly offended, it seems, was Khaek, the scurrilous prince who had equivocated in the plot against Kung and had then denounced the three princes in their plot against Uthumphon. Recognizing the mounting dangers posed by the kingdom's deteriorating governance, he persuaded several senior ministers to join him in a plan to return Uthumphon to the throne. Troubled in their minds and unsure how best to proceed, they decided to consult Uthumphon himself at Wat Pradu. The ordinarily phlegmatic Uthumphon was left perplexed. Ever the obedient younger brother and now a virtuous monk – and certainly having no taste for his proposed return to the throne – he decided to disclose the scheme to King Ekathat, with the strict proviso that the conspirators not be executed. The king had them imprisoned, while Khaek was exiled to the distant land of Ceilão.[43] In recalling Uthumphon's insistence that the king deal humanely with the coup plotters, it was said of him in later years: "Who can say he was anything but good? He was so even to the bad."[44]

Deliverance

During the closing months of 1759, after the monsoon rains had ended, Ayutthaya received reports that the forces of Burma's King Mang Rong (formally known as Alaungpaya) had overrun Siam's western, Andaman seacoast dependencies and that some of those brigands had crossed the Tenasserim range to the eastern shore of peninsular Siam. Mang Rong encountered so little effective resistance that he decided to extend his conquest with swift strikes into the kingdom's heartland. Siam's internal administrative weaknesses enabled nearly unimpeded headway by the Burmese invaders. Despite many tactical errors in their headlong advance – particularly the Burmese command's failure to ensure adequate provisioning and the limited coordination among its many regiments drawn from subject principalities – Mang Rong nearly succeeded in forcing Siam to its knees due to Ayutthaya's lack of effective counteraction.

Preoccupied with other matters, Ekathat paid scant attention to the initial warnings, but the mounting threat could not long continue ignored. News of a Burmese invasion crossing the Three Pagodas Pass in early 1860 compelled Siam's military command to rush an army to the Tenasserim uplands, but the information proved inaccurate, as the main Burmese advance had already pushed up the eastern coast from Phetburi toward the Gulf provinces, outflanking Siam's army unopposed. A series of belated encounters were unable to stop the Burmese from overrunning Ratburi and Suphanburi provinces and massing their forces to threaten Ayutthaya itself. In a panic, Ekathat called on Uthumphon to come to his aid for the sake of the kingdom. As a condition for exiting the monkhood to return to royal service, Uthumphon insisted on unrestrained authority, not out of vanity but in a sincere belief in his own merit. Ekathat agreed by elevating his brother's title, in effect, to the rank of viceroy. Through all his subsequent vicissitudes, Uthumphon's constancy remained admirable, neither being bloated by public adulationnor withered under adversity, holding to the opinion that it was his duty to offer himself to the service of his people irrespective of any reward, not only of riches but even of glory itself.[45]

Uthumphon's first act upon returning to royal office was the issuance of a directive to the governors of the inner provinces to contribute immediately a thousand serfs and slaves each for a special corps of 15,000 conscripts to strengthen the city's defenses.[46] Much of the provincial nobility was unresponsive to that call for support. Shortsighted as usual, they were more interested in their individual self-preservation than in their collective survival. To meet the state's military manpower needs, Uthumphon was compelled to drain the already depleted royal estates of their able-bodied peasantry. Furthermore, he exhorted the Ayutthaya populace to join in the capital's defense, a striking departure from conventional practice. The city's Portuguese, Chinese, Cham, Mon, and Malay communities responded with alacrity. Even the city's slave population showed enthusiasm for the enterprise when they were promised their freedom in recompense; Ekathat, to his lasting discredit, did not honor that pledge in the aftermath.

The Burmese forces reached Ayutthaya in April. A siege appeared inevitable, so Uthumphon directed all efforts to strengthen the city's fortifications. Powerful gun emplacements were concentrated at the Mahachak Bastion commanding the city's northeastern point, the Diamond Bastion overlooking the Mae Bia harbor at the city's southeast corner, and the Champa Phon Bastion at the mouth of the Lopburi River opposite the city's northwest corner. Recalling Ayutthaya's capitulation to the Burmese two centuries earlier, after a devastating crossriver bombardment of the Grand Palace, Uthumphon ordered the construction of an additional wall along the vulnerable north side of the Grand Palace overlooking the Lopburi River.[47] The new wall allowed a second echelon of cannon, manned by the king's Portuguese gunners, to fire withering volleys enfilade against the approaching enemy. Lacking sufficient bricks for the project, Uthumphon ordered their removal from the outer wall of the Grand Palace Forecourt, facing the city and thus providing no practical defensive cover, and from the wall surrounding his Rabbit Garden residential quarter. Much has been made of those heroic preparations to withstand the Burmese onslaught, but it should be noted that they were entirely defensive. Offensive tactics were left to the king's field commanders, who had already shown their ineffectiveness.

Ekathat was no warrior king. Many of his military commanders were equally unfit for such a role. They had been appointed by him on grounds of pedigree, seniority, and fawning congeniality rather than proven competence. With him, their ineptitude as military strategists was amplified by their reliance on esoteric divinations and astrological reckonings in the determination of propitious moments of attack, auspicious troop deployments, providential encounters with a weakened adversary, and the like. When once Ekathat had given way to fears of supernatural influence, his mind grew so clouded, so disturbed, and so easily alarmed that he thought any unusual or extraordinary thing a presage. His court was consequently thronged with mystics and diviners whose business it was to sacrifice and purify, and to foretell and even sway the future. So miserable a thing is superstition: like water where the level has been lowered, flowing in and never stopping, it fills the mind with slavish fears and follies, as was interminably the case with Ekathat.[48]

As a true warrior king, Mang Rong, Ayutthaya's adversary, despised such reliance on external influences in the course of warfare. His convictions centered on the efficacy of valor. He was lavish in his rewards but merciless in the face of failure; unsuccessful officers faced the prospect of summary execution. He took delight in personal command of marauding forays, ambuscades, and stockade assaults, modes of combat that required a high degree of individual initiative, cunning, and courage. He had less interest in empire building than in lightning conquest, the collection of slaves and other booty, and the victorious return home to prepare for his next adventure. His assault on Ayutthaya therefore emphasized shock warfare rather than protracted siege.

After his rapid advance across the Central Plain, he mounted a decisive attack as soon as he reached Ayutthaya, with its spearhead directly cross-river from the Grand Palace, as Uthumphon had anticipated. Mang Rong was in the habit of leading from the front, setting an example for his troops. On the last day of April 1760, Ayutthaya's Portuguese batteries atop the northern double-tiered ramparts of the Grand Palace fired a deadly cannonade of grape and chain shot against a forward Burmese gun emplacement across the Lopburi River. A chunk of that shrapnel penetrated the king's groin, wounding him grievously.[49] As soon as the gravity of the wound was ascertained the assault was lifted and the besieging army withdrew to escort their king back to the Burmese capital, Ava. Mang Rong died en route, along the Lamao River (Tak Province).[50] By such adventitious circumstances, Ayutthaya was saved. Many superstitious devotees among Ayutthaya's populace attributed the kingdom's deliverance to the protection provided by King Ekathat's personal protective deities, particularly the great Si Sanphet Buddha image presiding over the Grand Palace's Chapel Royal. Elaborate victory celebrations and propitiatory rites were convened. All that jubilation instilled in the Ayutthaya leadership a false sense of complacency, which served the kingdom ill in the years to come.

In July, after the festivities had died down, Uthumphon, having had enough of his superstitious brother and his incompetent subordinates, returned to the monkhood at Wat Pradu. On the eve of his leave-taking, Ekathat invited him to attend an audience at which he offered his younger brother any reward that he might desire in gratitude for his aid in Ayutthaya's defense.[51] Uthumphon replied that Ekathat's adherence to the Five Negations would be reward enough.[52] The king promised henceforth to follow the path of righteousness and, in affirmation, presented Uthumphon with the ancient golden Trailoka Pathimakon Buddha image. For more than two centuries it had graced one of the devotional chambers in the Chapel Royal and had served Uthumphon as a personal focus of contemplation in his daily meditations. It was conveyed in splendid procession by royal barge to Wat Pradu and was installed there on the dais in the monastic assembly hall.[53] Seated before that sacred emblem of his fidelity to the doctrine of the Buddha, Uthumphon made himself available to all who came to seek his guidance. At one such interview, not long after Siam's deliverance from the Burmese onslaught, he advised a visiting group of young princes that they had better carry on the rivalry of court life with the weapons in which they excelled – their tongues – and not by arms, in which they had so recently shown themselves to be deficient.[54] It is said that "he never shut his door against the petitions of the indigent, and so he came to be held a most saintly monk."[55]

Catastrophe (1767)

For the following six years, Ayutthaya carried on under a fragile peace. Those years saw the kingdom become increasingly fragmented as its provincial elites secured growing autonomy, leaving the center bereft of both authority and access to manpower for the collective defense. Ekathat remained oblivious to the threat posed by Burma's new king, Mang Ra (formally known as Hsinbyushin), the most capable of Mang Rong's many sons, who had declared as one of the prime goals of his reign the subjugation of Siam and destruction of Ayutthaya to avenge his father's death. Ekathat's delusion that there was naught to fear was interrupted in early 1765 by a massive two-pronged Burmese invasion – one offensive crossing the Tenasserim hills from the west coast to Ratburi, the other proceeding directly east from Ava to Chiangsaen, Chiangmai, and Lampang.[56]

The sack of Ayutthaya, April 7, 1767. (No Na Paknam, *Murals Explained* (in Thai). Bangkok: Muang Boran, 1993, p. 62).

The two approaching armies spent a year consolidating their positions along the Siamese periphery while they methodically encircled the center. In February 1766 they converged on Ayutthaya, one from the north and the other from the southwest, to set up a robust siege. Just as the defenders had done in response to the Burmese invasion exactly six years before, Ayutthaya gathered what food stocks it could and allowed hordes of frightened folk from the surrounding districts to throng into the walled city. Uthumphon, still a monk, relocated from the unprotected Wat Pradu to the comparative safety of Wat

Rachapradit Sathan within the city wall. He moved not out of personal fear or in search of comfort but only because his monastic brotherhood had come to a collective decision, which he was loath to contest. Once again Ekathat sought his brother's aid against the Burmese threat, but this time Uthumphon declined the invitation, pointing out, caustically, that as the deities had spared the kingdom once they would surely do so again. This time, however, no providential deliverance was at hand.

The Burmese did not loosen their grip. Instead, they used every opportunity to proclaim their intent to stay on to certain victory. In their defense of Ayutthaya, Ekathat and his ministers proved incapable of deciding

Remains of the Suriyat Amarin Throne Hall, King Ekathat's Grand Palace residence. (Editor's photo)

on a decisive military strategy. Repeated sorties as well as pitched battles along the waterways and among the grasslands surrounding the capital failed to dislodge the advancing enemy. Morale flagged, and with it died loyalty. In their wake, disorder and corruption flourished. With all that, the twin scourges of famine and pestilence assailed the people, as is usual when a besieged city is driven to subsist on any foul nutriment it can obtain, no matter how decayed or decomposed.[57] First to disappear were the city's rice stocks, livestock, fish, and fowl; then its dogs and cats; and finally, the very birds, frogs, snakes, squirrels, and rats from the fields. The hoped-for provincial reinforcements did not arrive; battles were lost; resources were wasted; famine, plague, confusion, fear, and despondence stole the people's strength. Finally, the desperately depleted city fell to the conquering enemy.

On the terrible night of the city's cataclysm, amid the flames and carnage, Ekathat managed somehow to flee the besieged city. Disguised as a commoner, he was placed unceremoniously in a shallow boat and paddled by his squires furtively downstream past the dying city's horrifying screeches and screams, flames and smoke, and rising miasmic stench. After hours of noiseless drift along unknown waterways his boat was brought to shore, and he scurried onto the rickety jetty of a deserted village temple. There his terrified attendants abandoned him to his own devices. The agonies of thirst, hunger, filth, and aches of unaccustomed toil competed with the overriding dread of capture to drive him to the verge of madness. Some 10 days later he was found by an enemy patrol, dead or dying in his sullied robe and slippers.

This Ayutthaya-era mural detail depicts a more than two-meter-tall golden funerary urn (*phra kot*), containing a deceased king's embalmed remains in seated meditation posture. The urn was set upon a dais under the central spire of a Grand Palace throne hall (except for King Ekathat, who died after Ayutthaya's Grand Palace had been destroyed). After more than a year of funerary rites, the urn was conveyed in grand procession to the royal cremation ground, where the king's remains were transferred to the soaring royal crematory monument (*phra men*) to be consumed in flames. (*Jana Igunma*, British Library Asian and African Studies Blog, Dec. 18, 2017 (https://blogs.bl.uk/asian-and-african/)).

His remains were carried to the Burmese camp and buried there. A half-year later, after the Burmese departure, they were disinterred by his surviving Siamese subjects and accorded proper Buddhist funerary rites on the royal cremation ground adjoining the destroyed Grand Palace.

> *The man deserved the fate, deny who can;*
> *Yes, but the fate did not deserve the man.*[58]

Uthumphon's fate, like the man himself, had a more dignified aspect. He was captured without resistance upon being discovered by the Burmese invaders seated sedately with his fellow monks chanting mantras before the presiding Buddha image in Wat Rachapradit's ordination hall. Brought before the Burmese commander and interrogated at length, his reputation for integrity was found to be well justified. Along with many thousands of other Siamese captives rounded up at Ayutthaya he was transported to Ava, and with them he disappeared from the pages of Siam's history. The following epitaph befits this eminently good but politically disinclined man:

> *Had you for Siam been strong, as wise you were,*
> *The Burmans had not conquered her.*[59]

Chapter 2
Burmese Ramayana

Editor's introduction
A close student of Myanmar's history recently boasted, in reflecting on his country's long history, that the Burmese are "well-qualified to be called a martial race." He notes that the word "myanma," the name by which the ethnic Burmans have traditionally referred to themselves, "suggests their ability and acumen to overcome all difficulties including the tactical problems in war ... with determination, perseverance, patriotism and strong will."[1] Paired with that martial characterization stands the classic observation of an earlier, British observer that "Siam [is] a nation which, though unable to contend with the Birmans ... in war, [has] cultivated with more success the refined arts of peace."[2] Such pithy judgments, voiced from opposite sides of the Tenasserim Divide and its associated cultural disparities, skim the surface of a deep and troubled historic relationship.

Despite its vaunted military prowess, the eighteenth-century Burmese state was in its medieval politics as fragile as that of the Siamese. Although Burma and Siam differed in many particulars, the two kingdoms were systemically similar in the instability of their feudal institutions as reflected in their oscillating configurations of weak center and loosely linked periphery. Twice – in the 1560s and again in the 1760s – the two empires entered into full-scale war at the very moment that Siam's ruling coalition was finding itself in decline just as Burma was approaching full spate under a new, vigorously expansionist dynasty. In each instance the Burmese conquered the Siamese only to be repelled by fortuitous circumstances backed by a resurgent center under a fresh dynastic impulse. It is the second of those two confrontations, culminating in the end of Siam's Ban Phlu Luang Dynasty (1688-1767), that is recounted with exacting precision in this second chapter of Diogo's Chronicle.

Diogo notes in his Testament that he received much information for his penetrating account of the fall of Ayutthaya from his drinking companion, António da Costa, a Portuguese military officer who had escaped his Burmese captors to join the Siamese cause and ended up living under parole in Bangkok's Rosario settlement. Despite de Costa's self-interested denials to the Siamese authorities following his narrow escape from Burmese detention, it is apparent that his presence in the Burmese ranks at the siege of Ayutthaya made him privy to the many insiders' anecdotes that flow from Diogo's pen. With the benefit of de Costa's eyewitness perspective, Diogo's narrative of the unfolding of Siam's defeat presents a unique counterpoint to the conventional accounts based on the kingdom's royal chronicles.

The tale as told by Diogo starts in the 1750s with the sudden revival of the previously crumbling Burmese state under the charismatic leadership of King Mang Rong (r.1752-1760), founder of the Konbaung Dynasty.[3] Mang Rong's reign saw a meteoric revival of Burmese might, which by the mid-1750s had consolidated control over most of Central and Lower Burma. Military action against a resurgence of the long-subdued Mon kingdom of Hongsawadi, centered in the vast Irrawaddy Delta, resulted in the destruction of much of its territory under a scorched earth policy. The Mon capital of Pegu along with the port city of Syriam were razed in 1757, and with that conquest ended the might of Hongsawadi. The subsequent flight of many Mon refugees across the Tenasserim Cordillera into Siam provided an incentive for Burmese incursions across the upland divide, followed by full-scale invasion in 1759-1760 upon Ayutthaya's refusal to accede to Burmese demands for the return of Mon fugitives and the submission of tribute, including white elephants (a favorite Western caricature of Siamese-Burmese diplomatic relations).

As in Siam, Burma under the Konbaung Dynasty was organized as a feudal kingdom. The new capital of Ava paralleled Ayutthaya as the galactic state's ceremonial and administrative epicenter, with the surrounding provinces, dependencies, and allied principalities being governed under concentrically diminishing degrees of royal patronage and military control. Much like the administrative difficulties troubling Siam's Ban Phlu Luang Dynasty (discussed in Chapter 1), the fall of Burma's Taungoo Dynasty had proceeded from a fragmentation of authority among government agencies, unrestrained exploitation of the conscripted workforce, and progressive escape of commoners from royal service to the patronage of provincial lords promising less onerous conditions of servitude. The Konbaung kings set out to undo those deficiencies through stern military-backed reversion to central state control. Many of the centralizing initiatives applied by the early Konbaung kings to civil administration, military organization, revenue generation, and cultural integration were remarkably reminiscent of the radical policies that had been proposed by Ayutthaya's Prince Kung in 1755 to arrest Siam's political rot.

The Burmese kingdom's resurgence saw, first, the reestablishment of central control over the entire Irrawaddy River basin and its neighboring uplands. Under that reform, hereditary local chiefs were replaced by appointed governors, a new corps of central officials was deployed to monitor local affairs, and local elites were disciplined to regiment their peasant cohorts into an expanded royal service corps.

Military reforms were introduced to replace fixed troop quotas with flexible conscription procedures as a means of accommodating fluid demographic circumstances. The officer staff was professionalized, raising Burma's tactical capabilities beyond those of Siam, which continued to rely on senior officers ill-prepared for their dual civil/military responsibilities. Munitions procured from European gunrunners came to play a prominent role in warcraft, and firearms tactics, marksmanship, and gunsmithing were improved under the tutelage of European officers and artisans, both mercenaries and war captives.

To finance the improved administration and strengthened military, state revenues were diversified from reliance on agricultural taxation to include commercial revenue sources. Agricultural tax receipts rose with the opening up of new tracts to cultivation and the relocation of upland peasant communities to the more fertile lowlands. Trade tax revenues rose with improved external transport via Yunnan into China and through the port of Syriam to South and West Asia. Monopoly privileges and tax farms in a diversity of revenue-generating fields were auctioned off to commercial syndicates, and royal shipping ventures were formed to trade both along the Irrawaddy River and with overseas markets.

As a fourth approach to state centralization, provincial governors were instructed to promote the cultural Burmanization of the peripheral regions. For all its vaunted military might, the Burman aristocracy continued to fret over its vulnerability in the midst of a constellation of politically unreliable alien constituencies and vassal states. The Burmese solution to such insecurity, real or imagined, was repeated armed intervention, coerced resettlement, and cultural assimilation, including the mandated adoption of such specific Burman practices as language, dress, and names – most vividly illustrated in the integration of Lower Burma's ancient Mon civilization, and the series of insurrections that it provoked (as further discussed in Chapter 6).

Ethnic assimilation, however, is invariably a two-way street. Burmanizaton included the accommodation of Burman culture to its neighbors through selective borrowing and adaptation. For instance, the Burmese – like the Siamese – had many centuries earlier adopted Theravada Buddhism from their Mon neighbors to serve as their state religion. Similarly, they had benefited from a wide variety of technical borrowings, ranging from Mon brickwork and monumentalism, to Lao textiles and lacquerware, to Mon, Khmer, and Siamese administrative institutions. Burmese adoption of the Siamese masked dance-drama for staged portrayals of the *Ramayana* following their 1767 conquest of Ayutthaya is a cultural borrowing of immediate relevance to the events highlighted in this chapter. The *Ramayana* had long been revered by the

Burmese people as an epic poem of mythic repute. Its influence on traditional Southeast Asian ethics and aesthetics, like the cultural impact of the Homeric epics throughout Europe, can scarcely be overstated. It provided not merely a vivid romance but a chivalric guide to social conduct and potent symbol of cultural community; it confirmed the aristocratic hierarchy that had been imposed on the region's nascent kingdoms; it instilled interpersonal relations – elder-younger, male-female, parent-child, lay-priest, elite-commoner – with moral content; its depictions of valiant warfare, supernatural events, fate and free will, comedy and tragedy, found a receptive audience among all classes of society; it complemented the Buddhist ethos of beneficence, fraternity, and equanimity with the Brahman lore of statecraft, power, and conflict. In an age reliant on troubadours for much of its news and entertainment, it furnished young and old, men and women, haves and have-nots with a shared diversion from the drudgery of daily affairs.

In Siam, the *Ramayana* had been elaborated into a theatrical performance of vivid imaginative power. As a masked dance-drama, it had matured into an operatic ballet presented in episodes and tableaux performed by dancers outfitted in magnificent costumes to the accompaniment of poetic recitation and instrumental music. It was brought to Ava by the captive court dancers and musicians of conquered Ayutthaya in 1767 and continued to be performed by them and their descendants at the court of Ava, and later at Amarapura and Mandalay, to great acclaim. So, when the king of Ava sought to pursue his ambitions against Siam with commanders symbolically bynamed Hanuman and Thosakan (the Ramayana epic's principal martial protagonists) and then later requested the captive King Uthumphon to introduce the Siamese rendition of the Ramayana epic as a masked dance-drama to the Burmese people, he brought Thai and Burman culture into closer alignment in support of his imperial ambitions.

Invasion

To grasp the enormity of Siam's collapse under the Burmese assault of 1767, it is useful to trace back events to the origins of Burma's Konbaung Dynasty. Mang Rong (formally known as King Alaungpaya), the architect of that dynasty, had started his illustrious career as a mere village chieftain. Although of limited formal education, his charismatic leadership, military prowess, and legendary ferocity enabled him to rise to sovereign position over Burma from his inland capital at Shwebo, a day's voyage upriver from his son's later, greater capital at Ava. His lasting achievement was the reorganization of Burma's moribund Taungoo kingdom into a prosperous, expansionist state. Burma under Mang Rong found in incessant warfare and incursions into neighboring states its means of sustenance and growth, and in the frightful exhilaration of combat it discovered the inspiration to build a resurgent empire.[4] He brooked no failure, as was confirmed by his habit of executing any commander so unfortunate as to have lost an engagement or any officer found to be shirking his duty to the slightest extent. He led by example, which ultimately spelled his undoing. The fatal front-line accident that prevented him from concluding his conquest of Ayutthaya in 1760 only whetted his successor's thirst for the subjugation of Siam.

After the brief, ineffective reign of Mang Rong's eldest son, his second son Mang Ra (King Hsinbyushin) revived the dynastic dream of imperial conquest. Of Mang Rong's many sons, Mang Ra was the most capable, and the most militant.[5] As king, Mang Ra continued his father's bellicose policies toward building a strong, unified state. While the father had raided for booty, the son was bent on empire. He announced his intensions by moving his capital to Ava, a storied seat of ancient Burmese empire. Some say that Mang Rong's devastating campaigns against Hongsawadi, Arakan, Manipur, and Siam left the Burmese kingdom thirsting for a peaceful interlude. Others contend that Mang Ra considered the Burmans to be "ever the best of subjects when employed in military expeditions, but irascible and turbulent in the idleness of peace."[6] Whichever of those contrasting strains is correct, Mang Ra sought war.

A pretext for war was found in Ayutthaya's refusal to submit periodic tribute, including the vassal's symbolic offerings of white elephants, and gold and silver trees. The true motive, however, was his "unquenchable thirst for empire and the distracted ambition of being the greatest man in the world."[7] Mang Ra's aggressive empire-building fomented war along several fronts – west to Arakan and Manipur, north to Yunnan, and east to Lan Na, Lan Chang, and Siam; as director of that far-flung enterprise he remained at Ava to coordinate his forces from the center.[8] That decision demanded commanders who could be relied on to carry out his directives with unquestioning loyalty far from home. Two of his father's ablest and most experienced commanders, General Maha Noratha (otherwise known as Mong Maha Nawratha) and General Sihabodi (or Ne Myo Thihapate), were his choice for the Siamese front.

Mang Ra typified the Burmese infatuation with the ideal of aristocratic chivalry harbored in the ancient Indic epic poem, the *Ramayana*. He had been weaned on recitations of its heroic stanzas. Its tales of honor, decorum, statecraft, and valor had been absorbed into his very soul; its mystique was never far from his thoughts, and he fancied himself an avatar of the epic's hero, Rama. In a moment of inspiration, he was struck by a quaint notion stemming directly from the *Ramayana*: Maha Noratha possessed many attributes of Hanuman (Rama's monkey general) while General Sihabodi closely resembled Thosakan (Rama's adversary, the demon king of Lanka).[9] The king took to referring to his two commanders by those mythical names, and his courtiers followed suit in their campfire conversations, as that pair of evocative diminutives was wonderfully descriptive of the two generals' contrasting personalities and military prowess.[10] He decided to exploit the mutual antipathies arising out of their opposing natures – Hanuman wily, devious, agile; Thosakan direct, uncompromising, inflexible – to ensure their individual loyalty to him, and to divert their attention from the throne toward their passion for besting one another.

Hanuman (General Maha Noratha), diminutive in stature and smooth-skinned but of masterful presence, was esteemed for his tactical virtuosity and negotiating skills, a crafty warrior ever willing to talk his way out of battle in order to conserve his forces. He spoke easily in open discourse, to great effect; his silver tongue was as greatly feared as his well-honed sword by those who challenged him in debate. Thosakan (General Sihabodi), a leathery, battle-scarred veteran who favored direct, frontal attack to gain any objective, was esteemed as a commander of masterful ability, though of a harsh and heated nature, much preferring to lead by fear rather than by love.[11] He possessed skill in the art of persuasion, but far more in private conversation than in public discourse, and was said to be the best of talkers, and of speakers, the worst.[12] That distinction was borne out in the two generals' contrasting approaches to warfare: Thosakan relied on shock tactics to win his battles, often at considerable human cost, while Hanuman's offensives usually relied on sorties marked by stealthy stratagems and tactical elegance. Thosakan gained the king's grudging respect for his warrior's audacity; Hanuman was admired as a model of strategic flair.

Despite the two generals' notable differences, they shared several essential traits. Both possessed a defining sense of dignity and personal honor. Both commanded the unstinting confidence of their officers and troops. Both had amassed proven records of military success in the service of the Konbaung kings. Both were exemplars of the ancient dictum: "How great a part of valor experience is."[13] Despite their contending personalities they maintained formally correct relations. The spirited exchanges between the cunning persuader and the assertive brawler that enlivened general staff conferences became a subject of delighted gossip throughout the army. It was evident to all that the two commanders formed an incongruous yet complementary duo, symmetrical opposites of virtually providential design.

In planning his assault on Siam, Mang Ra decided on a two-pronged, pincer movement aimed at Ayutthaya from north and south. Hanuman was assigned the less onerous southern approach. Although a Burman, he had spent much time among the Mon people and had gained fluency in their language, which suited him to that assignment. As a matter of policy, he directed his troops to refrain from plundering the country. He marched onward unresisted; many, hearing of his leniency, deserted the defenders to join his ranks.[14] At Ratburi, capitulation to the Burmese forces was negotiated by a delegation of local elders in the absence of the governor and his chief officers, who had fled their posts. The news of Ratburi's bloodless defeat was received at Ayutthaya with censure and reproach as an ignoble, treasonable act. The Ratburi populace, however, facing massacre in the face of overwhelming odds with no sign of aid from Ayutthaya, welcomed the surrender. At a parley with the besieged town's emissaries, Hanuman put the question, "whether he should pass through their country with spears upright or leveled, and invariably he received the same response."[15]

Some Siamese and Burmese battle formations, as diagrammed in various 18th-century Burmese and Siamese manuals of warfare. (Courtesy of Prof. U Thaw Kaung, Yangon)

Hanuman's willingness to negotiate the peaceful submission of that key Siamese strongpoint had the advantageous effect of inducing other townships, such as Nakhon Chaisi, Phetburi, and Suphanburi to follow suit. In each case, he advanced his army to the provincial frontier and then sent a herald to announce his demands. The defenders, terrified at his approach, delivered up to him the required booty and entered into alliance with him.[16] The conditions of surrender typically included, for the elite, an initial indemnity, periodic offerings of tribute, and hostages; for the commons it meant, in addition, the possibilities of military conscription, ransacking of the granaries and livestock, and the other usual hardships attendant on the nearby billeting of enemy garrisons. In all this, Hanuman invariably got his way. The uninformed among his men asked "why he took so many towns by surrender, and never one by storm, which might enrich them with the plunder."[17] Considerable persuasion was required of him to convince them of the greater benefits that lay behind his enlightened policy.

Thosakan, on the other hand, was well fitted to the northern posting. His own mother was Shan, which was why he could speak several Lao dialects so well. He was widely known among the subject peoples and was well regarded by their ruling elites; they had gifted him with a full complement of Shan and Lao princesses as concubines. In one respect, however, he miscalculated the mentality of the peoples he had been designated to subjugate: unlike Hanuman, who allowed the conquered towns to retain their local lords, Thosakan imposed his own officers as military governors. That harsh practice provoked repeated rebellion in the frontier principalities, favoring their shift of allegiance to Siam.

Following the directives of Mang Ra, the general staff devised a three-year, two-pronged campaign to bring down Siam. The king's sole regret, it was said, was his inability to accompany the march through the conquered territories, though he planned to join Hanuman and Thosakan at the gates of Ayutthaya for the decisive blow.[18] The two armies were instructed to envelop Ayutthaya for the purpose of reducing its defenses through constant harassment, time wasting, and attrition of resources.[19] The elemental intent, on which victory or defeat would necessarily turn, was progressively to strip away Ayutthaya's outlying provinces, weakening the center's capacity for manpower mobilization while increasing that of the Burmese and thereby reducing the residual strength of the capital itself. That strategy greatly accelerated the pernicious process of internecine conflict and disintegration already intensifying within the unraveling Siamese empire.

The northern invasion got underway in mid-1764 following Thosakan's suppression of insurrections in several Lao vassal states. Then, after the flood season, the southern campaign was launched with the subjugation of Siam's Andaman protectorates of Martaban, Tavoy, and Tenasserim. Hanuman then crossed the Tenasserim hills to gain control of Phetburi and Ratburi while Thosakan consolidated Burmese suzerainty over Lan Na, centered at Chiangsaen and Chiangmai, and Lan Chang, centered at Luang Prabang and Vientiane. With the arrival of the dry season toward the close of

1765, two 20,000-man vanguards converged on Siam's Central Plain from north and south, impressing subject regiments into military service as they proceeded. They arrived at Ayutthaya in good time, but it would be months before the two generals could hope to consolidate their position for a full-scale siege of the capital. The flood season would be imminent before they could possibly turn their thoughts to the final phase of their campaign.

In arms and field tactics the Burmese held a decided advantage. Neither Hanuman's swift Manipuri cavalry nor Thosakan's fierce Shan marauders encountered any opposition that could withstand them in the open field. Their forward cavalry regiments were sent out repeatedly on sorties to reconnoiter, harass, terrorize, and loot the outlying districts. Through such forays the invaders were regularly revictualed. The two Burmese armies were also well equipped with firearms acquired from British (Calcutta-based), French (Pondicherry-based), and Portuguese (Goa-based) suppliers.[20] Through the services of both Portuguese and French officers captured or hired to train their troops in the latest tactics of massed cannon and musket fire, they had mastered advanced infantry tactics. The Siamese were less favored in that regard. Most of their small-arms stockpiles consisted of obsolete matchlocks rather than the newer flintlocks and had been ill-maintained for decades; large quantities had rusted to scrap for want of periodic applications of grease. Ayutthaya's Portuguese community, which had long been relied on for its firearms prowess, had rusted in its fighting strength as well, and the British (Calcutta-based), Dutch (Batavia-based), and Portuguese (Macau-based) firearms dealers on whom Siam had come to rely were not always responsive to arms requests.[21]

Siege

In their rush toward Ayutthaya the two converging Burmese armies encountered little more than sporadic resistance from Siam's provincial militias, while King Ekathat and his courtiers, seated in solemn assembly at the spearhead of the Burmese advance, conferred over the niceties of alternative defensive strategies. The time that Siam wasted in mobilizing for war played into the invaders' hands. Through the pair of carefully calibrated offensives, both Burmese armies arrived at the outskirts of Ayutthaya simultaneously at the height of the dry season, with the first flowering of the mango groves. Hanuman approached along two fronts from Ratburi, his deputy command surging east from Suphanburi to set up a forward position at Ban Kuk Kai (the Si Kuk Camp), while he himself voyaged up the Chaophraya River to establish his headquarters at Bang Sai. Concurrently, Thosakan pushed his forces down from Chiangmai via Phitsanulok to Bang Pahan. with a forward position at the Pho Sam Ton Camp, to which he later moved his headquarters. As they approached Ayutthaya, the two Burmese armies' combined fighting strength rose from around 40,000 to more than 70,000 with the addition of conscript contingents drawn from the principalities that they had passed along their line of march.

Map 2. The Burmese Advance on Ayutthaya, 1766

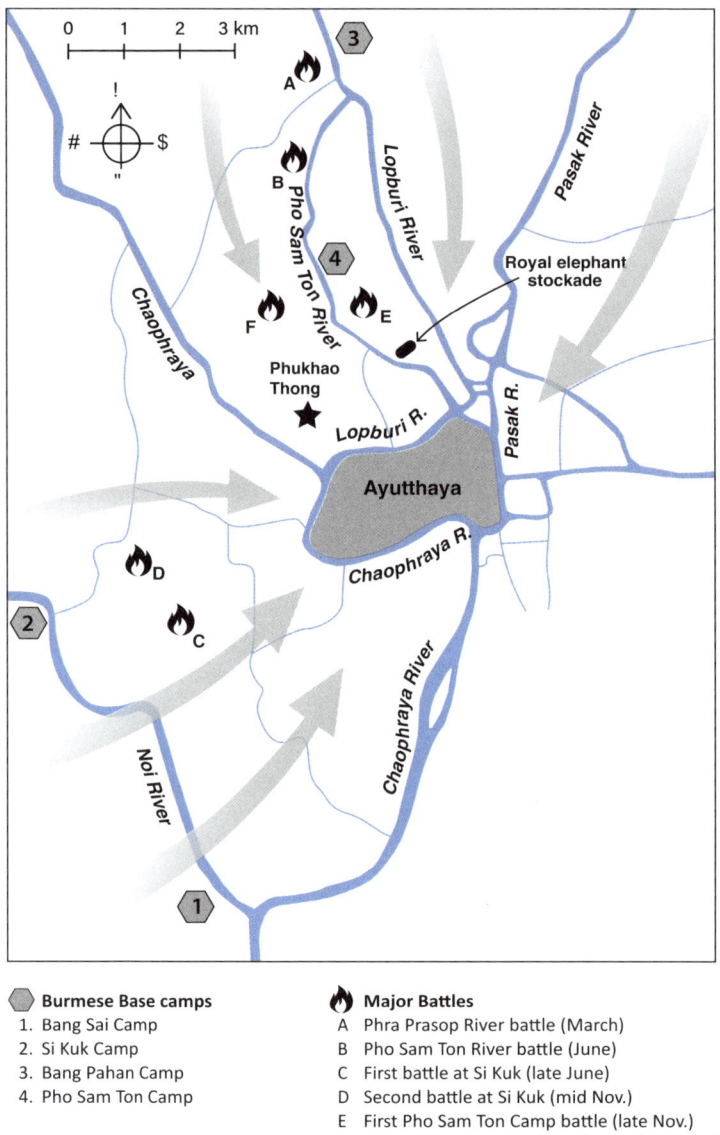

Burmese Base camps
1. Bang Sai Camp
2. Si Kuk Camp
3. Bang Pahan Camp
4. Pho Sam Ton Camp

Major Battles
A Phra Prasop River battle (March)
B Pho Sam Ton River battle (June)
C First battle at Si Kuk (late June)
D Second battle at Si Kuk (mid Nov.)
E First Pho Sam Ton Camp battle (late Nov.)
F Second Pho Sam Ton Camp battle (mid Dec.)

In April the two commanders met at Phukhao Thong, the great monument overlooking the Lumphli rice fields north of the city, to coordinate their further operations under the very noses of the city's defenders.[22] At that conference they agreed that Thosakan would besiege the northern and eastern sectors of the walled city while Hanuman would press forward from the west and south. A three-phased plan was agreed on: first, to envelop, confuse, and harass during the hot season (April-June); second, to besiege, weaken, and terrorize during the rainy season (July-October); and third, to assault, overwhelm, and defeat during the dry season (November-March). The

94 *Diogo's Chronicle*

two generals agreed to meet again after the November floods – upon the anticipated arrival of King Mang Ra – to reassess the situation and finalize the capital's conquest.

At Ayutthaya, Ekathat and his senior advisors had succumbed to the most fatal of military self-delusions – underestimation of the strength and will of the opposing forces. The king advised his ministers: "If over the course of this year you abstain from fighting the besieging enemy, his army's strength will wither and he will gladly depart of his own will."[23] A minority, led by the governors of Sukhothai, Phetburi, and Kamphaeng Phet, cautiously proposed a more aggressive course of action; their views were bruskly overridden.[24] As matters developed, the defenders vacillated between Ekathat's wait-and-see strategy and a series of rash sallies brought on by the court's growing self-doubt.

Hanuman and Thosakan chose to play a waiting game, repeatedly baiting the armies of Ayutthaya, if they wished to engage in open battle, to advance far from the walled city and its broad moat, hauling all their cumbersome gear behind them, to meet the enemy in set-piece battle.[25] The siege was thereby reversed, with the besiegers establishing their forward camps as a string of stockaded strongpoints within cannon range of the city wall, and the besieged repeatedly throwing safety to the wind in fruitless forays.[26] The Burmese stratagem succeeded. Not once in the many assaults on their camps did the Siamese forces gain a decisive victory. The repeated Siamese offensives succeeded only in wearing down their strength in the carnage of battle. Even stalemate spelled victory for the Burmese, for it enabled them to retain their positions while it depleted the Siamese ranks. That reversal of the opposing positions, pulling the defenders out of their encircled city to attack the fortified Burmese positions, created the anomaly of a cluster of small sieges in hopes of relieving the greater one.

Following Ayutthaya's several preliminary probing attacks against both the northern and southern Burmese armies, all unsuccessful in dislodging the invading forces, six major battles were fought in the capital's outlying districts over the course of the yearlong siege: the battle of the Phra Prasop River (March 1766); the battle of the Pho Sam Ton River (June 1766); the first and second battles of Si Kuk (late June 1766 and mid-November 1766); and the first and second battles of the Pho Sam Ton Camp (late November 1766 and mid-December 1766).[27] The Siamese general staff erred in thinking that each of those assaults, in turn, would turn the tide, for each battle squandered resources, and each painful defeat lowered morale.[28] It is indicative of the Burmese strategy that not until the final assault on the beleaguered city did either Thosakan or Hanuman allow any of those defensive victories to lure them prematurely into a retaliatory thrust to the city wall.

Of all those engagements, the first battle of Si Kuk was the most eagerly anticipated Siamese engagement but turned out to be one of its greatest defeats – though officially proclaimed a stalemate. It was at that massed encounter that Ayutthaya's defenders glimpsed for the first time an intimation of their kingdom's mortality. The Siamese forces fought under the command of General Tanthawong (Tan), with Lieutenant

Colonel Taksin (Sin) as one of his adjutant officers. Tan, a scion of the old Sukhothai aristocracy and hereditary governor of Sukhothai, was serving as acting Minister of War, the former minister having recently died. His eldest daughter was a favorite concubine of Ekathat, which allowed him a greater degree of freedom to voice his opinions at ministerial assemblies and follow his own council in war than he would otherwise have dared. Known as an aggressive military commander who advocated the crushing of his adversaries through overwhelming odds, he led the militant faction at court, in opposition to the king's preferred defensive strategy.[29] Tan's momentous defeat at Si Kuk reinforced Ekathat's preference for a defensive strategy, which boded ill for Ayutthaya's survival.

Tan placed the bulk of his forces along the two wings, leaving a weak center to draw the enemy's interest. He deployed his regiments in a "buffalo horns" array, requiring forward-leaning flanks, concentrating the bulk of their foot soldiers at the weak center, along with contingents of musketeers. The artillery was positioned at the rear, with the elephant corps and cavalry ranged along either flank. The Burmese countered with a wide but shallow "crow's-foot" formation – massed infantry (pikemen, lancers, archers, swordsmen) forming the center, the Portuguese artillery and Manipur cavalry on the right wing, additional guns supporting the Mon elephant corps and Arakan musketeers on the left.[30] Then, on the advice of his augurs, Tan delayed battle for three days by halting his army in the open fields a cannon shot from the enemy position. That time wasted under the hot dry-season sun on short rations left his foot soldiers weakened and discontented. Meanwhile, the Burmese defenders continued to raise their ramparts and plant bamboo mantraps in the surrounding irrigation ditches and across the sabotaged fields, planning to draw the enemy toward those designated killing zones at the crucial moment. The long-delayed day of battle finally arrived with a break-of-dawn advance by Ayutthaya's massed infantry forces.

The Burmese marched with ominous quiet out of their fortifications. At the moment of engagement their ranks did not fall directly upon the Siamese vanguard but, veering right, endeavored to draw them toward a cavalry charge from the left wing. The tumult raised a great cloud of dust, which shrouded both armies from clear view. It was then that General Tan, in the heat of battle, allowed his excitement to conquer his judgment. He failed to signal his flanks to press the attack, and so they did not enter the fray immediately or in a body but rather in straggling companies when the foot fight was already well underway.[31] The advancing Siamese infantry, lacking momentum, stalled and was slaughtered piecemeal. Enfolded between the pressing enemy flanks, their center broke, and the ranks fell back in disarray. The sun at their back and the enveloping dust gave the Burmese rearguard great advantage, hiding them from the enemy's sight. From afar their unencumbered foot regiments could not be discerned, so they advanced without fear. Before the Siamese center could realize how vast a multitude it had engaged, it found itself overwhelmed. The greater part was cut to pieces without hope of escape, for large numbers of the foot soldiers

Map 3. The siege of Ayutthaya, late 1766

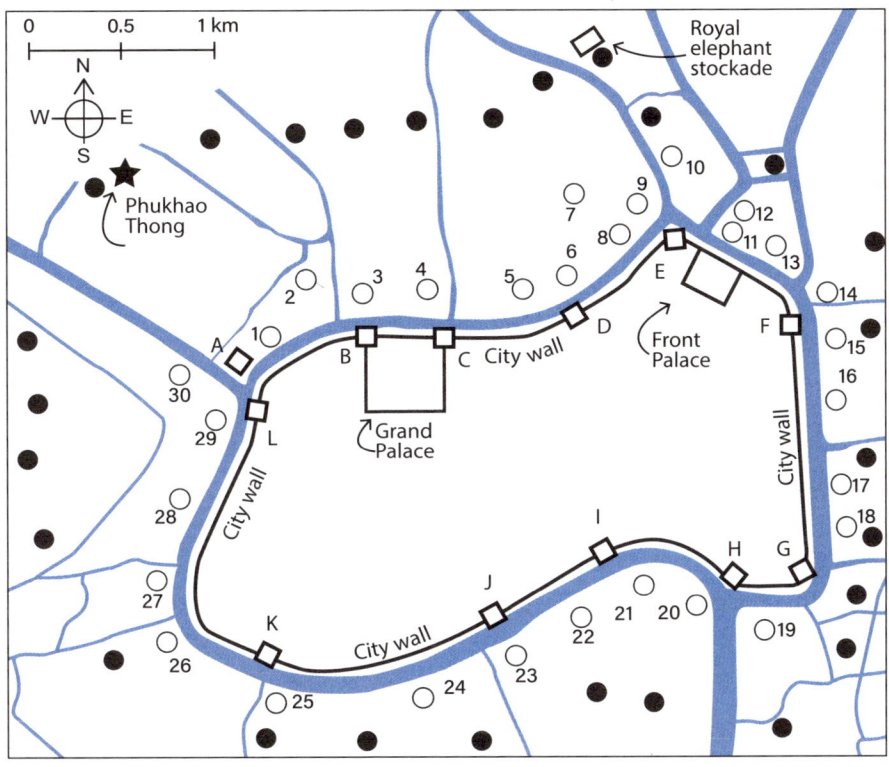

Burmese forward camps derived from Soe Thuzar Myint, 2011, p. 115.

○ **Siamese redoubts**
1. Wat Pa Phlu
2. Wat Sala Pun
3. Wat Tinw Tha
4. Wat Na Phra Men
5. Wat Rong Kong
6. Wat Intharam
7. Wat Mæ Nang Ploem
8. Wat Pa Khlong
9. Wat Phrao
10. Wat Sam Wihan
11. Wat Mondop
12. Wat Khæ
13. Wat Saphan Khloea
14. Wat Krachom
15. Wat Nang Chi
16. Wat Thamma Niyom
17. Wat Phichai
18. Wat Khruay
19. Wat Phanan Choeng
20. Wat Bang Kacha
21. Wat Nang Kui
22. Wat Khun Phrom
23. Wat Prot Sat
24. Wat Puthai Sawan
25. Wat Sampao Lom
26. Wat Chai Wathanaram
27. Wat Lat Chong
28. Wat Kasat Thirat
29. Wat Thamma
30. Wat Tha Karong

☐ **Major Siamese bastions**
A. Pom Champa Phon
B. Pom Pak Tho
C. Pom Tha Khan
D. Pom Pratu Khaw Ploeak
E. Pom Maha Chai
F. Pom Ho Ratanachai
G. Pom Ho Rachakhroe
H. Pom Phet
I. Pom Chakra Noi
J. Pom Ok Kai
K. Pom Wang Chai
L. Pom Sat Kop

● **Burmese forward camps**
The camp names, as recorded in the Burmese annals, are provided in Soe Thuzar Myint, 2011, p. 115.

had been tied fast to one another with long chains to prevent their breaking ranks.[32] At the rear, "enforcers" had been deployed to cut down any of their own conscripts seeking to flee the butchery. Up to a third of Ayutthaya's infantry and half its officers fell in combat or were taken prisoner in that clash. With the center annihilated, the Burmese turned to the flanks, and there, unsupported, the losses were not much lower for Siam's elephants, cavalry, and artillery. The Burmese losses, all told, came to less than half the Siamese numbers.

Burmese Ramayana 97

Soon after that pivotal battle the rains came. Ayutthaya returned to its defensive posture, setting up 50 gun batteries raised on stockaded mounds at regular intervals along the outer banks of the city's surrounding waterways, each manned by several hundred well-armed troops under a captain's command.[33] The Siamese strongpoints were charged with defending the city moat's crossings, detecting and discouraging any massing of Burmese troops, and deterring sorties.[34] The Burmese responded by erecting a ring of 30 raised, palisaded positions, many alongside prominent temples, along the outer rim of the city moat. The opposing strongpoints rained murderous gunfire upon one another. With the bulk of their troop reserves confined across the city moat and behind the wall, the Siamese positions isolated outside the city were subjected to relentless bombardment. After the annual floods had receded, those positions were, one by one, abandoned or overrun.[35] Then the Burmese trained their guns, some raised on timbered towers higher than the city wall, on the city itself.

The necklace of Burmese forward positions gradually tightened to strangle the besieged city. In addition to destroying the defenders' forts, the Burmese assailants were assigned the task of denying the city access to troop reinforcements as well as food supplies and stocks of munitions. They did not, however, hinder exit, on the theory that the departure of the city's defenders not only reduced its fighting capacity but equally important, its morale – a tactic known as "drying the pond to catch the fish." Sorties dispatched from the city to probe the Burmese encirclement found the gates shut and bolted or bricked up upon their return; so ropes were thrown down to hoist them over the wall one after the other.[36] Many fighters returning to Ayutthaya not in a body but as disorganized bands of stragglers were caught like birds in a net before they could reach the wall, because the Burmese had concealed squads of armed boatsmen along all the watercourses leading to the city.[37]

While sporadic armed confrontations between besiegers and besieged captured the most excited notice, a more insidious danger – the depletion of food reserves – increasingly preoccupied the attention of the commanders on both sides. From the very outset of the Burmese encirclement, Ayutthaya had found itself beset by hordes of starving, despondent panic-stricken peasants dragging their wretched possessions behind them. Sparsely populated tracts in the city's eastern precincts, and later its southwestern royal garden tracts, were opened to accommodate the miserable hovels of the demoralized refugees. Those additional thousands of empty stomachs multiplied the strain on the capital's dwindling rice reserves, with no recourse in sight. The Burmese besiegers encountered similar supply problems, made all the more urgent with the arrival of troop reinforcements. Having been inured to living off the land, they had brought with them few provisions. Once their repeated marauding had depleted the occupied territories of all possible plunder, they had been left with no recourse but to restore the abandoned paddy tracts surrounding the walled city and cultivate rice for their own subsistence.

Defeat

Mang Ra had made it known from the outset that he would join Hanuman and Thosakan at Ayutthaya for the climactic assault. As the 1766 flood season waned, however, he found himself tied down at Ava facing a mounting Chinese threat from the north. Reluctantly, he ceded the final seizure of the Siamese capital to his generals. Cavalry couriers were dispatched to inform the commanders of the changed circumstances with orders to speed victory in his absence. His directive was to defeat Ayutthaya without compromise, to prevent Siam from ever again rivaling Burma in might and grandeur. In an unfortunate oratorical flourish – conveyed to his crouching scribes perhaps in a moment of reckless inebriation – he proclaimed that Ayutthaya should be destroyed, leaving no brick unscorched, no man with wife, no child with parents, no farmer with bullock, the city razed, all captives and spoils to be carried off. It was understood by all but his most obtuse officers that such royal hyperbole was not to be taken literally. The king's commanders were capable men who, it would be expected, could parse the king's grandiloquence for its kernel of motivational rhetoric.

Yet the message was sent to the field commanders verbatim. Each interpreted his liege lord's instructions with careful study, each in close conformity with his own military philosophy. The one set his affections on a strategy of maximal achievement; the other, on optimal results. One aimed at the honor attaching to irresistible force of arms while the other sought to apply force selectively in pursuit of practical ends. Hanuman considered sufficient the comprehensive dismantling of Ayutthaya's defenses along with the capitulation of its citizenry and a crushing indemnity. The city's treasure and a sizable share of its citizenry were to be carried off while leaving behind a residual vassal population to fill the political void. Thosakan insisted on a more dramatic reading of Mang Ra's instructions by insisting on all-out assault, giving no quarter in the utter obliteration of the city and enslavement of its people. At a general staff conference, he accused Hanuman of faint-heartedness in time of danger. Swallowing the rebuke, Hanuman pronounced ominous words: "Strike if you will, but hear!"[38] However, Thosakan was past listening. Knowing that Hanuman would be impotent to oppose him, he roared that he would attack regardless. In falling back on that most primitive expedient, Thosakan bested Hanuman before his eager officers. Hanuman could not help but express his mortification upon finding his own glory thus totally eclipsed.[39] He departed the conference in silent humiliation.

Not many days after that acrimonious debate and its draconian resolution (January 4, 1767 by the Christian calendar), a great fire broke out in the besieged capital, attributed to the impact of unremitting bombardment. The fire raged through the city center, raising pandemonium among the oppressed populace. All told, it left more than 10,000 households homeless and multiplied the people's despair with the destruction of the warehouses containing the bulk of Ayutthaya's dwindling rice reserves. Many took that incident as an ominous sign of their collective fate if drastic remedial action should be further delayed. Ekathat consulted his ministers, and in concert they decided to proffer Ayutthaya's honorable surrender. The decision to send ambassadors to negotiate with the Burmese generals was taken not so much out of any hope of obtaining magnanimous conditions as out of necessity, to prevent the city's death by famine.[40] Royal heralds were dispatched to each of the two Burmese commanders' headquarters to propose that a parley be convened at Phukhao Thong, equidistant between the two Burmese headquarters and the besieged city. Ekathat and his officials certainly realized that the proposed armistice would cost much treasure but believed that it would at least return Siam to the diplomatic status quo ante; that was the best prospect in view.

For reasons that the Siamese court grasped only after the event, their envoys were requested to meet the Burmese command not at Phukhao Thong but at the royal elephant stockade, near the Pho Sam Ton Camp. There, Thosakan and his officers received a delegation led by Siam's Ministers of War and Interior. Hanuman was not in attendance. The Siamese envoys offered a peace treaty that would return Ayutthaya to the vassal status it had accepted two centuries before. Thosakan shocked them, however, by announcing that such a treaty would be unacceptable. His démarche recited that Siam had betrayed its century-old obligation of vassalage, having long failed to maintain its periodic offerings of tribute. Furthermore, Siam had supported the recent Mon uprising against Ava by offering sanctuary to Mon absconders and had refused to offer up to Burmese justice the rebellious rulers of the Andaman principalities. Under those circumstances, he announced, nothing less than unconditional surrender would be acceptable. Such suicidal terms beleaguered Ayutthaya could not accept, for the Siamese ministers recognized full well in that dire pronouncement Thosakan's intention to loot all of Ayutthaya's wealth and enslave its inhabitants. The council therefore concluded without agreement, and the Siamese delegation returned to the besieged city despondent, the bearers of Siam's death sentence, and their own.

Only after their return to the doomed city did the reason for the parley's changed venue and Hanuman's absence become evident. Discreet inquiries confirmed that Hanuman had boycotted the meeting because of his dissent from Thosakan's uncompromising stand. In their frenzy to thread their way out of the lethal trap into which Siam had fallen, Ekathat and his councilors imagined that in Hanuman's dispute with Thosakan they had gained a secret ally. They decided to contact him at his Si Kuk headquarters in hopes of gaining a more accommodating hearing, but preparations for that representation were betrayed to Thosakan. Within a few days (by the strangest of coincidences, it was whispered, with bitter irony) Hanuman fell mortally ill. None of his physicians would venture to offer him any remedy, as they thought his case desperate and feared the suspicion and ill-will that would befall them should they fail in their cure.[41] He perished in quick agony, of unknown causes. If he had been poisoned, as is generally supposed, it was for naught, as all suspicions of his betrayal were unfounded; he was an honorable man and faithful to his king, his colleagues, and his troops to the end. For fear of deadly reprisals, the possible causes of Hanuman's mysterious death were not investigated, despite swirling suspicions among the southern army's staff officers and throughout the ranks. The high fever, spasms, hallucinations, frothing mouth, and bloody flux that preceded his death were left unexplained.[41] Speculation withered away, however, after his cremation and the interment of his remains at the Si Kuk Camp in a reliquary monument overlooking the Noi River, followed by the designation of second-in-command General Pakanwun to replace him under the authority of the now supreme commander, Thosakan.

An enshrined image of General Maha Noratha ("Hanuman"), commander of Burma's southern invasion army until his death in 1776, and the ruined chedi that is said to have contained his cremains, at Wat Ban Si Kuk, Ayutthaya. (Editor's photos, 2012). At the time that these photos were taken, the chedi and shrine containing the general's image still occupied a corner of the temple grounds. Upon a return visit in 2022, the entire assemblage had been dismantled to accommodate the temple's renovation. The fate of the cast-metal votive figure commemorating Hanuman is unknown.

As an adjunct to his masterful handling of the peace parley, Thosakan managed to negotiate the secret defection of one of the Siamese envoys, Ayutthaya's Minister of Lands (Ngok), responsible for the administration of land taxes and collection of the capital's rice reserves. During a recess in the deliberations, Ngok was surreptitiously escorted to a private chamber where he found Thosakan seated resplendent amid a luxury of looted wealth. Thosakan was a person of singular skill at discerning a man's cupidity by his countenance and the glint of his eyes. Ngok's thoughts were easily deciphered, as he could not resist the temptation to gawk at the mounds of treasure surrounding him. Perceiving Ngok's infatuation with a magnificent silver bowl of Chiangmai manufacture, Thosakan asked him to take it in his hand and consider its weight. Ngok, "being amazed to feel how heavy it was, asked him what weight it *came to.* To you …," said Thosakan, "… it shall *come with* twenty times its weight in gold."[43] The price to be paid for his betrayal, Ngok soon learned, was his pilferage and profferment of many tons of Ayutthaya's dwindling rice stocks, and his commitment to open one of the city's key watergates to the invaders upon request.[44] When the time came, it was the Ratanachai Watergate, blocking one of the city's major transport canals at its confluence with the Pasak River near the Front Palace, that he managed to open on the pretext of the imminent arrival of a rice-raft convoy to ease the city's food crisis. Perhaps the weight of his betrayal was eased in his mind with Thosakan's disingenuous assurances that the lives and property of the city's inhabitants would be spared.[45]

The final phase of the siege, following the failed peace talks in January 1767, saw the Burmese attack the last-remaining Siamese forward positions along the city's outer rim. Over the following month, from late January into February, the besiegers systematically overran the Siamese strongpoints to the city's north and northeast, advancing their own forward camps to those positions, each occupied by a thousand or more troops. During the following month they similarly captured the fortifications to the city's southwest and southeast. Then in early March they took those to the west of the city, and then later in the same month they completed their encirclement by overrunning the remaining outposts to the south. Upon those captured forward positions they set up firing platforms for their own cannon, raising them on high posts to intensify their bombardment of the city from a deadly trajectory. Ayutthaya was left with no more than its broad moat and cannon-mounted wall as its last line of defense, complemented by sporadic night-time forays across the river by its remaining intrepid warrior contingents.

In desperation, the king's counselors requested Captain Maha Montri (Chot), a famed warrior though of junior standing, to lead a motley flotilla of Ayutthaya's remaining forces across the city moat in an audacious assault on the Burmese forward positions threatening the northeastern point of the city at Wat Mae Nang Ploem, Wat Sam Wihan, and Wat Mondop. The strike force was gathered in the long-vacant Front Palace, from which it would be able to slip across the Lopburi River under the protection of the gun batteries of the Mahachai Bastion on a daring foray into the very teeth of the massed antagonists. Great care was taken in the preparations for that heroic, do-or-die assault by divining the auspicious moment for attack through the reading of elaborate auguries. Supernatural protection was provided to the fighters in the form of sacred mantras, amulets, tattoos, potions, and vestments, which initially seemed effective as the Siamese fighters forced a Burmese retreat from both Wat Mondop and Wat Sam Wihan at the cost of minimal casualties. As they were girding to extend their victory with an onslaught on Wat Mae Nang Ploem, the arrival of Burmese reinforcements from the Pho Sam Ton Camp cut short their advance and ultimately forced their withdrawal back to the city.

King Ekathat, in great distress, then called for a last-gasp public propitiation of the city's tutelary deities. Buddhist rites were conducted in the Chapel Royal with

Map 4. The climactic assault on Ayutthaya, April 7, 1767

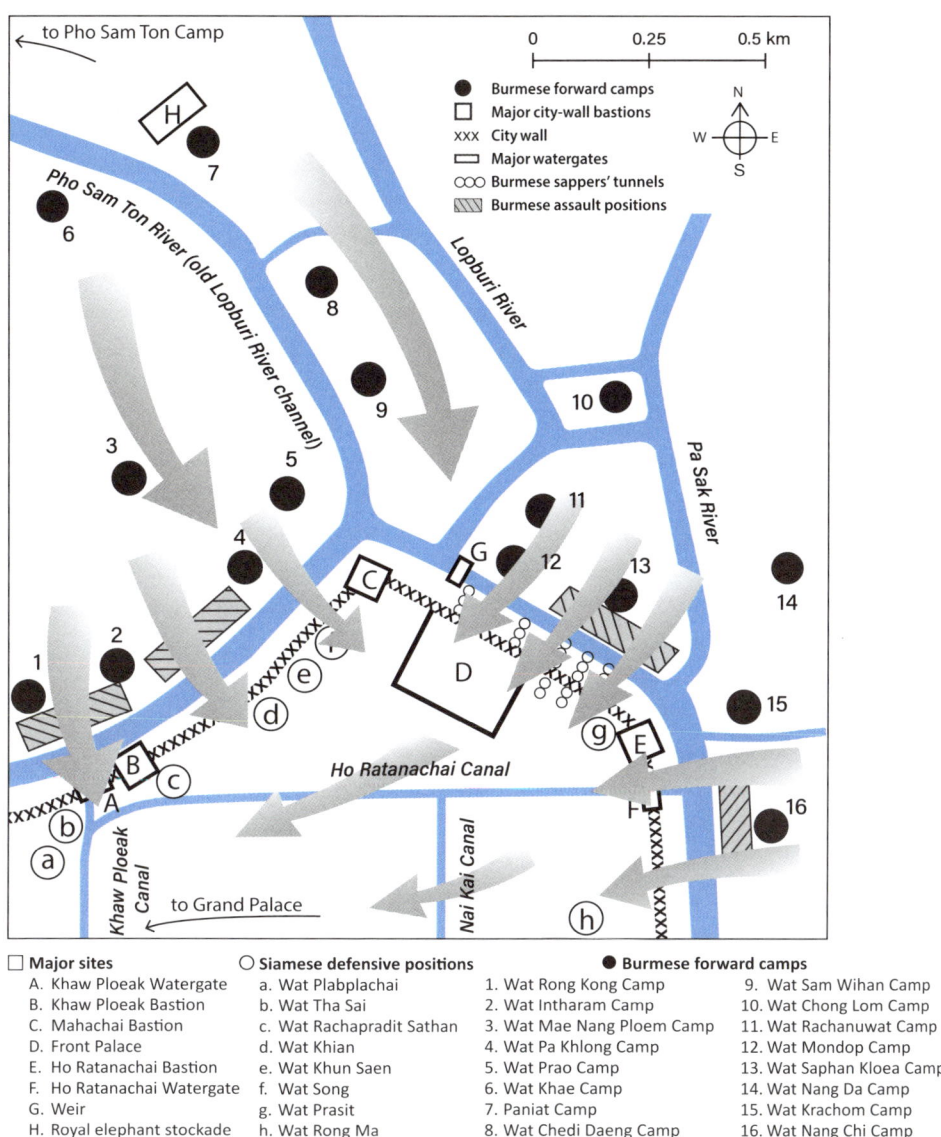

☐ **Major sites**
A. Khaw Ploeak Watergate
B. Khaw Ploeak Bastion
C. Mahachai Bastion
D. Front Palace
E. Ho Ratanachai Bastion
F. Ho Ratanachai Watergate
G. Weir
H. Royal elephant stockade

○ **Siamese defensive positions**
a. Wat Plabplachai
b. Wat Tha Sai
c. Wat Rachapradit Sathan
d. Wat Khian
e. Wat Khun Saen
f. Wat Song
g. Wat Prasit
h. Wat Rong Ma

● **Burmese forward camps**
1. Wat Rong Kong Camp
2. Wat Intharam Camp
3. Wat Mae Nang Ploem Camp
4. Wat Pa Khlong Camp
5. Wat Prao Camp
6. Wat Khae Camp
7. Paniat Camp
8. Wat Chedi Daeng Camp
9. Wat Sam Wihan Camp
10. Wat Chong Lom Camp
11. Wat Rachanuwat Camp
12. Wat Mondop Camp
13. Wat Saphan Kloea Camp
14. Wat Nang Da Camp
15. Wat Krachom Camp
16. Wat Nang Chi Camp

lengthy recitations by the city's assembled monks before the presiding Phra Si Sanphet Buddha image, followed by a sacred circumambulation of the chapel's galleried walkway. The Brahman priests were requested to seek the intervention of the deities Vishnu, Siva, Indra, and Ganesha. The spirit of the city pillar was mollified with elaborate sacrifices. The Chinese, Muslim, and Christian communities were urged to pray to their gods. Finally, the great cannon known as the Conqueror of Hongsa,

Burmese Ramayana 103

associated with its own miraculous powers, was hoisted upon a bastion before the Grand Palace to fire into the Burmese strongpoints across the city moat. When the gun repeatedly misfired, the superstitious king and his advisors were left distraught.

At about the same time, the Burmese were strengthening their forward position at Wat Mondop, directly across the Forward Moat from the Front Palace, the narrowest crossing along the water-girded city perimeter. They clogged the weir at the moat's upstream end in an effort to dry the passing current to a trickle, a task facilitated by the converging rivers' dry-season ebb.[46] The reduced water level exposed the steeply sloping riverbank fronting the city wall, shielding it from the deadly aim of the guns of the nearby Mahachai and Ho Ratanachai bastions. Detachments of Burmese sappers slipped across the depleted waterway under cover of darkness to establish a sheltered foothold along the protected shoreline fronting the wall and immediately started the perilous task of digging six parallel tunnels from the shoreline to the wall. Three of those tunnels were to be filled with kindling that could be set alight at the appropriate moment to collapse the timber pilings of the riverside Front Palace wall, and the rest were extended beyond the neighboring city wall into the city itself. On the opposite shore, troops were massed behind stacks of bamboo rafts piled as high as walls (to be strung together as pontoon bridges), scaling ladders, and other gear readied for the impending crossriver assault.

The city finally fell on April 7, 1767, the inauspicious eve of the Siamese New Year.[47] At the hottest afternoon hour of the hottest day of the year, the Burmese forces initiated a sustained crossriver bombardment from their positions around the full perimeter of the island city, though the focus of their onslaught was the city's northeast quadrant. They poured in burning missiles, setting the area ablaze. Simultaneously, they set fire to the tinder-packed tunnels at the base of the city wall. By dusk, sections of the undermined wall fronting the Front Palace started to crumble. Shortly after the evening change of watch, Thosakan himself fired a gun signaling the climactic assault. His massed troops, impassioned by the lust of impending battle, streamed across the moat on vast numbers of hastily deployed pontoon bridges and raft convoys in a concerted attack on the damaged sections of wall, where many of the assembled defenders had plummeted to their deaths with the collapsing parapets. Advance contingents scaled the ruined walls without thought of consequence. Others crawled through the tunnels to dig themselves through the final meters to the surface and strike the defenders from the rear. The Siamese fighters, worn and wearied with the massive onslaught, could not long withstand such overwhelming odds, and the assailants passed over the remaining lines of defenders like a plague of locusts. One of the last strongpoints to fall was the Diamond Bastion. With its lines of large cannon trained on the harbor and Thosakan's crossriver forward camps, its gunners were ill-prepared to repel the hordes of invaders that had overrun the city's northeast defenses and now attacked the river-facing guns from the rear. Withstanding the onslaught, the fort's gunners fought bravely, only to be cut down in merciless hand-to-hand combat.[48]

Detail of a panoramic painting evoking the Burmese assault on the Grand Palace of Ayutthaya, April 7, 1767. (National Memorial Museum, Thailand; artist unknown; photographed by Trisorn Triboon – Wikipedia Commons)

Gazing across the river at the suffering city, Thosakan is said to have commented dourly on the calamity, as he could well imagine how foul its face would be in a few hours under his soldiers' heel. Among the officers of his army there was not one who dared deny the city's plunder to the troops' demands, nor to their commander's insistence that it be burned down and leveled to the ground.[49] About midnight, when much of the city wall had been reduced and the surrounding precincts secured, Thosakan entered the breach with all the panoply of trumpets and drums sounding, followed by the triumphant howl of an army let loose with lances leveled and swords drawn. There was no numbering the slain, which to this day can be conjectured only from the space of ground saturated with their blood. Nor did the multitude that fell to slaughter exceed the number of those who, at the extremity of desperation and despair, slew themselves.[50]

The Burmese officers were unable to restrain their exuberant troops. Ignoring their commanders, the Shan marauders, joined by other levies, ran riot. They slaughtered the vanquished and ransacked the palaces, temples, markets, and homes at will while all around them the city burned. Their captives were tortured to reveal the locations of their wealth; a favorite cruelty was burning the feet of the tethered victims to open their mouths. Freedom was promised to those who informed on their fellows. The temples were desecrated despite the fact that the Burmese shared with the Siamese a reverence for the Buddha and his teachings. Many of Siam's most venerated religious icons were stripped of their gold and silver casings. The ashes of the destroyed Grand Palace throne halls and shrines were passed through sieves to recover the gold that had melted from their walls and furnishings in the blaze.[51] Even the tin tiles from their roofs were melted to ingots for their lesser value. The temple grounds were piled with soon-to-be rotting corpses, the waterways bobbed with awful blossoms of bloated cadavers. A putrid stench drifted across the defiled city. Flocks of scavenger fowl feasted. With the rape of Ayutthaya, those who had long opposed Thosakan's brutal philosophy of war, believing him responsible for much ghastly carnage, now added to their enmity, contempt.

Amid the night's turmoil, many of those not killed, maimed, or captured managed to escape. The Burmese took only about 30,000 captives.[52] The elite prisoners were placed under guard at the Pho Sam Ton Camp, where the senior members of Ayutthaya's royal family were placed; the nobility were confined with the rest as little better than slaves. They totaled no more than 10,000. The remaining 20,000 commoner captives were collected at the Si Kuk Camp. In addition to the captive population, elephants, horses, firearms, munitions, and such precious goods as ornaments, jewels, and bullion were specifically reserved for the Crown. Lesser valuables were allowed to the troops who had seized them. Many of the invading soldiers returned to their camps weighed down by sacks of coins, utensils, textiles, and other loot collected from their victims. More than a few of the heavily laden pillagers drowned while swimming the river out of sight of their comrades.

Mang Ra's generals well knew the need to avoid massacre in the sweeping up of captives as spoils of war. Prisoners – aristocrats and commoners alike – were too precious a commodity to squander on indiscriminate slaughter. In the nightlong rampage following the city's collapse and through the following several days that dictum was ignored. The Burmese accounts indicate that the king himself was among the casualties; Ekathat, unrecognized in the mayhem, was said to have been shot dead in the chaos of fleeing noncombatants.[53] Thosakan was reportedly vexed at the excessive carnage that his unleashed foot soldiers wrought. He had not anticipated that after months under strict restraint, his levies would burst their bounds in a frenzy of bloodlust, leaving their officers powerless to restrain them. The subsequent massacre of tens of thousands of the city's inhabitants explains the relatively small number of prisoners transported to Ava and Yangon. Thosakan thought otherwise; he reasoned that many Ayutthaya citizens had slipped to safety through his fingers in the city's final throes. In his anger, he proclaimed that they would not be spared, that he would leave behind him a nemesis more frightful than himself – namely, famine.[54]

Soon thereafter the Burmese departed with their booty for Ava. With its ruling class and manpower base emasculated, Siam was left rudderless, and havoc prevailed.

> The populace was afflicted with a variety of ills by the enemy. Some wandered about, starving, searching for food. They were bereft of their families, their children and wives, and stripped of their possessions and tools.... They had no rice, no fish, no clothing. They were thin, their bodies wasting away. They found only the leaves of trees and grass to eat....

In desperation many turned to dacoity.... They gathered in bands, and plundered for rice and paddy and salt. Some found food, and others could not. They grew thinner, and their flesh and blood wasted away. Afflicted with a thousand ills, some died and some lived on.[55]

Captivity

At the last moment, immediately upon the completion of his mission, Thosakan was ordered by King Mang Ra to withdraw his invading army from Siam in order to bolster Ava's defenses against a massive Chinese imperial invasion into Burma's northern reaches. It took more than a month beyond the conquest of Ayutthaya, however, for Thosakan to fully comply with that order. In the short time available before the military evacuation, huge mounds of treasure were readied for transport: several tons of gold ingots melted from palace spires, Buddhist monuments, and household treasure troves; a considerably larger quantity of silver, bronze, copper, lead, and tin; and many tons of gemstones, leather goods, textiles, and artifacts; as well as some 1,200 cannon and vast quantities of smaller arms.[55] The southern army barged much of its huge consignment of loot downriver to Nonthaburi, a day's sail, to redistribute among its overburdened vessels. One item, the cracked barrel of the great bronze Phirun Saen-ha cannon, which had been retrieved from the Crystal Pond in Ayutthaya's Grand Palace, was considered too cumbersome to transport all the way to Burma, so it was filled with gunpowder and blown to smithereens. The bronze shards were then divided among several vessels for onward shipment.

The 30,000 Siamese war prisoners were divided between commoners, adepts, and aristocrats for the march to Burma. Some 10,000 members of Ayutthaya's royal family and nobility, royal artisans, literati, and senior monks were carried off with the northern army via the Mae Lamao River route through Tak, Thaton, and Taungoo, directly to Ava. The remaining 20,000, consisting of hordes of peasants and day laborers, craftsmen, village monks, tradespeople, and the like, were assembled at the Si Kuk Camp to accompany the southern army by the Meklong River route, passing Ratburi, Kanchanaburi, and Martaban to Yangon and Pegu. Many of the captives were strung together by bamboo neck yokes or hobbled by thongs passed through their ankles to prevent flight. Despite such impediments, a number of stragglers along the southern route managed to escape and find their way back to Siam; few are known to have made it back from the frightful march to Ava.

In due course, the two armies with their contrasting captive consignments departed, at different dates, by different means, and via different routes, bound for their different destinations.[57] The southern forces, under the command of General Pakanwun, departed downriver at the end of May by junk, barge, and raft bound for Phetburi and then overland for Tawai and Pegu. The northern contingents, under Thosakan, moved off for Ava weeks later, leaving behind at the Pho Sam Ton Camp a 3,000-man brigade under the command of Colonel Thong-suk (Sukhi), whose assigned duty was to scour the countryside for additional prisoners and hidden wealth, for later dispatch to Ava. Mang Ra proved less enthusiastic about Burma's victory over Siam than Thosakan had expected, given that suspicions over the untimely death of Hanuman lingered and that the number of captives carried off to Ava was unacceptably small. After receiving perfunctory honors, Thosakan was sent off to the northern front.[58] Pakanwun received equivalent honors and retained his command at Pegu. Most of the subordinate officer corps was accorded brief furlough before being reassigned to follow Thosakan to the China campaign.

The abdicated King Uthumphon, snatched from his monastic life, was carted off to join the other royal captives in harsh confinement at the Pho Sam Ton Camp. On the difficult cross-mountain march to Ava he was treated with greater dignity, proceeding much of the way by elephant, as befitted his status. Those who survived the ordeal made the best of their adversity with a new life at their Sagaing internment camp, situated on a bluff overlooking the west bank of the Irrawaddy River, within view of Ava. There, the remnants of the Ayutthaya royal family, nobility, and senior clergy, plus an artisan contingent of gold-, silver-, iron-, bronze-, and tin-smiths, casters, sculptors, woodworkers, painters, weavers, dyers, physicians, scribes, dancers, musicians, and others with rare skills, were interned. The Siamese officer staff was segregated for cantonment at the army's Shwebo command center. Uthumphon was provided with a monastic residence befitting his stature and, by royal appointment, was designated titular head and spokesman of the Siamese captive community. In audience before Mang Ra, he was assured that his people would receive reasonable treatment so long as they complied unflinchingly with all royal requests for service.

View of the bluff fronting Sagaing, situated directly across the river from the ancient Burmese capital of Ava. (Editor's photo). The rugged Sagaing hillside was assigned as the initial settlement site for the several thousand Siamese aristocrats and royal retainers who had been carried off to Ava as war captives in 1767.

The Burmese had been familiar with the *Ramayana* as a work of epic import for many centuries, but they lacked a tradition for its dramatization. Marvelous tales of the Thai masked dance-drama had been related to Mang Ra for years. He was eager to judge for himself, so Uthumphon, in his capacity as spokesman for the Siamese captive community, was requested to organize a royal performance of the renowned Thai *Ramayana* dance-drama for the court of Ava. Luckily – or unluckily – among the many artisans carried off to Ava were court musicians, dancers and acrobats, puppeteers, mask-makers, and costumera well versed in the classical Thai theater. Some years after the Siamese captives' arrival, a vast circular tent spreading out from a stout center post was erected at the newly constructed Amarapura Grand Palace, some 10 kilometers north of Ava, to accommodate the week-long *Ramayana* performance before a royal audience. Staged as an elaborate romance featuring the abduction of Sita and its consequent wars between Thosakan's demon army and Hanuman's simian legions, the repertoire performed before Mang Ra and his assembled court about a year later took up 65 consecutive evening sessions. For that performance, the Siamese dance troupe secretly adapted certain obscure motifs to cast the evil Thosakan implicitly as representative of Burma's King of the White Elephant, while the lyrics for the heroic, long-suffering Rama and his clever warrior-general Hanuman were subtly adjusted to

The *Ramayana* pavilion at the Grand Palace at Amarapura. (*Le tour du monde, nouveau journal des voyages*, Paris, 1860). An engraving after a drawing by Joseph Navlet illustrating the visit of Captain Henry Yule to Burma in 1855, representing the Bengal office of the East India Company. The picture's historical value is greatly enhanced by its inclusion of the pavilion that a half-century before had provided royal seating for the Thai *Ramayana* masked dance-drama. The soaring "mast" in the right background is believed to have served as the center-post supporting the wide-spreading canopy that covered the "umbrella" theater where Siamese dance ensembles presented their elaborate performances.

represent Siam and its allies seeking to free Rama's beautiful abducted Princess Sita, symbolizing Sagaing's captive Siamese community. Fortunately, the hidden metaphor was not detected by the Burmese court, but it gave great satisfaction to the performers. The presentation was a memorable event. Its staging before the king and court of Ava was a resounding success, even though the musical recitation of the epic stanzas was in Thai, and it immediately became the rage of the day among the Burmese aristocracy.[59]

Mang Ra was quick to recognize the value of this popular new entertainment form as a device for the promotion of loyalty among his kingdom's disparate peoples. Through popularization of the *Ramayana* in Burman adaptation and Burmese dialogue, the beliefs, values, and aspirations of its main characters could be harmonized with the imperialist designs of the Konbaung kings. So, under Mang Ra's sponsorship, itinerant troupes were dispatched to the provinces to propagate this innovative entertainment. It was soon adapted to marionette performances to make it more readily accessible throughout the far-flung village world. Both as masked ballet and as puppet theater, performed to the accompaniment of music and poetic recital, it became intensely popular among all classes of Burmese society.[60]

Well pleased with the accommodating behavior of his Siamese war captives, Mang Ra allowed their leader increasing latitude.[61] Uthumphon continued as their leader, greatly beloved, to his long life's end. He was remembered, as king and monk, as a great man, ever warm in kindness, rare to anger. In punishing, he was always moderate and never inflexible; in distributing benevolence, he was single-mindedly obliging. He exerted himself unreservedly for the security and preservation of what he considered his noblest possessions, those over whom he had been fated to reign.[60]

Remains of one of the four boundary pillars surrounding King Uthumphon's crematory monument at Amarapura. (Editor's photo)

Chapter 3
Upstart Regime

Editor's introduction
No one could have imagined in April 1767 that the fall of Ayutthaya would spark a fresh beginning only six months later with Colonel Taksin's victorious eradication of the last remaining Burmese strongholds from the Siamese heartland, followed by the relocation of his command center far downriver to Thonburi, where he decided to reestablish the kingdom's capital. In this chapter of his recounting, Diogo reviews the kingdom's remarkable rebirth over the exuberant initial decade of Taksin's 15-year reign at Thonburi. Starting from nondescript beginnings, the new regime faced a cascade of existential trials. Taksin's overriding preoccupation was the reconstituted kingdom's security against external threat, compounded by the need to reinstate domestic law and order. Pursuit of those dual imperatives required an adequate militia, which in turn depended on the manpower attendant on the kingdom's political reintegration. His second priority was economic revitalization, ranging from food security and trade recovery to price stability and fiscal viability. Merging with that challenging agenda was Taksin's ambition to develop his Thonburi capital as the restored kingdom's ceremonial, administrative, trade, and cultural center.

Diogo focuses in this chapter on the initial, buoyant decade of Thonburi's emergence from the ashes of Ayutthaya (1767-1776) – the assemblance of an entourage of comrades, the emergence of new elites, the new capital's physical fabrication, and the kingdom's political reunification, while certain key events marking the course of that energetic recovery are examined in Chapters 4, 5, and 6. The later phase of Taksin's reign (1776-1782) is discussed in Chapter 6, while Chapter 7 deals with Thonburi's mounting disruption, culminated in the coup, counter-coup, and reign change of 1782.

Throughout all that, Diogo emphasizes that Taksin could not have realized his ambitions without the unflinching support of a circle of capable, committed, trusted confederates – a band of brothers, as he aptly refers to them. Rather than simply referring to those many retainers as the narrative unfolds, Diogo presents a roster of full-blown character sketches of Taksin's key comrades. Those biographical portraits are evocative of Plutarch's emphasis on the personalized perspective in recounting the course of history, tracing the manner in which his protagonists shaped events. They illuminate the diversity – in class, ethnicity, aptitude, temperament – of Taksin's inner circle and its members' complementary roles in shaping Siam's resurgence. It was their collective courage, capability, fortitude, and loyalty rather than such conventional considerations as age, experience, social pedigree, and cultural ties that constituted Taksin's principal criteria in the selection of his comrades-in-arms. From among his many confederates, he appointed his closest, most talented colleagues to the most senior posts in a command structure designed along the military lines of the Ayutthaya tradition. His ministerial appointments and provincial governorships formed a new feudal peerage replicating on a diminished scale the coalition of fiefdoms destroyed with the Burmese conquest. In drawing those character sketches, Diogo augments his personal recollections with the reminiscences of a group of well-versed informants (listed in his Testament), themselves all Ayutthaya-era survivors.

The virtual annihilation of Ayutthaya's governing elite required the creation of a new ruling class. Taksin dealt with that need in haste, but with care. The elevation of his closest, most capable comrades, complemented by the reinstatement of several senior Ayutthaya survivors, to the highest positions of power and privilege was largely completed within a year following his coronation. That restoration recreated the essential elite hierarchy of its Ayutthaya prototype. For practical purposes, Diogo's disordered listing of the select pool of favorites whom he elevated to the highest positions has here been arranged according to the conventional arrangement of royalty, nobility, and clergy. His commentary on each of the major actors and their influence on the course of events is placed within that frame. The small number of personages referred to in that listing is suggestive of the diminutive size of Thonburi's elite, and perhaps also of Diogo's less than comprehensive grasp of the upstart regime's high society.

Taksin's decision to relocate Siam's capital to the downriver Thonburi swamplands obliged a definitive break from four centuries of Ayutthaya tradition. Construction of the new capital in place of the old was a visionary objective to which the new regime quickly turned its attention, but effective action to that end was repeatedly postponed in the face of other priorities. Diogo suggests in his description of the disjointed details of Thonburi's physical development that the capital's intended replication of the Ayutthaya prototype failed to achieve its objective; it was one of Taksin's major failures. Thonburi grew, but it failed to gain the majestic glamor or attractive power that had uniquely characterized its forerunner. Its inhospitable terrain, miniscule population, inadequate resources, competing priorities, and deficient planning combined to undermine his ambitious intent. That shortcoming contributed much, in retrospect, to the lasting impression that the Thonburi period was no more than an interstitial moment in Thai history.

Reintegration of Siam's fragmented feudal coalition of provinces and penumbra of tributary dependencies in the wake of Ayutthaya's destruction proved to be Taksin's greatest early challenge – and arguably his greatest success. It was essential in the first instance as a means of precluding the kingdom's further political disintegration, and more generally to strengthen its defenses against foreign incursion, maintain domestic tranquility, and pursue prosperity. To those ends, Taksin mounted a sequence of military expeditions – initially in the North against the insurgent kingdom of Fang; in the South against Nakhon; in the East against Phimai, Udong, and Ha Tien – expanding and strengthening the realm to progressively greater scale while defending the Western frontier against the continuing Burmese threat. Those successes came at the cost of Taksin's campaign injury, which Diogo argues was fated to contribute to his ultimate downfall. In this chapter, Diogo seeks to capture in a handful of pages the essentials of that initial rush of conquest and mishap, leaving the further developments to be detailed elsewhere.

Comrades

Toward the end of October 1767, a half year after the fall of Ayutthaya and about four months after having taken Siam's Eastern Seaboard port of Chanthabun by force, Colonel Taksin set off in command of some 40 junks for the Chaophraya River carrying a combat force of more than 2,000 fighting men thirsting for battle against the straggling elements of the recently decamped Burmese army. Accompanying Taksin on that fateful voyage were the 500 troops who had survived with him the months of shared hardship in flight from Burmese pursuit to the safety of Siam's unconquered Eastern Seaboard provinces, plus the inner circle of comrades who had joined him in the conquest of Chanthabun. Through the extraordinary support that he had received at that thriving seaport from the local Taechiu merchant community, he had acquired the men, arms, and vessels to mount a naval expedition bent on restoration of the devastated Siamese heartland to its former glory.[1] That magnificent adventure was destined to occupy every moment of the remaining 15 years of his life.

Taksin and his comrades at the assault on Chanthabun, June 1767. (No Na Paknam, *Murals Explained* (in Thai). Bangkok: Muang Boran, 1993, p. 78)

Taksin's miniature armada hastened up the Chaophraya River driven by the monsoon's early November tidal surge and, having routed the undermanned Burmese garrison at Thonburi, continued its advance upstream eager to confront the remaining enemy strongholds at Ayutthaya. The Burmese camp at Pho Sam Ton was defeated in vicious combat shortly after the start of November, and the Si Kuk supply depot was taken shortly thereafter. In the immediate aftermath, Taksin's triumphal procession through the ancient capital was stunned into silence at the sight of the devastation left in the wake of the capital's earlier defeat. Ayutthaya had been laid waste. Its former glory had been reduced to rubble and ashes, its populace eradicated, its environs degraded into a charnel ground haunted by the ghosts of a dead past. Reoccupancy was unthinkable. Insufficient manpower remained to repopulate and reconstruct the defenseless island city. It was clear, furthermore, that life among the old capital's ruins would have been a perpetual dirge to Siam's calamitous fall.

In council with his comrades, Taksin reviewed the situation and the options open to them. It was agreed that the most viable alternative would be to relocate their command base to the Thonburi fortress at the mouth of the Bangkok Yai Canal, a day's sail downriver. That remarkable resurrection of the Siamese power center at a remote outpost well removed from Ayutthaya's magnetic attraction could not have been accomplished by Taksin without the close collaboration of his exceptional associates, several hundred strong and of disparate background, drawn to his side by their common yearning for vengeance during a time of great adversity. A number of his closest comrades-in-arms were fellow survivors of Ayutthaya's dispersed Royal Pages Corps and Royal Guards regiments. Many other warriors of less illustrious background flocked to his banner in their wake. Droves of Ayutthaya survivors of a less military bent joined to contribute their resources and capabilities to the common cause. Among the most memorable members of that band of brothers, starting with Taksin himself, were the following:

Taksin (Sin *sae* Tae) as an infant, with his parents, Tae Hai-hong and Nok-iang, 1734 (Department of Fine Arts, *King Taksin the Great* (in Thai). Bangkok, 2017, p. 6)

Taksin, a man of common blood but uncommon character, was recognized by his peers from an early age as destined for great things.[2] His detractors later grumbled "how unbecoming it was that a man of such raw years, one who was as yet, as it were, untrained, uninitiated in the first sacred rites and mysteries of government should, in contempt of the laws, intrude and force himself into the sovereignty."[3] He refused to allow such aspersions to alter his course. Not born to greatness and glory, he was brought to it by a passion after honor. His many exploits did not induce him to sit still and reap the fruits of his past labors; rather, they raised in him incentives to further victories and greater glory, as if the present were all spent and only the future mattered.[4] In military endeavors, he quickly gained renown as a brilliant tactician and

Taksin leading his comrades into battle at Ayutthaya, October 1767 (No Na Paknam, *Murals Explained* (in Thai). Bangkok: Muang Boran, 1993, p. 74).

a warrior of magnetic mien. "For his perilous adventures, feats of arms, and successive triumphs, as gentle after victory as he was terrible in the field, he had no rival."[5] The people flocked to his banner. His charismatic leadership as a commander of tested valor, integrity, dedication, and vision, devoid of the vices of hesitancy, vacillation, and skepticism, inspired unrivaled devotion among his followers. He had the uncanny ability to rouse armies to battle and lead them to victory. In support of his ever-vigilant war footing he surrounded himself with a fierce and faithful following of military acolytes and cultivated a particular rapport with Siam's Taechiu merchants, who saw in him their means to economic salvation. Within that inner circle of disciples lay his greatest strength during the early years of his reign.

With his innate grasp of the arts of war he modernized Siam's battlefield strategy and its tactics of armed combat. In his military endeavors his reputation for single-minded resolve accorded well with his absolute authority. In bestowing rewards and conferring honors upon those who proved themselves intrepid under his command he was magnanimous; he was no less sparing in rebuking those who shirked their duties. He applied inflexible severity in all that related to social justice and to that end was rigorous in upholding the ordinances of the kingdom.[6] He remained ignorant of many things done in his name, not because he was indolent but because he gave a free hand to those in whom he placed his confidence. For there was much simplicity in his character. He was slow to see his own faults, but when he did see them, was extremely repentant, and ready to ask pardon of those he had injured.[7] Those who demonstrated their worth through their valor, diligence, and loyalty were favored with his notable generosity – and then there were those whom he did not favor. His steadfast refusal to fawn on pedigree or title or riches may well have contributed to his downfall.

Sanguan (later known as Thong-in) was the longest-serving, most steadfast member of Taksin's inner circle, dating from the very start of the Burmese invasion to the very end of the Thonburi reign. He had started his career as a non-commissioned army officer but managed on his own merits to rise through the ranks over the course of his career to colonel; he was perhaps Taksin's comrade of least distinguished status, a provincial of no noble connection, lacking in courtly etiquette.[8] His military career was built not only on his reliability and discretion but also on his extraordinary size and strength. A champion kickboxer and swordsman who was taken on as Taksin's aide-de-camp early on, he retained that position for more than a decade, standing at Taksin's side as personal bodyguard in every battle. Taksin found "no reason ever to complain, in the employments he gave him in the war, of any want of courage, energy, or military skill."[9] The siege of Phitsanulok in 1776 spelled the end of Sanguan's military career with his wounding; he then was rewarded with appointment to the chieftainship of Phichai.[10] In the following years he gained the popular byname of Colonel Phichai of the Broken Swords[11] in recognition of his former valor in battle. Lacking the refined graces of many of his noble comrades, he was admired for his frank, insightful assessment of every unfolding situation.[12]

Mut, Taksin's second intimate on his path to power, was descended from a distinguished Ayutthaya lineage. Mut's father had been chief of Ayutthaya's Cham community with the title of Colonel Racha-wangsan, serving as commander of Siam's naval forces during the final years of the Burmese siege. Mut had been trained in the same cohort of the Royal Pages Corps as Taksin, progressing to the Royal Guards rank of Major Sak Nai Wen. In late 1765, he was selected to lead a squadron of troops to the Eastern Seaboard dependencies to convey the region's annual tax receipts back to Ayutthaya's royal storehouses. His return to the capital was prevented, however, by the Burmese siege, and when Taksin reached Chanthabun in flight from his Burmese pursuers a year later, Mut and his men were still there. With his troops, Mut joined Taksin's coalition of comrades, contributed his consignment of 320 *chang* of gold to the cause,[13] and then continued to provide faithful service as a favored military aide. He and his men joined Taksin's armada in the eradication of the remaining Burmese forces, and when Taksin established his base at Thonburi, Mut installed them at Kudi Yai, a naval cantonment along the Bang Luang Canal directly behind the new Grand Palace. There, Mut was awarded the title of Colonel Siharat Decho, admiral of Thonburi's naval forces. After the Southern expedition of 1769-1770, in which he played a leading role, he was raised to the eminent position of General Chakri Si Ongkharak, Minister of War, Taksin's second in command. His death less than a year later created a vacuum within the ruling coalition that Taksin found difficult to fill.[14] In commemoration of Mut's exceptional service, his senior son Chui inherited the family's traditional title of Colonel Racha-wangsan and was promoted to Minister of the Capital, with his title revised to Racha-bangsan.[15] In 1779, after nearly a decade of unremarkable service, Chui was seized on charges of misconduct (the particulars unknown) along with a number of members of his retinue, and all were executed. The resulting disaffection within the Cham community and associated elements fed the unrest that led to the 1782 coup.

Li-ang, Taksin's trusted financial counselor and principal benefactor, was a seasoned Taechiu junk captain with commercial connections reaching from Canton to Ayutthaya and every port-of-call in between.[16] He had been a former business associate of Taksin's father and thus in 1767 was among those who welcomed Taksin to Chanthabun, where he played an instrumental role in supporting Taksin's takeover and mobilizing support for his cause among the Eastern Seaboard's Taechiu merchant community. As leader of a consortium of his fellow traders, he provided his junks and able-bodied seamen toward forming Taksin's armada to Ayutthaya, and joined the expedition to eradicate all remaining Burmese elements. Taksin was well aware that, but for Li-ang's support, his would have been a lost cause from the outset. In recognition of that debt, and in partial repayment of Li-ang's financial support, Taksin at the very start of his reign appointed him Minister of Trade, with the title of Colonel Phiphat Kosa. In that capacity Li-ang played a leading role in resolving the new regime's tangled economic crisis. A major action toward that end was his sponsorship of an immigrant indenture scheme whereby landless Chinese peasants could be brought to Thonburi on trading junks to form a coolie labor pool for the rapidly expanding Left-Bank Taechiu anchorage.[17] Through that arrangement, Li-ang helped recruit a Taechiu militia, which was eventually upgraded to a prized royal regiment. In contrast to those successes, his several ministerial efforts failed to secure Chinese diplomatic recognition of Taksin as Siam's legitimate ruler and thereby allow formal resumption of Siam's profitable royal trade at Canton. Li-ang eventually sought respite from his many onerous ministerial duties. Upon retiring from his ministerial duties, he was rewarded with the governorship of Siam's Eastern Seaboard provinces, extending to Ha Tien, carrying the esteemed title of Colonel Rachasethi.[18]

Mapu, as with Li-ang, was an immigrant but differed much in having arrived overland in hardship rather than as a prosperous seaman. He had formerly held the title of Colonel Noradecha, chief of a Mon border district under the Burmese thumb.[19] In the 1750s he had joined an insurrection against his Burmese overlords and in defeat had led his people in flight across the Three Pagodas Pass to Siamese sanctuary. Through the consecutive Burmese invasions of 1760 and 1765-1767 he helped coordinate the coalition of Mon partisan militias fighting alongside the Thai in defense of Siam's western hill country. Having secured Thonburi, Taksin turned his attention to a threatened recurrence of Burmese incursion and found Mapu to be a reliable ally in defense of the western front. He invited Mapu to move to Thonburi as leader of the Mon militias guarding the Three Pagodas Pass and other, lesser approaches to the Siamese lowlands. At Thonburi, Mapu was awarded the Thai title of

Colonel Phetracha, and he and his entourage were provided a settlement site clustered around Wat Klang, situated in the wetlands directly behind the newly dug Thonburi citadel moat, within easy reach of the Grand Palace. In short order, Mapu's sober council drew him into Taksin's inner circle of confidantes. As his first assignment he was placed in command of the capital's waterways patrols, a police duty that had been carried out haphazardly in the absence of a full-fledged Ministry of the Capital. It was Mapu who suggested to Taksin the domestication of a tract of paddy fields in the Thonburi outskirts to overcome the capital's food deficit. The failure of that project in the area's saline water and clay soil was one of Mapu's great disappointments, but he compensated for it by devising a more successful brick-works project along the upper reaches of the Mon Canal to support the construction of Thonburi's citadel wall, Grand Palace, and major temples. Mapu spent his final years ailing, until his death in 1770, while his son Madot (Captain Bamroe Phakdi) carried out his duties on a custodial basis.

The brothers Duang and Bunma, like Mapu, were not among Taksin's initial inner circle of comrades but rose to favor quickly over the ensuing years as their abilities were sensed, tested, and acknowledged.[20] They had been born in 1737 and 1743, respectively, as the fourth and fifth children of Colonel Akson Sunthon (Thongdi), an Ayutthaya noble, and Dao-roeang, daughter of a local Hokkien merchant.[21] Both brothers advanced through the Royal Pages Corps during the final Ayutthaya reigns, Bunma opting for a warrior's vocation while Duang followed a more scholarly course. Duang, upon the conclusion of his training, was deputed as liaison to the Ratburi provincial administration, performing the duties of magistrate. There he married the daughter of a local landowner and survived with his family the 1765-1767 Burmese invasion in the safety of rural seclusion. His younger brother Bunma was appointed to a posting in the Royal Guard just as the Burmese siege was getting underway. He fought his way through the Burmese onslaught and managed to escape the massacre only by drifting downriver concealed in an abandoned sampan. From his hiding place along the Thonburi shore he learned of Taksin's arrival and hurried to join his command. His genial fellowship, warrior's skills, resourcefulness, and devoted service soon gained him a junior staff post, where he came to Taksin's notice. Through Bunma, Taksin learned of Duang's survival at Ratburi. Remembered as a former fellow Royal Page of promise, Duang stood high on his list of potential comrades. He acted on that impulse by requesting Bunma to stop off at Ratburi, en route to Phetburi on another urgent assignment, to invite Duang to join the upstart regime at Thonburi. Duang, overcoming his natural caution in the face of Bunma's fervent appeal, accepted Taksin's invitation. It was thus Bunma who recruited Duang, rather than the other way 'round, as would have been the normal course between siblings of such disparate age.

An interview with Taksin resulted in Duang's induction into the new government as Major Racha Warin, commanding one of the two companies of the Royal Guard, with the other company headed by Bunma as Major Maha Montri. The brothers were soon promoted to the dual ranks of Colonels Aphai Ronarit (Duang) and Anuchit Racha (Bunma). In that capacity, they were honed in advanced aspects of campaign strategy and battle tactics during lengthy tutoring sessions at the feet of their master. They soon discovered the reason underlying Taksin's personal interest in enhancing their command capabilities. He was preparing them for command positions in the whirlwind of military campaigns that were to shape the kingdom's reintegration. Before the year was out, the brothers were assigned dual command of an expedition to eradicate the threat posed by the fledgling kingdom of Phimai. In the wake of that victory, Duang was assigned to deal with urgent priorities at Thonburi and in 1770 was appointed Minister of the Capital. Then, following the death of Taksin's military confidant Mut, he was raised to Minister of War. The several years following the Ha Tien victory of 1771 offered Duang a period of respite from battle, until he was recalled to active service in late 1774 for the Chiangmai campaign, followed by the Bang Kaew battle of early 1775, and then the climactic Burmese assault on Phitsanulok in 1776.

Duang was of a stoic disposition, his actions without fail being weighted with restraint. "It was difficult to excite him to laughter, his countenance seldom relaxed even into a smile; he was not quickly or easily provoked to anger, but if once provoked, he was no less difficult to pacify."[22] "Likewise, in temperance, industry, and frugality he surpassed even those who were much senior to himself."[23] There was in his natural character, in fact, something stately, austere, reserved, and unsociable, which raised him above his peers but made his company less agreeable than his brother's.[24] In contrast, Bunma built his military career on the bravado of a dashing cavalry commander. He was accustomed "to drink and bandy jests with [his men] without regard to age or the indignity of his place, and to the prejudice of important affairs that required his attention."[25] The scars he bore as lifelong souvenirs of perilous exploits earned him the popular byname of Phraya Soea (Tiger General). Among the most memorable of his early triumphs were his capture of the Khorat fortress during the Phimai campaign of 1768, his audacious forays against the fanatic insurrectionists of breakaway Fang in 1769, and his heroics at Udong in 1771 against the Vietnamese backers of Cambodia's puppet regime. His combat tactics, favoring flanking cavalry charges, inspired his men with the example of his personal valor. Operational experience in clandestine operations, furthermore, trained him as a master of surveillance and espionage, which he put to effective use years later.

Although Bunma was a man famous for his courage in battle, he was prone to imprudent judgment in peace, given to ungrounded opinion and immoderate ambition.[26] His troops revered him, even though many suffered easy death under his impetuous command. Yet, despite his leadership aptitude, he found it difficult to follow orders. He obeyed only those injunctions with which he concurred and deviated from those that, in the heat of the moment, he considered inconvenient. As in war, in peace he was ever alert to the main chance, ready to seek advantage from the smallest turn of fortune, hard with friend and foe alike. Taksin counselled Duang on more than one occasion to constrain his younger brother's reckless exploits, for his own wellbeing no less than for the safety of his armies and the kingdom. It was a common convention for generals to display their rank at staff meetings with their sheathed swords spread across their knees. In Bunma's case, one could never be quite certain that he might not draw his weapon to spill blood in angry debate. He was, in fact, a man who would have been as satisfied to die by the sword as he was to live by it.

Elites

Within two months of his dramatic return to the Siamese heartland from Chathabun exile, Taksin was consecrated as king at Thonburi. He underwent a more formal coronation a full year later, in late December 1768. On that solemn occasion, in continuance of ancient Ayutthaya tradition, he adopted the reign name of King Boromaracha IV. The frightening occurrence of an earthquake a dozen days after his investiture accentuated the mystical import of that event in the minds of the superstitious populace. As his first edict, the new king installed his close kindred as his royal household and appointed a cluster of his most trusted comrades as a new senior nobility to fill the ranks depleted in the past several years' bloodbath. Continuity from the former regime was confirmed with the additional appointment of a number of surviving Ayutthaya nobles to the ranks of the new nobility, reconstituting the rudiments of Ayutthaya's traditional administrative apparatus. A palpable sense of conviction, purpose, enthusiasm, and devotion to the common cause and its valorous leader freed that new elite from the confusion, discord, and discouragement that had gripped the jaded Ayutthaya aristocracy in its final years.

Victory in war brought new challenges in peace. As the issues confronting Taksin in his unanticipated monarchial role clarified themselves over the initial months and years of his reign, he was compelled to gravitate progressively from military commander to the unaccustomed role of supreme arbiter on a range of policy issues reaching far beyond his former experience.

King Taksin the Great, an iconic image engraved on the face of a 100-baht banknote, issued February 26, 2015. (Shutterstock)

Overseeing an increasingly complex civil administration taught him in short order the wisdom of delegating authority to those of his comrades on whose judgment he could best rely. It taught him equally the wisdom of restoring as quickly as possible the traditional chain of command. From the moment of his coronation, he set about assembling his royal court, reconstituting the ministerial formation, reinstalling the provincial governorships, reinvigorating the Buddhist monastic order.

A grave concern was the paucity of capable, experienced senior officials; few had survived the Ayutthaya decimation. Few among his band of brothers had had much exposure to governance beyond the most junior levels; most had had none. The newness of it all bred in them an exhilarating mix of enthusiasm and trepidation. The exceptional fact that Taksin's inner circle of colleagues, confidantes, and councilors cut across all the major sections of the emergent Thonburi populace contributed to their bonding as a competent directorate. Inevitably, however, that initial camaraderie sorted itself into an ordering of assignments, a distancing of domains of responsibility, which eroded the initial bonds of brotherhood with nascent dissonance, rivalry, and factionalism. The ensuing tale of discord and disaffection unfolded gradually, but inexorably, among the various stakeholders competing for privilege and perquisite.[27]

Royalty – The Thonburi royal household was designed in keeping with its Ayutthaya prototype, but given the circumstances, was far less grand. Yet, it retained much of the peculiar character of its earlier incarnation. It inhabited three worlds: the world of everyday fact, which directs the lives of us all with its morning ablutions, midday occupations, and evening amours; the world of ceremony and ritual, which absorbed much of its daily activity with repetitive routines that dulled the mind and clouded the senses; and the world of gossip and rumor, which distracted and distorted its perceptions, generated misunderstandings and secret antagonisms, and did much to give the aristocracy its reputation for perversity. Those qualities distinguished the aristocracy – the nobility nearly as much as the royalty – from the hardworking, commonsense lives of the vast bulk of the commons.

The aristocracy's core constituency, the king's immediate family, was tiny compared with Ayutthaya's vast royal kindred, most of whom had been killed with the Burmese conquest, carried off, or scattered beyond recovery. In their place, Taksin installed as the core of Thonburi's new royal household his few surviving kin: his mother, his two wives, and his sole son, who had together fled to Phetburi. His mother Nok-iang was proclaimed Princess Mother Thepamat and took on the task of officiating over the Inside – the Grand Palace women's quarter – until her death in 1775 and replacement by Lady Songkandan (Thong-mon) as superintendent of that secluded realm.[28] His two wives Son and An were elevated to Queen of the Center and Queen of the Right, respectively. Overwhelmed by their precipitous rise from provincial life to Thonburi royalty, they served as Nok-iang's compliant attendants and later assisted Thong-mon in her palace superintendence. Taksin doted on Chui, his sole son (born of An), with every intention of ensuring his eventual succession to the throne. Chui's

Table 2. The Thonburi royal family

Taksin's immediate family [1]
Princess Mother Thepamat (Nok-iang)
Queen of the Center (Son)
Queen of the Right (An)
Consorts (numerous)
Children (listed in order of birth sequence)
    Unnamed (died young) – son of Son (born before Taksin's enthronement)
    Unnamed (died young) – son of Son (born before Taksin's enthronement)
    Prince Inthara Phithak (Chui) – son of An (born before Taksin's enthronement)
    Prince Noi (son of Son)
    Prince Amphawan – son of Tim (daughter of Lady Songkandan [Thong-mon])
    Prince Thasaphong – son of Chim (daughter of the deposed ruler of Nakhon
        Si Thammarat [Nu])
    Prince Sila – son of Amphan (daughter of the viceroy of Nakhon Si Thammarat [Chan])
    Princess Oranika – dau. of Amphan (daughter of Nakhon Si Thammarat viceroy)]
    Prince Thasaphai – son of Chim (daughter of the deposed ruler of Nakhon
        Si Thammarat [Nu])
    Princess Samliwan – dau. of Amphan (daughter of the viceroy of Nakhon Si Thammarat
        [Chan])
    Prince Naren Rachakuman – son of Chim (daughter of the deposed Nakhon Si
        Thammarat ruler [Nu])
    Princess Praphai Phakat – daughter of Ngoen (her paternity unknown)
    Prince Suphanthuwong, and later Prince Kasat Anuchit (Men) – son of Chim Yai
        (daughter of General Chakri [Duang], Minister of War and later King Rama I)
    Princess Panchapapi – daughter of Chim (dau. of the deposed ruler of Nakhon
        Si Thammarat [Nu])
    Noi (not recognized as prince) – son of Prang (daughter of the deposed ruler of
        Nakhon Si Thammarat [Nu]).
    Thong-in (not recognized as prince) – son of Yuan (daughter of the deposed ruler
        of Nakhon Si Thammarat [Nu]).

Ayutthaya royal family members
    Prince Anurak Songkhram (Ramlak)
    Prince Ram Phubet (Bunchan)
    Prince Nara Suriyawong (Saeng)
    Prince Surin Songkhram (Prathum Phaichit)
    Prince Chesada Kuman (personal name unknown)
    Princess Thabthim [dau. of King Phrachao Soea]
    Princess Suriya [daughter of King Boromakot]
    Princess Chanthawadi [daughter of King Boromakot]
    Princess Phimthawadi [daughter of King Boromakot]
    Princess Fakthong [daughter of King Boromakot]
    Princess Mit [daughter of King Uthumphon]
    Princess Prathum [daughter of King Uthumphon]
    Princess Chim [granddaughter of King Phetracha]
    Princess Bupha [granddaughter of King Thai Sa]
    Princess Ubon [granddaughter of King Thai Sa]
    Princess Mani [granddaughter of King Thai Sa]
    Princess Krachat [granddaughter of King Thai Sa]
    Princess Mongkhon [granddaughter of King Boromakot]
    Princess Phayom [granddaughter of King Boromakot]

1 The names of 16 children of unknown mothers (and no further mention) have been excluded from this list.

elevation to the august title of Prince Inthara Phithak (Protector of the King) in 1775 was an emblematic step in that direction.[29]

Beyond that inner royal family circle, Taksin's consorts rose to a considerable number, as had been common practice in previous reigns. Nobles from far and wide presented their daughters at court to learn the arts of aristocratic life, serve as ladies-in-waiting, and hopefully gain royal favor. However, he fathered far fewer children than had been the custom for most of his predecessors. For reasons of state, particularly Taksin's commitment to even-handed dealings with his many comrades-in-arms, he avoided the daughters of most of his senior officials. One exception was Nu, the governor of Nakhon Si Thammarat, several of whose daughters bore Taksin children.[30] Another was General Chakri (Duang), his Minister of War, whose eldest daughter bore Taksin a son, Men, who was duly awarded the title of Prince Suphantuwong.

Surviving members of the Ayutthaya royal family were sought out by Taksin's minions to augment the Thonburi royal family, but few were found. No more than two dozen Ayutthaya royals were discovered in provincial seclusion for invitation to join the resurrected court at Thonburi. Among them were more than a dozen princesses, but only five surviving princes (commonly referred to as Taksin's "nephews").[31] Thonburi's Ayutthaya-era princesses and their retinues formed an exotic presence within the Grand Palace women's quarter, conveying through their refined behavior, in both word and action, a wealth of knowledge on proper courtly decorum. The five princes were adopted into the royal family with great fanfare, along with high royal rank and riverfront palaces alongside the Grand Palace. One of them, Prince Nara Suriyawong (Saeng), was in 1769 appointed royal overseer of Nakhon; Princes Anurak Songkhram (Ramlak) and Ram Phubet (Bunchan) were favored by the king for inclusion in his inner circles of military commanders. Several played supporting roles in later military campaigns.

Within four months of his December 1767 investiture, after the dilapidated Thonburi fort had been renovated to a site fit for royal habitation, Taksin dispatched his staff aide Bunma by caparisoned junk to Phetburi to invite his mother and his two wives and son to join him at Thonburi. They arrived accompanied by a retinue of provincial ladies who would form the core of Thonburi's Grand Palace staff for years to come. Upon Taksin's formal coronation nearly a year later, his mother and wives were elevated to their royal titles as Princess Mother, Queen of the Center, and Queen of the Right, and his son Chui was formally invested as prince.

The court retainers, staff, and servants initially were few, for much the same reasons as those that restricted the size of the royal family. In the absence of experienced palace staff from former reigns, the king's primary agent in management of the royal household, until her death in 1775, was his mother, Nok-iang, who, with her friend Thong-mon ever at her side, was quietly tutored in her new royal role by the most senior of the resident Ayutthaya-era princesses. In that capacity, she recruited a bevy of titled palace ladies for the handling of essential royal household functions pertaining to protocol, children's education, religious paraphernalia, the kitchens, the sanitary facilities, and the Inside's female guard force. Of Thong-mon's six children, one daughter was accepted as a consort by Taksin, raising Thong-mon's status at court even higher. With Nok-iang, Thong-mon tended the lingering agonies of the injury that Taksin had sustained on the Nakhon expedition of 1769, and she continued to fulfill that duty faithfully after Nok-iang's death. More than any other courtier, she relieved Taksin of the burdens of royal household management and sought to ease his many ceremonial duties under the disturbed conditions that marked the reign's final years.

Nobility – Taksin did not adjust easily to the personal transformation required of his elevation from military strategist and battlefield commander to deified sovereign and executive overseer of a revived kingdom. While he retained firm command of military affairs, at least through the initial phase of his reign, the substance of civil administration devolved largely upon his senior officials. Increasingly, he assigned administrative oversight to those trusted subordinates, though he retained personal control of the planning, or at least the final word, for all major policies and programs. He appointed his nobles largely from among the comrades drawn to his side during his early years in power. Greatly favored were those who had endured with him the initial hazardous escape from Burmese encirclement and the subsequent privations of Chanthabun sanctuary. Early on, that inner circle was joined by a number of survivors: Ayutthaya nobles who considered Taksin's rise to power the sole practicable option for the kingdom's restoration. Over the ensuing years, numbers of lesser affiliates were appointed to administrative positions in recognition of their expertise and as reward for their pledges of fealty.

Thonburi's administrative alignment re-established the traditional Ayutthaya arrangement centering on the Ministries of War, Interior, Trade, Capital, Palace, and Lands.[32] As at Ayutthaya, a number of additional departments independent of those key institutions executed specific technical functions – among them the Royal Guard, Palace Guard, Royal Secretariat, Judiciary, and Departments of Royal Scholars, Religious Affairs, and Artisans. The most pressing affairs of state were discussed by the king and his council of ministers in the privacy of the Royal Audience Hall, guarded from eavesdroppers by an encircling detachment of liveried sentries.[33] Seldom did a minister venture to introduce any deviation from the consensus, though the king himself preferred candor and had expressed himself to that effect. Under that protocol, decisions were, with rare exception, reached in perfect accord with Taksin's assessments. Whether those decisions were invariably carried out with equal aplomb is less certain.

Unlike the responsibilities assigned to specific departments, the functional distinctions between ministries were vague and in constant flux. Their jurisdiction over the provincial governors, who constituted a subsidiary echelon of noble authority, vacillated with continuing uncertainty within the hierarchy of feudal patronage. Most remarkable was the small number of Taksin's principal councilors and direct

Table 3. Ministries and ministers of the Thonburi reign, 1768–1782

Ministry	Years in office	Ministers
War (*kalahom*)	1768 – 1770	Vacant
	1770	Gen. Chakri Ongkharak (Mut)
	1771 – 782	Gen. Chakri (Duang)
Interior (*mahadthai*)	1768 – 1771	Vacant
	1771– 1782	Gen. Surasi (Bunma)
Trade (*phra khlang*)	1768 – 1771	Col. Phiphat Kosa (Li-ang *sae* Tang)
	1771 – 1776	Col. Phichai Aisawan (Ching-chong *sae* Yang)
	1776 – 1779	Col. Siri Aisawan (Hok-chu *sae* Tae)
	1779 – 1782	Vacant[1]
Capital (*moeang*)	1778 – 1770	Vacant[2]
	1770 – 1771	Col. Yomarat (Duang)
	1770	Col. Yomarat (Bunma)
	1771 – 1779	Col. Yomarat (Chui)
	1779 – 1782	Vacant[3]
Palace (*wang*)	1768 – 1776	Vacant[4]
	1776 – 1785	Col. Thamma Trailok (Bunrot)[5]
Lands (*na*)	1768 – 1782	Unknown

1 During the period of vacancy, some ministerial duties were delegated to a senior Malay functionary of the Harbor Department.
2 During the period of vacancy, the ministerial duties were divided among the directors of the royal warehouse, eastern trade, and treasury departments.
3 During the period of vacancy, some ministerial duties were delegated to Colonel Ramanwong (Madot).
4 During the period of vacancy, some ministerial duties were delegated to Prince Nara Suriwong (Saeng), and then Major Maha Montri (Bunrot, later raised to minister).
5 Bunrot continued as minister into the First Reign with the new title of Gen. Thammathikon.

administrative subordinates. The number of his ministers over the term of his reign exceeded not more than a dozen or so, and his provincial governors amounted to no more than twice that number. Most retained their positions to the end of their lives, though several were removed from office on charges of misconduct, with execution their sorry fate.

Clergy[34] – As the Thai people's spiritual refuge since time beyond memory, Buddhism forms their moral anchor in daily affairs, with such force that it is often said that to be Thai is to be Buddhist. The Buddhist monkhood and its temples form the seat of village and city life and the mainstay of learning and communal support. Just as the great river nurtures the annual rice harvest and the king in his divine majesty oversees the land's tranquility, it is said, the Thai people regard Buddhism as the natural essence of their lives. At its core, as propounded by its clergy – its monastic brotherhood – lie its greatest virtues, tolerance and peace-of-mind, which are exemplified in the people's wonderful equanimity and in the diversity of peoples and religions that Siam has peaceably absorbed over the generations, to the advantage of all. Just as in other kingdoms with other religions, however, the Buddhist canon and clergy offer convenient instruments for the Crown's command over the people. The carnage that marked the fall of Ayutthaya, despite the Buddhist beliefs professed by both the Thai and Burmese, marks a historic affirmation of that abiding paradox.[35]

The pillage of Ayutthaya destroyed virtually all its Buddhist temples, as well as its Christian churches, Hindu sanctuaries, Muslim mosques, and Daoist shrines. Those that were not consumed in the flames were pillaged for their treasures. Many clerics died in the havoc, and many more were carried off into captivity. Those who survived formed the fount of the kingdom's religious revival. The Thonburi regime allowed no constraint to interfere with the revitalization of its state-sanctioned religious orders. Sanctuary was offered to an array of clerics and other adepts who had found their way to the new capital. Taksin ordered the dispatch of missions into the countryside to persuade revered monks to reassemble their brethren at Thonburi. He sponsored the reconstruction of many of Thonburi's abandoned temples for monastic residence and urged others to follow his example.[36] The investiture of a new supreme patriarch to ensure the effective administration of Siam's revived Buddhist clergy was among Taksin's immediate priorities.

Restoration of the traditional monastic order was essential to the clergy's participation in the kingdom's revitalization. The monastic brotherhood was in principle an assemblage of peers, but in practice it required leadership. The former venerable abbot of Ayutthaya's Wat Pradu – his monastic title unknown, his personal name Di – had miraculously survived the 1767 slaughter. As the most distinguished cleric to have found his way to Thonburi, he was selected as Thonburi's first supreme patriarch and was installed at Thonburi's centrally located Wat Bang Wa Yai. Less than a year later, it was discovered how he had managed to escape the fall of Ayutthaya unscathed. Word reached the throne that he had succumbed to Burmese threats of torture by revealing the hiding places of wealth left behind by fleeing households.[37] Upon discovery of that act of betrayal, he was summarily demoted from his post as Supreme Patriarch to that of an untitled monk. That great scandal was swiftly resolved with Di's replacement by Si (former clerical title unknown), a candidate of unblemished qualifications.[38]

As the venerable abbot of Ayutthaya's Wat Phanan Choeng (situated directly alongside Ayutthaya's Taechiu port district) Si had escaped the Burmese siege in its closing months on a junk bound for Nakhon Si Thammarat, where he had found refuge at the venerated Wat Mahathat. In 1769, upon Taksin's conquest of Nakhon, Si was invited to Thonburi and was upon arrival appointed Di's replacement as the abbot of Wat Bang Wa Yai and Supreme Patriarch of Siam's monastic brotherhood with the title of Phra Thamma Trailok. Si brought with him from Nakhon an authoritative recension of the Buddhist scriptures for copying, as few canonical texts were available at Thonburi. Accompanying him from Nakhon were several fellow monks who over the following years worked with him in reviving Thonburi's temples.[39] Two years after his installation as head of Siam's monastic brotherhood, Si was requested by Taksin to dispatch a party of missionary monks to the North to sponsor monastic reordinations and reeducate the people in the Buddhist precepts in the aftermath of the heretic Chao Phra Fang insurrection. The success of that unprecedented clerical venture enhanced his reputation as a royal advisor and forged his lasting association with the brothers Duang and Bunma.[40]

Reconstruction

The river bend reaching downstream from Bangkok Noi to Bangkok Yai, with Wat Bang Wa Yai at its midpoint, linked the opposing ends of the great Thonburi oxbow canal. The old fort situated at its downstream point had distinct military and trade potential. Foremost among Ayutthaya's downriver strongpoints, it had for several centuries served as a customs post and junk waystation for vessels plying the river route between the Gulf of Siam and Ayutthaya, while its guns and garrison had helped defend the Siamese heartland against threat of armed incursion. Furthermore, the fort had long guarded the river's main inland waterways extension the Bangkok Yai Canal/Dan Canal/Sanam Chai Canal/Tha Chin River route – to the western seaboard provinces. Beyond the damaged fort and adjacent ships' anchorage, Thonburi's riverside in the Ayutthaya aftermath consisted of little more than a jungled shoreline. Taksin's directive to forsake hallowed Ayutthaya in favor of that desolate frontier outpost provoked much anxious debate among his comrades, but his mind had been made up. His choice of Thonburi as his command post remained a contentious decision for years but, in hindsight, is today universally recognized as a brilliant stroke.

The dilapidated Thonburi fortress required comprehensive reconstruction as a royal compound in the Ayutthaya mold. Taksin took initial steps by relocating the garrison upriver and then preparing the premises for the installation of his family within a sturdy stockade backing his centrally located personal living quarters and audience hall. As one of his first steps toward upgrading the military post to a royal redoubt, the riverside Wichai Prasit Bastion was strengthened with a line of gun emplacements at the Bangkok Yai Canal confluence. Along the opposite bank of that canal, alongside the Hokkien junk anchorage, he erected boatsheds for his berthed rivercraft, as well as storehouses for the tax receipts, tributary offerings, and spoils of victory that he expected to accumulate.[41] He ordered the excavation of a defensive moat behind the fort reaching upstream from the Bang Luang Canal to the Bangkok Noi Canal, demarcating the riverside Thonburi citadel.

Taksin had no particular aptitude for the planning and execution of the new capital's construction, nor did he have the patience for that task in the midst of the recurrent crises in which the new regime had become embroiled. For that project he turned to the small group of surviving Ayutthaya court prelates who had been recruited to staff the Department of Pundits.[42] As his initial duty, the adept heading that department, the Venerable Phra Maha Rachakhru (Sombat), arranged the king's coronation rites. He and his colleagues were then deputed to lay out Thonburi's geomantic contours, all in replication of Ayutthaya's former dimensions – to the extent possible, given the new capital's unique configuration. After many days of study, the survey team reported their findings to Taksin. The king listened patiently to Sombat's learned disquision on the new capital's proposed celestial contours. It was recommended that in its guise as the new Ayutthaya, the walled city of Thonburi should reach well beyond the existing moated area to a broad moat to be excavated at least double the distance inland from the river, joining the Bangkok Yai and Bangkok Noi Canals to form an urban island about half the size of the Ayutthaya prototype. The makeshift Thonburi moat should then be expanded into a more substantial transport canal bisecting the city between the existing riverside citadel and a new noble quarter, with a commercial zone beyond, centering on the Bang Luang Canal/Don Canal confluence near Bang Yi Roea Mon and reaching to the outer limits of the oxbow bend. Key features of the citadel's configuration should be a new Grand Palace fronting the river alongside Wat Bang Wa Yai, backed by a city pillar, with lesser palaces stretching along the riverfront. It was advised, furthermore, that the current Grand Palace be replaced by riverport facilities to support the traders' quarter situated up the Bang Luang Canal. Taksin concluded Sombat's grandiose presentation with effusive thanks and assurances that the pundits' proposal would receive careful attention. However, only a few of the report's exhorbitant recommendations were ever acted upon.[43] The implicit snub affected Sombat and his fellow adepts deeply. They played a muted role at the Thonburi court through the remainder of the reign, until the eve of the 1782 coup.

Instead of expanding the city westward, as proposed in the pundits' plan, the city spread eastward over the ensuing years, across the river. That process, favoring the development of a Taechiu-dominated Left Bank port district, was complemented by the rafting of massive loads of bricks from the dismantled Ayutthaya city wall for improvement of the Thonburi Grand Palace and its principal gun battery, the Wichai Prasit Bastion, and the extension of a crenelated city wall of plastered brick upriver to the newly built Prakan Bastion.[43] Once those key defenses had been completed, work was started to extend the citadel wall along Thonburi's rear moat and its linked canal sides. Despite the consignment of much of the work to Taksin's Taechiu supporters, who enlisted expert Chinese architects and masons to supervise coolie contingents for the task, the work proceeded slowly due to recurrent supply interruptions and manpower diversions with the intervention of competing priorities. Great effort was expended to support the riverside wall section on deep-set, close-lined timber pilings, as the soggy shoreline was prone to rapid erosion under the weight of the high-piled brickworks. The many pilings proved inadequate against the river current,

Evocation of the Thonburi Grand Palace in its prime. (*Muang Boran Journal*, vol. 43, no. 4, 2017, front cover detail)

however; within two decades of the wall's construction most of its shoreline stretch had collapsed.

Well before construction of the Thonburi citadel wall, work was begun to upgrade the old fort to accommodate palatial quarters within a massive crenelated wall including gunned parapets, spired gateways, and other features proclaiming royal status. The palace was laid out to replicate, on a diminished scale and lesser level of luxury, the layout of its Ayutthaya prototype. Its central throne hall and royal residence were backed by the women's quarter and fronted by a forecourt containing the Chapel Royal, law courts, storehouses, an arsenal, guardposts, and other administrative facilities. The remainder of the citadel's terrain was cleared of jungle growth, leveled, raised, and crossed with several lesser canals reaching from the river to the rear moat, ready for residence by the new regime's senior elite and their retinues. It took only a few years for the citadel's waterfront to be occupied by several princes' palaces and a string of noblemen's residences, backed by their retainers' clustered dwellings and servants' huts shaded within lush gardens. The citadel was completed with the renovation of its five temples – Wat Bang Wa Noi, Wat Bang Wa Yai, Wat Mon, Wat

Chaeng, and Wat Tai Talat – a municipal prison, a Royal Guards cantonment, elephant and cavalry enclosures, and several marketplaces.

The Thonburi conurbation extended from the river inland well beyond the citadel bounds, primarily lining the banks of the Bang Luang Canal.[45] Along that major waterway, Taksin allotted settlement sites to a polyglot collection of Ayutthaya survivors – Thai, Mon, Malay, Persian, Cham, Hokkien, Portuguese – who had by one means or another managed to evade Burmese capture. Similar arrangements were subsequently made for other refugee communities – Thai, Mon, Lao, Arab – along the rear of the citadel moat, following the Mon Canal inland, and along the banks of the Bangkok Noi Canal. In return for their assurances of fealty to the fledgling state, all those seekers of sanctuary were offered food, land, and protection, while their leaders were awarded noble status along with assigned government functions – often

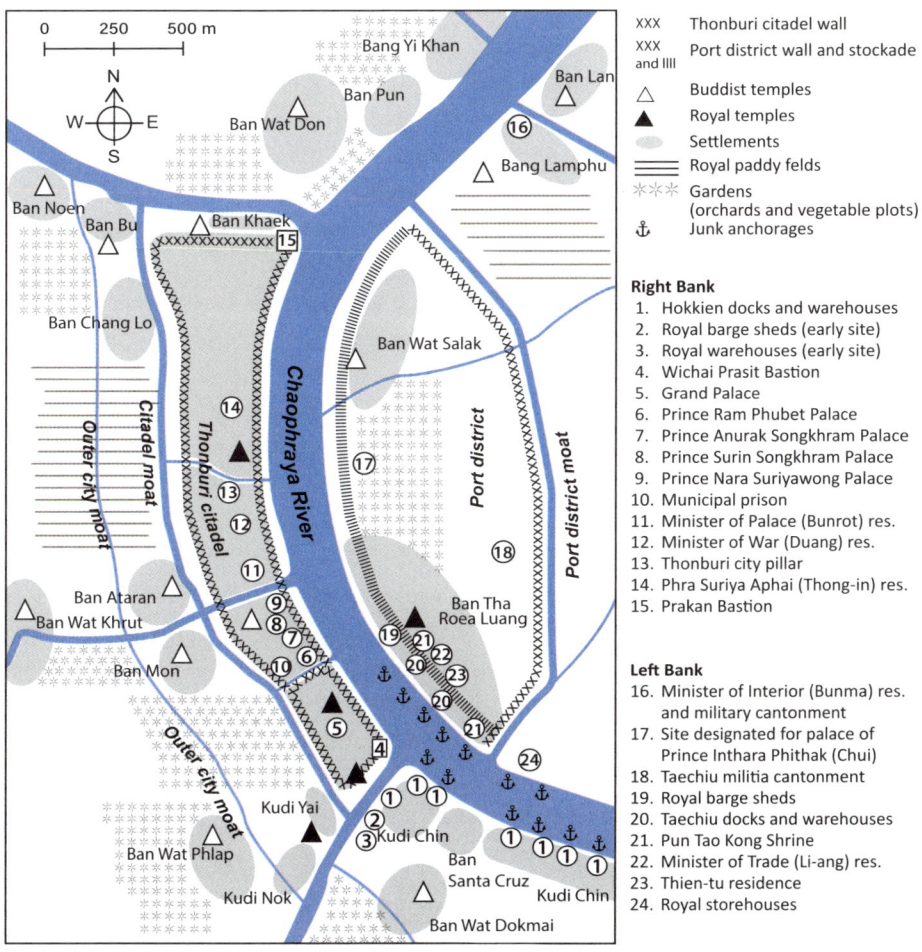

Map 5. Thonburi revival, c. 1776

in continuance or amplification of the positions they had occupied at Ayutthaya. Their affiliation with the Thonburi regime was predicated on the understanding that they and their followers would contribute to the defense of the capital as standing militias; some of those brigades came to play important roles in the many military campaigns that Taksin mounted over the course of his reign.

As one such public service, Thonburi's Mon community was mobilized early during the reign to provide its labor toward the straightening, expansion, and extension of an ancient zigzag of drainage channels to form the Mon Canal, reaching from the river through the citadel and past the inland villages to join the western bend of the great oxbow canal, opening new tracts to settlement and cultivation. Several years later, as that area became populated, it was decided that the ring of extramural villages had increased sufficiently to warrant the excavation of an additional, outer moat – as had been advised by the pundits' survey – to demarcate the expanding conurbation. A shallow channel was dug and lined with barbed bamboo thickets as an initial step toward creating an outer moat as deep and wide as the Mon Canal, but other priorities intervened during the reign's later troubled years to block full realization of that plan. The unfinished project remained a vague symbol of Taksin's unrealized aspiration to expand the Thonburi citadel into an approximation of the Ayutthaya ideal.[46]

The tidal salinity of the lower delta's sedimentary soils restricted rice cultivation to scattered rises and ridges. That impediment had not been anticipated with the hurried downriver move to the kingdom's new capital. Severe rice shortfalls – a strategic blunder following on the mistaken assumption that rice yields in the Thonburi area would approximate those of the Central Plain – led to near-famine conditions and precipitous price increases over three consecutive harvest failures (1767/68, 1768/69, and 1769/70). Among the many urgent responses to that recurring crisis were the distribution of emergency rice allotments from the royal granaries, strict policing of government-imposed price ceilings, vigorous negotiations with neighboring states to expedite rice purchases, and heavy state borrowing to cover the costs of rice imports.[47] A preliminary directive issued in 1768 ordered Thonburi's senior officials to supervise all able-bodied men in the cultivation of arable tracts behind the Right Bank's citadel and along the Left Bank downriver from the Banglamphu Canal. Those royal rice fields, settled and farmed by the king's men (peasants conscripted to royal service), never came close to satisfying the capital's consumption requirements. In retrospect, the compelling urgency of Taksin's assemblage of rice policies confirmed Thonburi's inferior rice-growing capacity.[48]

The low-lying, marshy, sparsely populated Left Bank riverside directly across from the Grand Palace was allotted to Taksin's Taechiu comrades for development as a mariners' anchorage. There, alongside the royal barge landing, they drove a line of close-set pilings into the riverbank and filled the sodden tract behind with dredged landfill to form a habitable frontage for a row of docks and jetties, warehouses, and living quarters that soon expanded into a bustling junk port, sanctified by its distinctive

Taechiu shrine dedicated to the merchants' guardian deity. Far upstream along the Left Bank, at the mouth of the Banglamphu Canal, from where a cannon shot could reach across the river as far as the Bangkok Noi Canal mouth, Taksin established a military guardpost to defend the capital's upriver approaches. He assigned its command to Bunma, who took up residence alongside the position's gun battery and troop cantonment. The neighboring tract of royal rice fields that he was charged with developing continued in later years to be populated by a cluster of conscripted peasant villages.[49] The remaining Left Bank riverside, however, long remained far less densely settled, much of it left vacant for haphazard conversion by Chinese smallholders to riverside vegetable plots, pig sties, and poultry runs.

Some years later, having achieved his initial objective of reintegrating the kingdom, and not long before the outbreak of renewed Burmese hostilities, Taksin turned to the enlargement of Thonburi's physical bounds beyond its constricted Right Bank confines. Along the less encumbered Left Bank he renovated two old temples (Wat Salak and Wat Pho) and installed a riverside row of royal barge sheds backed by royal storehouses situated directly across from the Grand Palace. With the sizable contingents of indentured coolies available to his Taechiu merchant associates, he sponsored the digging of a Left Bank moat behind the port area, broader and deeper than the Right Bank citadel moat that had been hurriedly dug some six years previously, defining the extended perimeter of Thonburi's new port district. A sturdy plastered-brick wall was raised along the new moat's inner bank. In view of the problems that had arisen with the riverside subsidence of the Right Bank's citadel wall, the Left Bank waterfront saw the raising of no more than a timber stockade.

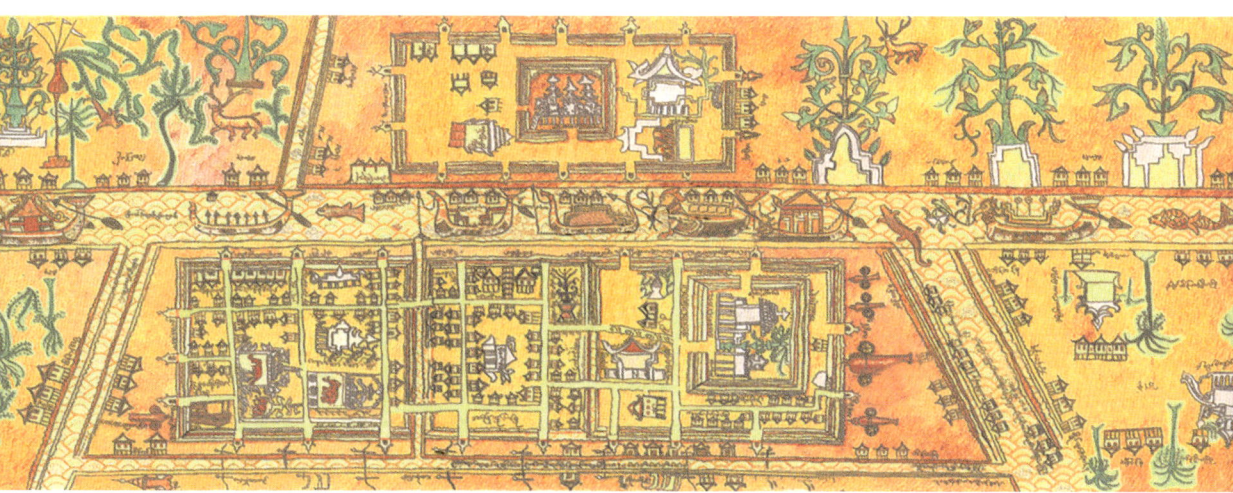

Thonburi in a Burmese spy map, c.1782. (Courtesy of the Asian Studies Center, Chulalongkorn University). Discovered several decades ago in the Rangoon state archives, this detailed hand-drawn contemporary map of Taksin's Thonburi is believed to have been diagrammed surreptitiously by a Burmese enemy agent, possibly posing as a trader.

Upstart Regime 133

He also sponsored the establishment of a cantonment for the Taechiu militia (later formalized as a royal regiment) to the rear of the newly walled Left Bank precinct and initiated action toward the construction of a Left Bank riverside palace for Prince Chui, his eldest son. With the emergence of that urban extension, Thonburi's progress to prosperity accelerated, though by the end of its revival phase the new capital's rise to a stature akin to Ayutthaya still remained a distant dream.

Reintegration

Many of Siam's outer provinces and neighboring tributary principalities had responded to Ayutthaya's collapse by distancing themselves from the center. Left to their own devices they had turned renegade, strengthened their defenses, formed new alliances, and redirected their trading networks. Some claimed independence with the elevation of their former chiefs to sovereigns. The resulting political disintegration was Taksin's greatest challenge in the years immediately following his accession. Loss of manpower, more than loss of territory, lay at the heart of that predicament. Manpower control was vital, for it contributed revenues, military forces, and labor for public works. To attract the people back to Thonburi's ambit of influence, the annual period of corvée labor service – the most onerous imposition imposed on the peasantry – was eased from six months to four. Among the many measures taken to regain command of the subject provinces and principalities were the registration of all able-bodied commoners (based on a population census relying on the wrist tattooing of all able-bodied men), the granting of tax exemptions on certain types of productive activity (such as fishing, inland transport, and marketplace trade), and the dispatch of conciliatory missions to restore the fealty of obstinate provincial leaders.

Not all outlying areas were easily induced to join the new regime. Among those that dared assert their independence, several went so far as to display hostile intent. Those threats required Taksin's immediate response. An early example was the troubled purchase of rice from the far-off Gulf-coast principality of Ha Tien in early 1768. The rice-laden junks that Ha Tien sent were suspected to be heavily gunned and packed with marines bent on assaulting Thonburi. Hostilities were averted by dispatching Thonburi's junk fleet to the Chaophraya River estuary, where the rice was transferred under force of arms to Taksin's vessals for conveyance to its intended destination. Ha Tien explained away its vessels' military capability with the excuse that it provided a safeguard against the risk of piracy. The episode left lingering mistrust, which was confirmed by Ha Tien's further covert support of the Phimai rebellion of 1768. A similar threat was posed by the expansionist efforts of the breakaway province of Phitsanulok against its neighboring loyalist neighbors. Despite Thonburi's desperate shortage of military manpower, Taksin in October 1768 deputed his military subordinates, Duang and Bunma, to mount an assault on that upstart principality. However, the fortress city of Phitsanulok proved impregnable against their inadequate forces. To conserve their manpower, and their honor, the brothers withdrew.

Map 6. Reintegration of Siam under the Thonburi regime, 1768–1771

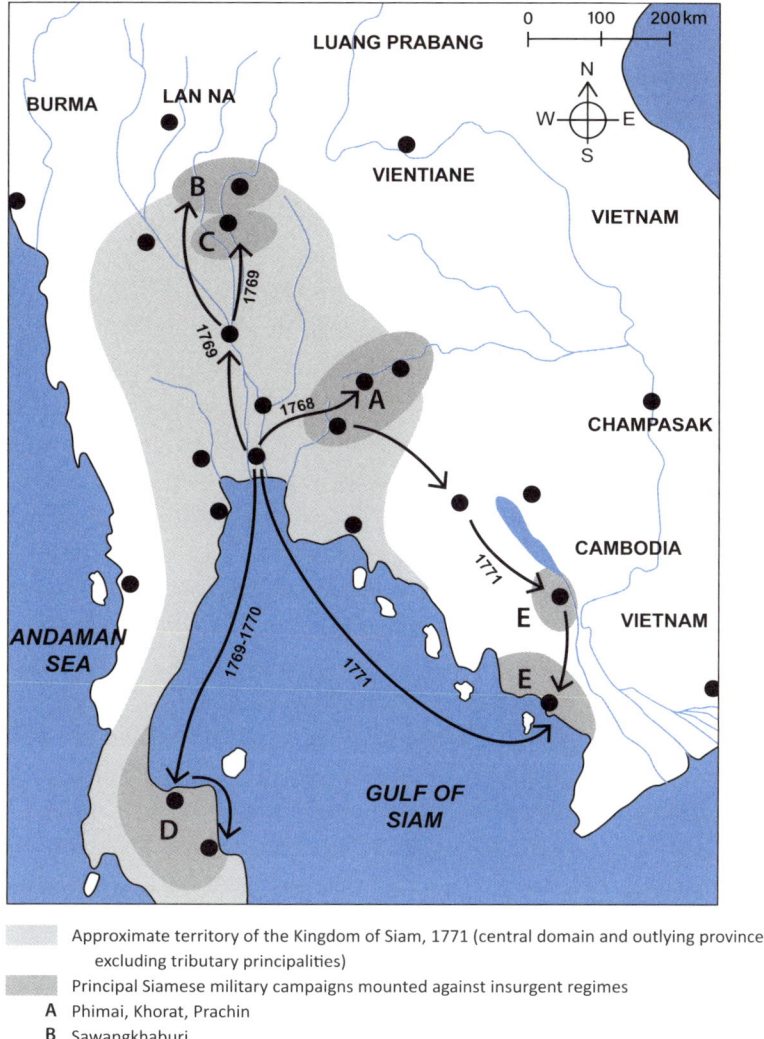

- Approximate territory of the Kingdom of Siam, 1771 (central domain and outlying provinces, excluding tributary principalities)
- Principal Siamese military campaigns mounted against insurgent regimes
- A Phimai, Khorat, Prachin
- B Sawangkhaburi
- C Phitsanulok
- D Nakhon, Surat
- E Udong, Ha Tien
- → Campaign routes (and dates)
- ● Principal population centers

Phimai, 1768[50] – Rather than recall Duang and Bunma directly to Thonburi from the aborted Phitsanulok battle, Taksin journeyed by state barge upriver to Nakhon Sawan, bringing with him troop reinforcements and additional arms. There, the brothers met him with foreboding of punishment for their failed mission but were instead assigned another urgent task – subjugation of the renegade kingdom of Phimai. Taksin's stern warning that they should not again meet disappointment, given their bolstered strike force, was heeded with prudent preparations. In late September the strengthened regiments sped off by muddied march through the seasonal rains, bound for the assault on Phimai's forward base at Khorat. The campaign culminated in a resounding victory, ensured no less by the defenders' disarray than the assailants' prowess. With that conquest the brothers vindicated themselves. They were rewarded with appointment to joint directorships of the Royal Guard, and two years later with elevation to even more illustrious office. Under their oversight, their senior officers were appointed to the governorships of Khorat and Prachin, ensuring secure reintegration of the eastern frontier into the Siamese fold.

Nakhon, 1769-1770 – The loss of Nakhon posed a more formidable problem. As the presiding port of Siam's peninsular provinces, Nakhon had been one of Ayutthaya's most precious assets. The ancient port city possessed an excellent junk harbor and was favored with a hinterland rich in agricultural abundance and jungle produce. Its populace represented Siam's southernmost Thai Buddhist extension reaching toward the Malay Muslim world, ensuring the tributary alliance of neighboring Patani and the other sultanates beyond. In the wake of Ayutthaya's collapse, however, the ruler of Nakhon had proclaimed his independence. After the victory over Phimai, Taksin was eager to continue his unification of the kingdom with Nakhon's return. To that end, he sailed off in July 1769 in command of a fleet of 25 gunned junks carrying two royal regiments, with Colonel Siharat Decho (Mut) as his admiral, on a maritime expedition to subdue rebellious Nakhon. A smaller flotilla was dispatched from Chanthabun with additional troops, scheduled to join him en route, at Surat.

Brisk winds sped Taksin's royal fleet southward. Aboard his flagship anchored off Surat awaiting the Chanthabun squadron's imminent arrival, a sudden gale blasted through the junk's rigging. Taksin, weathering the torrent alongside the helmsman, was struck and severely injured by a falling spar torn from its lashings. The shattered beam left a wad of wooden splinters piercing deep into his thigh. Not all the sharp slivers could be removed; they left a nest of festering ulcers that tormented him with recurrent bouts of excruciating pain, delirium, and impaired judgment. Months of convalescence and the unremitting endeavors of his physicians with applications of camphor, tamarind pastes, and other medications of local, Chinese, Indian, Arab, and Western origin failed to heal the suppurating abscess. Taksin was cautioned by his physicians never again to travel by horse or elephant. To his endless vexation, his military exploits were henceforth confined to conveyance by royal palanquin or barge or ship, and to sedentary command from the rear.[51]

Nevertheless, the Southern campaign proceeded to successful conclusion. Guided by Taksin's bed-ridden instructions complemented by Mut's diligent seamanship and front-line command, Nakhon's harbor and land approaches were blockaded. The city capitulated without severe damage. Its populace was spared but for the seizure of a token contingent of war prisoners and the transfer of its ruling family to Thonburi detention. Nakhon was proclaimed a full-fledged province of Siam, and Prince Nara Suriyawong (Saeng), one of Taksin's royal "nephews," was installed as its overseer.

Taksin stayed on at Nakhon for several months to recuperate from his injury before returning to Thonburi by painful stages early the next year, to the great relief of one and all. Mut was rewarded with appointment to high office.

Udong, 1769 – For a century and more, weakened Cambodia had been drawn ever more tightly into the Siamese tributary orbit.[52] Following the Burmese conquest of Ayutthaya in 1767, however, the factionally torn Khmer kingdom gravitated toward Vietnamese vassalage. While vacillating between the opposing political camps, disturbances broke out between the parties led by King Narai Racha (Ton) and Prince Ram-Racha (Non), his Siam-leaning viceroy. Ton called upon his Vietnamese sponsors to aid him in his struggle for the throne, while Non was forced to flee to the protection of Siam. Facing the prospect of losing Cambodia's rich trade, Taksin requested Ton to present him with the traditional tribute of silver and gold trees in vouchsafe of his fealty. In rebuff, Ton announced: "We are descended of a most noble dynasty. It is not proper that we should submit to King Tak, a mere Chinese merchant, and thus dishonor ourselves."[53] A decisive response was called for, but Taksin was about to depart on his Southern campaign. He settled the matter by dispatching a force of two royal regiments led by Duang and Bunma against Udong to install Non on the Khmer throne. As soon as Taksin was well embarked on his southward voyage to Nakhon, the two brothers' overland expedition to subjugate Udong got underway, adding provincial detachments as they sped past Khorat, and then overrunning defenseless Siemreap and Battambang without casualties. As they approached Udong they received the (false) news that Taksin had been killed in the fighting at Nakhon. Despite all efforts to keep his shipboard mishap and lingering malaise secret, wild rumors of his death had filtered back to Thonburi; the gossip had been carried as far as Cambodia. With their worst fears apparently realized, Duang and Bunma aborted their advance against Udong and rushed home to defend the supposedly leaderless heartland, much to Taksin's later displeasure.[54] The Cambodia stalemate was left in abeyance, calling for resolution on another day.[55]

Sawangkhaburi, 1770 – A half year after that pair of expansionist adventures South and East, Taksin's attention turned North, to a fast-spreading insurrection crossing the Lan Na borderlands toward Siamese Sukhothai and dissident Phitsanulok. At Sawangkhaburi, a renegade monk claiming esoteric powers capable of infusing warriors with martial invulnerability had gathered hordes of followers, proclaimed himself Chao Phra Fang, the messianic lord of the spurious kingdom of Fang. He proceeded to extend his realm into neighboring areas by force, threatening the provinces further south. Taksin, believing himself recovered from his injury, decided to lead a military expedition, with Bunma as his second-in-command, to put down the apostate monk and his zealot army. He set off from Thonburi with several royal regiments in early August, with arrangements to add conscript contingents along the way, in the hope of completing the campaign before the monsoon could interfere. En route, he ordered Bunma to divert to Phitsanulok and subjugate that stronghold, which he had failed to accomplish on an earlier occasion. Weakened from earlier assaults by Fang's zealot forces, Phitsanulok was taken with ease. Bunma proceeded to burnish his warrior's luster by repulsing Burmese forays sent from Chiangmai and Lampang. As reward, he was appointed military governor of the North, stationed at Phitsanulok, with the title of General Surasi, carrying a status equivalent to Minister of Interior. In the aftermath of the heretic Fang insurrection, Taksin consulted the Venerable Phra Thamma Trailok (Si), the recently appointed Supreme Patriarch of Siam's Buddhist clergy, who dispatched a delegation of monks to the North to re-ordain the provincial monastic order and reeducate the populace in traditional Thai Buddhist practice. That extraordinary peacemaking mission did much to return the rebel province to the Siamese fold without further bloodshed.

Ha Tien and Udong, 1771[56] – Thonburi's string of victories over Phimai, Nakhon, and Fang brought with them increased manpower, trade, and tax revenues. They validated Taksin's reign in the eyes of former skeptics and strengthened the kingdom's constellation of alliances. They infused a new-found luster of self-confidence into Thonburi's public life. Taksin drew on that energy to prepare a further adventure. Within two years of the aborted Udong expedition of 1769 and less than a year after his triumph over the lord of Fang, a fresh two-pronged campaign was mounted in early 1771 to reclaim the Cambodian throne for Prince Ram Racha (Non). It differed from the earlier instance in its greater ambition – to extend the subjugation of Udong with the conquest of neighboring Ha Tien. Accompanied by the exiled Prince Non and two royal regiments, Duang and Bunma were dispatched on an overland march from Prachin via Battambang to subdue Udong and unseat King Narai Racha (Ton). Bunma was left to deal with that issue while Duang rushed on toward Ha Tien. Paralleling Duang's overland march, Taksin, at the head of a fleet of war junks, accompanied by Colonel Kosa Thibodi (Li-ang) as his admiral, sailed across the Gulf past Chanthabun and Kampong Som to Ha Tien, which was taken in a swift marine assault of classic proportions.

The subjugation of Udong and conquest of Ha Tien culminated Taksin's four-year struggle to consolidate the Siamese mandala to its former dimensions. His strategic shift from defense of the homeland to expansionist moves against recalcitrant neighbors had proved successful. Thonburi's ever more assertive military actions had achieved the kingdom's reintegration.

Chapter 4
Royal Scoundrels

Editor's introduction

Just as Siam had for centuries contended watchfully with its Burmese and Mon neighbors to the west, it had maintained cautious, sometimes adversarial relations with the Lao and Khmer realms to the north and east. Relations on the Cambodian front had a particularly storied past with Ayutthaya's adoption of Khmer court ritual and aesthetic symbolism as well as administrative reforms, particularly during the reign of King Trailokanat (1448-1488). Many Khmer loan words from that time, including titles and technical terms relating to royal protocol and public administration, persist in Thai speech and literature to the present day. Also associated with that time are a number of place names identifying Khmer settlement sites along the eastern frontiers of Siam as well as along the lower reaches of the Chaophraya River. Furthermore, several strategic canals dating back to those days were likely dug by Khmer war captives – the Pa Sak River extension forming the eastern moat of Ayutthaya, the Bangkok shortcut canal that over the course of the following century widened into the main Chaophraya River channel passing Thonburi, and the Samrong Canal linking the Chaophraya River via the Bang Pakong River to the thinly populated Khorat Plateau stretching eastward to the Mekong lowlands.

Under the weakened conditions left by the fifteenth-century Siamese depredations, Cambodia over the subsequent centuries proved easy prey for repeated Siamese slave raids. The persistent population drain prevented a return to the Khmer kingdom's glory days. That sorry state of affairs was compounded over the course of the eighteenth century by Vietnamese southward expansion along Cambodia's eastern flank into the Mekong Delta. Generations of Khmer countrymen of all classes were ground relentlessly between the millstones of Siamese and Vietnamese imperialism as the growing rivalry between the two powers played itself out on Cambodian territory, splitting the Khmer court into opposing westward- and eastward-leaning factions as it struggled to accommodate the two evils. Repeatedly, Ayutthaya and Hué intervened in Cambodian dynastic disputes, the best-known instances coming in 1709, 1716-1717, 1771-1773, and 1779. Each of those incursions was accompanied by devastating manpower raids and border encroachments, contributing to Cambodia's depopulation and isolation while it added to the peopling of Siam's agrarian hinterlands. The largest share of Siam's sizable population of resettled war captives, as the eighteenth century wore on, arrived from Cambodia, and most of them were settled in the kingdom's eastern dependencies. By the close of the century, the successive Siamese assaults had likely reduced Cambodia's population from its former million and more to no more than half a million.

The later decades of Cambodia's eighteenth century saw repeated invasions, coupled with outbursts of internal disorder under inept rule; it was a period of bloodshed and devastation as Siam and Vietnam contested control of the lower Mekong basin. The successive Cambodian kings, virtually powerless under the thumb of Siamese and Vietnamese military overseers, are said to have wasted their impotent reigns on cruel oppression, petty intrigue, and sensual diversion. To placate the rival Siamese and Vietnamese interlopers, the Khmer offered generous tribute, both substantive and symbolic, to both suzerain powers simultaneously. Such dual vassalage required duplicitous diplomacy, which contributed to a lasting Khmer reputation for guile. Despite brief respites from imperial oppression in the 1760s and 1770s as Siam contended with Burmese invasions from the west while Vietnam struggled through the damaging Tay Son rebellion to the east, Cambodia's chronic internal discord only intensified further, fomented by opposing court factions and ambitious provincial nobles.

Cambodia's unsettled politics radiated to the very core of the Siamese state through the sizable Khmer émigré presence at the court of Ayutthaya. Some elements of that community consisted of Khmer aristocrats carried off as political hostages; others had been gifted by vassal kings as royal consorts and court functionaries; yet others had arrived seeking refuge from their kingdom's deadly civil strife. They and their retinues brought with them their language, customs, and patronage networks, as well as an added layer of complexity to an already faction-riven Ayutthaya court. A natural consequence of their presence was an interlacing of the royal families of Siam and Cambodia through the concubinage of Khmer royal and noble women to successive generations of Siam's kings, princes, and high officials. Khmer women at the Siamese court proved particularly adept at using their charms, persuasive powers, and family connections as subtle means of influencing perceptions and policies in both kingdoms. At Ayutthaya's Grand Palace their presence contributed to a royal household of multiple ethnic affiliations and political alliances, compounding the perennial tensions of rank and privilege among palace women and royal offspring of conflicting status and suspect loyalty.

Within the court at Ayutthaya the struggle for influence over the Cambodian throne gravitated for several decades of the eighteenth century around several competing grandsons of Cambodia's King Thommo Racha III (Tham). Like him they braved alternate periods in exile, moving easily within the Khmer circle at the Siamese court as they shuffled the Cambodian throne among themselves. In 1766, the current Siamese favorite, Prince Non, escaped the Burmese siege of Ayutthaya by taking passage on a merchant junk bound for Chanthabun. There, in mid-1767, he joined Colonel (later King) Taksin's campaign to resurrect the Siamese kingdom, with the understanding that Taksin would in turn sponsor Non's quest for the Cambodian throne. As king, Taksin rewarded Non's loyalty by sponsoring his return to power at Udong in 1771 as King Rama Racha. That designation was opposed by his cousin Ton, who had usurped the throne as King Narai Racha II. With his Vietnamese backers, he held the throne until a Siamese-Vietnamese armistice in 1773 re-installed Non as consensus king, with Ton as his viceroy. The generations of pent-up enmity soon shattered that détente, bringing about a resurgence of Siamese-Vietnamese conflict. In the consequent years of civic turmoil, Ton died of unknown causes in 1775 (or 1776), followed by Non's assassination in 1779, sparking a further dynastic crisis. Siam responded with a major military intervention led by Taksin's senior commanders, Generals Chakri (Duang) and Surasi (Bunma).

Through those many decades of ceaseless turbulence, great swaths of the Cambodian peasantry were swept up into Siamese captivity and resettled in Siam's frontier lands on the Khorat Plateau – Thailand's present-day Northeast (Isan) – an ill-governed no-man's land traditionally plagued by brigand bands. The plateau formed a distinct ecological zone of lesser agricultural productivity intermediate between the fertile Thai and Khmer lowlands. Its northern reaches in the eighteenth century comprised a sparsely settled Lao frontier area, while its southern districts served as a westward extension of Khmer settlement. The region's relatively sparse Lao population expanded greatly in 1779 and again in 1827-1828 with bursts of forced resettlement following Siam's conquests of Vientiane, Chiangkuang, and Champasak. That Lao influx soon eclipsed the region's Khmer population, transforming the entire Khorat Plateau into a predominantly Lao zone of habitation under Siamese hegemony.

The Mun River, a Mekong tributary flowing west-east through the region's center, served as a rough dividing line between the region's Lao and Khmer settlement areas. Inadequate soil nutrients, high levels of salinity, and uncertain rainfall ensured that both culture zones suffered persistent poverty – the Lao as glutinous rice farmers in the flatlands to the north and the Khmer supplementing their wet-rice economy with hunting and forest foraging in the rolling hills to the south. To the agrarian troubles faced by those settlers were added the exactions regularly imposed by their Siamese overlords, whose command post at the regional trading center of Khorat marked Siam's eastern frontier in accord with the Indic geomantic symbolism that the Thai had inherited from Angkor. Sporadic insurgencies punctuated the endemic brigandage troubling the overtaxed Northeast's Khmer dependencies. It became customary practice for Ayutthaya to depute to Khorat a ranking prince, backed by a military garrison and administrative staff, with the mission of conciliating the local warlords, ensuring tax compliance, and imposing a semblance of law and order across the troubled borderlands.

The tale of Princes Khaek and Sisang, who together played a vital role in representing Siam's interests along its eastern frontier during the closing decades of the Ayutthaya era and the first years of its Thonburi aftermath, covers an especially tumultuous period in Siamese-Cambodian relations. In an elaborate pantomime of Siamese-Cambodian royal diplomacy, those two princes were born as the paired product of a marital alliance between a parallel pair of Siamese sovereigns and Cambodian princesses. According to Diogo's account, the full-sisters Chiap and Chaem, daughters of Cambodia's exiled King Thommo Racha, were in 1709 offered as consorts to King Thai Sa and his younger brother and viceroy, Prince Phisanu Thibodi (Phon, later Thai Sa's successor as King Boromakot). That dual marital alliance created Khaek and Sisang, casting those two sons as fraternal confederates for life. It also tied them to Sisang's flawed younger brother, Tui, who shared their adventures in the aftermath of Ayutthaya's fall and contributed to their discreditable end.

Diogo's Chronicle details the scandalous lives of that trio of royal scoundrels. Diogo candidly admits at the outset that relations between the exiled Cambodian aristocracy at Ayutthaya and the royal household of Siam were so factional, fickle, and personalized as to be virtually unfathomable. However, his tale of Khaek and Sisang provides rare glimpses into a political milieu that has hitherto been largely unknown. The "brothers" were bred for cross-cultural careers. Much of Khaek's life was focused on Siam's northeastern dependencies, where from 1733 to 1759 he served as royal overseer of the kingdom's Khmer community and to which he returned as a royal renegade in 1766, with dire consequences. Sisang, along collateral lines, served as Siam's resident envoy to the Cambodian court at Udong from 1733 to 1767 and after the fall of Ayutthaya continued to play a devious role in Cambodia's factional quarrels to 1769. Through those two enigmatic princes, Ayutthaya in its final decades sustained its political sway over the Khmer populace, not only along Siam's eastern frontier but far beyond. In examining the parallel lives of Khaek and Sisang, with their dual Siamese-Cambodian royal pedigree, Diogo's Chronicle presents not only a character study of two gifted, unscrupulous aristocrats at the court of Ayutthaya but, more broadly, an insider's view of eighteenth-century Siam's eastward imperial ambitions.

Pretensions

The records of Cambodia's relations with Siam are so vague that "scarcely is anything asserted by one of them which is not called into question or contradicted by the rest."[1] One thing, however, is certain: the persistent efforts of the Ban Phlu Luang dynasts to extend their sway over Cambodia ensured a notable Khmer émigré presence at the court of Ayutthaya. The most illustrious instance was Cambodia's King Thommo Racha from 1704 to 1706, and again from 1709 to 1738. During the decades of his exile, extending across the reigns of Siam's Kings Suriyen Thibodi, Thai Sa, and the early years of Boromakot, Thommo Racha bided his time at Ayutthaya as Siam's Khmer protégée in the ongoing contest for the Cambodian throne. Between those interludes in exile, Ayutthaya managed to install him on his rightful throne three times. Each of those terms ended with his replacement by a Vietnamese-sponsored royal Khmer surrogate, attesting to the difficulties that Siam persistently faced in maintaining its Cambodian suzerainty during those turbulent decades.

In affirmation of his fealty to Siam, Thommo Racha offered two of his daughters, Princesses Chiap and Chaem, to King Thai Sa in 1709, a year that coincided with both Thai Sa's coronation and Thommo Racha's own Siam-sponsored reinstatement on the Khmer throne.[2] Chiap was accepted as a concubine by Thai Sa; she presented him in due course with two sons, Princes Sisang and Tui. Chaem was passed on to Thai Sa's younger full-brother and viceroy Prince Phisanu Thibodi (Phon, later King Boromakot); she bore, in short order, Princes Khaek and Pan.[3] Upon the death of King Thai Sa in 1733 and the ascension of Phon as his successor, the new sovereign reunited Chiap with her sister Chaem in the Grand Palace and adopted Sisang and Tui as his own sons, raising them as brothers of Khaek and Pan.[4] With their clutch of notable sons and their personal entourage of several hundred ladies-in-waiting, servants, and slaves, Chiap and Chaem became the matriarchs of the Khmer faction at court. Their four sons were reared as the closest of siblings. Within the court's lively Khmer community, they grew up as much Khmer as Thai in language, culture, and outlook.

Of the four brothers, Khaek, the first-born (born in 1710), demonstrated the dominant personality.[5] By no means was Khaek a physically prepossessing man, yet he was favored with a sly intelligence and compelling presence. Self-important and sanctimonious in a court seething with arrogance and intrigue, he adored the adulation of his retainers and was thus excessively indulged by the sycophants in his employ. Persistent rumor, never substantiated, that he was actually Thai Sa's bastard, transferred to Boromakot in infancy along with his mother Chaem, may have whetted his insatiable thirst for preference. He was determined to make his way to glory, seeing all others, regardless of their bonds of kinship, friendship, or allegiance, as mere stepping-stones to his ends. How far he was serious in his pretensions to greatness, and how convinced of the brand of royal bastardy, how far his indignation was a self-imposed justification for his villainy, all are impossible to gauge. The fact that a

Table 4. Cambodia's dynastic succession, 18th century

King	Reign	Lineage	Primary patron
Thommo Racha III (Tham) (First Reign)	1702-1704	---	Siam
Chey Chettha IV (Sor)	1704-1706	---	Vietnam
Thommo Racha III (Tham) (Second Reign)	1706-1709	---	Siam
Ramathibodi I (Em)	1709-1722	Son-in-law of Thommo Racha III	Vietnam
Settha II (Chey)	1722-1738	Son of Ramathibodi I	Vietnam
Thommo Racha III (Tham) (Third Reign)	1738-1747	---	Siam
Narai Racha II (Tong) (First Reign) [Ramathibodi II]	1747-1749	Son of Ramathibodi I	Siam/Vietnam
Chey Chettha V (Sanguan)	1749-1755	Son of Thommo Racha III	Vietnam
Narai Racha II (Tong) (Second Reign) [Ramathibodi II]	1755-1758	---	Vietnam
Uthai Racha II (Ton)[1]	1758-1771	Son of the viceroy (So) of Chey Chettha V	Siam/Vietnam
Rama Racha (Non) (First Reign)	1771-1772	Grandson of Thommo Racha III	Siam
Narai Racha II (Tong) (Third Reign)	1772-1773	---	Vietnam
Rama Racha (Non) (Second Reign)	1773-1779	---	Siam
Narai Racha III (Eng)[2] [Ramathibodi III]	1779-1796	Son of Uthai Racha II	Siam
Uthai Racha III (Chan)[3]	1796-1834	Son of Narai Racha III	Siam

1 Vassal of Siam up to the fall of Ayutthaya (1767), vassal of Vietnam thereafter.
2 The early years of his reign (to 1794) were governed under a Siamese regency.
3 The early years of his reign (to 1806) were governed under a Siamese regency.

man such as he could have had a nature so warped is a dark mystery. He was, in fact, the eldest of Boromakot's eligible successors, each of the king's earlier sons having either died young or retreated to the monastery. However, his younger half-brothers Kung, Ekathat, and Dok-madoea all eclipsed him in royal rank, as their mothers were queens, while his mother was merely a first-class consort.[6] Relegation to secondary status in the line of royal succession regardless of his chronological seniority plagued him throughout his life, as it stymied his overweening ambition to rise someday to viceroy and thereby, in due course, to the throne. It was that failing more than any other that decided his fate. Inexorably, years later, it led him repeatedly to stretch his pretensions a step too far, first in his unwarranted intervention in the struggle for the Siamese succession, and finally in his self-enthronement as ruler of the stillborn kingdom of Phimai.

Khaek's mind was from his earliest years imbued with a keen interest in political affairs. Eager from the first to obtain the highest office, he was transported with thoughts of glory and inflamed with a passion for distinction.[7] As a youth, he served his novitiate at Wat Lokaya Sutha (located directly behind the Grand Palace, beyond the Tho Canal) and thereby received his essential education in the Buddhist precepts, literacy, and other disciplines appropriate to his social class.[8] It is said that the abbot, recognizing his brilliance, divined his horoscope as portending his future ascension to the throne.[9] That prognostication, combined with Khaek's natural aptitude and high status among his fellows, reinforced in him, unhappily, the obsessive craving for preeminence that had marked him since childhood.

Upon his father's investiture as king in 1733, Khaek was appointed royal commissioner (in effect, regional viceroy) of Siam's northeastern dependencies and their extensive Khmer population, with the elevated title of Prince Thep Phiphit.[10] While much of his time continued to be spent at court in Ayutthaya, the competent staff of administrators and military officers that he had inherited with his post represented him as best they could in securing law and order among the many Khmer principalities dispersed across the wilds of the Khorat Plateau. Equally important was their responsibility for collecting the Khmer settlers' periodic tax assessments, collected in kind as cardamom and lac, gum benjamin, sandalwood, deer and rhinoceros hide, and other valuable forest produce destined for Ayutthaya's royal warehouses and export to overseas markets. An adjunct responsibility was the collection of transit taxes on merchandise movements between Cambodia and the Siamese heartland. His many years as superintendent of Siam's eastern tributary principalities had schooled him well in the region's complex politics, built him a resilient patronage base among the region's Khmer elites, and taught him how to profit from the many commercial opportunities that attended his official duties.

In both character and pedigree Sisang was of much the same stamp as Khaek; yet he was held in lesser esteem. Many of his contemporaries regarded his sly demeanor with misgivings. His efforts to cover his maneuverings for preference and profit beneath

A caravan halt along a cross-Khorat Plateau trade route, early 19th century.
(Henri Mouhot, *Travels in Siam, Cambodia, and Laos, 1858-1860.* London, 1864, p. 267)

A military convoy approaching the walled city of Khorat, 19th century.
(Courtesy of *Silpawattanatham magazine*, Bangkok)

a dignified mien were complicated by his susceptibility to the frequent goadings to indiscreet action proposed by his brothers Khaek and Tui. His subordination to Khaek's often reckless schemes did nothing to dampen his inherent guile. His dream of elevating himself someday to the Cambodian throne, analogous to Khaek's designs on the throne of Siam, came to nothing. Although Sisang was several years Khaek's junior, his career shadowed closely the latter's trajectory. In parallel with the award of Khaek's princely title and posting as Ayutthaya's commissioner at Khorat (later known as Nakhon Rachasima), Sisang was elevated to Prince Thip Phiphat – not to be confused with his "brother" Prince Thep Phiphit – with assignment as ambassador to the Khmer throne at Udong (also known as Banteay Phet), Camboda's capital.[11]

He was charged, first, with monitoring the Khmer court's factional tensions and with offering such Siamese-slanted counsel to the Cambodian throne as occasion might allow. In addition, he was entrusted with the dual duties of ensuring the regular flow of Cambodian tributary submissions to Ayutthaya and fostering Cambodia's trade with Siam. Those duties provided him with frequent opportunities to add to his personal wealth. In the conduct of his diplomatic posting, he was, similar to Khaek, fortunate in his capable staff, as he would have failed miserably if left to his own devices in negotiating the complex Cambodian political scene. As an adjunct assignment, he served as envoy to the Chinese-Vietnamese outpost of Ha Tien.[12] On his occasional travels between Ayutthaya and Udong – usually by sea to Ha Tien and from there up the Bassac River rather than via the rugged overland route across the Khorat Plateau – he was invariably accompanied by his brother Tui and a sizable retinue of courtiers, councilors, and bodyguards. Those trips were infrequent, however. As was the case with Khaek, Sisang spent much of his time at Ayutthaya, where he could be counted on to serve faithfully as abettor of Khaek's machinations. Ever the crafty diplomat, he consistently managed to fade into the background as Khaek pursued his risk-laden political schemes.

Sisang's ambassadorial appointment to Udong enabled him to cultivate the leaders of Cambodia's Cham community, a perennially neglected, disaffected minority presence at the Cambodian court.[13] Relying on Ha Tien's fleets of flat-bottomed barges, he expedited the export of Cham produce – principally textiles, livestock, hides, sticklac, and cardamom – down the Bassac River and its distributaries to Ha Tien and from there by junk on to Canton. Exploiting the opposite export route with the support of Khaek's Khorat-based troops, he ensured the safe passage of Cham bullock caravans across the Khorat Plateau to Prachin and from there to Ayutthaya. The Cham community benefited greatly from that commercial patronage. Bolstered by Sisang's intimations of future reward in return for the Cham leaders' support for his partisan aspirations, they assured him, in confidence, of their allegiance. That private understanding came to play a crucial role in his plans for personal glory.[14]

Beyond their parallel career paths, Khaek and Sisang displayed personal affinity and mutual affection. Both were known for their canny minds – though not half so clever as generally claimed. Less widely heralded were their often devious, disreputable dealings. They were equally prone to intrigue and duplicity, and equally deficient as warriors. These two men's virtue – or, rather, the lack thereof – even looking to the most minute points of difference between them, bore the same color and character, so as not to be distinguishable. Both had a passion for distinction in civil life, and both countered that ambition with a want of sincerity in peace and courage in war. Both were notorious for their inconstancy in maintaining friendships, and for their base and underhanded proceedings. Just as Khaek was to be blamed for his treacherous, arbitrary, rebellious behavior, so was Sisang no less blameworthy for his meanness of spirit.[15] They were equally oblivious of the pain they inflicted on their underlings and on the Khmer and Cham settlers over whom, in one way or another, they held sway. Nor were they alone in that odious quality; much of the Ayutthaya aristocracy shared that unfortunate trait, as envy, ambition, greed, and malevolence were hallmarks of the age. The former time of pure and upright manners had declined and yielded to a crude appetite for riches and luxury.[16]

No less profound an influence on Sisang's judgment than the instigations of the nefarious Khaek was his lifelong incubus, his younger brother Tui.[17] Wherever Sisang went, so went Tui, a slouching, sinister companion to the other's slithering gait. Tui suffered speech and hearing impediments, which he kept carefully hidden behind his taciturn demeanor. While still a youth of 10 or so, he had shocked a clutch of court ladies strolling through the palace gardens upon being discovered gleefully tormenting a litter of newborn pups seeking to suckle their anguished dam, whose teats he had scorched to uselessness. Long remembered, too, was a youthful outburst occasioned upon his encounter with a gaggle of chattering playmates devouring a fresh purchase of pungent, thorny durian fruit. When they ignored his advances, he responded by flailing out with a discarded strip of spiked durian rind, which struck several of them full-face, leaving one blinded and several others with life-long scars. From such childhood depravities Tui matured into an accomplished connoisseur of cruelties, an infamous scavenger of barbarisms. A number of healers, herbalists, and mystics were consulted in hope of effecting a cure. For a time during his childhood, he had been placed in the care of monks who had attempted unsuccessfully to tease the meanness from his soul. Evidently irremediable, and incorrigibly ungovernable, he was spurned, and errant behavior became his way. He made it his habitual practice to attend the trials of ordeal, the frightful tortures conducted at the municipal prison adjacent to the royal cremation ground abutting Wat Phra Si Sanphet, sufficiently distant from the Grand Palace throne halls to muffle the victims' anguished screams from royal ears. The satisfaction he derived from others' sufferings was evident to all.

Tui's saving grace, if such it can be called, was his elder brother Sisang, his sole companion, the only person able to restrain his worst perversions. From childhood the brothers had developed a powerful bond fortified by a private language of hand and head gestures entirely inscrutable to others. Under Sisang's guidance, Tui had learned to conceal his handicaps beneath a stoic demeanor, leaving many who met him unaware of his affliction. Awkward, inarticulate, and unresponsive, he was rarely called on to assume any serious responsibility. He was, in short, a man of a highly irregular character, full of inconsistencies within himself, and much given to prodigality. He cringed before those to whom he stood in need and domineered those who stood in need of him, so that it was difficult to determine whether his nature had more in it of pride or servility. He displayed no gentle manner, emitting a sense of suppressed violence. His unmerciful disposition was both feared and hated.[18] Whenever left to his own devices he was accompanied by a retinue of personal bodyguards handpicked by Sisang to temper his outbursts, though their best efforts rarely managed to stifle his unpredictable temperament. He was shunned by one and all; no woman would willingly come near him, given the miasma of viciousness that clouded his presence. Had he not been so monstrous in his cruelties, he would have been a piteous creature.

It is tempting to describe the bond between Sisang and Tui as a simple case of filial devotion, but was it as simple as that? Sisang on his own was an incomplete man; given his craven nature, his impulsive, ill-advised actions in moments of crisis can only be understood through the inclusion of Tui as his diabolical second self. Tui was said to be as clever as his elder brother, and in matters of chicanery more resourceful. Thus, may it not have been that Tui led Sisang down the path of deceit, conflict, and inevitable defeat? Would the timid Sisang have dared to aspire to the Cambodian throne without Tui's encouragements to that end? Would he have thought to suborn the Cham elders to his cause but for Tui's instigation? Would he have risked joining forces with Khaek's army at Khorat without Tui's urging? Did the events that ensued – the brothers' cunning escape from capture, their headlong flight to Ha Tien, their collusion with Siam's enemies, and ultimately the collapse of their dreams of glory in military defeat – follow from Tui's fevered imaginings? Although testimony to corroborate those inferences is wanting, the many tales of the brothers' collaboration in all else are suggestive.

Conspiracies

Amid Cambodia's intensifying political travails as the eighteenth century wore on, both Khaek and Sisang stealthily recruited a sizable clientele of Khmer and Cham provincial leaders bent on distancing themselves from the crumbling Cambodian center. The two princes became adept, in complicity with those local strongmen, in amassing substantial personal fortunes – Sisang from his Udong-based ambassadorial posting and personal participation in trade relations between Siam and Cambodia, Khaek from his Khorat-based oversight of the overland trade routes and participation in the collection of local land taxes, produce levies, transport duties, and tributary prestations. All that was placed in jeopardy, however, with the prospect of the two princes' removal from their sinecures upon the elevation of their senior-ranking half-brother, Prince Ekathat, to the Siamese throne in 1758. Prince Dok-madoea, their favored candidate for the throne, could have been relied on to retain his father's appointments in office, but Ekathat had his own coterie of favorites eager to appropriate those lucrative posts.

As King Boromakot declined into advanced age, dissension over the royal succession grew increasingly rancorous. Khaek, adopting the role of senior brother among Boromakot's many sons – elder in age though not in rank – managed to outmaneuver the various contending camps by independently spending much time and effort ingratiating himself with his father, the king. His gilded tongue gained the doddering king's confidence, earning him many royal favors. Questions were quietly raised at court whether his audacity demonstrated more faithfully his filial devotion or his fraternal treachery:

> *Who praise their fathers but the generous sons?*
> *Who praise their fathers but degenerate sons?*[19]

When in 1755 the viceroy, Prince Sena Phithak (Kung), was sentenced to a fatal flogging for his alleged illicit liaison with Queen Sangwan, Khaek assumed the role of royal family spokesman in petitioning the king for leniency, but to no avail. Asked why he had volunteered to take on that extraordinary duty, he averred that his seniority in age designated him leader of his generation in royal family matters, irrespective of royal rank. It was with that palace crisis that he took on the self-styled vocation of impresario for popular causes, invariably serving his personal interests. His policy seemed to be: if I cannot myself be king, then at least I can be king maker. In that capacity, he banked the fires of his higher ambitions – but the flames could not be damped for long; they flared up years later, as we shall see, first at Kandy (the uplands kingdom of Lanka Island, to which he had been exiled), and then again, some years thereafter, at Khorat and Phimai (where he had established a new kingdom).

Khaek entered Ayutthaya's succession dispute initially as a minor player in the doomed struggle to save Kung from his terrible fate; but as he found his voice he came to luxuriate in his ringmaster's role. As events unfolded, the self-serving cravings for recognition that underlay his superficial charm and demagogue's rhetoric became increasingly evident. It is certainly necessary for a political leader to be an able speaker. However, as Khaek's more discerning critics remarked: "It is ignoble for any man to relish the glory of his own eloquence and, worse yet, apply his public eloquence to his personal gain."[20] With King Boromakot's fading health in the months following Kung's execution, and then in the unsettled state of affairs following the king's death in 1758, Khaek took on, successively, the function of supplicant, moral arbiter, adversary, and agitator in the sequence of royal conspiracies that placed Dok-madoea on the throne as King Uthumphon, and then hatched a hapless scheme that culminated in the disastrous plot to unseat Uthomphon's successor, Ekathat. Those successive subversive deeds compounded his earlier insidious acts of self-promotion to consign his memory to everlasting disrepute.

Throughout that series of succession crises, Khaek persisted in pursuit of his self-interest above all else. Always more shrewd than wise, he insinuated himself into the good graces of, first, the viceroy (Kung), then the king (Boromakot), and finally the successor (Dok-madoea). In the process, however, he distanced himself from many of the lesser princes and made an implacable enemy of Prince (later King) Ekathat. His rashly expressed preference for Prince Dok-madoea confirmed, as he well knew, King Boromakot's own inclinations regarding the royal succession. Accordingly, when Dok-madoea was finally installed as the new viceroy, Khaek could proudly claim to have played a part in that appointment. Again when, upon the death of King Boromakot in 1758, Dok-madoea succeeded to the throne as King Uthumphon, Khaek made much of the counselor's role he had played in ensuring that smooth transition.

Khaek sought to ingratiate himself with the devout Uthumphon by seeking his guidance on such eccesiastical issues as temple patronage, monastic appointments to high clerical office, and the adaptation of Khmer to Thai monastic practice. He based his approach to Dok-madoea on their childhood bond, years earlier, as fellow novices at Wat Lokaya Sutha, where Dok-madoea's bent towards celibate renunciation had first manifested itself to gain him an exemplary monastic reputation. Never of a particularly devout inclination himself, Khaek nevertheless feigned a fervent desire to propagate Thai Buddhism among his Khmer minions as a means of gaining Uthumphon's affection.

Subsequently, when a clique of junior princes – Ekathat's cronies, including Khaek's disaffected younger brother, Pan – pledged to oppose Uthumphon's elevation to the throne and collude to dethrone him in favor of Ekathat, Khaek temporized. Ever a master of duplicity, he came to hear of the princes' plot through Pan, who foolishly thought to gain his endorsement, if not his active participation in the conspiracy. Instead of backing the coup, however, Khaek betrayed his brothers to King Uthumphon. The collaborators, including Pan, were apprehended red-handed, tried and convicted of treason, and executed. Despite his pivotal role in preventing a dynastic crisis, Khaek's standing at court did not rise in the wake of that sordid affair. Many considered his actions tantamount to fratricide.

Within two months of his enthronement, Uthumphon – never having coveted the throne in the first place and having been appalled at the unprincipled actions that his new duties required of him – abdicated in favor of Ekathat and evaporated back into the monkhood at Wat Pradu. As an erstwhile supporter of Uthumphon, Khaek now believed his life to be in peril at the hands of Ekathat. Rumors swirled that he was about to become the principal target of a royal purge. To save his skin, he followed Uthomphon's example and entered the monkhood at Wat Krachom –

located a convenient five-minute walk from the abdicated king's quarters at Wat Pradu. His later actions confirmed that guile, deceit, and faithlessness followed him into the temple. Monastic ordination was for him a political expedient rather than, as it was for the pious Uthumphon, a spiritual calling. Unlike his fellow monks at Wat Krachom, he surrounded himself with a personal retinue of servants and slaves, including young women. No dedicated monk, he openly flouted the monastic Code of Conduct. Only his high aristocratic status protected him from expulsion from the Buddhist brotherhood.

A year later, while still in monastic retreat, Khaek again became entangled in a cabal of high-ranking nobles bent on the removal of Ekathat and reinstatement of Uthumphon to the throne. He was sought out by the conspirators to approach Uthumpon in hopes of gaining his support or at least his tacit approval of the proposed coup, but that hope went begging, as Uthumphon adamantly rejected the very thought of restoration. He was astounded that Khaek, now sworn to renunciation of worldly affairs as a fellow monk, should have taken a personal interest in such a sordid intrigue. He saw clearly the cunning temper of the man through his monastic disguise. As Uthumphon is rumored to have later said: "Until I saw his monastic robe so carefully arranged and observed him adjusting its folds with one finger, I could not imagine it could enter into a man's mind to subvert so blithely the teachings of the Buddha."[21]

As a man of impeccable moral conduct regardless of personal peril, Uthumphon duly reported the matter to the king, his brother. The conspirators were immediately arrested and imprisoned. Only Uthumphon's exaction of the king's pledge that his revelation would not lead to their deaths saved them from execution. Forewarned, Khaek fled in his monk's robes but was soon apprehended and placed under detention with the others. In consideration of his monastic status, no harm came to him. However, his continued presence at Ayutthaya preoccupied the king; Ekathat feared Khaek's scheming ways and sought to rid the realm of his disruptive presence. A message had recently arrived from Sri Lanka, addressed by the king of Kandy, to the lately deceased King Boromakot, inviting a monastic delegation to attend a conclave at one of the Kandyan kingdom's most venerated temples.[22] That invitation was taken as a propitious opportunity to consign Khaek to distant exile. Accompanied by a party of monastic scholars, Khaek and his inner circle of personal retainers were placed on a visiting Dutch merchant ship bound for the Lankan port of Batticaloa and expelled from Siam. He was warned in no uncertain terms that he should prolong his overseas sojourn indefinitely, and the sealed royal letter of introduction that accompanied him to Kandy included a request that he be permitted to stay on in monastic retreat beyond the conclusion of the conclave to pursue further Buddhist studies. In the light of Khaek's later escapades, his sophist parting dictum that "Only those who do nothing make no mistake" was long remembered.

Exile

The court at Kandy had not been apprised of the unsavory circumstances that had prompted Khaek's voyage, so he and his monastic retinue were in early 1760 received at the port of Batticaloa in grand style and conveyed in regal procession to the upland kingdom and their living quarters at the royal Buppharam Temple. It was understood by one and all that Khaek was a foremost prince of Siam and a learned monk of great repute. With those credentials he easily formed strong connections at the court of Kandy and, given his infamous aptitude for partisan intrigue, soon became caught up in royal wranglings. Within half a year of his arrival he had become involved in a plot hatched by a coterie of disaffected courtiers to overthrow the king of Kandy. It is rumored, rather implausibly, that the conspirators intended to enthrone Khaek as the new king but that the plot failed. Whatever the case, the chief culprits were executed, while Khaek and his retainers were spared death only in observance of their clerical status and diplomatic niceties, and left to rot in prison. As Khaek's devotees later averred, "his Kandy interlude proved him to be of a vehement and impetuous nature, possessed of a clever mind and a strong and aspiring bent for action and great affairs."[23] Others, however, affirmed him to be a reckless royal rascal, an unscrupulous scoundrel, a misfit among his peers. While perhaps not an outright villain by the freewheeling virtues common in the Thai world of his day, he consistently skirted the margins of probity.

After a year's harsh confinement at Kandy, Khaek and his entourage were released, and with the onset of the eastward monsoon in early 1762 they departed on a Dutch barque bound across the Bay of Bengal for Mergui, the main Andaman seaport of Siam's Tenasserim dependency. Ignorant of the circumstances surrounding his unannounced arrival, the governor of Tenasserim welcomed him as a harbinger of revived ties with Ayutthaya, which had been left to languish since the recent Burmese depredations. Khaek was quick to recognize his good fortune and played his sham role as a wandering Siamese monk of aristocratic bloodline with panache. During his Tenasserim stay he exited the monkhood on the entirely inappropriate grounds that the local monastic facilities and low-ranking Buddhist clergy were beneath his royal dignity. Actually, he appears to have defrocked simply because it no longer afforded him any demonstrable benefits. His return to the lay life enabled him to indulge more freely of all the diversions and debaucheries that Tenasserim had to offer a visiting Ayutthaya dignitary.

Several years of anonymous residence at that remote refuge ended in late 1764 when Khaek once again found himself in an untenable position, pinched between the gathering threat of both Burmese and Siamese captivity. On the one side, in a budding military offensive aimed at the Siamese heartland, armed Burmese forays were advancing rapidly down the Andaman seaboard. On the other, a Thai military detachment was rumored to have been sent from Ayutthaya to affect his capture and conveyance to the capital to face charges of having violated the terms of his parole.

Map 7. The travels of Prince Thep Phiphit (Khaek), 1760–1768

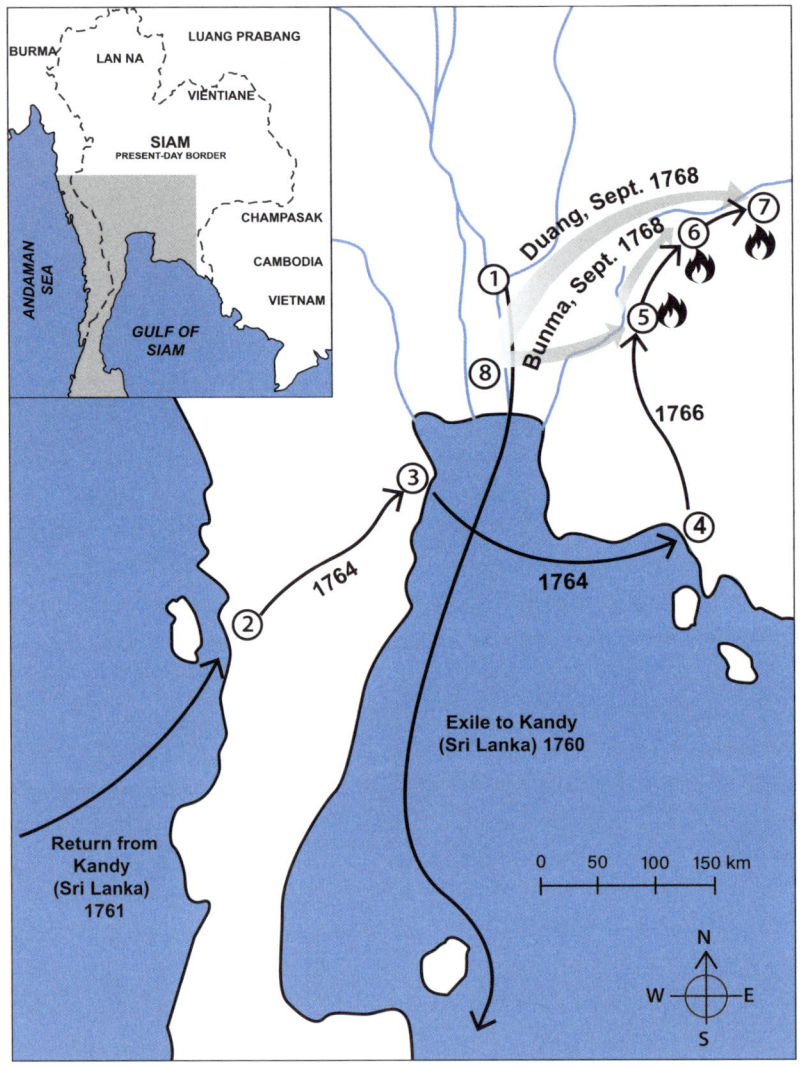

Note: Khaek was disgraced and exiled from Ayutthaya to Sri Lanka in 1760. In 1761 he returned to Siam without authority and established himself at Chanthaburi. There he organized an army and in 1766 overran Prachin, Khorat, and Phimai to establish his new kingdom of Phimai. An army was sent from Thonburi in 1768 to eradicate that kingdom, and Khaek was captured and executed.

→ Khæk's travel routes
Thonburi military campaign route
Battle sites

① Ayutthaya
② Tenasserim
③ Phetburi
④ Chanthabun
⑤ Prachin
⑥ Khorat
⑦ Phimai
⑧ Thonburi

154 *Diogo's Chronicle*

Map 8. The travels of Prince Thip Phiphat (Sisang) and Prince Tui, 1759–1769

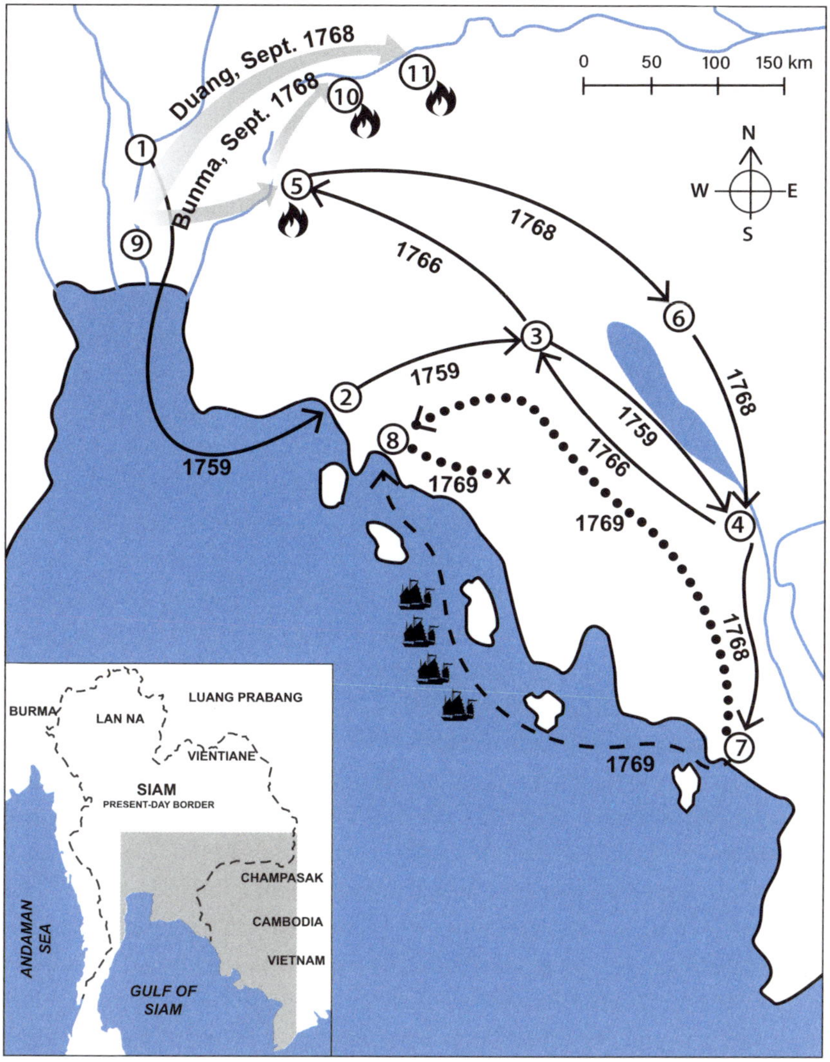

Upon the defamation of their brother Khaek, the brothers Sisang and Tui departed Ayutthaya hurriedly in 1759 for Sisang's ambassadorial posting at Udong, and never returned. They traveled to Prachin in 1766 to rejoin their brother at his nascent Phimai kingdom and escaped Thonburi's attack on Prachin by taking refuge at Ha Tien in 1768. In 1769, Ha Tien sent them with two armies, by land and water, to conquer Chanthabun and Trat. There, both brothers lost their lives.

- ⟶ Sisang's and Tui's travels together
- --> Sisang's war junk voyage to Trat
- ••••> Tui's land march to Trat
- Thonburi military campaign route
- Battle sites

① Ayutthaya
② Chanthabun
③ Battambang
④ Udong
⑤ Prachin
⑥ Nakhon Luang
⑦ Ha Tien
⑧ Trat
⑨ Thonburi
⑩ Khorat
⑪ Phimai

Royal Scoundrels 155

To escape the fast-closing net he slipped across the hills to the Gulf port of Phetburi and from there sailed across the Gulf to Chanthabun, placing himself within reach of his erstwhile liegemen at Khorat and his brothers Sisang and Tui at Udong.

Khaek's stay at Chanthabun, from late 1764 to early 1766, coincided with Burma's invasion of Siam and siege of Ayutthaya. Careful study of that looming catastrophe led him to fashion an audacious plan. His long exile at Kandy and the provincial backwaters of Tenasserim and Chanthabun had left him eager to resume his exploits toward realization of his long-dreamed royal destiny. As the Burmese siege of the capital of Siam intensified, he contrived a foolhardy scheme aimed at earning him a hero's welcome back at court, a royal pardon, and possibly even appointment to the vacant post of viceroy of Siam. His vision was to lead a grand army from the east to rescue Ayutthaya from the Burmese siege. In the throes of that overweening rapture, never for a moment did he pause to consider the complexities of its execution or the possibility of defeat. Capitalizing on his influence over the governor of Chanthabun, he managed initially to recruit a well-armed militia of Chinese settlers and seamen comprising the first several regiments of his planned army. To that force he hoped, with great optimism, to draw an additional 10,000 men from the Khmer-peopled lower Khorat Plateau dependencies, a 3,000-man Cham levy to be mobilized by Sisang and Tui at Battambang, plus several additional thousands of Siamese warriors from Siam's neighboring provinces.

In all that, Khaek was ill-informed and ill-advised. Believing his rabble of poorly led, inadequately trained, woefully armed men sufficient to save the day at Ayutthaya, he grievously underestimated the strength of the Burmese besiegers. In any case, many of the promised troop contingents failed to materialize. Ignoring all potential pitfalls, he marched his Chanthabun militia off to Prachin in June 1766, expecting there to marshal his forces and await the arrival of Sisang and Tui with yet additional fighters. "On that march, lacking experience of military leadership, he commanded his army of volunteers more like a band of brigands than as a company of regular soldiers."[24] His deficient generalship grew evident to his officers and confederates in short order, leading several of his Khorat allies to renege on their promise of troops and supplies. That laid the groundwork for the debacle in which his ill-conceived enterprise would end.

One of Khaek's first actions upon arrival at Prachin was his dispatch of a courier to the besieged court at Ayutthaya with the news, typically audacious and typically ill-considered, that he was mobilizing an army to rush to the capital's rescue. It was inconceivable to him that the beleaguered city would reject his offer of aid. His prospects quickly dimmed when, in what was perceived as a studied royal rebuff, no response was received.[25] The snub provoked Khaek to extend his fantasies along an alternative line, one that visualized a new kingdom radiating from his Khorat strongpoint across the flatlands stretching from Saraburi to the Mekong lowlands to challenge the waning kingdoms of Siam and Cambodia. With the fall of Ayutthaya not many months later, that fantasy took on heightened plausibility. Its very audacity attested to the frenzied state of Khaek's delusional ambitions.

He was further convinced of the feasibility his project, however, when several Ayutthaya courtiers who had long been secretly dissatisfied with Ekathat's leadership and sympathetic to Khaek's cause – most prominently General Ratana Thibet (Krit), Minister of the Palace – slipped out of the besieged city with their families and retainers to join Khaek at Prachin. The arrival of Krit's émigré troupe was an important coup for Khaek, as it went far toward legitimizing his position as contender for the throne of Siam. An additional boost was the arrival of Sisang and Tui from Udong, though accompanied by a disappointingly small contingent of Cham warriors. In the wake of Kheak's collaboration with the abortive coup attempt at Ayutthaya, Sisang and Tui had in 1759 departed hastily for Udong. During the subsequent eight years of Khaek's exile at Kandy, Tenasserim, and Chanthabun, they had remained in the Cambodian capital to nurture their patronage networks and continue their lucrative trade ventures, until rushing off with their reinforcements in 1766 to throw in their lot with Khaek.

Khaek initially sought by all means to make himself popular at Prachin through his commanding presence, his beguiling eloquence, his royal bloodline, and his familiarity with Khmer language and culture. Indeed, he had in him something that was appealing to a populace that loved to be courted. He demonstrated in his presence before his cohorts how effective persuasion can be if well spoken. Not all his listeners, however, were enamored. One skeptic, upon being asked which of Khaek's orations he liked best, responded: "The shortest."[26] Another who refused to be convinced by his overtures was General Kamhaeng Songkhram (Ngoen), the governor of Khorat, one of the many Siamese nobles who had been cast adrift with the siege of Ayutthaya. That stalwart soldier told his comrades that something stank in Khaek's glib words. Indeed, having gained control, and his mind growing haughtier, Khaek abandoned his popular dialogues in favour of regal monologues, odious to the people.[27] To Ngoen, who loved honesty above all else, Khaek seemed all too subtle, extolling what was just only when it was profitable and judging truth to be no better than falsehood, a philosophy that enabled him to set a value upon both according to his interest.[28] Seeking guidance from Ayutthaya on how to proceed against Khaek's menacing military presence at nearby Prachin, Ngoen received sealed orders to detain him as a royal renegade Somehow, those orders became known to Khaek, and he preempted them by leading his forces against Khorat, which he overpowered with the connivance of the garrison's Khmer detachments.

Khaek deputed his depraved brother Tui to deal personally with Ngoen's insolent opposition. The interrogation and execution were conducted by Tui with excruciating savagery, condemning his blameless prey to be broiled under a fiery spit in the manner mentioned in ancient Buddhist legend, to serve as an example for all those who might dare resist Khaek's will.[29] For Ngoen's senior aides Tui concocted

Execution by fire, observed by deities, from a temple mural illustrating the Chula Paduma Jataka. (Google Images). This temple mural detail is evocative of Prince Tui's atrocious killing of Khorat's governor, General Kamhaeng Songkhram (Ngoen).

an even more atrocious penalty. They were placed in large, sealed jars with only their heads protruding, plied with food through funnels thrust deep into their mouths, and then forced to drink honey till it ran over their faces, soon covered by multitudes of flies. And as their bowels evacuated what had been eaten and drunk, vermin sprang up in the rotten corruption of their excrement and entered their entrails to consume their bodies.[30] Tui's name henceforth was rarely mentioned, and, if so, never without disgust. All steps were taken to have his memory eradicated.

Khaek received deferential visits at his Prachin base from the rulers of many of Siam's Khmer dependencies. Despite his absence of nearly a decade, those former allies still recognized him as their royal patron and now added fear to their sentiments. Through them he mustered additional troops, though far fewer than expected. To ensure those peasant conscripts' loyalty, he promised them fertile farmlands and freedom from future taxes as reward for their military service. That was a small price to pay for his prospective vindication and acclamation as a hero, and his acquisition of a kingdom. The serfs he had promised to enrich and empower by his favor had been made not only his fellow soldiers in the prospective expedition in aid of Ayutthaya but also now his bodyguard in his usurpation. For all those marauders' misdeeds and all the lawless violence committed in his name, however, they received compensation less than they believed to be their due. As objects of Khaek's erratic leadership, they grew eager to have anyone in his place. They resolved no longer to hazard their lives for the satisfaction of his luxury and pleasure.

In January 1767 the Burmese besiegers at Ayutthaya learned of the military mobilization at Prachin under the command of a dissident Siamese prince. Considering that matter an unpleasant distraction from their imminent conquest of the Siamese capital, they dispatched a detachment of three regiments to dispense with that distant irritant. Khaek, struggling to control his undisciplined army, had failed to emplace an adequate sentry system and thus was not informed of the rapid Burmese advance up the Bang Pakong River in time to mobilize effective defensive measures. His ill-prepared forces fled their camp in riotous disorder in the face of the unexpected assault. With the remnants of his army, Khaek retreated to a fortified position fronting the strong-walled frontier post of Khorat. Believing they had resolved the issue and eager to partake of the plunder awaiting them at Ayutthaya, the Burmese assailants withdrew, allowing Khaek's tattered army to lick its wounds at Khorat while Ayutthaya suffered its final agonies.

In place of Ngoen, Khorat's executed governor, Khaek installed General Ratana Thibet (Krit), Ayutthaya's defected Minister of the Palace, as that stronghold's new military commander. Sisang was installed as commander at Prachin, leaving Khaek free to establish a royal redoubt for his household at the ancient Khmer sanctuary of Phimai.[31] However, Khaek's division of his forces between the widely separated bases of Phimai, Prachin, and Khorat left him vulnerable to piecemeal attack. From his Chanthabun exile as a royal renegade to his investiture as ruler of a dawning kingdom had required little more than a year's concerted effort; his fall from that height of remarkable achievement, recounted below, took no more than a few days. Surely there had never before been a prince upon whom fortune had made such short turns, nor any other life or story so filled with swift and surprising changes from small matters to great, then from splendor to humiliation, and then again from utter defeat once more to power and might, all to be followed by sudden, final descent into oblivion.[32]

Ruins of the principal Khmer shrine and its frieze at Phimai (Etienne Aymonier, *Le Cambodge*, Paris, 1901, vol. 2, p. 122). The fortifications and temple ruins at Phimai, dating from the 12th century, stamped that ancient imperial Khmer waystation as a natural royal capital for the short-lived kingdom established by Prince Thep Phiphit (Khaek) in 1767. Standing alongside Khaek's palace as a potent symbol of his proposed Thai/Khmer realm, the temple ruins were in far better repair at the time of his brief reign then at the turn of the twentieth century, when these photos were taken.

160 *Diogo's Chronicle*

Requital

Newly arrived at Phimai, Khaek received the astounding news of the sack of Ayutthaya, the death of King Ekathat, and the capture of the abdicated King Uthumphon. Recognition that, as the senior surviving son of King Boromakot, he now stood in direct line for the vacant throne of Siam stirred him to immediate action. His first task was to reinforce his position at an impregnable base from which to strive for his goal. Khorat's defenses were hardened, and a formal administrative hierarchy was installed to rule the fledgling state. Reconsidering his options, he moved his arsenal and rice reserves to adjoin his royal residence and personal bodyguard at Phimai and declared that ancient Khmer stronghold his imagined kingdom's capital.[33]

At the same time, the bulk of his infantry, artillery, elephantry, and cavalry was divided between Krit and Sisang at their respective Khorat and Prachin camps. After two months of intensive preparations, with the rudiments in place, he proclaimed himself king of his new domain with an investiture rich in ritual and panoply.[34] The eastern dependencies over which he had previously exercised oversight on behalf of Ayutthaya were incorporated into the new kingdom as subject principalities. Their chiefs were dubbed governors of the new state's provinces, creating a sovereign political orbit intermediate between destroyed Siam and impotent Cambodia. It was said by many of his dupes, in hindsight: "in civil strife e'en villains rise to fame."[35]

As meteoric as had been the rise of Khaek's Phimai kingdom, so was its fall little more than a year later. In September 1768, Thonburi's recently crowned King Taksin launched the first of several major military offensives to rid the kingdom of insurgent threats. This campaign was intended to eradicate Khaek's upstart regime with the dispatch of several royal regiments all under the command of the brothers Duang and Bunma (then still Colonels Racha Warin and Maha Montri).[36] Taksin's urgency in mobilizing that expedition was evident in its inappropriate timing, at the height of the rainy season, a time eminently unsuited for military exploits as it was considered unwholesome for strenuous exertion, unhealthy for long-distance travel through mud and flood, destructive of munitions, and coincident with the Buddhist Lent, the annual three months' period of retreat and reflection. Assignment of that perilous campaign to two lightly tested commanders while other duties required his attention must also have weighed on Taksin's mind. Evidently, the new King of Thonburi considered the surprise attack a vital expedient toward removing his most immediate opponent from the scene. It was a gamble that paid off handsomely.

Phimai learned quickly of Thonburi's military mobilization. In anticipation of the foe's imminent arrival, Khaek assembled his Khorat garrison for one of his distinctive, silver-tongued harangues. Resplendent in his royal regalia and fully prepared to rouse his massed troops to action with his storied eloquence, he mounted a hastily built reviewing pavilion. The spot selected for his peroration, however,

Royal execution by pounding with sandalwood clubs, the likely procedure applied to Prince Thep Phiphit (Khaek). (Courtesy of *Silpawattanatham magazine*, Bangkok)

The royal execution illustrated here differs from the procedure ordinarily described, whereby the victim, seated cross-legged within a black velvet sack with hands raised in salutation, awaited the executioner's blow of a sandalwood club against the base of the skull.

had been ill-chosen; it proved to be an abandoned charnel ground used in ancient days as the outpost's execution site. A gathering flurry of whispers swept through the crowded ranks, informing all of the inauspicious portent. With the troops' attention distracted by those ominous murmurs, Khaek's stirring rhetoric fell flat. Despondency seized his cohorts, who recognized the unlucky omen, and for the remainder of that day they sulked in their camps and declined to gird themselves for the coming battle.[37] When the Thonburi regiments finally advanced on the Khorat defenses the following morning, Krit's troops performed poorly. Many fled at sight of the approaching enemy, and Krit himself seemed to quake in prospect of battle. Additional contingents had to be rushed in to mount an adequate defense against the lesser opposition. Krit was accused by Khaek's lieutenants of having been sluggish in the engagement, possibly because age had impaired his courage. More likely, however, his reticence reflected simply how hard it was for him, who had lived with one generation of men, to plead now for caution before another.[38]

Khaek's strategy of dividing his forces between the three distanced strongpoints of Khorat, Prachin, and Phimai, separated from one another by a day's forced march, proved faulty. The Thonburi army defeated the dispersed defenders piecemeal. Bunma stormed the walls of Khorat and routed Krit's garrison; Krit himself was killed in the melee. Sisang's Cham regiment at Prachin was overwhelmed by the combined forces of Bunma and Major Inthara Aphai (Pramot), and in the aftermath Pramot managed to capture both Sisang and Tui. At the same time, Duang pressed the onslaught against Phimai and was successful but for the momentary escape of Khaek.

To forestall the likely eventuality of an eastward retreat by the struggling Phimai forces, Duang deployed a flanking cavalry squadron to their rear. That tactic proved prudent, as Khaek and his principal officers were caught in headlong flight toward the Khmer heartland. His Siamese captor, Captain Pin, was promoted to the vacant rank of Major Kamhaeng Songkhram. Khaek's surviving Khmer and Cham troops were treated harshly to set an example for all the inhabitants of Siam's eastern dependencies. Their officers had their limbs lopped off, and then their heads. The troops received only severe canings, and then had their thumbs severed to prevent them from ever again handling weapons of war. After a period of sulking servitude under the short rations deemed appropriate punishment for their mutiny, they were released to their families and farmsteads with clear warning to abide in future by the strictures of their Thonburi masters. Khaek, on the other hand, was transported to Thonburi in shackles. There, his defiant refusal to pay obeisance to King Taksin was followed by his execution by sandalwood bludgeon, a death befitting a rebellious prince of Ayutthaya.

Sisang and Tui did not meet such an abrupt end. Captured by Major Inthara Aphai (Pramot) after the battle of Prachin, they and their surviving guardsmen, some 30 in number, were placed in confinement awaiting the arrival of Duang from Phimai. The two princes were surprised to find themselves treated with utmost courtesy. That favorable arrangement, given their otherwise desperate situation, inspired Tui to devise a devious scheme to effect their release. He silently communicated his plan to Sisang, who duly requested a parley with Pramot. In whispered conversation, Sisang offered Pramot their most cherished personal possessions, their golden, gem-studded royal regalia, for their freedom. The officer showed interest but expressed fear for his life. A maneuver was proposed whereby Pramot and a trusted team of his men would kill their fellow captors; then the regalia would be handed over and hidden. Sisang swore on his word as a prince of Ayutthaya – which was easily offered, as the kingdom was now defunct – that he would have his men hogtie Pramot and his team and then flee. Pramot would later explain to his commander that his killed troops had been the culprits, that they had placed him and his stalwarts in fetters with the intent of ridding the captive princes of their jewels but had then been killed by the captives instead. What the credulous Pramot had not reckoned on was the two princes' perfidy. They fled with their men as arranged, but they carried with them the jewels that had been their captors' promised reward. In the aftermath, Pramot and his men were rigorously interrogated to reveal the truth, and they were then executed. Upon receiving a report of the incident, King Taksin ordered that the standard penalty of 30 strokes of the cane be imposed on the expedition's commander, Duang, for having failed to prevent such a perfidious escape. But the punishment for that infraction was expunged in view of his victory over Phimai.

Sisang and Tui with their small party of fleeing guardsmen sped on horseback to Siemreap and from there found their way past Udong to Ha Tien. There, Mac Thien-tu, the ruler of that distant maritime principality, already acquainted with Sisang as Siam's royal envoy and former frequent visitor as Ayutthaya ambassador as well as commercial speculator, offered them sanctuary. Flattered to be hosting such illustrious guests, Thien-tu offered them generous hospitality; under such blandishments they recovered their nerve and resumed their intrigues. Sisang managed to insinuate himself into Thien-tu's confidence and over the course of lengthy policy discussions convinced his host to take retaliatory action against the upstart Thonburi regime.[39] Thien-tu was seduced by Sisang's vainglorious pretensions – "the innate disease of princes, ambition for empire."[40] Through Sisang's insidious counsel, Thien-tu was persuaded that the field had been left open to him while Taksin was preoccupied with other matters.[41] Under those propitious circumstances, it was argued, a naval expedition to take control of the Eastern Seaboard ports could easily regain Ha Tien's ascendency. Intrigued, but too old to lead in combat, he invited Sisang to take titular command of his junk fleet against Chanthabun, while Tui was assigned a regiment of Cham troops to march through the Cardamom Mountains from Battambang for an assault on neighboring Trat. The two princes of royal blood, in their military demeanor surrounded by their personal fighting retinue, instilled the campaign with an aura of invincibility, though effective command remained in the hands of the experienced officers assigned as their subalterns. Thus arose, in September 1769, Sisang's and Tui's final misadventure. Whether their rash assumption of unfamiliar duties marked a real revolution in their minds, or rather simply reflected their insatiable hunger for great things, remains a matter of conjecture.

Having no practical knowledge or previous experience in naval warfare, Sisang was left to rely wholly on the Cantonese sea captains and pilots who led the way. Tui was similarly relegated to dependency on the Cham officers assigned to lead their troops on the overland march through uncharted jungles. In propitiation of the Cham guardian spirits, three young buffalo were ritually slain, each in turn tethered to the ritual post and cleanly beheaded by a single stroke of the battle axe. A wondrous portent then was witnessed by the assembled battalions: the heads of the sacrificed beasts, lying separated from their bodies, were seen to thrust out their tongues and lick up their own gore.[42] Consternation afflicted the troops, and many slunk off to escape the inevitable defeat that the swaggering princes had failed to contemplate. Tui, it seems, was abandoned by his officers in the desolate Cardamom rainforests and left to an uncertain fate. He vanished, leaving no trace of his body or possessions, only the stench of his memory and the mystery of his fate. As a result, the land assault was abandoned, leaving the sea forces to continue the fight on their own. As it happened, however, Sisang's sea assault on Siam's Gulf ports, too, was aborted when a deadly epidemic struck the flotilla while anchored off Trat. Sisang was among the many who did not survive the scourge.

The port of Chanthabun, mid-19th century (Henri Mouhot, *Travels in Siam, Cambodia and Laos, 1858-1860.* London, 1864, p. 137). This lithograph of the placid Gulf waters fronting the port of Chanthabun (modern Chanthaburi) shows the port and its anchorage at the far right, secluded in the distant haze behind island foliage. The Alpine massif dominating much of the skyline is the lithographer's dramatic, entirely fictitious embellishment of the jungled alluvial countryside that reached deep inland toward low rolling hills.

Chapter 5
Warlords of the South Seas

Editor's introduction

The South China Sea meets the Gulf of Siam at Cape Ca Mau, the southernmost tip of Vietnam, where the roiling crosscurrents and uncertain winds of the converging waters challenge maritime navigators. Sheltered along the western lee shore, some 300 kilometers due north of the peninsula's sunbaked Land's End, the placid estuary of Ha Tien for centuries formed a mariners' haven, the coast's only port worthy of that distinction. Today Ha Tien survives as an obscure township marking Vietnam's coastal border with Cambodia. In the eighteenth century it provided a favored anchorage for Chinese junks sailing the trade routes skirting the Cambodian seaboard. Both the port and surrounding territory, stretching eastward along the Cambodian littoral from Kampong Som to the Ca Mau Peninsula, were in ancient times known as Banteay Meas (the Golden Domain), a Khmer placename apparently deriving from the Malay Pantai Mas (Gold Coast), a pirates' toponym. As the principality hived off from Cambodia in the early eighteenth century to become an autonomous political entity, it came to be more commonly known by the Vietnamese term Ha Tien (Bewitched River).

With its seaworthy harbor sheltered behind a cluster of limestone-cliffed islands and a prominent headland, today much eroded, Ha Tien and its hinterland, rich in jungle produce and agricultural surplus, became in the years following the fall of Ayutthaya a fulcrum of contention between Vietnam, Siam, and faltering Cambodia. For the Khmer during the generations before the mighty Mekong's deltaic distributaries came to offer safe passage to the sea via Saigon (formerly known as Preykor), My Tho, Vinh Long, and Can Tho, the port of Ha Tien served as a vital vent for trade. For the Nguyen lords of Hué, the capital of eighteenth-century Quang-nam (forerunner of Annam and imperial Vietnam), Ha Tien marked the frontier of southward expansion across the vast stretches of the Mekong Delta. For Siam, Ha Tien afforded a tempting backdoor into the Cambodian kingdom, a perennial object of Siamese imperial yearnings.

Ha Tien rose to prosperity in the eighteenth century as a fortuitous consequence of China's dynastic transition from Ming to Ching and the train of events to which that political watershed gave rise. Under the latter reigns of the Ming Dynasty (1368-1644), overseas trade and transport had been curtailed during extended periods as the empire turned inward. The first eight decades of the succeeding Ching Dynasty (1644-1911) saw the reinstatement of that policy with a campaign to suppress the Ming reactionary provinces in China's southern borderlands. The pressures brought to bear on the Ming partisans and other undesirables hounded by the draconian Ching justice system led many thousands to run the government's naval blockade in flight to the South Seas. There, some joined the old Chinese trading enclaves at local ports while others cleared and drained virgin delta lands for smallholder cultivation or struck off into the interior to seek their fortune gathering exotic jungle products and mining the region's valuable ores and gemstones. Two distinct Chinese overseas migration patterns appeared in that context. The "trader" pattern was exemplified by seafarers, merchants, and artisans, many fleeing political persecution by settling down, marrying locally, and building close relations with local rulers for maximum mutual benefit. In their wake, the "coolie" pattern arose from the migration of junk-loads of marginal peasants and landless laborers fleeing poverty in search of wage-work in the port towns as dockworkers, hawkers, or men-at-arms; independent settlement in the seaboard provinces as market gardeners; or onward migration into the hinterlands to forage jungle produce and extract ores and gemstones for the export market.

Crosscutting the characteristic occupational, trader/coolie distinction of China's Southeast Asian diaspora was its ethnic composition, readily apparent in the differing provincial origins, dialects, and cultures of its participants. The members of each group clustered, quite naturally, among their fellows of like dialect, perpetuated their own customs and kindreds (though Chinese women were few among them), and formed their own communal guilds and trade networks. Cantonese speakers (from Kwangtung Province) came to predominate the exile communities along the Vietnamese and Philippine coasts, while the more adventurous Hokkien speakers (from Fujian Province), with their larger, more seaworthy junks, ventured further afield to the Gulf of Siam, Malay Peninsula, and Indonesian Archipelago. Within that Chinese migratory flow, overseas trade and transport at Ayutthaya, Southeast Asia's premier port during the several centuries preceding its fall, came to be dominated by a Hokkien merchant community working in close collaboration with the Siamese aristocracy's lucrative export monopolies and as facilitator of the Siamese state's periodic trade and tribute missions to Peking. Indicative of the Hokkien community's mercantile role at Ayutthaya was its concentrated presence in the capital's port quarter, the rise of a number of Hokkien tycoons to prominent positions in Siam's Ministry of Trade, and the staffing of that ministry's lower levels by Hokkien factors, warehousemen, accountants, customs officials, interpreters, junk captains, pilots, and able-bodied seamen.

After decades of political suppression marked by the closing of China's southern ports and prohibition of overseas trade, the Ching emperor in 1727, in the face of recurrent provincial crop failures, famines, and local uprisings, finally rescinded those draconian restrictions to satisfy the urgent demand for rice imports. The earlier Hokkien and Cantonese migrations to the South Seas were then joined by a third Chinese emigrant constituency, the Taechiu (alternatively Teochiu, or Chaozhou), a fiercely independent people native to the poverty-wracked, famine-prone borderlands dividing Kwangtung from Fujian, intent on maintaining their distinct cultural identity developed under endless adversity. As belated interlopers along the Gulf coast, they were relegated to the lesser ports and the periphery of the major trade centers. At Ayutthaya, for instance, the emerging Taechiu presence was in the mid-eighteenth century restricted to the rowdy, disreputable seamen's quarter of Suan Phlu, situated downstream from the walled city's Mae Bia Harbor (at the confluence of the Chaophraya and Pa Sak rivers), while Ayutthaya's well-established Hokkien merchant community was permitted to erect its homes and warehouses within the walled city's southeastern commercial quarter, dominating that harbor. Post-Ayutthaya Thonburi (1767-1782), with its blatant favoritism for Taechiu interests, presented a telling departure from that convention. There, the Taechiu community was assigned a preferred waterfront anchorage and residential quarter directly across the river from the new Grand Palace, while the Hokkien (Fujianese) merchants remained confined to their long-established Kudi Chin anchorage and cramped riverbank settlement immediately downriver from the Thonburi citadel.

Taechiu trading junks, in contrast to those of their Hokkien and Cantonese rivals, were relatively compact and maneuverable; they featured only one or two masts, had smaller capacity and smaller crews, and generally frequented provincial ports offering shallow harbors inaccessible to larger vessels. Ill-equipped to compete effectively with the heftier Hokkien and Cantonese long-distance voyagers, they customarily specialized in coastal shipping and often pursued fishing as a supplementary pursuit. In addition, the Taechiu junk fleets sailing the Gulf waters had a reputation for piracy, just as they did along the South China coast. There must surely have been more than a tinge of truth in that belief. Along the Gulf coast and its abundant sprinkling of islands useful for camouflage and hideout, piracy introduced a serious challenge to Ha Tien's role as a safe haven for passing mariners, and Taechiu freebooters were singled out for the brunt of the blame. A relentless struggle to suppress that perennial irritant was waged through resort to convoys, armed escorts, amphibious assaults, public executions, and the like. In all that, it is difficult to sift Cantonese Ha Tien's anti-Taechiu commercial bias from its anti-piracy policies.

The threat posed to the profits of the Gulf's Taechiu trading network by the extension of Cantonese marine power to Ha Tien and beyond in the eighteenth century generated a hostile reaction. From the Cantonese viewpoint, Taechiu trading incursions must have seemed equally provocative. The commercial rivalry played itself out in the years following the fall of Ayutthaya as an escalating conflict between Thonburi and Ha Tien; more personally, it coincided with unfriendly relations between King Taksin of Thonburi and Thien-tu *sae* Mac, the ruler of Ha Tien. Over the course of Ayutthaya's Ban Phlu Luang Dynasty (1688-1767), Ha Tien had, through astute diplomacy, managed to avoid direct confrontation with Siamese flotillas conveying troops to the Cambodian front. As Ha Tien flourished during the 1700s, however, Siam came to see it not simply as an obstacle to its Cambodian ambitions but as an increasingly serious threat to its commercial interests – to the point where, with the rise of Thonburi, Ha Tien found itself beset by the menace of direct Siamese attack. Ha Tien's very success as a Cantonese overseas emporium made it a prime object of Thonburi's imperial pretensions. The political leverage exercised by Thonburi's Taechiu merchant community played no small part in that anti-Ha Tien outlook. With strong backing from its Taechiu allies along the Gulf coast, Thonburi in 1771 launched a decisive naval assault aimed at destroying once and for all Ha Tien's competitive position. Thus ended Ha Tien's entrepôt-based prosperity, with repercussions that rippled through the remainder of the Thonburi reign, and beyond.

Diogo's observations in this chapter bring Thonburi's conquest of Ha Tien into focus as a notable triumph along Siam's path to imperial power. In narrating the course of that multifaceted conflict, he draws a number of comparisons between the two leading protagonists, Taksin and Thien-tu, within the context of the Gulf coast's Taechiu parvenus and its well-established Cantonese/Hokkien commercial alliance. As a subsidiary theme, Diogo's Ha Tien tale clarifies the intensifying Siamese-Vietnamese struggle for Cambodia. Diogo examines closely Taksin's and Thien-tu's contrasting ethnicities (the former of Thai-Taechiu birth; the latter Vietnamese-Cantonese), temperaments (one an intrepid warrior; the other a canny merchant-prince); and policies (one bent on rebuilding a collapsed empire, the other immersed in mercantilist dominance). While that comparative character study dominates much of the discussion, it serves as an essential device for Diogo's examination of the larger political dynamics of the Thonburi regime. He treats the strained relations between the two rulers, in effect, as a parable of the eighteenth-century Taechiu /Hokkien commercial rivalry that played a little-known but vital role in Siam's progress from Ayutthaya to Thonburi to Bangkok.

Conquest

Colonel Taksin, assigned to aid in the defense of Ayutthaya during the waning years of the Ban Phlu Luang Dynasty at the western frontier outpost of Tak, showed himself to be a man endowed with many virtues, of which the most eminent was valor in warfare. In recognition of his martial prowess, he was raised at an exceptionally young age to the senior ranks of the nobility.[1] Taksin's elemental military strategy placed agility and surprise before numbers. He sought to force the enemy into combat when he found his own forces stronger and avoided direct confrontation when he believed his troops the weaker. If the enemy advanced, he was nowhere to be found; whenever and wherever they camped, he molested and alarmed them; he obstructed their lines of supply, hindered them from foraging, and cut them off from water; if they besieged any town, he besieged them in turn and put them to extremities of want.[2] From his personal witness to the folly of Ayutthaya's static defense against incessant Burmese advance, he learned to carry the fight consistently to the enemy. Having several times been bested in battle against the Burmese at Ayutthaya, he protested that he would never again suffer the penetration of any enemy into the kingdom's heartland, nor be reduced to defending the capital's walls; accordingly, he decided always to draw out the army into the field.[3] So he did, with the result that his many campaigns were far-flung and kept him distant from Thonburi for extended periods of his reign.

Unwavering in his opinions, brooking no fool, Taksin's brilliance as a military tactician quickly gained him as many friends as his self-confident, uncompromising nature earned him enemies. The decline and fall of Ayutthaya left in him a lifelong loathing for the narrow-minded ritual, nepotism, and petty governance practiced by the Ban Phlu Luang dynasts. His unconcealed disdain for Ayutthaya's idle, pleasure-seeking aristocracy provided a tireless target for his detractors; they rebuked his gravity as pride, his plain talk as self-will, his studied advice as reprimand.[4] Adding to those insults, his enemies at Ayutthaya insisted that his commoner origin left him ineligible for high office. They subsequently sought to corroborate that prejudice by referring to his flight from Burmese encirclement during the final days of Ayutthaya as a treacherous desertion of his post. His comrades contended, to the contrary, that Ayutthaya's defeat had been facilitated by those of the highest pedigree, and that his daring escape in the face of overwhelming odds had been a tactical victory. In view of his later accomplishments, it can surely not be gainsaid that his survival to fight another day proved infinitely preferable to what would otherwise have been certain defeat, and death.

At Ayutthaya, Taksin was relieved of his prestigious command in retribution for his insolent complaints regarding the weak defense of the city. Instead, as the defenders' difficulties mounted, he was assigned in October 1766 to head a regiment of untested volunteers in securing the island capital's southeastern perimeter. Within the span of a month, he managed to introduce discipline and order, taught his men to stand fast in the face of assault and obey his signals and watchwords; and out of a confused body of coolies, thieves, and yokels he wrought a regular, well-disciplined fighting force.[5] Their resolute resistance at Wat Pa Kaew nevertheless proved inadequate against a massive Burmese onslaught. Then, in January 1767, with his back to the city moat at Wat Phichai, surrounded and about to be overrun, Taksin led his men in a desperate charge through the Burmese lines, outwitting his pursuers in a sustained dash through the wilderness to the provincial outpost of Prachin several days to the east.

From there the exhausted brigade proceeded down the Bang Pakong River to the Gulf coast in search of support from Siam's Eastern Seaboard dependencies, which had remained distant from the Burmese invasion. The ports of Chonburi and Rayong had little to offer, but Chanthabun boded richer fare. Camped within easy gunshot of the town wall, Taksin conducted protracted negotiations with the governor's envoys for food and munitions. Despite his pleadings, the town fathers spurned his every overture. It became evident that the provincial governor and his minions had abandoned the hapless cause of Ayutthaya in favor of an alliance with the rising power of Vietnamese-backed Ha Tien. In proof of that change of allegiance, Chanthabun had evicted its Taechiu junk fleets to the lesser anchorage at Trat, a day's voyage down the coast.[6] In June 1767, with Ayutthaya lost, his food stocks depleted, and his patience worn thin, Taksin roused his men to take Chanthabun by force. The neighboring coastal towns were quickly brought under his sway as warlord of Siam's Eastern Seaboard domain.

Taksin had aimed for the Eastern Seaboard as a rallying point from which to strike against Siam's Burmese invaders. He had not been aware that his arrival would intrude upon an ongoing dispute to the east. Before his occupation of Chanthabun he had known scarcely more of the Gulf coast's Taechiu-Cantonese conflict than the participants in that conflict had known of him. An unanticipated byproduct of his conquest of Chanthabun was the disruption of the Cantonese junk traders' aspirations to extend their dominance along the Gulf coast.[7] Much to his surprise, Taksin was fêted as a Taechiu hero for having ousted Chanthabun's Cantonese-allied governor, though he had always considered himself more Thai than Chinese and was only superficially fluent in the Taechiu dialect. That unanticipated local fame was destined to color the subsequent course of his career.

In his dealings with the miscellany of adventurers scattered along the Gulf coast, Taksin quickly learned not to trouble himself with the self-righteous port governors but rather collaborated with the seaboard's true masters, the unassuming merchant-seamen perpetually preoccupied with market dealings and their warehoused inventories, and the swashbuckling junk captains responsible for conveying their precious cargoes along the hazardous coastal shipping lanes. Chief among them was Li-ang *sae* Tang, a formidable mariner whose junk fleet regularly plied the sea lanes linking Siam with China. The possibility that Li-ang may formerly have been involved in piracy as a sideline to his frequent coastal trading expeditions was an issue that did not trouble Taksin. He welcomed the stalwart captain's friendship and support, which proved critical to his rise to power. In reward for Li-ang's faithful services he was in due course appointed to the high office of command of the Eastern Seaboard provinces, cementing Taechiu control over the Gulf coast west of Ha Tien.

Meanwhile, at the Cantonese-controlled port of Ha Tien, Li-ang's actions favoring Taechiu dominance over Siam's Eastern Seaboard ports were viewed as little more than a passing irritation. Ha Tien's ruler, Thien-tu *sae* Mac, was the son and natural successor to his father Mac Cuu, the founder of Ha Tien as a flourishing seaport. Approaching his sixth-cycle birthday, Thien-tu had superintended his realm's rising fortunes since 1735, one year short of Taksin's entire lifetime.[8] Over those years he had grown into a great-bellied, grey-bearded, ivory-dentured autocrat, as befitted an eminent Chinese merchant-prince. He exuded the counterfeit charms of many an elder statesman – courteous, and yet intimidating; pleasant, yet aloof; superficially forthright, yet consistently devious; relying on the deference shown by his interlocutors as an invitation to dominate every colloquy.[9] Only a fool, however, would ignore the power wielded by this pretentious old man. Under his command sailed an imposing fleet of armed maritime junks that traded profitably at all the principal ports lining the South Sea.[10] In his grasp rested the fortunes of his prosperous maritime principality.

Ha Tien Bay and its limestone cliffs, featured on a Republic of Vietnam postage stamp. (Editor's photo)

Vietnam's Mac Cuu Memorial at Ha Tien, commemorating the principality's 18th-century founder and father of Thien-tu. (Google Images)

Persistently underestimating Taksin's reputation, resolve, and resources, Thien-tu embarked on an escalating sequence of provocations aimed at undermining the fledgling Thonburi regime. The following sequence of events includes the most vexatious of his affronts to neighborly relations in the years leading to the fall of Ha Tien.[11]

1767-1768 – As the fate of Ayutthaya under Burma's implacable siege crystallized, Thien-tu joined Cambodia in shifting his allegiance from Siam to Quang-nam.[12] From the moment of Taksin's enthronement at Thonburi, Thien-tu discontinued tributary relations with Siam on the grounds that the upstart Thonburi kingdom was no suitable substitute for Ayutthaya, as Taksin was merely a Chinese interloper.

1768 – In response to Taksin's urgent call for rice imports to stave off famine at Thonburi, Thien-tu sent several junk-loads of paddy, escorted by a convoy of troop-laden warships. Taksin was advised that this so-called goodwill mission might actually be a stratagem to seize Thonburi in ambush. To preempt that eventuality, the flotilla was intercepted at the mouth of the Chaophraya River and was there dispossessed of its rice cargo and turned away.

Late 1768 – After Thonburi's defeat of Khaek's forces at Phimai, Khaek's renegade brothers Sisang and Tui were offered sanctuary at Ha Tien. Thien-tu declined Taksin's demand that they be extradited to Thonburi on the spurious grounds that they had received sanctuary under the protection of Ha Tien's resident French priests.

1769 – Thien-tu sent a series of disparaging messages to the Chinese authorities at Canton concerning the recent regime change in Siam in a move to avert any imperial validation of Taksin's assumption of the throne. As a result, Taksin's repeated appeals for political affirmation and trade prerogatives received a haughty snub from the representative of the imperial Chinese throne.

Map 9. Ha Tien and its neighborhood, 1771

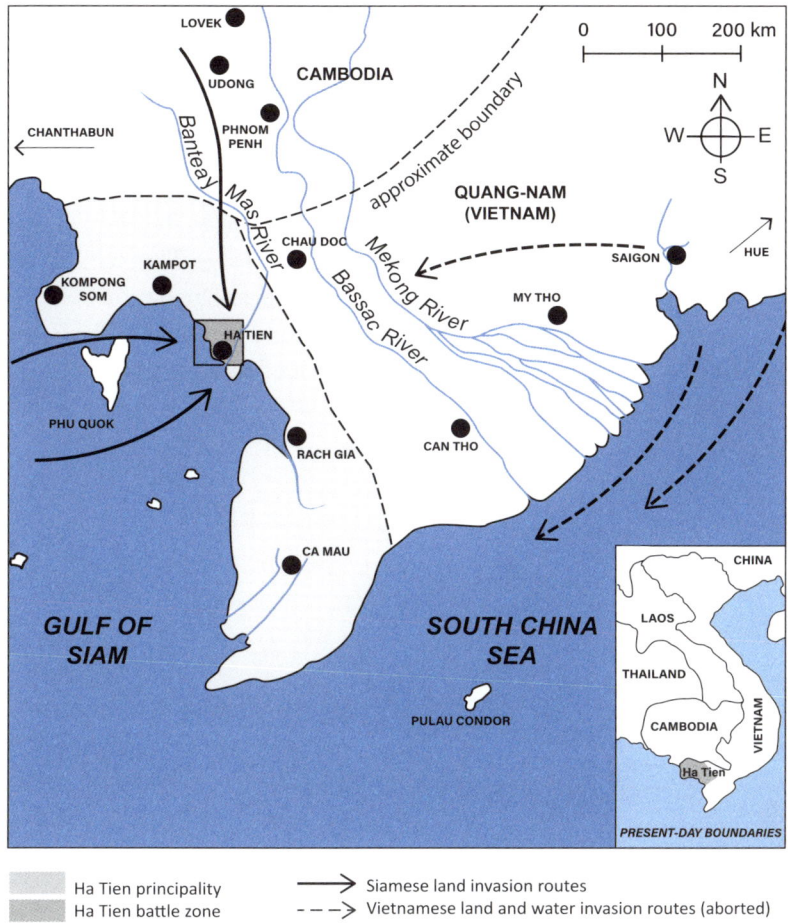

Late 1769 – Following Taksin's departure from Thonburi to subdue Siam's rebellious southern provinces, Tien-tu dispatched a war fleet carrying 3,000 troops to annex Chanthabun and its neighboring port of Trat. The Chanthabun defenders could muster little more than 1,000 men, but the Ha Tien expedition failed due to the outbreak of a devastating epidemic among the besieging forces, saving Siam's Eastern Seaboard ports with scarcely a shot fired.

Thien-tu's provocations proved vexatious but not disabling to the Thonburi regime. Eventually, however, Taksin's forbearance at those recurrent aggressions ran out. Spurred by Li-ang and other Taechiu counselors, who were naturally eager to rid the Gulf of the Cantonese menace, he decided to resolve the issue by annihilating Ha Tien's threat in a single bold stroke. Absorbing the distant port into the Siamese fold would also secure for Siam an unobstructed eastern gateway into Cambodia. After a year's preparations, a naval expedition was mobilized at Thonburi in September

Warlords of the South Seas 175

1771. Unlike Siam's previous wars, this campaign did not have manpower acquisition as an immediate aim. It saw, instead, a distinct territorial advantage in acquiring this far-eastern maritime outpost as a deterrent against intensifying mercantile rivalry. That prospect merged naturally with Taksin's secondary aim, the replacement of Cambodia's Vietnamese vassal, King Outey Racha (Ton), with Siam's protégé, Prince Non. In pursuit of that second objective, a 3,000-man force led by Duang, recently raised to General Chakri, Minister of War, marched directly across the Khorat Plateau and through western Cambodia, escorting Non to the royal seat at Udong. Ton fled downriver to the safety of Vietnamese-held Can Tho, while Non was installed on the Cambodian throne as King Rama Racha. Duang then led his taskforce down the Banteay Mas River to join the assault on Ha Tien, but the battle had been all but decided by the time he arrived. Accompanied by Li-Ang, he returned to Udong to settle the Cambodian political crisis.

Map 10. The Thai conquest of Ha Tien, 1771

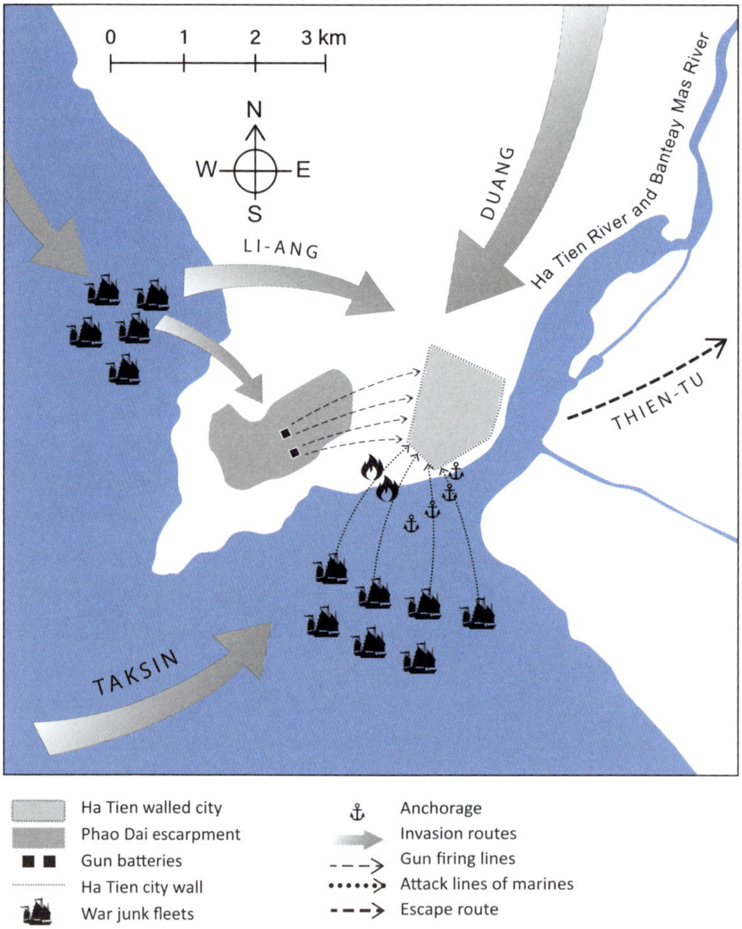

The expedition's main objective was pursued under Taksin's personal command of a junk fleet that sailed from Thonburi for the Eastern Seaboard carrying a 1,000-man marine contingent plus boatloads of munitions and many cannon. It was joined at Chanthabun by a 20-vessel squadron carrying a 3,000-man Taechiu militia under the command of Li-ang.[13] Forewarned of the coming attack, Ha Tien sought aid from both Udong and Hué, but the promised reinforcements were still being awaited when the Siamese armada approached silently in the midst of a nighttime downpour in mid-October 1771 with all lamps doused.[14] Flatboats carrying marines and ordnance were beached behind the Phao Dai escarpment topping the promontory on the west shore of the harbor, out of sight of the port. Siege cannon, powder, and shot were stealthily trundled to the peak of that commanding position. As the predawn murk faded into a misty sunrise, the Siamese fleet was discovered anchored on the far side of the harbor, beyond range of Ha Tien's batteries. Thien-tu's adjutant, it is said, exclaimed in fright, "We have fallen into our enemy's hands." Not yet aware of the cannonry threat from the headland, Thien-tu replied, "And why not they into ours?"[15]

A day later, having received no response to their demand for capitulation, the besieging forces launched a vicious bombardment from their hilltop batteries directly into the town, complemented by a longer-range and less accurate barrage from the shipborne guns fronting the harbor. During a lull in the gunfire, Thien-tu instructed his herald to row out toward Taksin's flagship under a flag of truce and declaim in a taunting tone, "If you are indeed a great general, disembark your ships and fight us like men." In response, Taksin cried out, "If you are one, make me do so."[16] After several days of devastating bombardment, including a lucky shot that exploded the town's powder magazine, to devastating effect, Siam's troops landed after nightfall along the western flanks of the fortified city. The ramparts were breached, the defenders took flight, and the pulverized citadel was taken.[17] Ha Tien had been out-maneuvered, out-gunned, and out-fought. A 500-man garrison was installed under the command of Li-ang, whose title was now raised to Colonel Rachasethi, confirming his authority over the Eastern Seaboard reaches. In the aftermath, Li-ang ordered that Ha Tien's harbor be narrowed and shallowed with the scuttling of a number of stone-weighted hulks to form a permanent navigational hazard. That obstruction effectively ended the port's role as a favored Gulf coast junk haven.

During the nighttime melee marking Ha Tien's fall, Thien-tu, surrounded by his personal retinue, his women and children cowering behind the gunnels, slipped away by low-prowed barge through the wetlands canal tracery into the thinly populated, lawless Cambodian/Vietnamese borderlands flanking the Mekong Delta to Chau Doc. From there they sped down the flood-swollen Bassac River to Can Tho, where they secured the protection of the Nguyen warlords of Saigon and Hué. His passage to the safety of Can Tho paralleled the route taken a fortnight before by Cambodia's ousted King Outey Racha (Ton) upon the Siamese takeover of Udong. A much-diminished man, the deposed Khmer king died in Vietnamese exile not long thereafter. Outey Racha's unhappy fate preoccupied Thien-tu with such melancholy thoughts as might be expected of a man who for the past 36 years had grown accustomed to the rewards of commerce and the comforts of sovereignty and now, in old age, faced disruption and defeat for the first time. In one day, he had been stripped of all the glory and power that he had acquired with painstaking care over decades of industry.[18] Built of stronger metal than Outey Racha, however, he did not allow the loss of his realm to leave him a broken man.

Thien-tu and his family fleeing Ha Tien upon the port city's fall, October 1771 (No Na Paknam, *Murals Explained* (in Thai), Bangkok: Muang Boran, 1993, p. 84)

Détente

As previously mentioned, Thonburi in 1767, upon Taksin's takeover, had been a sparsely populated shell of its former self.[19] To rebuild the stronghold and its environs as the site of his proposed new capital, he had directed his men to scour the surrounding countryside three days' journey in every direction for surviving remnants of Ayutthaya's former inhabitants. Starving bands of homeless wanderers from all quarters had been persuaded to join him with promises of food, protection, and preferment. Many of the displaced artisans, adepts, and clerics among them were assured of royal patronage, and those who had occupied lowly standing as slaves or war captives at Ayutthaya were offered the chance to have their former status raised to the social station of freemen. The new citadel's immediate environs soon came to be surrounded by villages of Thai, Lao, Mon, Malay, Cham, Indian, Persian, Khmer, Chinese, Portuguese, and other survivors of the recent holocaust inflicted on Ayutthaya. Those of Taksin's comrades-in-arms who had been appointed by him to senior ranks were charged with oversight of the newly arrived communities, entailing all the responsibilities and rewards that such authority carried in its train. With such innovative measures a new social order was created, patterned after the old.

Thonburi's rapid transformation from outlying customs post to chief entrepot of a resurrected Siam benefitted from its influx of Chinese expatriates, principally the Taechiu seamen attracted from the Eastern Seaboard. Taksin's remarkable popularity among that populace in the wake of his Chanthabun victory opened his eyes to the political opportunities implicit in the Taechiu business connection. The financial support that accompanied his continued patronage of the Gulf-coast junk traders after the establishment of his Thonburi base was eagerly reciprocated. Many of the traders accepted his invitation to move their ventures to Thonburi, and they prospered as the port traffic swelled. He welcomed their offers of assistance, never hesitating to consider how he would generate the resources to repay their munificent loans. All he cared to know was that their financial backing would provide him the means to address effectively the reviving kingdom's most pressing problems.

It is probable that more survivors of the fall of Ayutthaya died of famine and pestilence in the years immediately following that disaster than had been slaughtered in the event itself. The peasants' rice crops, seed reserves, paddy fields, and buffalo herds had been destroyed in the devastation, and so the ensuing several years saw consecutive crop failures. Thonburi faced a desperate need for resolution of that dire situation. Beyond satisfying the urgent needs of the destitute peasantry, Taksin needed to feed his troops, his officials, and the slaves conscripted to build his new capital. To placate those vulnerable, volatile constituencies, he turned to his Taechiu comrade-in-arms, Li-ang, who broached the idea of a Chinese traders' consortium to offer the struggling regime temporary financial relief. Thonburi's Taechiu and Hokkien merchant communities were approached. The former responded with enthusiasm; the latter considered the proposed return too low to warrant the risk, and declined. Taksin never forgave the Hokkien traders' avarice; with few exceptions, they were excluded from senior office through the remainder of his reign.

Taksin knew little of business affairs and so relied heavily on Li-ang for commercial guidance. In his name they negotiated loans with the Taechiu consortium for such purchases as rice and arms at the concessionary annual interest rate of 12 percent, well below the going commercial rates of 24–36 percent. However, no one troubled to keep him informed of the growth of that debt as interest accumulated, nor, over the ensuing years, of the credit syndicate's mounting disquiet over the repeated postponement of its repayment. When, eventually, Taksin was fully apprised of the discontent that Thonburi's tardy reimbursements of its unbridled borrowing had generated, he protested that, of the many burdens of sovereignty, the greatest was that even those who were accounted his most reliable friends and trusted confidantes rarely ventured to speak freely or tell unpleasant truths.[20]

In addition to the considerable store of arms that Taksin accumulated as booty from his early conquests, he requested Thonburi's Taechiu mariners to procure inventories of cutlasses, cannon, muskets, and munitions on his account in the course of their trading voyages, thus adding to his debts. Dutch Batavia and Portuguese Macau provided active markets for such purchases. Arms were also surreptitiously acquired at various lesser ports along the China coast despite Peking's official proscription against such dealings. At the same time, Taksin purchased the mercenary services of many arriving shiploads of bonded Taechiu workmen who were trained by his officers to form a steadfast royal militia. Those indigents had been indentured by trading firms at Changlin, Thenghai, and other ports of China's Taechiu Prefecture for transport to Thonburi with the offer of reimbursement of the cost of the voyage plus the promise of a plot of fertile land in return for 10 to 12 years of contractual service.[21] Taksin's functionaries acquired those arms and men through the financial arrangements negotiated with Thonburi's Taechiu merchants, greatly magnifying the state's debt to its Chinese benefactors.

The mounting struggle to repay Thonburi's creditors came to preoccupy Li-ang's attention in his capacity as Minister of Trade. One seemingly painless solution was the granting of tax farms to major creditors in liquidation of their outstanding loans. Thus, with royal approval he added a number of new items to the list of farmed-out taxes long dominated by the gambling, spirits, and fishing taxes: boat building, brick making, lime slacking, and charcoal firing to palm-sugar tapping, and honey gathering, among others. A host of Taechiu creditors of the Thonburi regime entered the lesser ranks of the nobility as lieutenants, majors, and captains in designation of their newly acquired status as tax farmers.

Another solution was the imposition of increased exactions on Thonburi's many outlying dependencies. Ha Tien was singled out for particularly stern treatment in that regard. The port's remaining resident merchants in the wake of the 1771 defeat took to complaining of Thonburi's severe tribute demands as well as the excessive port fees and fines exacted on behalf of the suzerain state as nothing more than Taechiu piracy by another name. In deference to Ha Tien's protests, Taksin stated that, as a king, he venerated only two deities, Persuasion and Compulsion. Ha Tien responded that it was served by two greater powers, Poverty and Penury, which prevented it from honoring Thonburi's extravagant demands.[22] To Ha Tien's dismay, Taksin's patron deities proved superior.

Siam's diversity of in-kind tax and tribute exactions, dominated by the paddy tax collected annually from every farming household, were gathered in Thonburi's royal storehouses, where the proceeds were held for periodic redistribution as stipends to royals, nobles, the clergy, lesser officials, military units, and other worthies, as well as emergency stockpiles. The annual surplus remaining after those deductions was assigned to overseas shipments in exchange for essential imports. A favored means of compensating the Taechiu traders' consortium for their earlier financing of rice imports was the granting of preferential participation to their vessels in the junk convoys that were annually organized to export the royal warehouses' surplus inventories of rice, hides, dye woods, aromatics, lac, ivory, and other prized commodities to major overseas markets, particularly the great Chinese port cities of Canton and Amoy.

More effective than any of those direct approaches to dealing with Thonburi's debt problem, however, was the indirect means of reining in state spending. Most troublesome among Thonburi's expenditures, so far as Li-ang was concerned in his role as Minister of Trade, was the high cost of Taksin's protracted military adventure in Cambodia. He repeatedly urged Taksin to ease his fruitless effort to best Quang-nam in the contest for the Cambodian protectorate, which was draining the kingdom's manpower, rice stocks, and other resources at a frightening rate. The strain of that Sisyphean task eventually led him to seek personal relief, and in 1771, after the Ha Tien campaign, he resigned. His deputy, Ching-chong *sae* Yang, was appointed as his successor with the title of Colonel Phichai Aisawan, while Li-ang was honorably transferred to command the Eastern Seaboard provinces with the title of Colonel Rachasethi. Fortunately for Thonburi's financial standing, a negotiated settlement of the protracted Cambodian confrontation became increasingly attractive to both Siam and Vietnam as other military priorities intensified, and the financial drain eased.[23]

Cambodia's interminable dynastic conflict drew to a fragile settlement in 1773. Under the contested dominion of Siam and Quang-nam – the vassal state's competing suzerains – a formal détente was negotiated at the neutral site of Phnom Penh, with all participants attending under pledge of safe passage. The Siamese delegation was led by General Surasi (Bunma). Quang-nam was represented by several Nguyen generals. Thien-tu, greatly subdued in his irregular status as a fugitive from Siamese pursuit, participated as an advisor to the Quang-nam delegation. Under the compromise worked out between the negotiating parties, Prince Non (Siam's protégé) was confirmed as Cambodia's King Rama Racha, with Prince Ton (Hué's newly selected protégé)[24] being appointed viceroy. As a codicil to the accord, Siam conceded the return of Thien-tu to rule Ha Tien as dual Siamese-Vietnamese vassal.

A contrite Thien-tu sailed off for Thonburi with the returning Siamese delegation in December 1773 to pledge fealty to Taksin in a formal investiture to his new post.[25] At his introduction before the enthroned King Taksin in the ministerial audience chamber of Thonburi's Grand Palace, the two very unlike men struck up a surprising rapport.[26] After years of animosity, it was extraordinary that Taksin, at least in his public remarks, now came to hold Thien-tu in some esteem – ostensibly for his courageous defiance in the face of the overwhelming Siamese assault of 1771 and for the grace with which he had survived his subsequent vicissitudes. Conversely, Thien-tu, after years of conspicuous contempt, expressed public admiration of Taksin's achievements in reviving Siam after the Burmese disaster, for building the kingdom's vibrant new capital at Thonburi, and for his statesmanship in engineering the Cambodian détente.

At the royal banquet that followed, Taksin amazed the attending dignitaries with a lengthy disquisition on the many remarkable similarities that he shared with his new vassal, as if they had been born under a single horoscope. Thien-tu, swallowing his pride, responded with warm words in kind. Much that might have been considered less complimentary to one or the other was left unsaid, though it must have preoccupied the minds of the more knowledgeable courtiers that both men's fathers had been nothing more than uprooted Chinese adventurers who had by pure chance formed advantageous local connections, established themselves as traders, obtained tax farms, and married local noblewomen; that those fathers' illustrious sons had found themselves, through no fault of their own, on opposite sides of an ancient partisan divide; that Thien-tu was more than three decades older than Taksin and had held firmly to the old ways, while the younger Taksin had blended wholeheartedly into the local lifestyle and had triumphed while Thien-tu was now prostrate before him in contrite submission.

The public events were followed on subsequent days by a series of private discussions at which the two statesmen were accompanied only by their most senior councilors. Among the issues dealt with were the following. First, Thonburi would guarantee the protection of Ha Tien against any military threat in return for an annual tributary offering. Second, Thonburi and Ha Tien would provide one another's vessels preferential treatment in the form of reduced anchorage fees and favorable dockside facilities, and at sea would join in efforts to suppress the Gulf's endemic piracy. Third, Thien-tu would support Taksin's efforts to gain formal recognition from the Chinese emperor by approaching the Cantonese authorities on his behalf. Fourth, on the issue of dual vassalage, Thien-tu agreed to distinguish between Thonburi's "indelible" vs. Hué's "unreliable" backing. In ratification of that understanding, Thien-tu committed to future consultations with Hué to confirm his primary fealty to Thonburi – a promise easier made than kept. In closing, Taksin emphasized that he prized loyalty no less than valor, that he was as generous in his rewards to his faithful followers as he was severe with those who betrayed his trust. Taksin's lingering uncertainties of Ha Tien's loyalty to its new overlord must have been much on his mind.

Upon Thien-tu's departure to take up his new post at Ha Tien, he left behind at Thonburi as hostages several of his sons and their families and one of his daughters as a court lady, though she never progressed to royal concubine. Support for that family circle was provided by a sizable staff of Cantonese/Vietnamese soldiers, merchants, artisans, and monks. A well-furbished royal guesthouse laid out in Cantonese style – a solid, four-square, brick and teak compound surrounding a central courtyard, centrally located along the Thonburi riverfront – was built for his use whenever visiting Thonburi. His hostage sons at Thonburi continued to dwell there in his absence. The supporting entourage was provided with a residential tract some distance downstream.

Asylum

Little more than a year after Thien-tu's return to Ha Tien, a great civil war erupted in Vietnam and spread rapidly southward to engulf the Mekong Delta. Several years of military maneuvering for control of the vast delta reaches followed. Ha Tien found itself cut off from its Nguyen protectors at Saigon and Hué and left to its own devices by Siam while being subjected to increasingly ferocious rebel raids. In a series of attacks staged during the 1776/77 dry season, the rebel armies succeeded in overrunning great swaths of the Ha Tien hinterlands. The port itself finally fell to the insurgents in October 1777. As the rebel armies surged toward his capital, Thien-tu and much of the town's populace fled to the haven afforded by the nearby island of Phu Quoc. Repeated appeals for aid finally induced Li-ang to dispatch a naval squadron from Chanthabun to convey Thien-tu and more than a thousand of his followers to Siamese asylum. They were received at Thonburi in early 1778 with full honors. Duang, typically cautious in expressing his views, remarked under his breath during the preparatory discussions that, if he were Taksin, he would not so readily embrace his former adversaries. "Nor would I," replied the magnanimous Taksin, "if I were Duang."[27] Truly, Thien-tu posed no threat; he had become a creature more to be pitied than feared. Nearing his eightieth year, he was worn out, as he himself confessed, with age and illness. In his advanced years he had become timid and unenterprising, and suffered from an indisposition that left him entirely immobile. It must have been difficult for him who had lived vigorous and supreme among one generation of men to plead now as a helpless supplicant before another.[28]

Thien-tu and his family returned to the royal guesthouse they had occupied on their earlier visit, near Li-ang's Left Bank residence directly across the river from the Thonburi Palace.[29] His senior aides were quartered alongside, and his hundreds

The great bronze bell standing on display in the Royal Audience Hall of the Thonburi Grand Palace, presented as a tributary presentation by Thien-tu to Taksin in 1777. (Shutterstock)

of lesser followers were provided a residential site a short boat ride downriver in an orchard tract well beyond the city's walled confines. That settlement came to be known as Ban Yuan.[30] In gratitude for Taksin's magnanimity and in proof of his own fidelity, Thien-tu presented to his Siamese suzerain a great bronze bell carrying an emblematic inscription in Chinese calligraphy.[31] In addition, he presented him with his youngest daughter in concubinage. She joined her elder sister who had been left hostage at the Thonburi Palace as a lady-in-waiting upon his earlier visit five years before.

Many more asylum seekers from the Mekong Delta turmoil joined Ban Yuan over the following year. With those additions, that Cantonese/Vietnamese village came to form a notable extension to the riparian city. Nguyen partisans all, the villagers pleaded with Taksin's ministers to extend Siam's military aid toward the recovery of Ha Tien from the rebel cohorts. Eventually, as the resurgent Nguyen armies succeeded in routing the rebels from the Mekong Delta, a number of Thonburi's Ha Tien exiles departed stealthily homeward, without royal sanction. The majority, however, stayed on at Thonburi, not simply for fear of offending Taksin but out of love and respect for Thien-tu in his advanced age.

The Ha Tien exile community met a cold reception among Thonburi's Taechiu merchants, but the Hokkien junk traders at Kudi Chin welcomed them with cautious hope for commercial collaboration. The Cantonese merchants were well known for their diligent enterprise and extensive overseas connections. Other than access to export commodities from local sources, which was a problem they soon solved (as the following pages will reveal), all they lacked toward the realization of their commercial ambitions were maritime junks, most of their vessels having been destroyed by Vietnam's rebel forces and the remainder having been commandeered by the Siamese navy. They believed that reserving cargo space for their merchandise on the annual convoys of Hokkien junks bound for Chinese ports would enable them gradually, year on year, to rebuild their livelihood. However, Thien-tu instructed his followers to be cautious in developing such Kudi Chin contacts because of the strains evident between the Hokkien community and the Thonburi regime. So, they searched for alternative opportunities, which ultimately proved their undoing.

In addition to its peripheral location, Ban Yuan's distinctive lifestyle set it apart within the Thonburi cityscape. At the village center stood a communal shrine regularly used as the site for local festive events and political gatherings, dedicated to the Daoist deity Ma Cho.[32] In addition to that defining venue, the village boasted two other religious sites. At its eastern outskirts stood Wat Kham Lo, founded by the Mahayana Buddhist monks who had accompanied Thien-tu on his first Thonburi visit in 1773 and had stayed on with his hostage retinue.[33] A second Mahayana Buddhist center, Wat Khanh Hoi, was founded as a meditation retreat in the gardens behind the village by the refugees who accompanied Thien-tu's second arrival in 1778.[34]

Thien-tu was a frequent visitor to Ban Yuan's Ma Cho Shrine and served as patron of the two village temples, but he generally avoided Thonburi's other religious sanctuaries. In an effort to mend his relations with the Taechiu merchants, however, he made a show of visiting the local Taechiu community's Pun Thao Kong shrine, situated amid the riverside dockyards behind Wat Pho.[35] There, in a placatory gesture, he paid homage before the presiding sacred image and with sumptuous festivities donated to the shrine an image of Kwan U, a Daoist deity venerated for his honesty, integrity, and valor in war, revered by both the Cantonese and Taechiu speech groups and known to be much favored by King Taksin.[36] The installation of that image offered occasion for conciliatory gestures on all sides, but the fellow feelings thus engendered did not last long.

The tense triangular relations between Thonburi's Taechiu, Hokkien, and Cantonese communities gradually approached a critical juncture.[37] Li-ang, as Siam's overseer of Ha Tien, had coordinated closely with Colonel Phichai Aisawan (Ching-chong), his successor as Minister of Trade, in harsh but always honest enforcement of Ha Tien's tax and tribute obligations. Ching-chong's death in 1776 raised hopes that his successor would prove to be a more lenient taskmaster. However, the new minister, Hok-chu *sae* Tae (Colonel Siri Aisawan), a Taechiu merchant who had previously served as director of the Royal Warehouse Department under Ching-chong's oversight, proved to be a covetous, malicious, utterly corrupted man. Although no favorite of Taksin's, he had been sponsored for that post by Duang in his ministerial capacity, and so his appointment was approved without objection.[38] Hok-chu's appointment in 1778 came at a portentous moment for the Ha Tien exiles, coinciding with their arrival at Thonburi. At the helm of the ministry and with intimate knowledge of the personnel and procedures of its Royal Warehouse Department, he stood unopposed in his ability to divert export inventories for unauthorized, surreptitious sale to Thonburi's Cantonese merchants at inflated prices, with the proceeds entering his own coffers. Thonburi's Taechiu junk traders soon discovered that new threat to their commercial hegemony. They complained that Ha Tien had, after all, not been bested; its venue had merely been relocated to Thonburi. Taksin was not pleased upon learning, as he was eventually destined to do, that an inordinate portion of the state's export revenues were being pilfered into private hands. All the conditions for a violent showdown had been set in place.

Retribution

The cascade of unsavory events that culminated in the final retribution by Thonburi's Taechiu junk traders upon their Cantonese rivals was not long in coming. A trickle of insidious gossip had been circulating through Thonburi's port district entailing suspicions of disloyalty among the Ha Tien exiles from the day of their arrival. Those rumors were given a tinge of substance, about a year after the émigrés' arrival, with the appearance at Thonburi of a small party of shackled Vietnamese military officers led by Prince Chuan, an uncle of Prince Nguyen Anh.[39] That band of adventurers had been seized by Taechiu freebooters while sailing furtively among the many islands studding the Cambodian coast and had been brought to Thonburi by their captors in expectation of a substantial bounty. Chuan was able to convince Taksin's interrogators, however, that his voyage had been simply an ill-starred flight from war-torn Quang-nam. He and his men were released, under Thien-tu's personal bond, to join Thonburi's émigré community. It was not long before whispers were circulating to the effect that Chuan was in contact with Vietnamese partisans plotting against Siamese interests. To ascertain the truth of those reports, he was threatened with ordeal by fire. Under that irresistible inducement he admitted his involvement in Vietnam's machinations against Siam and its Cambodian interests and was condemned to execution.

Taksin was advised by his ministers that although no proof had been elicited to inculpate Thien-tu directly in Chuan's treasonous dealings, the aged merchant-prince, along with his senior officers, should also be put to death, as they bore responsibility for their guest's actions. To the annoyance of Thonburi's rumormongers, Taksin demurred. So, they further embittered the already fraught atmosphere with a suspect letter from a Nguyen general addressed to Thien-tu, a missive that sought Thien-tu's support for a proposed Vietnamese naval assault on Thonburi. Taksin's councilors advised caution, suggesting that the letter might well be fraudulent, as it lacked many of the seals and honorifics of aristocratic protocol usual in such communications. Taksin took no joy in the prospect of Thien-tu's trial and possible execution; he therefore decided to elicit the truth of the matter through a personal interview. However, Thien-tu had reached the fatal decision that his destiny had been preordained. Bodily afflictions and public calamities naturally embitter the minds of men and predispose them to such peevishness that hardly any word can be addressed to them to which they will not take offence.[40] So it was with Thien-tu in his advancing years. In his anguish, he refused to speak in his own defense, setting in train the inevitable consequences.

At around the same time, in Cambodia, renewed rebellion, abetted by Vietnamese intervention, culminated in the assassination of Siam's protégé King Rama Racha (Non), and the return of Cambodia to Vietnamese protection. Reports of Vietnam's de facto abrogation of the 1773 détente and complicity in Non's murder reached Thonburi in May 1780. That news dealt a harsh blow to Siam's Cambodian aspirations, and to Taksin's prestige. Preparations were immediately initiated for a retaliatory strike aimed at returning Cambodia to the Siamese fold. In the meantime, to deflect the damage to Taksin's standing, a search was mounted to identify scapegoats; with that, the Taechiu rumor mills started grinding again. It was whispered anew that the decrepit Thien-tu, despite his continuing confinement at Thonburi, had somehow been involved in the Vietnamese intervention into Cambodian affairs. He was accused of having conducted a secret correspondence with Fa Thalaha (Mu), the rebellious governor of Cambodia's Bassac Province (bordering Ha Tien and Vietnam) and conspirator with the Vietnamese interlopers.[41] Taksin initially gave the accusations of Thien-tu's betrayal little credence, but his advisors deemed it essential to clear the politically charged Thonburi air with a trial of the accused.

Thus, Thien-tu's three sons and 50 of his senior officers were in November 1780 detained and interrogated under ordeal by fire. Unable to withstand the agony, they admitted complicity with the Vietnamese. Days later they were all beheaded and buried at the charnel ground of Wat Samploem, not far downstream from Ban Yuan. Prince Chuan was executed separately in accordance with royal protocol. In deference to Thien-tu's age and incapacity, Taksin permitted him an honorable death by self-administered poison.[42] Among Thonburi's inhabitants there were many in addition to the Taechiu merchants who applauded Thien-tu's death, looking upon him as a glowing ember which had only wanted blowing to burst into flame. For when he had been in his prime it had not been his warrior's skill that had made him Siam's enemy but his guile and experience, together with his innate malice toward Siam, conditions that do not decay with age.[43] In the wake of Thien-tu's death many of his remaining followers slipped away to Vietnam, leaving Ban Yuan severely depleted of population.

Taksin's preoccupation with the alleged perfidies of the Ha Tien exiles was soon overshadowed by rumors that Hok-chu, under the cover of his commercial negotiations as Minister of Trade, had been collaborating with them in support of the Vietnamese enemy. It was whispered that Hok-chu's junks had carried Chuan's couriers between Thonburi and the Cambodian front via Ha Tien. Upon investigation it was found that those vessels had been conveying not only secret agents but, more heinously, rice cargos pilfered from Thonburi's royal warehouses. The rice had been shipped onward up the Banteay River by flatboat to Chau Doc, where it was stockpiled to feed the Vietnamese forces advancing up the Mekong in support of the Cambodian rebels. Thonburi's Taechiu merchants had not overreached in their whispered defamations of Hok-chu; rather, they had simply opened the door to formal discovery of his betrayal. In addition to his dereliction of duty in allowing enemy couriers to travel on his junks, he was charged with looting the royal warehouses of their rice inventories, transporting and selling those stocks to enemy combatants, and redirecting the profits to his personal coffers. He was imprisoned, subjected to excruciating ordeals, found guilty of treason on all charges, and condemned to a miserable death. In a separate bloodbath of executions from the one that had decimated the Ha Tien leadership at Wat Samploem only days before, he was put to death along with 16 accomplices and subordinates at the desolate Wat Sampheng, downstream near Rosario. In so doing, he complied with the ancient counsel that, while rewards should be served out little by little, so that they may be fully savored, punishments should be served all together, so that the less often they are tasted, the less they will offend.[44] In the aftermath, Taksin delegated the principal functions of the vacant Ministry of Trade to a colorless Malay official formerly serving with the Harbor Department and considered a neutral party.

Hok-chu's removal from office and the further cleansing of the Royal Warehouse Department staff marked a change in Taksin's leadership. They were the first public expression of his profound vexation with the nobility's increasingly flagrant defiance of his principles of propriety. With that incident he had reached the limits of his tolerance for the unbridled profiteering and factionalism that was coming increasingly to characterize his reign. His exasperation with the widespread lack of compliance with his expected standards of rectitude left him believing himself the victim of evil conspiracies. As a military commander, he had achieved much, but in civil governance he had proved inadequate. He lamented: "In war, solidarity holds sway; in peace it is every man for himself." In fact, the failure of his halting efforts to purge the kingdom's resurgent corruption contributed materially to his downfall less than two years later.

Chapter 6
Turning Point

Editor's introduction

After King Taksin had consolidated the Siamese kingdom with his campaigns against the nascent eastern kingdom of Phimai (1768), the breakaway southern principality of Nakhon Si Thammarat (1769), and the northern Chao Phra Fang insurrection spreading from Sawangkhaburi (1770), followed by his invasion of Cambodia and conquest of Ha Tien (1771), he slowed the pace of Thonburi's military adventures in both frequency and intensity. The people celebrated their new-found peace with a determination to improve their communal lives, and Taksin turned his energies to matters of domestic reconstruction. That comparatively peaceful interlude was interrupted in 1775 by renewed Burmese aggression, which initially disturbed Siam's northern and western frontiers and then pivoted to a full-blown invasion of the kingdom's upper-central provinces, aimed at an all-out assault on the upcountry linchpin of Phitsanulok. Taksin was forced by those unexpected developments to turn his attention back to full-scale military mobilization.

The fortress city of Phitsanulok (Vishnu's World) was situated along the Nan River some 275 kilometers upstream from Ayutthaya, as the crow flies, with Sukhothai and Kamphaeng Phet to the west. It dominated the upriver reaches of Siam's lush Central Plains, watered by the Chaophraya River's Ping, Wang, Yom, and Nan tributaries. Phitsanulok had for centuries been esteemed as Siam's most important northern strongpoint. It had long served, in effect, as the kingdom's adjunct capital, linking the Central Plains with the narrow northern river valleys of Lan Na, which were occupied by a politically aligned cluster of Tai Yuan-speaking principalities long subjugated to Burmese vassalage.[1] Symbolic of its privileged status, Phitsanulok had historically been governed by a younger brother and viceroy of the reigning king, who ruled the principality as his feudal benefice. The most famous instances of that arrangement had been Prince Naresuan, son of King Maha Thammaracha (r. 1569-1590), and Prince Phitsanu Thibodi (Phon), son of King Thai Sa (r. 1709-1733). King Taksin's installation of his favored liegeman Bunma as governor of Phitsanulok in 1771 – in the absence of an eligible prince – was an effort aimed at continuing that tradition with Bunma's appointment as General Surasi Phitsana Wa-thirat (roughly equivalent to "The King's Valiant General in Charge of Phitsanulok").

During the Burmese southward march toward Ayutthaya in 1765-1766, the mighty army led by General Sihabodi (elsewhere said to have been dubbed

"Thosakan") had found Phitsanulok's defenses so formidable that he decided to bypass that obstacle in his onward rush to victory. Subsequently, in the political vacuum left by the abrupt withdrawal of Burmese forces after the fall of Ayutthaya, Siam's governor at Phitsanulok – a temporary incumbent who had been installed during the last Ayutthaya reign – claimed independence and declared himself king of Phitsanulok and its surrounding territory. His adventure soon failed, however, as repeated raids by Chao Phra Fang, an aspiring warlord at nearby Sawankhaburi (Uttaradit), weakened Phitsanulok's defenses, and a virulent epidemic that spread in their wake resulted in his death and the demise of many of his henchmen. In the aftermath, during Taksin's 1769-1770 campaign against Chao Phra Fang, leaderless Phitsanulok readily acquiesced to reintegration into the Siamese fold.

For Burma's King Hsinbyushin (referred to by Diogo as Mang Ra), abandonment of the Ayutthaya campaign in 1767 in the face of mounting tensions along the Chinese border festered as an irksome scab in need of healing. The conclusion of peace negotiations with China several years later enabled Mang Ra to return his attention to the unfinished subjugation of Siam. In view of his depleted military resources, however, he decided on a more prudent but no less decisive course of conquest than he had pursued at Ayutthaya a decade before. Unlike the grand, two-pronged Ayutthaya campaign of 1765-1767, the Burmese lightning strike in December 1775/January 1776 from Martaban over the Tenasserim Divide toward Phitsanulok was intended to split the Siamese realm across its soft center, weakening it for piecemeal subjugation. Burma's forces, led by the new Minister of War, Asae Wunki, was limited to only about 40,000, about half the might that had been assembled for the previous invasion. Nevertheless, they posed as daunting a challenge for Siam as had the forces that had earlier attacked Ayutthaya, given Siam's similarly diminished resources. Although the Siamese forces were consistently outnumbered, Taksin demonstrated in this conflict the full range of his military virtuosity. That advantage, combined with the superior morale, agility, and fortitude of both his officers and conscripts, enabled Siam to withstand the Burmese onslaught throughout much of the combat. Yet, in the end, Burma's greater numbers prevailed.

Diogo, the compiler of this Chronicle, asserted in his Testament that his Rosario drinking companion, Major António da Costa, a former Burmese war captive, provided him with much of his information on the events of the Phitsanulok invasion. In fact, the construction of the present chapter suggests that it is a close rendering of da Costa's own diary of the Burmese invasion, plus several insertions derived from information provided to Diogo by Prince Chakra Chesada (La). As a Burmese prisoner of war, da Costa had been impressed into military service as an officer of minor standing. That experience afforded him intimate familiarity with Burmese military life and Burmese modes of warfare. The fact that his captors assigned him light duties as a troop training officer does not appear to have clouded his judgment; rather, his functions provided him privileged access to intelligence on the current course of affairs, which he stored away for his future use. Though holding no affection for his captors, and only grudging respect for their commanding general, da Costa may be presumed to have offered in his reminiscences an unvarnished report on the invasion's unfolding.

In affirmation of da Costa's contribution to the following pages, it is worth noting that this chapter differs stylistically from the rest of *Diogo's Chronicle* in its relatively dry, terse, militaristic recitation – though Diogo appears to have inserted occasional flourishes with his lighter hand. Da Costa's contribution is evident in the detailed description of the Burmese side of the conflict, which would otherwise have been unknown to Diogo. The absence of Plutarch paraphrases and character-focused vignettes in this chapter, except in the description of events surrounding the Siamese escape from Phitsanulok (added to da Costa's account based on information provided by Prince Chak and other survivors) is indicative. Despite Diogo's evident smoothing of the presentation to fit the larger text, da Costa's conflicted loathing and admiration for his Burmese captors' military prowess and personal predispositions glimmer through his otherwise arid presentation.

Beyond its stylistic idiosyncrasies, da Costa's account of the course of the Phitsanulok invasion displays several departures from the traditional interpretation presented in Siam's dynastic chronicles and associated sources. Most readily apparent is the precise Western calendrical timeline – apparently sourced to da Costa's daybook – to clarify the complex interplay between Burmese and Siamese troop movements and strategic adjustments in the ongoing military contest. Further, da Costa's account differs from the conventional view that the 1775-1776 conflict arose spontaneously out of two independent insurrections, one in the Mon provinces of the Burmese south and the other in the Lan Na vassal states to the Burmese east, by claiming that both rebellions were purposely amplified by Mang Ra as opportunities to deflect Siam's preoccupations away from the planned line of attack. Thus, according to da Costa, the two rebellions were not simply coincidental events preliminary to the Phitsanulok strike but coordinated actions designed from the outset as diversionary stratagems within the larger plan of conquest.

A third contrast between da Costa's account and the conventional interpretation revolves around the leadership conflict that arose among the Siamese General Staff during the Nan River battle. As da Costa would have it, the disagreement arose out of Taksin's decision to pull back, overruling the insistence of his deputy commanders, the brothers Duang and Bunma, on holding Phitsanulok at all costs. In resolution of that rupture in battlefield decorum among the members of his inner circle, Taksin devolved full authority over the arena's northern sector – and all responsibility for the consequences – upon the brothers. That "turning point" encapsulates a fundamental transition from the ruling elite's comradeship of the Thonburi revival (recounted in Chapter 3) to the factional discord culminating in the 1782 reign change (examined in Chapter 7). As described in the present chapter, apparently on the basis of information provided by Prince Chak but nowhere referred to in the conventional sources, Taksin's insistence on the tactical imperatives of mobility, evasiveness, and avoidance of confrontation whenever troop strength favored the enemy was contested in this case by Duang and Bunma due to their personal attachment to Siam's northern capital, their feudal domain. The fact that they subsequently found their position untenable in the face of the overwhelming odds, as had been foreseen by Taksin, was an embarrassment subsequently cleansed from the record.

Lastly, da Costa's account departs from the conventional sources in displaying some ambivalence regarding the events leading to the city's abandonment. Were Duang and Bunma abandoned in the wake of their resistance to Taksin's strategic adjustment? Was the escape a reluctant confirmation of Taksin's tactical discernment? Did the city's evacuation achieve the invaders' aims, or did it open new lines of resistance for the defenders? The heroic action of saving the citizenry from the Burmese scourge was surely a desperate, last-ditch gamble in the midst of a losing cause. Should the escape be better seen as a brilliant victory, as emphasized in the conventional sources, or as a debacle? Diogo's Chronicle leaves the questions unresolved.

As with the fall of Ayutthaya a decade preciously, only the last-minute intervention of an unforeseen emergency within Burma saved Siam from annihilation. That extraordinary coincidence is studiously ignored in the conventional accounts, possibly because of its interference with the contrasting parables of Ayutthaya's moral decline and Thonburi's – and then Bangkok's – virtuous resurgence. It may also be a contributory reason why the Phitsanulok invasion has been largely glossed over in Thai popular history.

Subterfuge

Mang Ra was a cruel despot. He stamped his rule on Burma and its conquered territories with the harsh suppression of his subjects through confiscatory taxation, harsh conscription of men, and vile treatment of women. His aggressions against neighboring states were universally despised for their implacable ferocity. The pillage, devastation, and depopulation that his armies habitually left in their wake, compounded by the slave-like subservience that his military governors persisted in imposing on the subjugated peoples, led to successive waves of desperate rebellion. Such troubles intensified after Burma's premature withdrawal from Siam following his 1767 victory over Ayutthaya. Burma's hasty departure left a political vacuum that spawned further unanticipated troubles in the vanquished territories. But, most regrettably for him, it inadvertently allowed Siam's resurrection. Mang Ra decided to correct that error by brutal means.

A year or two after his negotiated peace with China's Ching emperor, Mang Ra conferred with his Minister of War, Asae Wunki,[2] to devise a plan to revive the interrupted effort to annihilate Siam. It was agreed that Burma's truncated military power in the aftermath of the Chinese wars required that aspirations for total conquest be pursued on a reduced scale. It was therefore decided that, instead of employing the previous two-pronged, northern/southern pincer campaign against Ayutthaya, the new assault would take the shorter, more direct route via the Myawaddy Pass across Siam's upriver rice plains to divide the kingdom and then proceed to destroy systematically its upper and lower halves. In support of that line of attack, a strategy of subterfuge was devised to draw Siam's military forces away from the center toward the northern and southern frontiers. The strategy was activated by intensifying Burma's military actions against the insurrections already underway along its eastern (Lan Na) and southern (Mon) frontiers. The planners expected that the superficial similarities between that pair of strikes and the Ayutthaya pincer campaign of 1765-1767 would lure Siam into deploying its forces toward both its northern and western frontiers in hopes of avoiding a repetition of the catastrophic loss of its capital city.

In Lan Na, Mang Ra's military governor, General Mayu Nguan, located at Chiangsaen on the banks of the Mekong River, was supplied with additional consignments of men and materiel. With that strengthened force he was directed to intensify his oppressive rule, and thereby draw Siam's interest. The unrest intensified into a coordinated rebellion when the chiefs of Chiangmai, Lamphun, and Lampang offered their vassalage to Siam in return for protection. The chiefs of Lan Na were close kin, said to be seven brothers, with their senior member being Prince Kawila of Lampang (later transferred to Chiangmai). They sealed their bond with Siam with the presentation of the traditional ceremonial tribute (in the form of gold and silver trees) as well as women in marriage. In ratification of that bond, a Siamese army headed by General Chakri (Duang) and his younger brother General Surasi (Bunma) marched north from Phitsanulok to support the Lan Na rebels, with King Taksin following with additional forces from Thonburi. The Burmese had not anticipated the strength of the Siamese response. Their base at Chiangmai fell to the combined attack on January 15, 1775,[3] compelling Mayu Nguan to retreat to his Chiangsaen redoubt, which was left as Burma's primary Lan Na outpost in its further struggles against Siam.

To the south, the restless Mon provinces stretching from the Irrawaddy Delta and Andaman seaboard into the Tenasserim hills faced similar upheaval. There, Mang Ra directed his military governor, General Sihabodi,[4] to conduct a full-scale conscription of all adult males, ignoring the standard practice of rotating months of military service with months of leave to allow them to harvest the rice crop. A popular uprising against that tyrannical rule was ruthlessly crushed by the Burmese occupiers. As anticipated, many of the dissidents fled across the hills to Siam, just as their forebears had done in earlier uprisings. A large body of Mon insurgents escaped across the Tenasserim Divide via the Three Pagodas Pass into Siamese sanctuary in a late-December 1774.[5] That flight of perhaps 10,000 refugees provided the Burmese strategists with the pretext for which they had been waiting to escalate their incursion with a provocative cross-border reprisal.

General Sihabodi had arrived in Yangon with his officers a dozen days before that insurgent flight to set up his headquarters and initiate preparations for the planned campaign. Shortly thereafter, the first of many contingents of raw conscripts arrived to fill out his army, and the march to Martaban, on the Andaman coast, at the mouth of the Salween River, got underway. There, they established a forward base where the conscripts were transformed into an effective fighting force. The peasant draftees were introduced to military discipline and drilled in basic battlefield tactics: close-rank and hand-to-hand combat, musketry, cannonry, entrenchment, sapping, and the other arts of war.[6] Much of the training was provided by a small group of French, Portuguese, Spanish, and other Europeans who had been taken, through one misfortune or another, into Burmese captivity. That preparatory regimen was kept secret from Siam's espionage network, which had in any case withered with the collapse of the Mon insurrection, while the Burmese conducted their own intensive surveillance of Siamese army dispositions, especially the movements of King Taksin and his senior staff officers. By the start of the next rainy season, in mid-1775, a 25,000-man Burmese fighting force had been assembled, equipped with an enormous cache of arms, munitions, and food stocks.

Many months earlier, as soon as the annual rains had receded and the slippery hill trails had dried sufficiently to allow his troops a solid footing, General Sihabodi had ordered General Khongwun, his deputy commander at Martaban, to lead a brigade of 5,000 men up the Ataran River and across the Three Pagodas Pass in pursuit of the recently absconded Mon rebels. General Khongwun's cross-mountain adventure was harassed by Mon skirmishers but could not be deterred from pressing on to Pak Praek, at the confluence of the Khwae Yai and Khwae Noi rivers.[7] Their orders were to draw a Siamese counterstrike in support of the outnumbered Mon, so they continued their advance into the lowlands, raiding for loot and captives just as they had done successfully during the Ayutthaya campaign a decade before. Upon reaching Bang Kaew, a hard day's march southeast of Pak Praek, General Khongwun learned that a strong Siamese force was approaching Ratburi. To defend against that threat, he divided his regiments among three well-fortified camps situated at Pak Praek, Bang Kaew, and Khao Cha-ngum to await the anticipated combat.

King Taksin learned of the Burmese cross-border incursion as he was returning down river to Thonburi in mid-February 1775 from his Chiangmai triumph. Within days of reaching Thonburi, he rushed on to Ratburi to deal with the developing crisis.[8] The month-long fast march from Lan Na to Ratburi by way of Thonburi left his three Royal Guard regiments in need of brief recuperation. During that respite, his scouts' thorough reconnoiter of the area corroborated the information provided by the local Mon chiefs and convinced him of the gravity of the situation. To halt any further advance by the Burmese forces, he ordered the mobilization of 6,000 troops from the western seaboard provinces, under the command of some of his most trusted subordinates. Further support came a dozen days later with Duang's rushed arrival from Chiangmai at the head of a 3,000-man army and Bunma's dash with an equal force from Phitsanulok. For the Burmese, it was a successful start to their planned division and devitalization of Siamese military capabilities.

General Sihabodi was pleased to learn that his cross-border diversion was being met by a hasty Siamese response. To bolster the Burmese fighting strength, he ordered the dispatch of an additional brigade through the pass. Confronting one another across the Mae Klong River rice tracts, General Khongwun at Bang Kaew and King Taksin at Ratburi oversaw a continuing series of scouting and raiding probes that gradually defined the theater of action. Prominent among the Thai contingents were two regiments led by Prince Inthara Phithak (Chui) and a third regiment under Prince Anurak Songkhram (Ramlak). Both princes carried senior royal titles at the Thonburi court but were junior in military experience and hesitant combatants; their appointment to such prominent army commands reflects Siam's leadership shortages of the day. Two other, more battle-hardened officers brought in to support their efforts were Colonel Ramanwong (Madot), leading three Mon militia regiments, and Colonel Thibet Bodin (personal name unknown), director of the Royal Guard and not long to live, heading two regiments charged with defending Taksin's Ratburi headquarters. Duang and Bunma established their joint headquarters at a forward position from which they could besiege the Bang Kaew camp. The beleaguered Burmese soon ran short of rice rations and resorted to subsisting on boiled swamp grasses and the flesh of their elephants and horses, though plentiful well-water remained available. Incoming mortar, cannon, and musket fire killed many, and the survivors were kept busy digging graves to ward off pestilence.

The Siamese strategy aimed to prevent the Burmese from consolidating their forces by besieging each of their three camps separately, starving them individually, and assaulting them as they weakened. One by one, the Burmese stockades were pulverized by the besiegers' guns, the camps were overrun, and many prisoners were taken. The Bang Kaew camp was the first to fall, at the peak of the hot season, days before the New Year. General Khongwun and his officers were captured, interrogated, and put to death, but their troops were spared that fate; instead, they were held in close confinement for transport to remote locations as war captives. Most of the troops manning the remaining two Burmese camps, however, managed to fight their way through the encirclement and flee into the hills. At the height of the battle, the Burmese troop strength was about 9,000, while that of the combined Siamese forces reached 20,000. Of the total Burmese force, some 1,600 died in the three besieged camps, and more were killed in the retreat, but the majority managed to find their way back to Martaban. The Ratburi encounter was claimed by the Siamese as a resounding victory. For Asae Wunki at his Martaban headquareters, however, it was little more than the distraction it had been meant to be, serving the larger purpose of spreading the Siamese military front north and south, distracting their strategists, consuming their munitions, and fatiguing their forces. He considered his losses a price well worth the damage inflicted on Siamese capabilities and the uncertainties he had implanted in the Siamese military mind.

Invasion

The Burmese defeat at Chiangmai in January 1775, followed by the fall of Bang Kaew in March, were considered minor setbacks by Mang Ra. Those battles did not end the war; instead, they had the intended impact of dispersing the focus of Siamese military concerns between the far north and the southwest. They did nothing to deter Asae Wunki from continuing his preparations for a lightning strike through the weakly defended midsection, aiming for Sukhothai and Phitsanulok. To that end, he proceeded with his secret troop training and arms stockpiling at the Andaman coastal camps awaiting the end of the monsoon rains. Once the waters had receded and the muddy mountain tracks had dried sufficiently to permit concentrated troop transport, the Burmese strike force received its marching orders. They set off from Martaban in late December on a dash straight east across the Myawaddy Pass, which they had purposely neglected in earlier incursions while diverting the Siamese defenses to the far-off Three Pagodas Pass. From Tak they swept across Siam's north-central plain toward Kamphaeng Phet and Sukhothai, with the objective of more distant Phitsanulok. The strategy was to astonish the unsuspecting opposition with headlong force, focused pressure, and irresistible advance across a narrow front.

News of Asae Wunki's invasion reached Taksin as a complete surprise. The week that it took for Mon couriers to carry the news past the Burmese vanguard from the Myawaddy crossing to Thonburi left the Siamese armies unprepared to intercept the Burmese incursion in good time. Instantly recouping his poise, and confronting the emergency with his typical audacity, Taksin activated his forces and devised his war strategy with lightning speed. Within days of receiving word of the invasion, in mid-January 1776, he was hastening upriver from Thonburi by state barge, gathering a 12,000-man army as he proceeded through the Central Plains provinces. His forces preceded him, but they approached the Burmese line of march too late. Asae Wunki had already sped past the Tak waystation to take Kamphaeng Phet and Sukhothai. Taksin therefore set up his base camp near the downstream Nakhon Sawan transport hub, from which his battalions could set off in any direction at a moment's notice. By good fortune, Duang was currently bivouacked with his division at Phitsanulok, his regular stopover between Thonburi and the northern front. In the absence of his brother Bunma, who was engaged in continued military operations against Burmese-held Chiangsaen, he was contacted by Taksin with instructions to prepare for an expected Burmese assault. Bunma was informed and rushed home, but his regiments were delayed along the way in encounters with Burmese elements. His battalions assaulted both Sawankhalok and Sukhothai but were unable to penetrate the Burmese lines, so he disengaged and rushed on by a roundabout route to join his brother. To the north, his Lan Na allies, recently freed from Burmese subjugation, had been more successful in their engagements with the Burmese, preventing contingents from Burma's Chiangsaen base from pressing south to link up with Asae Wunki.

The Burmese offensive swept virtually unopposed across the Siamese lowlands toward its Phitsanulok objective. At his Sawankhalok headquarters in mid-January, Asae Wunki interrogated local Siamese officials regarding the current whereabouts of the elusive Tiger General (Bunma). He was already aware that Duang was entrenched at Phitsanulok, so he ordered his vanguard, encamped along the Yom River near Sukhothai, to await the arrival of reinforcements from Chiangsaen – which never arrived – while he sought clarification of Bunma's whereabouts and refined his battle strategy. A half month's idleness lay in store for his troops before the battle ignited. During those listless days, his junior officers were kept fully occupied in dealing with issues of low troop morale.[9] Throughout the depopulated countryside still recovering from the Burmese ravages of a decade before, marauding detachments of the invading army terrorized the surviving village communities.[10]

Within hours of his arrival at Phitsanulok, Bunma was urging his brother to join him in deploying their combined forces for an assault on the Burmese forward positions.[11] Duang cautioned against such rash action, suggesting that Taksin, already en route to their aid, would surely insist on making the command decision himself. Furthermore, Bunma's troops were exhausted from their long travel through the hills from Chiangmai, interrupted by repeated combat along the way. They needed a respite. Reluctantly, Bunma agreed to defer the decision. He rested his men while he sought to replenish their munitions and strengthen the riparian city's defenses. The city walls were strengthened with additional gun batteries lining the parapets along its length; booms were extended across the river to block the city's upstream and downstream approaches; the external artillery redoubts defending the city moat and

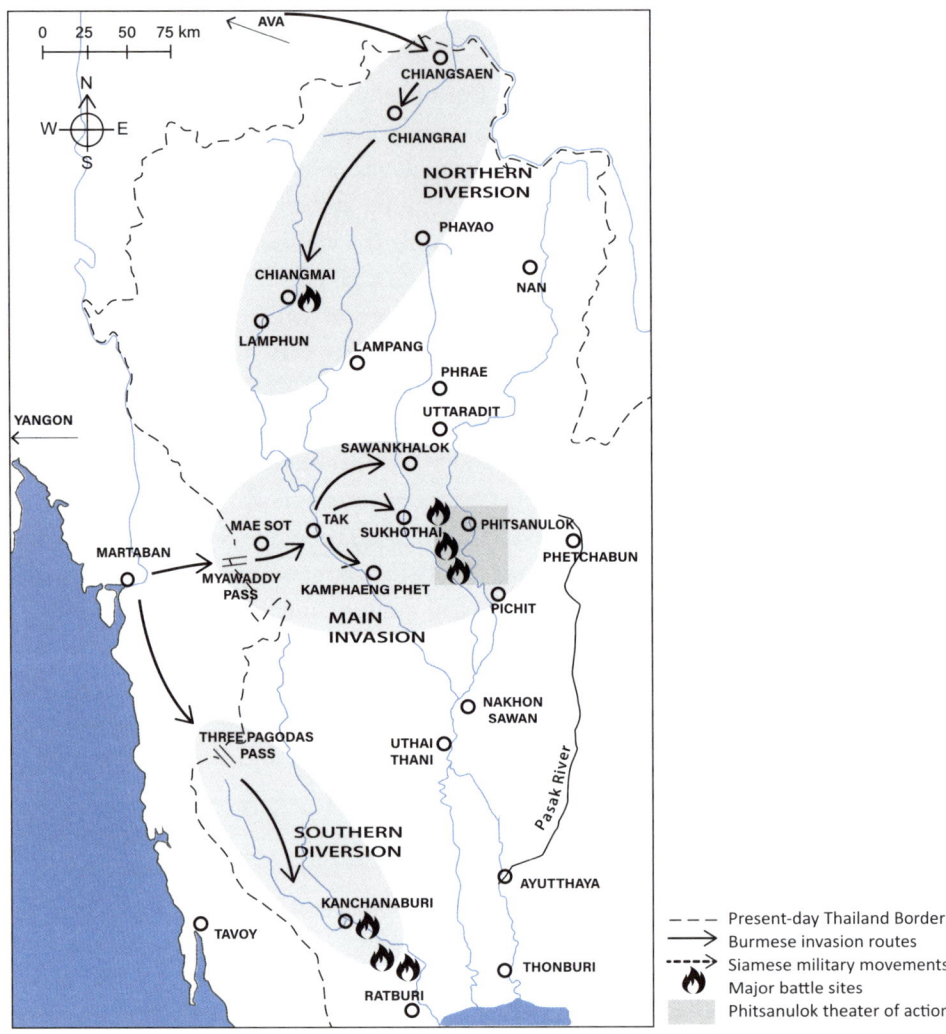

Map 11. The Burmese campaign of 1775–1776

its principal land and water gates were hastily reinforced with spiked entrenchments. With his brother's aid, he gathered the people within the walled city and provisioned them as best he could in anticipation of a protracted siege.

The Burmese siege gathered strength in stages. Bunma's withdrawal to Phitsanulok induced Asae Wunki to advance his main force of 30,000 men to a ring of three widely spaced stockaded camps within striking distance of the western city wall, with instructions to enforce an embargo on all passing traffic. As a provocation, he took to massing as many as 3,000 troops within open view of the city, though still well beyond gunshot, to gain a better sense of the city's defensive capabilities. Additional forward positions were set up as the besiegers gained their footing. The Siamese defenders sent out skirmishers to deal with the increasing nuisance of Burmese reconnaissance teams and harassing forays daring to approach the city walls, but they inflicted little damage on the cautious probers. On the broader front, the rice tracts and open countryside stretching across the full-day's marching distance from the Burmese base camps at Sawankhalok, Sukhothai, and Kamphaeng Phet to the Phitsanulok front were transformed into a wasteland isolating the besieged city from its western outskirts.

Duang and Bunma regarded Phitsanulok and its surrounding feudal fiefdom as their family birthright, as their father had served there in a senior capacity during the principality's brief interlude as an independent state and had died there during that time. Accordingly, they considered it their hereditary duty to hold the city, against all odds, as the linchpin connecting Siam with its Lan Na confederates.[12] At the peak of their troop strength they commanded a combined force of 20-or-so battle-ready regiments. Cut off by the invading forces from the agrarian flatlands to the west, the city's remaining supply lifeline lay along the narrow, winding Nan River extending far downstream to Nakhon Sawan. The transport of supplies from Nakhon Sawan required many days of toil against the current, an especially challenging task because of the river's twisting course, shifting shoals, hidden snags, seasonal surges and droughts, and stretches of jagged shoreline. To defend that essential waterway, the defenders laid out a protected corridor extending inland from each riverbank along its entire length northward from Pak Phing to Phitsanulok. In addition, the narrow Kraphuang Canal, reaching west from the Nan River at Pak Phing to the Yom River, was secured to provide a secondary downstream supply route. Along the vulnerable upper reaches of that narrow transport corridor, between Phitsanulok and Pak Phing, they set up a string of five heavily fortified guardposts – Ban Khaek, Wat Chulamani, Ban Bang Kradat, Ban Tha Rong, and Bang Sai – each assigned a battalion headed by a seasoned commander.[13]

A placid stretch of the Nan River not far from Phitsanulok. (Editor's photo)

It took not much more than six days for Phitsanulok's defensive preparations along that entire river stretch to be completed. Squadrons of armed flatboats were kept busy patroling the river channel against any Burmese attempt to harass the supply line or cross to the east bank. Mobile artillery detachments armed with jingals were deployed to strategic points along the winding river route, ready to move into position against any threat.[14] As additional protection, a 500-man cavalry corps was assigned to escort the supply-raft convoys along riverside paths. However, communication among the dispersed strongpoints along that lengthy river corridor consumed both time and manpower. Troop coordination across the extended theater of action proved to be a persistent weakness. By contrast, the fewer, concentrated Burmese troop positions were a strength on which Asae Wunki consistently relied.

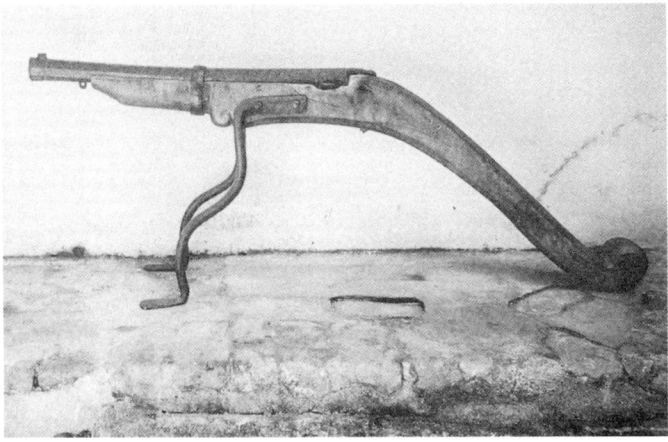

An 18th-century *jingal* (or gingal) muzzle-loading field artillery piece. (courtesy of the Colombo National Museum, Sri Lanka). Such heavy-duty firearms requiring tripod support served in 18th-century warfare as mobile artillery pieces capable of being discharged from set positions on open ground or from defensive embrasures, boat deck, or elephant-back. The illustrated example shows a small version weighing approximately 15 kgs and having a bore of 2-3 cm. in diameter. Larger jingals could weigh up to 50 kgs, capable of firing balls of 8 cm, each weighing up to half a kilogram.

While the threatened city girded its defenses, Asae Wunki ordered his massed forward units, within reach of the city wall, to consolidate their battle positions, leaving no more than a 5,000-man rear guard at Sukhothai. He had intended to replenish his besieging forces with supplies from Chiangsaen but was prevented from doing so by the continuing harassment of Taksin's Lan Na allies. Instead, he was forced to turn to the less reliable sources available in the devastated flatlands stretching toward the western frontier. His dwindling rice stores proved increasingly difficult to replenish, as

Siamese marauders were well placed to intercept his supply convoys trudging across the rolling plain. Despite that continuing distraction, his forward brigades achieved their objective in short order. They positioned themselves as a concentrated force divided among the three forward base camps – known simply as North, Central, and South – less than an hour's march west of the city wall, awaiting further orders. Asae Wunki rode forth from his Sawankhalok headquarters to observe the disposition of his forces, the city defenses, and the terrain of the future battleground.[15] A lurking threat was the possibility that Taksin's army approaching from Nakhon Sawan would link up with Duang and Bunma at Phitsanulok to mount a major counterattack. He therefore deployed 2,000 of his 5,000-man Sukhothai reserves to increase the troop strength facing Phitsanulok, with most of the remaining 3,000 deployed to Kamphaeng Phet to reconnoiter the Yom and Nan River corridors reaching toward Nakhon Sawan. He then ordered a pause, awaiting the hoped-for supply replenishments from Chiangsaen and further clarification of the Siamese fighting intentions.

Gauntlet

By early February 1776, Taksin had established his battlefield headquarters at Pak Phing, linchpin of the Nan River transport corridor, about a day's journey down the winding river from Phitsanulok. Asae Wunki had set up his forward headquarters at Nong Huai Yang, amid the rice fields behind the frontline battalions charged with besieging the city. As the siege intensified, he took to spending more of his time there than at his comfortable Sawankhalok base. From that post he could personally observe the extent to which the plodding, incremental pace of his advance was wearing down his troops without perceptible impact on the more agile Siamese adversary. Increasingly, he became preoccupied with his conscripts' chronic malingering, recalcitrance, and desertion, compounded by the declining rice stocks resulting from the harassment inflicted on his supply convoys by Siamese marauders.

After days of sporadic skirmishing along the Nan River battlefront, the tempo of combat rose with an audacious Siamese assault on the nearest forward camp. Led by Bunma's cavalry, the attack sped from the Phitsanulok fortifications across the fallow fields toward the Burmese South Camp. Mobile field cannon and mortars were dragged into position by horse and elephant with the aim of blasting entry through the camp's palisade. Several Burmese gun emplacements were sufficiently damaged to enable Bunma's fighters to charge into the Burmese lines for hand-to-hand combat, where their superior swordsmanship gained them the advantage. Although many warriors were lost in the bloody melee, the bulk of the Burmese forces remained largely unscathed behind their unbreeched stockade and could not be drawn back into open-field engagement. After a night's futile attempts to storm the ramparts, the Siamese assailants withdrew. The stalemate continued through the next several days with a series of indecisive encounters. It was a confused time for both sides as each searched fruitlessly for an effective opening.

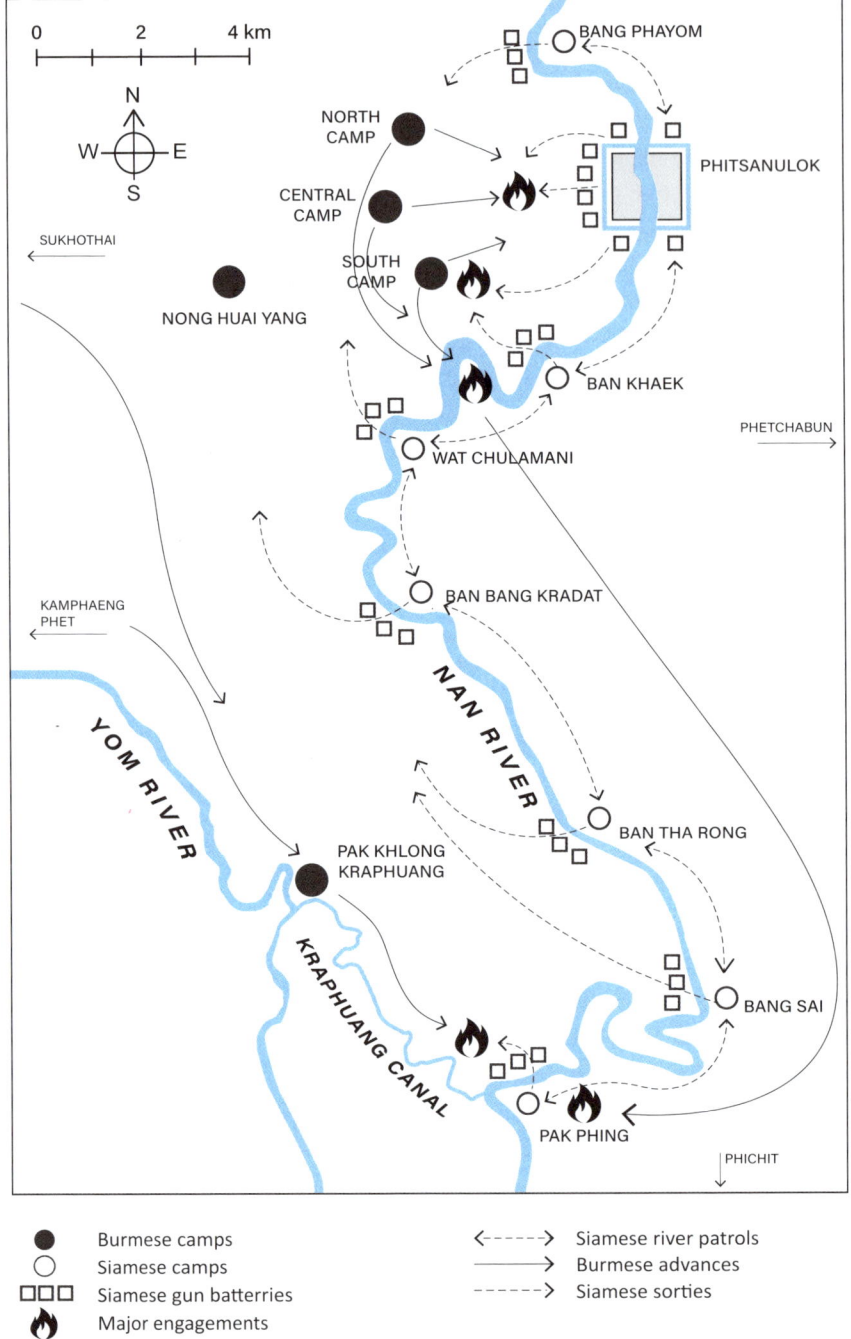

Map 12. The Phitsanulok theater of action, February–March, 1776

The situation clarified as Asae Wunki shifted his attention from his initial strategy of besieging the city's western approaches toward harassing its downriver supply corridor. That new front greatly widened the focus of combat, thinning Siam's defense lines. The firmly stockaded, gunned, garrisoned, and provisioned Siamese camps, set at cannon-shot intervals along the river's Left Bank, were linked with one another by ceaseless naval patrols, mobile shoreline gun batteries, and cavalry marches. Conversely, the open tracts stretching west from the river's Right Bank comprised a no-man's land, a broad terrain across which sporadic Siamese raids and Burmese sorties roamed in search of one another's weaknesses. The city's closest downriver strongpoint, Ban Khaek, nearest the Burmese forward camps, received Asae Wunki's concentrated attention. To weaken the Siamese defenses, he slipped some of his forces further south to outflank their lines. That tactic was, in turn, quickly parried by Taksin's redisposition of his troops. Each time Taksin moved contingents from the upstream strongpoints further downstream, however, Asae Wunki dispatched skirmishers to pressure the commensurately reduced upstream stretches. The constant positional adjustments posed a logistical challenge for both commanders but exerted a greater toll on the lesser strength of Siam's forces dispersed among a larger number of entrenched outposts.

Despite their successive downriver thrusts, the Burmese were unable to dislodge the defenders. The Right Bank line of stockaded forts and military cantonments was fronted along the opposite shore by clusters of mobile gun batteries shielded behind staked earthworks. Any attack on those emplacements could be readily supported by infantry crossings of the river from the Left Bank bases. The intermediate, less accessible, steep-banked river stretches were patroled by Siamese cavalry platoons, whose exertions were immense over the dozens of days of constant surveillance along the twisting riverbanks. Repeated Burmese sorties in search of weak points proved futile; musket volleys and grapeshot fusillades served the Siamese side as effective deterrents against all attempts to ford the fast-flowing waters. Days of repeated efforts produced inconclusive results.

Finally, the tide of battle turned. A convoy of rice-laden barges, rafts, and lesser rivercraft, protected by Siamese sharpshooters crouching among the trees and escorted along the riverside paths by several companies of foot-soldiers and outriders, proceeded upstream from Nakhon Sawan to Pak Phing without incident. However, the second leg of the gauntlet stretching from Pak Phing to Phitsanulok did not go as smoothly, despite the supportive string of riverside forts. On February 12, a company of hand-picked Burmese commandos managed to intercept the convoy as it wound around the sharp riverbend between Wat Chulamani and Ban Khaek. Skillfully evading Siam's patrols, their jingals managed to hull several heavily laden rice-rafts. The wrecked vessels obstructed the channel, preventing the rest from proceeding to their destination. One party of Burmese marauders managed to cross the neglected riverbend and establish a Left Bank beachhead, providing cover for the emplacement of sufficient field cannon to ward off further boat passage. With those obstacles, no further resupply convoys dared risk the Nan River gauntlet, introducing a new phase to the combat.

The strategic importance of that supply line interdiction was not lost on the opposing generals. In a remarkable instance of parallel battlefield decision-making, the Burmese and Siamese commanders engaged independently in a near-simultaneous pair of strategic adjustments. In view of his positional gain, Asae Wunki decided to extend his advantage downriver to the Kraphuang Canal. He ordered three regiments to rush toward the new front from Kamphaeng Phet, while two supplementary regiments were readied to join them from Sukhothai. Conversely, Taksin, recognizing the disastrous implications of the Burmese river interdiction, drew the bulk of his troops back to his Pak Phing base at the Kraphuang Canal's Nan River confluence. That short canal transport link between the Nan and Yom River corridors thus became a new flashpoint. With the focus of the fighting gravitating ever further downstream from Phitsanulok, the besieged city experienced some respite from intensive harassment, but it found itself increasingly isolated from relief.

Immediately after the hiatus attending the commemoration of Makha Bucha,[16] Asae Wunki on February 21 initiated the construction of fortifications for a large, palisaded camp at the Yom River confluence of the Kraphuang Canal.[17] Taksin learned of that undertaking a day later and without delay convened a General Staff meeting at Ban Tha Rong. Many of the particulars of that gathering remain obscure, but it is evident that the discussions did not go well. He opened the meeting with a summary of the shifting battlefield situation and a stern declaration that the resulting contours of engagement left beleaguered Phitsanulok indefensible. Its commanding officers should thus prepare for evacuation, while the downriver battalions should shoulder the brunt of the fighting along the new Kraphuang Canal front.

Taksin asked for his generals' views. Bunma, with Duang at his side, broke the silence that followed with an impassioned declaration that he believed Phitsanulok's sustainability to be still feasible. All thought of abandoning Phitsanulok in the wake of recent events, he suggested, should be laid to rest. He expressed the view that the main problem facing the encircled city was not manpower inadequacy but supply shortage. The path to victory, as he saw it, lay in outlasting the besiegers with intensified harassment, supplemented by the development of a new supply corridor via the Pasak River route through Phetchabun. Duang quietly concurred.

In the face of such unprecedented opposition, Taksin meditated for a moment, and in a deliberate cadence responded with a compromise strategy – a north-south division of the battlefield command. The defense of the beleaguered city and its supply corridor south to Ban Tha Rong would be assigned to the command of Duang and Bunma, and they were encouraged to explore the possibility of a Pasak River corridor. The southern theater, centering on the Kraphuang Canal and Pak Phing, would remain under Taksin's direct command. Taksin's abrupt proposal was presented, in effect, as an order, broaching no comment, leaving the assemblage astounded, and tongue-tied. The matter was thus decided; all were obliged to comply with their king's directive.

As the General Staff adjourned in somber disarray, its departure was interrupted by the rumble of distant gunfire announcing the onset of a concerted Burmese advance. The gathered commanders sprang into instant action. Taksin hastened to support his threatened downriver headquarters. Duang and Bunma rushed off to take up their command responsibilities at Phitsanulok. The others dashed to marshal their battalions for action at their respective riverside strongpoints.

Taksin reached the scene of battle well before sunrise to find that the Burmese had pushed down the Kraphuang Canal nearly to the Nan River confluence and his Pak Phing camp. With their overwhelming odds they had already overrun several of Siam's forward positions. The fighting continued into the early morning hours. Later that day, February 23, Taksin led the Royal Guard in a cross-river charge to relieve his remaining hard-pressed Kraphuang Canal gun batteries. Several Siamese regiments continued their counter-advance toward the Burmese base camp at Pak Khlong Kraphuang; their assault continued for three days but was unable to force any retreat of the far greater Burmese numbers. In the face of the impregnable Burmese position, Taksin deputed Colonels Ratana Phimon and Thep Orachun to take active command of the Khlong Kraphuang sub-theater while he withdrew to his headquarters to devise further strategy. At dusk that day, having received word of his departure, the Burmese mounted an assault on the royal camp, but they could not penetrate its defenses. Under the vigorous leadership of Taksin's two favored adjutant officers, Siam's downriver battlefront narrowly held its ground.

Duang and Bunma, after returning to Phitsanulok, had little time to firm up the northern sector's defenses before Asae Wunki activated a ruse, opening a new salient along the upriver corridor in a masterly three-phased feat of deception. First, he intensified the skirmishing along the city's western perimeter. Having focused the city defenders' attention on that flashpoint, he moved to the second phase by changing course with a sudden strike on the Ban Khaek outpost downstream via the cross-river beachhead that had been established nearby. Dozens of field-cannon were dragged forward to aid in pulverizing the Siamese breastworks. That engagement provided cover for the culminating third phase, under which he pushed the bulk of his forces through the cross-river breach, not to escalate the Ban Khaek fighting but to rush downriver along the Left Bank, unopposed, to double his attack on the downstream front with a surprise assault on the unprotected rear of the royal base at Pak Phing.

Asae Wunki's gambit bore results on February 27. After two days of inconclusive combat at Ban Khaek he mounted a concerted attack on a single riverside battery. Phitsanulok was informed that the 240-man artillery emplacement had been surrounded and was about to be overrun. Instead of instructing the cannoneers to withdraw, Duang ordered the mobilization of all available forces to support them in a decisive, do-or-die defense against the Burmese assault. In following that command

Siamese troops awaiting battle orders. (No Na Paknam, *Murals Explained* (in Thai), Bangkok: Muang Boran, 1993, p. 86)

Siam's position held, but at the cost of a severe depletion of personnel and munitions and a weakening of the neighboring riverside strongpoints that came to their aid. With their reduced resources, the riverside defenders were unable to withstand a broader Burmese river crossing. It was with that masterfully orchestrated Nan River probe that Asae Wunki was able finally to penetrate the hard-pressed Left Bank defenses and race downriver to attack the Pak Phing from the river.

The Siamese forces along the Kraphuang Canal front were placed under great stress to withstand a broader collapse of the river corridor. After more than a half month of continuous fighting, Taksin and the Royal Guard, three regiments strong, withdrew from the Pak Phing battlefield on March 14 to reassemble at a rearguard encampment near Pichit, a day's march downriver. With that defeat, entailing the loss of the Kraphuang Canal transport route, the abandonment of their Pak Phing strongpoint, and the definitive interdiction of the Nan River transport route, Siam's chances of successful defense against the Phitsanulok siege ebbed. The Siamese forces had lost the battle for control of the Kraphuang Canal against a brilliantly conceived Burmese action. It was Asae Wunki's greatest tactical triumph. The Burmese noose had been secured around the beleaguered northern capital. His advantage in numbers, reliance on massed strength, and rapid advances had bested Taksin's strategy on force dispersion, agility, and resolve. The defenders' hopes of breaking the siege of Phitsanulok had been crushed.[18]

Table 5. Major Siamese military campaigns and principal engagements, 1767-1782

Year	Campaigns/engagements	Commanders [a]
1767	**Eastern seaboard expedition** Seizure of Chanthaburi (June 1767)	Taksin
	Chaophraya heartland campaign Battle at Thonburi (October 1767) Battle at Pho Sam Ton (November 1767)	Taksin
1768	**First Ratburi campaign** Engagements at Bang Kung (January-February 1768)	Taksin
	First Phitsanulok campaign Battle at Tambon Keichai (October 1768)	Taksin
	Phimai campaign Battles at Prachinburi, Khorat, Phimai (December 1768)	Duang and Bunma
1769	**Southern campaign** Seizure of Nakhon Si Thammarat (September 1769)	Taksin
	En route to the battle of Nakhon Si Thammarat, Taksin suffered a grievous wound and remained incommunicado until early 1770.	
	First (aborted) Cambodia campaign Battle at Siamrat (October 1769) Retreat to Khorat (October-November 1769)	Duang and Bunma
1770	**Sawangkhaburi campaign** Battle at Phitsanulok (August 1770) Battle at Sawangkhaburi (August 1770)	Taksin and Bunma
1771	**First Chiangmai campaign** First battle at Chiangmai (early 1771)	Taksin and Bunma
	Second Cambodia campaign Seizure of Udong (November 1771) Battle at Ha Tien (October 1771)	Taksin, Duang, and Bunma
1774/75	**Second Chiangmai campaign** Second battle at Chiangmai (January 1757)	Taksin, Duang, and Bunma
1775	**Second Ratburi campaign** Battles at Bang Kaew (February-April 1775)	Taksin, Duang, and Bunma
	Third Chiangmai campaign Third battle at Chiangmai (October 1775)	Duang and Bunma
1776	**Second Phitsanulok campaign** Burmese siege of Phitsanulok (February-March 1776)	Taksin, Duang, and Bunma
	After the battle of Phitsanulok, Taksin did not participate in any further military campaigns	
	Battles at Kamphaeng Phet, Uthai Thani, and Nakhon Sawan (May-June 1776)	
	Fourth Chiangmai campaign Fourth battle at Chiangmai (October 1776)	Bunma
1777	**Nangrong/Champasak expedition** (February-March)	Duang
1778/79	**Vientiane campaign** Seizure of Champasak (early 1779) Siege of Vientiane (December 1778 – March 1779)	Duang and Bunma
1781/82	**Third Cambodia campaign** Seizure of Udong from Vietnamese partisans (February 1781)	Duang and Bunma
1782	**Coup and countercoup at Thonburi** (March – April 1782)	Thong-in and Duang

Breakout

The division of Siam's command structure between the campaign's northern and southern sectors freed Taksin to concentrate his full attention on the struggling downriver reaches. At the same time, the independent command of the northern battlefront that he had conferred on Duang and Bunma raised their prominence from adjunct participants in the military command structure to principal contenders. The previous day's disruptive General Staff meeting, where unprecedented dissension over battlefield strategy had erupted between the brothers and their king, had marked a turning point in the tenor of personal relations among the Thonburi leadership.[19]

In a final word of caution, the brothers had been counseled by Taksin that, if they were bent on the defense of Phitsanulok rather than its capitulation, they should by no means hazard a head-on battle against an adversary so formidable in the field as Asae Wunki, but instead use delay as a continuing tactic, for that would gradually diminish his resources, erode his patience, and cloud his judgment.[20] The practicality of that advice was greatly diminished when, upon their return to Phitsanulok, the brothers found, to their dismay, that the city's fighting strength had deteriorated considerably under conditions of mounting deprivation. Stocks of both rice and arms had been depleted. Famine and pestilence, as is usual when people are driven to subsisting upon any food they can get, had begun to assail the city.[21] Even more distressing, the city's military manpower – even with the redeployment of the surviving troops from its upstream strongpoints, totaling not many more than 2,000 fighting men – would not be sufficient to fortify its defenses against a concentrated Burmese onslaught. Without hope of immediate infusions of rice, munitions, and manpower reinforcements, the besieged city would soon be forced to submit. Realizing that they could not prevail, the brothers came to the humiliating conclusion that they would, after all, have to abandon the city, and destroy its fortifications and all other facilities of possible use to the enemy.

They proceeded to prepare an escape plan for Phitsanulok's citizenry and its troops. While Duang set about making the necessary military preparations, Bunma addressed the city elders on their likely fate should the Burmese succeed in their onslaught. Recalling the horrors that had accompanied the fall of Ayutthaya, the townspeople readily cast their lot with the brothers. They committed their lives in support of the military imperative. The details of a mass evacuation were decided before the day was done, and the necessary arrangements were quickly put in place. All the town's movables were gathered for the flight. After the townspeople and their paltry possessions had been assembled in readiness at the base of the east wall, all the bridges crossing the river and lesser waterways flowing through the city's midst were dismantled, to prevent easy pursuit.

At the moment of the first distant pre-dawn cock's crow, March 16, the plan was activated. A cacophony of pipes, flutes, and bugles sounded a thrilling military cadence from atop the west wall's parapets, facing the Burmese camps, announcing to the invaders the city's determination to take up the fight. The cannon batteries fronting the wall blasted a crescendo of fire toward the Burmese positions from morning to night. Late that evening, the city's barricaded troops were assembled and supplied with arms for battle. At the prearranged moment, they stormed forth from the western city gate in full panoply as if to fight a do-or-die battle. The onward-rushing infantry battalions were accompanied by charging squadrons of cavalry and trumpeting elephants, raising clouds of dust and confusion, guarding in their midst a pair of senior officers masquerading as Duang and Bunma – both of whom were preoccupied elsewhere in their urgent preparations for evacuation. Unsuspecting, Asae Wunki's army advanced steadily in standard Burmese set-piece "crow's-foot" battle formation, the infantry pushing forward in close ranks, spike-tipped muskets to the fore, cavalry and elephantry following, ready to thrust through on command at the propitious moment. The more agile, loosely organized Siamese fighting forces rushed into battle en masse, on foot, horseback, and elephant, swords and lances flashing in search of close combat. As the two armies were about to collide, the Siamese troops abruptly turned tail and bolted back toward the city gates as if in terror, many abandoning their arms to speed their flight. The feint proved a decisive success, with the cheering, jeering invaders chasing them to the city wall, The guns massed along the ramparts fired a withering stream of grapeshot into the jubilant Burmese ranks, cutting blood-soaked carnage, forcing the survivors into panicked retreat. Most of the

Burmese "crow's-foot" battle formation, the classic attack mode favored by Asae Wunki. (Courtesy of the Asian Studies Center, Chulalongkorn University)

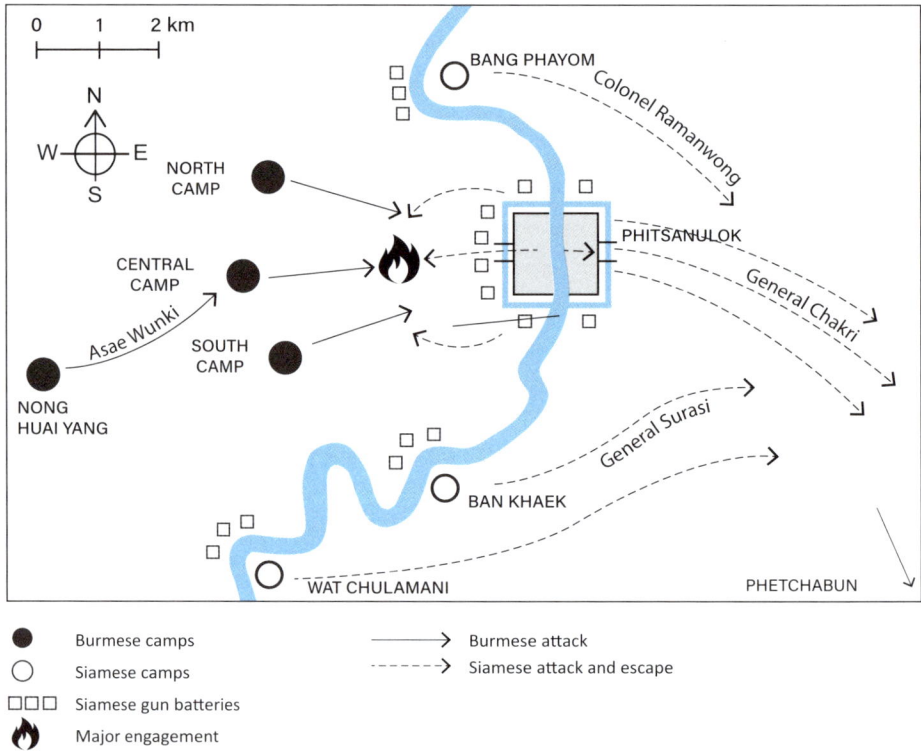

Map 13. The escape from Phitsanulok, March 15, 1776

city's remaining firepower was exhausted in that devastating barrage. Although the defenders lost dozens of men, the assailants suffered hundreds of casualties. Duang's grand deception had saved the day.

Hours earlier, a minor eastern city gate, hidden from Burmese observation behind a tamarind grove, had been prized open, allowing Siamese commando detachments to slip through in silent ambush of the widely spaced, thinly manned eastern-flank Burmese siege-posts. At other east-wall gate, the able-bodied townspeople, some 15,000 strong, were assembled to slip away in lengthy files into the night. In the midst of that mass escape, a violent thunderclap announced the onset of an early-season nighttime downpour. A deluge of wind-driven rain swept across the terrain. The city's two commanders turned that providential torrent to their advantage. While the unsuspecting enemy sentries, posted within musket-shot of the city wall, cowered beneath the dripping foliage awaiting the storm's passage, the townspeople were marshalled into compact bands, the gates were pushed further open, and all filtered through at utmost speed. The city's abandonment was organized in classic campaign formation: the forward armed elements were prepared to force passage through the besiegers' lines; the central battalions escorted the city's citizenry, with cavalry squadrons protecting the flanks; and the rear units defended all against pursuit while conveying their paltry arms and food stocks. Cutting through the heart of the undermanned Burmese siege posts, the two generals and their troops guided the escaping multitude in a muffled rush to the southeast, the start of an arduous three-day flight through rough hill country toward the beckoning Pa Sak River valley and Phetchabun sanctuary.

They left behind an empty city, its defenses dismantled, its markets and homes abandoned, its wells poisoned, its gardens hacked to stumps, only its temples and shrines spared – a hollow triumph for the Burmese invaders after their months-long siege. All that remained, sheltered among the cloister walls and deserted monastic dormitories of Wat Yai was a huddled encampment of perhaps 500 elderly, infirm, and ailing starvelings under the care of a bevy of steadfast monks, left with meager provisions to face the uncertain mercies of the invading horde.[22] Phitsanulok had fallen without the defeat of its defenders; they had fled a city stripped of booty. The conquerors took revenge on the peoples' successful escape by burning to the ground what was left and demolishing what remained of the city's defenses. The fate of those left behind is unknown. At his Nong Huai Yang headquarters, Asae Wunki pieced together the confused reports of his troops' hollow victory and drew up his retaliatory tactics. In the absence of clear directives from Ava to guide the next phase of the campaign, there was little that he could do, and little of value to be gained from pursuing the fleeing rabble.

The following several months were marked by indecisive action.[23] News had filtered down the military grapevine that Mang Ra was fatally ill. Both the Thai and

Phra Phutha Chinarat, the presiding Buddha image in the congregation hall of Wat Phra Si Ratana Mahathat (formerly Wat Mahathat, or simply Wat Yai), Phitsanulok. (Wikipedia Commons)

Burmese commanders showed reticence in taking major action while they awaited further word on that potentially new dynamic. Bivouacked within the deserted city, the Burmese invaders faced supply deficiencies nearly as critical as those that had confronted by the defenders. Bunma's roving raiders had greatly aggravated the Burmese forward camps' access to their Kamphaeng Phet food stores. Despite their reduced situation, the Siamese troops, dispersed into mobile marauders' contingents roaming a broad contested terrain stretching west from Phitsanulok to the Tenasserim Divide, continued to fight a defensive campaign of great courage, though their utmost efforts were insufficient to drive the enemy from the field.[24] Asae Wunki's intention of moving down the Nan River toward Pichit and Nakhon Sawan in pursuit of Taksin's Royal Guards regiments had to await manpower replenishments and provisions, especially munitions. His army became bogged down in dealing with its supply problems, a steady stream of stealthy defections, and sporadic response to the recurrent Siamese raids. Prospects for a victorious advance toward Thonburi grew increasingly bleak.

On June 20, as Asae Wunki was considering his options for dealing with the disintegrating battlefield situation and deepening military morale crisis, a flurry of royal couriers arrived from Ava bearing an urgent dispatch announcing the death of King Mang Ra ten days previously. He had died unrelieved of "the unquenchable thirst of empire, and the distracted ambition of being the greatest man in the world."[25] With that news the invading army was ordered to immediately abandon its hard-fought campaign and return to Ava by forced march. Asae Wunki and his elite regiments sped off without delay by the difficult upland route via the remote Mae Hong Son hill station, leaving his remaining forces under the command of his principal adjutant Kala Bo.[26] The bulk of the troops, carrying the loot and prisoners that they had collected at Sukhothai, were marshalled to retrace their earlier steps across the Myawaddy Pass to Martaban. As at Ayutthaya a decade before, they left in their wake a wasteland that would take generations to repair. In the vacuum left by the sudden Burmese withdrawal, Duang and Bunma reclaimed Phitsanulok. The younger brother led his mounted harriers in a blur of thrusts against the withdrawing Burmese contingents. The elder initiated a program to repair and repopulate the city. The people returned, and the town was rebuilt and refortified, though it took many years to restore to a semblance of its former glory.[27]

In late June, Taksin, headquartered with the Royal Guard near Pichit, learned that Asae Wunki's deputy commander Kala Bo and a garrison of some 2,000 Burmese regulars were encamped as a rearguard force in the vicinity of Kamphaeng Phet. With great urgency, he ordered one of his regiments to proceed from Nakhon Sawan up the Right Rank of the Ping River, another up the Left Bank, and a third, already patroling the Ping River corridor, to join them for a coordinated assault on Kala Bo's garrison, while his Royal Guard regiments sped cross-country from Pichit to join them. The Siamese assault was victorious, the cantonment was destroyed, but Kala

Bo managed to escape the encirclement with a portion of his forces. That was the last major engagement of the war. Taksin embarked by royal barge for Thonburi on July 1,[28] leaving the bulk of the Royal Guard to scour the ruined provincial tracts reaching from the former front lines to the western hill country in search of any other lingering Burmese brigand bands.

The former Phitsanulok battle terrain widened into a broader field of operations – covering the provinces of Kamphaeng Phet and Sukhothai to the west, Uttaradit to the north, and Pichit, Nakhon Sawan, and Uthai Thani to the south. Across that broad sweep, the more mobile, dispersed Siamese raiders, avoiding set-piece battle and unrelenting in their assaults, slowly gained dominance over the remaining Burmese encampments. Among the ill-led, virtually abandoned Burmese infantry contingents, brigandage became an increasingly common mode of warfare, and, with it, increasing brutality. Roaming bands of unsupervised foot soldiers laid waste to the land; in the absence of booty, they collected heads, hands and other body parts as trophies. For them, the tempo of war degenerated into a chaos of pillage, plunder, and massacre. To deal with that pestilence, Taksin issued a parting order that his field officers followed with zeal: "If Burmese forces are encountered, beat them back. If they flee into the jungle pursue them, and annihilate all."

One of those Siamese companies, scouting the western foothills of Kamphaeng Phet for lagging remnants of the enemy's rushed departure, found that they had left only a single regiment to protect their rear. Taksin ordered two of his Pichit regiments to obliterate that remaining garrison and eliminate all stragglers from the field. About seven days later, another Siamese regiment marching west to Uthai Thani encountered a Burmese contingent considerably larger than its own, its wagons packed with spoils of war for the homeward march. Realizing that they would be unable to gain a victory against the odds, the regimental commander dispatched his speediest couriers to inform Taksin at Thonburi. They rushed back with orders that the troops engage the Burmese caravan with darting sallies to lure it eastward toward Nakhon Sawan. There, a powerful Siamese reserve force was moved into place to ensure a swift Siamese victory. After having accomplished that task, the consolidated force proceeded upriver to attack another rearguard Burmese camp in the western Nakhon Sawan hinterlands. The fighting lasted many days. On July 27, Taksin dispatched the Royal Guard to Chainat to hearten his fighting forces and bolster their strength. He learned that the Burmese had abandoned their camp in retreat toward Uthai Thani. The combined Siamese forces assaulted the Burmese in the vicinity of Suphanburi. The Burmese could not prevail against such a powerful army and fled Siam by way of the Three Pagodas Pass. In mid-August, the Royal Guard led the way in a concerted push to Tak. From there, forays were mounted to harass the retreating Burmese forces, and 300 Burmese captives were collected. Siam had been cleared of the menace; Burma mounted no further serious threat for the remainder of Taksin's reign.[29]

The full course of Asae Wunki's invasion, from the lightning strike in December 1775 to the conclusion of his army's labored departure in August 1776, lasted nine months. Credit for victory was claimed by both kingdoms in a mutually disparaging dispute. From Siam's point of view, the Burmese taking of Phitsanulok was considered not a loss but a grand deception that had left the invaders in a vulnerable position. Duang and Bunma were praised as heroes. Siam had survived.[30] The Burmese, on the other hand, saw the invasion, despite its premature termination, as a successful emasculation of the Thonburi regime. It was believed to have weakened Siam's grip on the vulnerable North and had acquired much loot and many captives. On balance, this final Burmese-Siamese war of the Thonburi reign ended as a costly stalemate, with both kingdoms weakened.

Chapter 7
Reign Change

Editor's introduction
The Thonburi regime's initial decade of exuberant recovery from the Ayutthaya catastrophe, interrupted by the Burmese invasion of 1775-1776, was followed by a less resilient second phase of subdued expansion amid the rising challenge of internal unrest. Siam had escaped from the Phitsanulok crisis only by the skin of its teeth. The exultant aftermath was marred by a rising undercurrent of discontent engendered by the decline in administrative competence accompanying King Taksin's withdrawal from active leadership, coupled with the disbandment through death, distancing, and disaffection of his erstwhile band of brothers.

In this concluding chapte,r Diogo exhibits more openly than in his accounts of earlier events his partisan leanings. Previous chapters included candid depictions of characters and events marking Thonburi's revival, highlighting Taksin's charismatic leadership. Diogo continues that narrative here with sketches of various personalities and incidents associated with the Thonburi regime's decline and fall. Here Diogo seeks to set right what he claims to be the biased interpretation of Taksin's failings and the trajectory of his fall as depicted in the redacted Thonburi chronicle – the Phan Chanthanumat edition of 1795 (referred to in the Prologue to this volume) – and as has been repeated endlessly in further studies of that pivotal period. His revisionist interpretation challenges the aphorism that history is written invariably by the victors.

Modern accounts, relying on the redacted Thonburi chronicle, would have it that the brothers Duang and Bunma – Diogo refers to them in this chapter as the Chakri brothers – orchestrated the 1782 reign change as an act of social responsibility. Whether they were the primary instigators behind the events or simply complicit actors in the broader sweep of change remains a moot point. In either case, neither ideological principles nor humanistic sentiments were the order of the day in eighteenth-century Siam. Implicit in Diogo's account was a view of the Siamese feudal order as a coalition of self-serving factions interacting as the essential cohesive force within Siam's diffuse galactic polity. The ousting of Taksin and the remnants of his band of brothers in 1782 reordered that social hierarchy to place the Chakri faction at the pivot of power. It was not aimed at improving the public welfare, as defined under the tenets of modern-day populist ideology, though it certainly sought to reintroduce law and order to a disjointed commonwealth.

The popular belief that Taksin's purported insanity, symptomized by what modern psychologists would term paranoia and an accompanying disoriented spiritualism, was the infirmity that destroyed him is contested by Diogo. He presents a convincing alternative interpretation in maintaining that the charge of insanity was a calumny foisted on him by his detractors to legitimize their factional pretentions and, by and by, their takeover. The portrayal of Taksin as mad in the redacted Thonburi chronicle and later writings appears in that revisionist rendering to have been a major provocation behind Diogo's writing of his unorthodox narrative. His rendition of the events suggests that the theory of Taksin's madness may well have been a gross misrepresentation of the recurrent bouts of agony arising from his infected thigh injury, his unsuccessful medical treatments, and their effect on his attention to duty. The Catholic missionaries at Thonburi were, according to that reading, gullible parties to the malicious "Mad King Tak" gossip that circled for several years before Taksin's death. Their reports to Rome and Paris were influential among their foreign audience and filtered back to later generations at Bangkok to reinforce the official record. Unattuned to Thonburi's thorny politics and ignorant of many of Siam's cultural norms, the missionary priests would have been among the first to consider Taksin's actions cruelly excessive and even perverse. Their judgment may have been influenced by memories of the inhospitable reception that their unyielding theological beliefs had received at Thonburi. An edict issued by Taksin had followed the tradition of earlier Ayutthaya reigns in prohibiting them from proselytizing Christianity and prohibiting his Buddhist subjects from converting to Christianity; in addition, Taksin had reacted with swift force to the priests' threat of excommunication for those Christian officers of the Siamese Crown who might participate in the Water of Allegiance ceremony at the annual royal oath-takings.

Diogo presents here a series of synoptic sketches of the major protagonists involved in the regime's downfall – similar to his sketches of key participants in the emergence of the Thonburi regime in Chapter 3. Several of those personalities dated back to the regime's formative years, but most were late entrants into Taksin's inner circle. A number of those arrivistes – Kawin (Director of the Royal Arsenal), Bunrot (Minister of the Palace), Thong-in (Duang's nephew, and Deputy Governor of Khorat), Ramlak (surviving prince of Ayutthaya, Director of the Royal Guard), Madot (Director of the Palace Guard), Choeng (Colonel Cheng, chief of a recently arrived militia of Mon refugees) – are described here in portraits that anticipate their fated roles in the drama. All those latter-day protagonists had been left obscure in the redacted Thonburi Chronicle and later accounts. Diogo fills in enough of the missing information – much of it doubtless based on the recollections of his well-placed informants – to enrich our understanding of the evolving situation and humanize its design.

The coup and countercoup, and the reign change that followed – known collectively today as the Siamese Revolution of 1782 – came at a moment of relative calm along all the kingdom's frontiers. The South had been subjugated; Ha Tien had been brought to heel; Vientiane had been conquered; Lan Na had been pacified; Cambodia was being subdued; the western front had calmed under a new reign in Burma. However, it came, too, at a time of weakness at the Siamese center, with Thonburi in turmoil under enfeebled administrative control, the kingdom's inner defenses hollowed out in line with Taksin's longstanding expansionist policy, and his chief ministers Duang and Bunma far off biding their time.

Siam's 1782 coup d'état was, however, no American or French Revolution, despite the close historical timing. Diogo makes the difference plain in his emphasis on its elitist exclusivity, its absence of popular participation (except as a supporting cast), and its narrowly confined field of action. The reign change consisted of a clash between contending factions within the nobility. The redacted chronicle's references to "unrest" and "disturbances" describe not mass gatherings, public demonstrations, or rioting in the marketplaces and public squares (except for such isolated instances as the Ayutthaya rampage) but a growing malaise within the ruling class fed by the spread of rumor and gossip, mounting to disaffection, dissension, and insurrection, leading to armed confrontation between the most audacious elements of the power elite. Nothing fundamental in the Thai social order changed other than the hierarchical lineup of its leading personalities and their patronage networks. The traditional feudal paradigm persisted; the Buddhist/Brahman-inspired monarchy with its parallel viceroyalty lived on; the status hierarchy with its rigid divisions between elite and commons was unaffected; patronage relations within the factional alignments retained their hold; and administrative rapacity soon returned nearly to its former intensity. In the coup's aftermath, under Duang in his elevated stature as King Rama I, Ayutthaya's traditional legal system, Buddhist precepts, royal ritual, and administrative apparatus were revived, codified, and modulated to fit the changing times. The coup d'état was motivated not by consciously expressed ideologies but by inherent, instinctive impulses bred through centuries of Siamese state-making.

Throughout this chapter, Diogo demonstrates his Plutarchian bent by highlighting obscure events and personalities as touchstones, benchmarks, points of reference within the larger time frame. The fact that most of those details were excluded from the redacted Thonburi Chronicle – if Diogo's rendition is accepted as reliable – may well reflect their sensitivity to the "official" depiction of the course of events. The coup and countercoup, in particular, are passed over with scarce mention in the redacted chronicle and most later studies, whereas Diogo exposes them – through his unique access to suppressed information and documents later lost – as discrete episodes each carrying its own drama, each conveying the tale forward to its fated end. Through all that, Diogo's narrative defends Taksin against his detractors while it challenges the adulatory portrayal of the Chakri brothers presented in the other sources with what may be considered a more balanced view. In keeping with the Thai chronicles tradition, Diogo ends his narrative abruptly with the events of April 6, 1782, avoiding any closing peroration. As he no doubt intended, his iconoclastic perspective on the incidents that shaped the times may well inspire fresh insight into the course of later events.

Distractions

Torments – From his posting as a brigadier during the 1765-1767 siege of Ayutthaya to his royal command at the battle of Phitsanulok a decade later, Taksin had been involved ceaselessly in the planning, preparation, and prosecution of Siam's recurring military campaigns. That decade-long preoccupation satisfied his burning thirst for vengeance against the Burmese scourge, fulfilled his dreams of resuscitating the Siamese state, and served his ambitions for personal fame and fortune. Like most men of restless energy and deep reflection, he had matured in office. Years of military command, participation in bloody combat, loss of comrades in the slaughter, and rise to high station had refined his wisdom and honed his judgment. He had come to recognize that war must not only be just and laudable in its execution but must necessarily proceed from reasonable motives and lasting principles.[1] He had learned to despise the evils of arrogance, envy, calumny, and contention that often attended public business.[2] He had reached the realization that, in war, governance thrives on tyranny for the single object of victory, whereas peace, with its endless litany of competing values and interests, demands more compromising, conciliatory, accommodating leadership. Taksin had become imbued with the greatness of soul that makes a king think the obligations to his realm are stronger than the ties of kinship and friendship.[3] However, his life as a warrior had been arduous, subject to frequent privation and fraught with risk to life and limb, culminating in the grievous injury he had suffered during the Nakhon campaign of 1769. All came to a head years later in the aftermath of the Phitsanulok campaign of 1776, as his old trauma flared anew. His injured thigh was again oozing foul humors; he could barely stand, and even bedridden he suffered recurrent spasms of agony, prompting outpourings of wrath.[4]

Distracted by the torments of his revitalized affliction, Taksin played no active role in the final phase of the Phitsanulok campaign beyond receiving regular reports and issuing advisory dispatches to his lieutenants. By the time of the northern capital's fall he had already been evacuated from his Pak Phing command post for downstream Pichit, and from there had been barged at a calmer pace to Thonburi for recuperation. His physicians begged him to remain immobile, with herbal poultices covering the raw lesion from which they had stripped the rotted flesh.[5] Seeing no alternative, he transferred full command of subsequent field operations to his dual Ministers of War and Interior, Duang and Bunma.[6] That his departure from the field did not end in catastrophe says more for the sudden withdrawal of Asae Wunki and much of the Burmese army than for the competence of his subaltern commanders and the resolve of his troops. Despite the return of peace, however, subsequent events did not bode as brightly.

Adding to Taksin's distress as the Phitsanulok battle gathered pace was the illness of his mother, Princess-Mother Thepamat; and then, as the war passed its climax, the lingering melancholy following her death. A year earlier, in February 1775, she had fallen ill and departed Thonburi for convalescence at her Phetburi family home.

En route, she had stopped over at Ratburi, where her grandson Prince Chui was preparing the provincial defenses to withstand a Burmese incursion. Taksin arrived several days later – proceeding to the siege of Bang Kaew – to be at her side. Despite desperate medical efforts, she declined into terminal illness and died there in mid-March, at the height of the Burmese hostilities. Her remains were conveyed by royal barge to the Thonburi Grand Palace; her cremation, initially planned for March 1776, was postponed due to the continuing Siamese-Burmese hostilities and was finally rescheduled to take place at Wat Bang Yi Roea Tai in July.[7] In his grief at his mother's death, compounded by the suffering of his continuing physical torment, Taksin turned to scriptural studies and intensive meditation as palliatives.

That chain of sorrowful events accentuated the already palpable distancing in relations between Taksin and his Ministers of War and Interior, the Chakri brothers. The precipitating circumstances ran deep, but the terminating events were sudden, centering on the humiliating corporal punishment meted out to each of the brothers, the king's two most senior lieutenants. In the first case, Bunma, exhilarated with his heroic escape together with his brother from besieged Phitsanulok, rushed on to Thonburi to burst in upon the king unannounced in the midst of his daily meditation. For that impertinence, it is said, the incensed king ordered his arrest and caning. The king's motivation, however, likely lay deeper than such petty annoyance: Taksin was heard to mutter, "Yes, you saved yourselves. But you lost the war." That unhappy incident was followed a few months later, when Duang, recently returned from the Phitsanulok warfront, was assigned responsibility for the construction of the Princess-Mother's elaborate cremation pyre. The pyre's half-built framework, designed to rise higher than the highest temple stupa, collapsed during a torrential rainstorm; the irate king ordered Duang's caning as punishment. The humiliation of that unprecedented pair of thrashings of Taksin's principal field generals and chief ministers rankled. Many, however, thought the dual punishments not simply disciplinary acts for passing blunders of the moment but a veiled reprimand for the brothers' earlier opposition to the battle plan proposed by Taksin at the Ban Tha Rong General Staff conference at the height of the Phitsanulok conflict. Whatever the reason, the pair of canings left lasting grievance.

The absence of Taksin's avuncular confidante Li-ang *sae* Tang added to the king's distress. Following Li-ang's requested reassignment in 1771 to the reduced post of commissioner for the Eastern Seaboard region, his successor as Minister of Trade, Ching-chong *sae* Yang, replaced him as Taksin's most valued counselor. Ching-chong's death during a raging flux that passed through Thonburi in mid-1776, at the worst possible moment, came as an unexpected blow. Taksin's disquiet intensified when Ching-chong's replacement, Hok-chu *sae* Tae, proved to be an administrator of inferior quality, a man under whose flawed guardianship the state treasury failed to prosper. The Crown was coming under intensifying pressure from its Taechiu creditors; its debts had been refinanced several times but, despite the post-war economic recovery, remained in arrears. To Taksin's mounting frustration, Hok-chiu made little progress toward resolving that persisting issue. Discovery of the new Trade Minister's embezzlement of a sizable share of the state's rice reserves was more than the king could endure. In 1779 Hok-chiu was tried, found guilty, and condemned to execution, severing yet another strand in the fraternal comity that had defined the earlier years of the Thonburi reign.

Punctuated by a series of such disruptive incidents, Taksin's inner circle of former years fragmented into a fragile constellation of shifting factions increasingly bent on pursuit of their individual interests. Those who had bound the old Ayutthaya elite through common kinship, ancestral alliances, and peer-group internships in royal service had found their linchpin in the Chakri brothers, the powerful Ministers of War and Interior. Separately, the Taechiu merchant community had coalesced around the Ministry of Trade, while lesser factions had formed around other parvenue power blocs, attracting their own provincial associations. Taksin's governing consortium, in short, had unraveled.

Ministerial meetings – Whether from his physicians' efficacious potions and poultices, the benefits of deep meditation under the guidance of his monastic mentors, or his women's gentle ministrations, Taksin gradually regained sufficient strength to resume a modified pace of governance. Interaction with his executive officers, however, grew increasingly delicate, decorous, and detached. Ministerial conferences grew sporadic; informal consultations became less frequent; personal interaction lost its former exuberance, conviviality, and outspoken honesty. Bereft of his former hearty brotherhood, Taksin had been left abandoned of candid counsel. In an evident effort to draw the ruling coalition back to alignment, he convened a full-scale ministerial meeting in October 1776, immediately after the end of the rainy season retreat.[8] The administrative lineup at that gathering showed many changes from the band of brothers that had been Taksin's former strength, including the introduction of the newly installed Ministers of Trade (Hok-chu) and Palace (Bunrot, formerly filling that role without ministerial status); a new division between the Royal Guard (headed by Ramlak) and the Palace Guard (Madot); and a number of new provincial governors. At lengthy sittings over the course of several days, Taksin received detailed reports on each ministry's current situation and brief reviews of each major department's recent activities, followed by a collective assessment of the kingdom's prospective security concerns. In reserved tones, ignoring all doubts he may have harbored, the king expressed his satisfaction.

Some six months later, following the annual Water of Allegiance ceremony accompanying the New Year's celebrations, a second such gathering was convened to consider in greater depth the kingdom's stance regarding persisting tensions along the eastern borderlands in the presence of the reduced Burmese threat from the west. Taksin reviewed, first, Vientiane's mounting provocations over matters of royal protocol, trade, and tribute; Champasak's subversive encouragement of brigand bands along the eastern trade routes; and the escalating adversities being encountered by

Cambodia in its struggle to fend off Quang-nam's embrace. The Chakri brothers added detailed accounts of their recent activities to suppress banditry along the eastern and northern frontiers, coupled with a description of their patronage of the many minor principalities scattered across the borderlands. Their spirited summation was rewarded with a royal proposal that they devise a comprehensive eastern frontier strategy for the king's further consideration. At a third ministerial meeting a year later, again coinciding with the New Year's celebrations, Taksin reviewed the Chakri brothers' plan for the pacification of Vientiane and Champasak and endorsed its early implementation, advising only that in their subjugation of those recalcitrant princedoms they place greater weight on conciliation than on force.

The Vientiane campaign of 1778/79 – Other than occasional visits to Thonburi for royal audiences and family reunions, the Chakri brothers took to biding their time at their upcountry bases of Phitsanulok and Khorat, interspersed with scouting sorties across the volatile northeastern borderlands. Those marches sought to bring under Siam's sway the sparsely populated wilderness expanse stretching toward the Mekong River, occupied by petty principalities edging the Vientiane and Champasak spheres of influence.[9] In lengthy deliberations, the brothers devised plans for securing the eastward transport routes and the attendant bounty of transport tolls, trade profits, and manpower resources. Increasingly, their thoughts turned to harvesting the wilderness to raise their domains' agrarian productivity and rice export surplus. With Taksin's withdrawal from active command, they had been left free to consider such expansionist plans, serving both the kingdom's interests and their own. They welcomed Taksin's endorsement of their proposal for further conquest, despite his proviso that they deliver a share of their captive population into royal service.

In late November 1778, after the monsoon floods had receded, they set off with their battalions from Khorat on an extended military venture to subdue the downstream trans-Mekong Lao states, to increase Siam's revenue flows through firm control of the region's trade routes, and to increase the kingdom's manpower base with forced migration to the inner provinces. As Bunma marched east through the scrublands toward Nakhon Luang[10] and from there north to Champasak, Duang marched straight north from Khorat through the rolling hills toward Vientiane. Along both fronts, the Lao defenders, lacking the necessary complement of strategic leadership, firepower, and war-trained troops, crumbled against the battle-hardened Siamese forces. To the north, Luang Prabang acceded peaceably and accepted Siamese tributary status. Champasak capitulated to Bunma after a token confrontation in February 1779, and his forces then pushed up the Mekong River to reinforce Duang's assault on Vientiane, which fell in April. With the conquest of Vientiane, the brothers captured most of the royal family and hundreds of their retainers and servants, as well as many refugees from Champasak. From the city's hinterlands and surrounding provinces they swept up additional thousands of peasant households for resettlement in Siam's war-depopulated Khorat, Phitsanulok, and Saraburi hinterlands.[11]

Table 6. The Vientiane royal succession, 18th– early-19th centuries

King	Lineage position	Reign	Vassalage status
King Setttha Thirat II (We)	(founder)	1698-1730	
King ...... (Long)	(son)	1730-1740	
Viceroy (Nong)	(younger brother)	1740-1751	
King Siri Bunsan (Bun	(son)	1751-1779	
		1781-1782	(returned from exile as Siam's vassal king)
King Nanthasen	(son)	1782-1795	(Siam's vassal king)
King Inthawong	(younger brother)	1795-1805	(Siam's vassal king)
King Anuwong	(younger brother)	1805-1828	(Siam's vassal king)

Flushed with victory and anticipating a glorious Thonburi homecoming, the Chakri brothers conveyed in their wake an endless caravan of booty. Unbeknownst to them, however, Taksin had dispatched his son Prince Chui (soon to be elevated to the august title of Prince Inthara Phithak) to Saraburi to escort downriver to Thonburi the victors and their royal captives, as well as Vientiane's state palladia and other hallowed treasures. The Chakri brothers were offended by their relegation to subsidiary status in that aquatic procession, with pretentious but insignificant Chui occupying a royal barge accompanying the Lao palladia on their triumphal voyage to Taksin's reception at the Grand Palace. That public slight was well remembered in the brothers' later interactions with Chui, and it preordained his eventual downfall.

Amid ecstatic celebrations and great ceremony, the palladia of Vientiane – the Phra Kaew and Phra Bang Buddha images – were installed in the ordination hall of the Chapel Royal, on either side of the presiding Buddha image. Yet, not all the assembled aristocrats welcomed their arrival, as it was whispered that the veneration of those hallowed idols as trophies of war and symbols of subjugation would inspire evil consequences. It was also feared that the close juxtaposition of those two powerful deities would arouse conflict between them and endanger the kingdom.[12] Following Chui and the sacred trophies, and the lesser barge conveying the Chakri brothers, additional vessels bore Vientiane's hostage royals, led by Princes Nanthasen, Inthawong, and Anuwong, and their elder sister, the formidable Princess Khiaw-khom. The lesser captive contingents were conveyed to Thonburi on forced march.[13] There, the royal hostages were assigned to a large residential compound upriver from the Thonburi citadel, neighboring Bang Yi Khan, and their accompanying entourage was settled nearby, crossriver.[14]

As a personal conquest, Duang carried off from Vientiane to Saraburi, behind the silk-draped howdah swaying upon the back of his trudging war elephant, his new mistress, Kham-waen, lady-in-waiting to Princess Khiaw-khom. Through the devious designs of Khiaw-khom, Waen had been instructed, and then introduced to Duang, with the intent of turning his mind from his warrior's pursuits to the protection of her people. Enamored of Waen's feminine graces, Duang sent for her, there being no discernible cause that they might not converse without suspicion or offence. In the natural course of events, she found the wisdom and the will to accept his intimate embraces and humored him in all things according to his heart's desire.[15] Among her own people, unfortunately, she gained the reputation of "a celebrated wit and beauty, but in other respects nothing better than an ordinary harlot."[16] In fine, having obtained great power over Duang, she persuaded him to marry her and declare her his lawful wife, overruling the convention whereby Nak, his senior wife of many years, should occupy that position.[17] Nak, deeply aggrieved, abandoned Thonburi with her nine children for her parental home at Bang Chang, in Ratburi's Amphawa district, fortuitously avoiding the dynastic upheaval about to engulf Thonburi and transform her husband's life.

The Cambodia campaign of 1781/82 – Over the following two years, the Chakri brothers maintained their distance from Thonburi with only infrequent visits as circumstances might demand. Duang established his new operating base at Saraburi with Waen and her Lao entourage in attendance. His military cantonment at Khorat was converted to a forward camp fronting the Lao hinterlands, under the governorship of his reliable kinsman Pin, recently promoted to Colonel Kamhaeng Songkhram. Bunma, overseeing the kingdom's northern frontier and dealing on friendly terms with the chiefs of the Lan Na principalities from his base at Phitsanulok, often met with Duang to coordinate their further course of action in the volatile borderlands that they had recently brought under their sway. Their conversations gravitated increasingly to the possibility of asserting full Siamese suzerainty over turbulent Cambodia.

During his 1779 march past Nakhon Luang toward the conquest of Champasak, Duang had requested Cambodia's King Rama Racha (Non) to conscript a 10,000-man army in support of his adjutant, Colonel Kamhaeng Songkhram (Pin). Non assigned that manpower mobilization task to Mu, governor of Cambodia's Bassac region, stretching across the kingdom's northern territories from the Mekong River toward Vietnam. Siam's demand for Khmer troops incited deep resentment and then widespread resistance among the local populace. Under Mu's leadership, the peasantry rose in revolt with the watchword: "We are Khmer subjects, not Siamese slaves." The uprising peaked with the assassination of Non and all his sons, leaving Cambodia leaderless but for the upstart Mu. A year of chaos followed as Mu, now elevated to the grandiose title of Fa Thalaha, fought on while seeking Vietnamese patronage in the face of unrelenting Siamese opposition. Confronting Mu's unyielding militias, Pin's conscripted troops wearied of the forced long-distance marches, monsoon rains, jungle miasmas, short provisions, and long absence from home; they would push no farther. His efforts to raise additional Khmer levies faltered, and even the diminished forces that he was able to scavenge quickly evaporated with the desertion of many under his harsh discipline. He withdrew to Cambodia's western frontier at Battambang and established there a fortified camp to await future orders. Mu had temporarily prevailed against the Siamese incursion.

Battambang served well as a Siamese forward base during Cambodia's turbulent years of Vietnamese intrusion and dynastic uncertainty. It commanded the vital trade routes to Khorat and Saraburi, was peopled by a Khmer/Cham populace tolerant of a peaceable Siamese presence, and was governed by Baen, a firm partisan of Udong's anti-Vietnamese royal faction. In Cambodia's long-standing dynastic dispute, Baen had been a staunch supporter of Non (Siam's protégé for the Khmer throne) in the dispute with Prince Ton (Quang-nam's protégé).[18] Non's installation in 1771 as King Rama Racha had been a Siamese triumph; his assassination in late 1779 at the hands of Mu and his Vietnamese patrons came as a countervailing disaster. In the subsequent months of unrelieved chaos, Baen was forced to flee to Thonburi. There, despite the Chakri brothers' representations in his defense, he was imprisoned by an irate Taksin on grounds of dereliction of duty, caned a near-fatal 100 strokes, and had his earlobes sliced off as a permanent reminder. His release from detention into Duang's custody was eventually arranged, and he survived as Duang's man to play an important role in Siam's further Cambodian adventures.

Cambodia's chaos, against the backdrop of Mu's Vietnamese-backed insurgency, persisted through the political vacuum left by the assassination of Non. To consider an appropriate Siamese response, Taksin convened a ministerial meeting at which the Chakri brothers received approval for their proposal to settle the situation with a decisive military assault. Accompanied by Pin and Baen, Bunma marched off from Khorat in December 1780 leading a 10,000-man army. A steady flow of military communiqués to Thonburi over the following months reported indecisive progress against the elusive adversary. Finally, Duang announced that he had shifted his base from Saraburi to Khorat to resume his regular ministerial duties there with Pin at his side, leaving Bunma in command of continuing field operations accompanied by Baen. Astute observers at Thonburi surmised that the brothers had resolved to monitor the deteriorating situation at Thonburi from a more discreet vantage point.[19]

Taksin countered Duang's unauthorized withdrawal of Pin's regiments from the Cambodian front by dispatching his son Prince Inthara Phithak (Chui) with two of his Taechiu regiments by junk to Chanthabun, and from there overland to Battambang. The king's detractors took that opportunity to spread malicious gossip that Chui had been sent in expectation of his elevation to the Khmer throne, though there is no evidence to support such a claim. Chui's arrival was an unwelcome addition to Bunma's campaign, but one to which the brothers could not readily object. Secretly scorning Chui as a callow youth of no particular merit, Bunma persuaded him to assume responsibility with his Taechiu battalions for the Battambang stronghold and the neighboring borderlands while Bunma advanced eastward against the Cambodian rebels with his cavalry and infantry regiments. Over the ensuing months, Bunma's troops succeeded in scattering the bulk of the rebel forces and pressing the Vietnamese interlopers into retreat. Fa Thalaha (Mu) was captured and executed, along with his entire family. Baen was installed at Udong as guardian of Siam's new Cambodian royal protégé and king-apparent Prince Eng – only seven years old, the sole surviving son of the recently executed Prince Ton. Bunma and his battalions stayed on to maintain the peace, with Chui holding the Battambang base and Baen supporting him as Cambodia's acting Minister of War and regent for Prince Eng. Gradually, with the Vietnamese presence in recession, Cambodia's turmoil eased.

Disorder

Rumors – Taksin's decision to withdraw from direct military command at the height of the Phitsanulok crisis, by dint of the revived agony of his old leg injury, had filled him with great remorse, and had left him increasingly isolated. The years following that final battlefield foray bound him to his Thonburi palace – not, as some averred, for fear of assassination, but in deference to his physical incapacity. Only his personal physicians, his attending women, his meditation instructors, and a select few other confidants were allowed to share the secret. The small band of French priests at Thonburi, respected for their medical knowledge but additionally recognized for their covert role as foreign emissaries – little better than spies – were kept in ignorance and consequently aired outrageous opinions, based on hearsay, to explain his aberrant behavior.[20] Some of Taksin's closest attendants warned the king time and again of the malign rumor-mongering. As was later repeated in idle conversation, they claimed that among his subordinates there lurked some who were raising worms that hungered to consume his entrails. Perhaps that unfortunate rhetorical juxtaposition of his own purulent injury and the rotting body politic disinclined him from confronting the latter matter with resolve. There was guarded talk that he had lost heart, that he had sloughed off his taste for command and governance. Much whispering suggested that, in his strict seclusion, he trusted no one and had discarded his friends. Gossip drifted across the city like a toxic fog, claiming that he had turned against his former comrades, imposing on them cruel punishments for imagined offenses.

Taksin had found early on that frequent application of the cane offered a compelling lesson in obedience. As his reign proceeded, he resorted to that conventional means of corporal punishment with increased frequency and fervor. His standard remedy for insubordination was 30 strokes of the cane as light punishment and 60 strokes or more in serious cases. Although he was not by nature of a malevolent inclination, he maintained that "the generality of men are most ready to reverence those whom they fear."[21] Under special circumstances of noncompliance at the command level, he resorted to earlobe clipping,[22] though he was not averse to ordering execution in extreme instances. For cases of flagrant dereliction of duty, and treason, he preferred the standard protocol of beheading over such loathsome practices as impalement, flaying, boiling, and disembowelment, favored by many of his penal officials.[23] Only through the exaggerations bandied by his detractors did the repeated reports of his excessive or unwarranted punishments escalate into charges of deranged behavior.

Taksin often reprimanded his regimental officers for lack of diligence in pursuit of their objectives, for want of deference to their superiors, for unbecoming swagger in dealing with their subordinates. At such moments he was wont to remark: "How many generals have we here, and how few soldiers."[24] His uncompromising imposition of military discipline on deserters, malingerers, and looters was well known. One of his officers, on leading a battalion past his own home en route to battle, took the opportunity to visit his family, and lingered on. Upon hearing of that infraction, Taksin had the officer arrested, tried, and executed; his head was impaled upon a bamboo staff to rot on public display as a warning. Similarly, in consolidating the Siamese kingdom, Taksin repeatedly resorted to the defeated insurgents' harsh confinement to ensure their submission. He realized, as Machiavelli had stressed, that "when the prince is with his army and has under his command a multitude of soldiers, then it is absolutely necessary not to care about being thought cruel, for without this reputation, no one has ever kept an army united or ready for any feat of arms."[25] He carried that prescription from his military training into his peacetime administration. In his civil capacity he applied with rigor and rectitude, but with growing detachment, the authority that he had formerly wielded personally as a military commander.

In addition to having proved himself a charismatic leader, brilliant warrior, strategic thinker, and stern taskmaster over the early years of his career, Taksin had gained acclaim for his endeavors on behalf of Thonburi's Buddhist revival. From the start, he had emphasized the importance of Buddhism as a mainstay of the kingdom's renaissance. He had taken a special interest in inviting leading monastic survivors of the Ayutthaya holocaust to move to Thonburi as a new center for the preservation of the monastic tradition. The 1769 Sawangkhaburi insurgency was followed by Taksin's dispatch of a monastic mission to revitalize orthodox Buddhism in the North, and the Nakhon expedition later that same year returned from the South with a contingent of Ayutthaya refugee monks accompanied by recensions of rare Buddhist scriptures. Subsequent years featured the systematic renovation of Thonburi's temples as well as many others upcountry. In the difficult years following the death of the Princess-Mother and the subsequent Phitsanulok crisis, Taksin turned that virtue inward with personal inquiries into Buddhist doctrine and practice, which served him as a daily mental cleansing, a salve for his worsening physical affliction, an escape from the interminable flow of royal duties. His detractors turned that ethical enterprise against him, accusing him of unmitigated arrogance and even lunacy in accepting the blandishments of his clerical sycophants in declaring him a Stream Entrant.[26] There was even talk that his fawning mentors had suggested him capable of levitating during deep meditation, and that they had broken with canonical convention in prostrating themselves in obeisance before their king. Through such rumors, Taksin's critics distorted his efforts to master advanced theological doctrine and meditation techniques with condemnation for his hubris.

Within the Buddhist monkhood, the servility accorded to Taksin by his religious mentors grew into a matter of doctrinal debate, with many conservative voices raised in opposition. Taksin settled the dispute with the ouster of the supreme patriarch, Phra Thamma Trailok (Si, abbot of Wat Bang Wa Yai), who had been the chief opponent of claims to his "Stream Entrant" status, replacing him with the more pliable Phra Phonarat (Choen, abbot of Wat Hong).[27] At the same time, the abbotcy of Wat Bang Wa Yai was transferred to Taksin's principal meditation teacher, Phra Wanarat (Thong-yu, formerly the temple's deputy abbot). That royal intervention into monastic affairs triggered a public scandal that went far toward tarnishing Taksin's reputation. The entire affair was so clouded in secrecy, however, and the attendant rumors stretched to such outrageous proportions, that the facts of the case remain uncertain.[28]

Factions – The atmosphere of exuberance that had marked the early years of Thonburi's revival from the Ayutthaya disaster ebbed. It was as if the years of euphoria had worn themselves out, that the spasm of rejoicing over the kingdom's resilience had been overwhelmed by a gathering wave of self-doubt. Whispers of discord and intrigue at the highest levels grew increasingly prevalent, shading every hushed conversation within an oppressive penumbra of caution, uncertainty, ambivalence of mind. Rumors of astrologers' reckonings that the kingdom faced disaster under the conflicting horoscopes of its leading personalities caused considerable disquiet. Along with that tidal change in public sentiments rose a surge of religious excess featuring spiritual dispute and sectarian schism, as is the wont among people in times of apprehension, as if the kingdom had lost its way. It may well have been that those newly-risen public sentiments reflected the anxieties attending the changing competencies and shifting alliances within the ruling elite as the kingdom's administrative leadership encountered a generational reordering.

Taksin found much truth in the adage that in war your enemies reveal themselves, while in peace they hide among your friends; on the battlefield they seek your head, at court they steal your reputation. The loss of a number of his trusted comrades saddened him. The deaths of Mut (former Minister of War) and Ching-chong (former Minister of Trade) had been fated. The distancing of some others, such as Li-ang (transferred to oversight of the Eastern Seaboard), Sanguan (appointed as chief of Phichai), and Saeng (Prince Nara Suriyawong, designated to rule Nakhon Si Thammarat) had been necessary, but others had left his side under less clearcut circumstances. The estrangement of the Chakri brothers, retaining their ministerial portfolios but distancing themselves from Thonburi, was a particularly troublesome case.

Duang and Bunma remained inseparable companions throughout, though an element of fraternal rivalry often animated their personal relations. On many occasions Duang was chided by his younger brother for his hesitancy in taking definitive action, complaining that he had let slip the chance for easy pickings through procrastination. Under that persistent goading, Duang in time learned to act with alacrity when the occasion demanded. On a more sensitive note, when Bunma, in a pique, complained

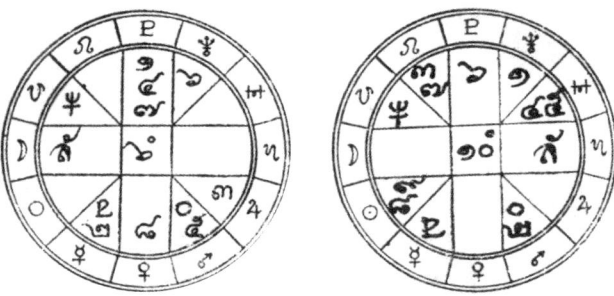

The conflicting reignal horoscopes (*duang phra chata*) of Kings Taksin and Rama I. (Courtesy of Phra Maha Rachakhru Phithi Si Wisuthikun, Bot Phram, Bangkok; scanned from *Book of 200 Horoscopes of Royal Persons*, (in Thai)). The two horoscopes are said to stand in opposition, portending inauspicious consequences, though knowledgeable Thai astrologers decline to identify the specifics of the conflicting celestial alignments.

that Duang had not obtained the honor of rising to the forefront of Siam's military forces through his own merit alone, Duang replied: "You speak the truth. I should never have achieved such fame had I not been your brother. Nor you, had you not been mine."[29] Such frictions finally led Duang to declare, in exasperation, "Because of our fraternal familiarity, you think you receive too little honor, and presently you grow angry."[30] However, their mutual devotion overcame those tensions; as in marriage, deep-set feelings of affection, obedience, respect, and tolerance preserved their union through all storms.

After their return from Vientiane and presentation of the campaign's trophies to the king, the brothers agreed to distance themselves as best they could from their increasingly thorny relations with Taksin. Bunma gravitated between Phitsanulok and Khorat in oversight of the ever-restless frontier. Duang retired to Saraburi, which he had adopted as a convenient administrative headquarters alongside the resettlement tract assigned to his captive Lao entourage. There, at his secluded estate overlooking the Pa Sak River, he spent much time with his mistress Kham-waen, far removed from his disaffected wife Nak. There too he entertained frequent visits from Bunma, delegations of political allies, fence-straddlers eager for his patronage, and lesser supplicants seeking his even-handed judgment in settlement of land disputes, debt claims, inheritance squabbles, criminal charges, and the like. Saraburi became the brothers' listening post for news of developments at Thonburi, and for word of any tremor of disaffection along the kingdom's frontiers. The brothers settled into a period of uneasy tranquility, which was bound not to last long.

Though the Chakri brothers managed to retain their posts – at a distance – the loss of many other old comrades through death or distancing forced Taksin to seek replacements. It was difficult to staff those vacant positions with suitable candidates, as zeal had flagged, enthusiasm had dulled, reliability had eroded. With the press of events, however, a new generation of senior officers was bound to emerge. Among the foremost of the arrivistes, carrying in their train presentiments of significant factional

Reign Change 229

realignment, and all slated to play consequential roles in the events to come, were the following:

Madot (Colonel Ramanwong, son of the Mon chief Saming Noradecha, Mapu) and **Choeng** (Colonel Cheng, formerly carrying the Mon title of Saming Choeng) had both been involved in the ongoing Mon struggle against Burmese oppression, and both had been forced to escape with their people across the Tenasserim Divide into Siamese sanctuary. Madot had accompanied his father in their 1750s flight to Ayutthaya, where he had been assigned the title of Captain Bamroe Phakdi as his father's adjutant, and their later move to Thonburi. Upon his father's death in 1770, Madot succeeded him as head of the local Mon community and commander of Thonburi's Mon regiment with the title of Colonel Ramanwong. He gained distinction as commander of the Mon detachments at the battle of Bang Kaew in 1775 and at Phitsanulok in 1776. The death of the director of the Palace Guard, Colonel Thibet Bodin a year later led to Madot's appointment as his successor, while retaining his distinctive title.

At around the same time, the arrival of Choeng, leading a large Mon refugee contingent in flight from a new wave of Burmese oppression, stirred unrest within Thonburi's established Mon community. The new arrivals were allotted a settlement site directly across Thonburi's Mon Canal from Madot's village, but Choeng refused to accept Madot's precedence on the grounds that he himself was of Mon royal blood, whereas Madot was no more than a minor noble.[31] In the conflict that led to Taksin's downfall less than two years later, Madot and Choeng took opposing sides. Madot and his regiments remained loyal to their king, though there were times when he appeared to vacillate, and for that he would pay the price without complaint. It has been said of him that "in all the vicissitudes of public affairs, the constancy he showed was admirable, not being elated with honors, and demeaning himself tranquilly and sedately in adversity."[32] Choeng, in contrast, long maintained himself aloof from Thonburi's growing political malaise, until he finally opted to lead his men into an alliance with the Chakri brothers, which helped decide Taksin's fate, and spelled his own good fortune.

Ramlak (Prince Anurak Songkhram, grandson of King Boromakot) was the most popular of the Ayutthaya royals affiliated with the Thonburi royal family. Although of junior standing within the small circle of Ayutthaya royals at Thonburi, he was the most quick-witted, spirited, and vivacious of them all. In military service he delighted in the dangers of war and thus gained Taksin' favor, which advanced him to the highest ranks of the officer corps. Taksin assisted him at every turn, helping to conceal or at least extenuate his occasional errors of judgment by setting off his good qualities to best advantage.[33] After years spent recovering from grievous saber wounds suffered during the 1767 assault on Pho Sam Ton, he returned to play a regimental commander's role at the 1775 siege of Bang Kaew and at the subsequent 1776 Phitsanulok battle. Many of the officers participating in those conflicts found him, with his royalist airs, unable to conform to command protocols, inclined to indiscretion in his talk, and often infected by the suggestions of his friends, and thus they came to shun him.[34]

Relegated to obscurity in the subsequent years of the Chakri brothers' elevated station, his ambitions diverted to command of the Royal Guard regiments at Thonburi, a post for which he vied with Madot, who had attained co-equal military rank as commander of the Palace Guard, creating thereby a natural rivalry. His close association with Kawin, director of the Royal Arsenal. in the quest for mastery of Thonburi resulted in his entanglement in the events culminating in Kawin's attempted coup d'état of March 1782, and his ruination.

Bunrot (Colonel Thamma Trailok, Minister of the Palace) was a rotund, smooth-edged, inscrutable courtier with a well-deserved reputation as a skilled royal minion. He claimed descent from Ayutthaya's Brahmin lineage through his father, a senior official in the old capital's Ministry of the Palace under whose tutelage he had gained proficiency in courtly etiquette. Somehow, he had managed to survive the 1767 disaster and found his way to Thonburi, where he gained sanctuary within the newly established royal household and slithered his way upward to become Taksin's aide in dealing with issues of royal protocol, carrying the title of Major Maha Montri. In that position, he gradually gained oversight of an agglomeration of departments, including the Royal Secretariat, Royal Pages Corps, Palace Guard, and Judiciary, as well as Pundits, Physicians, Dancers, and Musicians. Among his additional duties were superintendence of royal ceremonies and entertainments, maintenance of the royal premises, and arbitration of minor cases relating to court protocol. His unctuous manner, given to accommodating all views even when contradictory, obsequious even to his own servants, shielded him from all cause of offense. As an implacable champion of the king's wellbeing, he screened his master from the endless flow of palace intrigues. Finding himself unable to stem the rising tide of discontent and dissension surrounding the beleaguered king, Bunrot suggested to his master, in the reign's final desperate weeks, that he be granted leave on pilgrimage to the Shrine of the Buddha's Footprint (a distant upcountry excursion, a full day's travel beyond Lopburi). That secret, last-minute abandonment of his duties left him reviled by many, but safe from the coming storm and prepared to resume his post in calmer days. Slippery as an eel, he was a man whose inbred guile managed unfailingly to turn troublesome situations to his own advantage.

Kawin (Colonel Sankhaburi, often referred to simply as Colonel San) was of obscure origin, a self-made man. Physically unprepossessing, bearing unsightly scars from battle, but not lacking in confidence, courage, and cunning, he had by sheer will and unremitting energy managed to get his rank raised from line gunner to artillery captain. Nevertheless, not unlike many other aspiring men of more precious pedigree, he harbored a flawed soul, "a man famous indeed for courage in battle, but of no sound judgment, full of ungrounded hopes and foolish ambition."[35] He professed the highest regard for his betters, proffered them great devotion, and attended them with all deference, while underhand he kept up his dealings with his own coterie of associates, and with them pursued most assiduously his own interests.[36]

Kawin first came to Bunma's notice as a gunnery officer during the Phitsanulok campaign of 1776. Having cultivated the general's acquaintance through their shared exploits in both battle and debauchery, he often joined him as a familiar in the company of common soldiers, making the pair of bibacious officers a delight of the army. Through that convivial association, Kawin rose to the rank of colonel, carrying with it the minor fiefdom of Sankhaburi.[37] There, he soon gained a reputation for filling his coffers with illicit revenues, and his household with louche women and misbegotten offspring. There too, at Bunma's urging, he learned a new craft, directing the clandestine operations of informers on banditry and insurgency along the kingdom's frontiers, which greatly facilitated Bunma's sensitive responsibility, as Minister of Interior, for maintaining order in the hinterlands. In overheard conversation, Bunma once remarked to his brother that Kawin's highest virtue was his spymaster's skill. Duang replied: "That indeed is an admirable trait, but even more excellent would be the moral strength to keep his hands from collecting bribes."[38]

As Bunma's protégé, and with Duang's restrained endorsement, Kawin was eventually recommended for the directorship of the Royal Arsenal, a post uniquely fitted to the technical skills of a former gunnery officer.[39] In recompense for the Chakri brothers' support, he was requested to provide them with periodic confidential reports on Taksin's waning health and Thonburi's weakening administration. Expanding on that commitment, Kawin built a surveillance network across Thonburi that he used simultaneously as a rumor mill that ground out exaggerated market talk of Taksin's mounting cruelties and religious excesses. His access to privileged information and his rising ability to influence public opinion fed his arrogance, advancing his ambitions for greater power. If ever a man exemplified the aphorism that a person's character decides his fate, it was Kawin.

Insurrection – Although the ailing king remained scrupulously honest in his personal affairs, he increasingly eased his way by turning a blind eye to many of the excesses of his minions, which demanded, sometimes, not a little injustice.[40] Increasingly, he took to his writing desk to ease his troubled mind in composing essays grappling with esoteric aspects of Buddhist theology far removed from the distasteful business of political affairs. Under Taksin's neglectful oversight, his deputies' appointments and promotions of junior officers became more often a matter of purchase than a reward for performance.[41] The distancing of Taksin's Ministers of War and Interior, Duang and Bunma, and the extended vacancies of several other ministerial-level posts left him bereft of essential counsel. Those gaps in the executive hierarchy weakened his command over the lower administrative ranks. Complaints of abuse of office consequently multiplied in both frequency and gravity. The widening culture of corruption was blatant in the royal law courts, where justice itself became openly available for sale, and in the tax farming system, which in many cases degenerated into overt extortion of the peasantry. Those excesses were used by Taksin's detractors – many of whom were, paradoxically, among the very beneficiaries of the vices they decried – in the mobilization of adverse public sentiment. Reports of pilferage from state inventories at both the central and provincial levels, unwarranted coercion of village folk by their putative patrons, and other symptoms of a spreading malaise within the civil order rose to levels not encountered since earlier reigns, decades past.

The mounting unrest reached breaking point during the evening of February 22, 1782 – not at Thonburi, but at the upcountry town of Ayutthaya. It remained unknown at Thonburi until the dawning of the next day, upon the astonishing appearance of Ayutthaya's distraught and disheveled governor, Colonel

King Taksin at his writing desk in the Thonburi Grand Palace. (Department of Fine Arts, *King Taksin the Great* (in Thai), Bangkok, 2017, p. 58)

Inthara Aphai (Pricha), disembarking from his foam-spattered barge at the Grand Palace's Wasukri Landing, bearing the astonishing news of insurrection. He was ushered straight to the royal presence, where an informal audience had been hastily arranged for him before the king, attended by his Minister of the Palace and the directors of the Palace Guard, Royal Guard, and Royal Arsenal.[42] Taksin, lounging in frail repose against the bolsters on his couch rather than in his customary cross-legged pose upon the seat of state, appeared unwell, but not a word on the matter was whispered, nor even an eyebrow raised. No introductory word of welcome was wasted; Pricha was ordered straightaway to explain his abrupt arrival and unseemly request for an urgent hearing. In quavering tones, the governor offered his apologies, followed by a stammered statement to the effect that the previous day a mass of more than a thousand marauders had stormed the town. A local tax farmer and his family, and several other townspeople, had been murdered in the mayhem, and the governor's residence had been ransacked and set afire. Pricha, his family, and his retinue had all escaped with their lives, and at his first opportunity he had rushed off to inform the king.

Taksin interrupted the governor's monologue in search of more detailed information. Were the marauders a known gang? Who was their leader? Were they well-armed? Had there been widespread looting? What other motives may they have had? Why had they singled out the governor and a tax farmer as their targets? Had Pricha had no foreknowledge of their approach? Had he mobilized his retainers or the townspeople to resist them? Why hadn't Ayutthaya's Pho Sam Ton garrison been called into action? The governor was requested to respond to each and every one of those points.

Shaken by the king's probing questions, Pricha presented a rambling, stumbling response that may be summarized as follows: Tek-ki *sae* Lim, a survivor of Ayutthaya's old Hokkien merchant community, had during Thonburi's revival years reestablished himself at the ruined former capital as a rice trader and tax farmer, attaining the honorary title of Captain Wichit Narong. In 1780, he had expressed to the governor an interest in establishing a royal monopoly on prospecting for the buried wealth left behind in the besieged city in 1767, as a means of bringing under control Ayutthaya's current scourge of indiscriminate treasure hunting. Pricha arranged that tax farm for an annual fee of 500 *chang*[43] payable to the governor on behalf of the Trade Ministry's finance bureau. With that state-sanctioned power in hand, Tek-ki proceeded to auction off certificates of authorization to the many scavengers who had descended on the old capital – his personal benefits being a specified emolument plus a percentage on whatever was found. However, the issuance of monopoly rights to disreputable treasure hunters had only served to increase their vandalism. As for the insurrection, as he persisted in referring to the riot, he opined that it had been organized by treasure hunters disgruntled over their ill-treatment. The Pho Sam Ton garrison had been called out but was so seriously depleted of manpower and firepower that it could not advance against the brigands.

In muted riposte, Taksin dismissed the severity of the incident, referring to it as no more than a minor instance of public protest against incompetent governance. The assaults on the tax farmer's household and the governor's mansion had likely been a spontaneous demonstration of the townspeople's grievances over the plundering of their land. The quaking governor was reprimanded. He was judged derelict in the discharge of his duties, was placed in fetters, and was removed from the chamber, not to be heard of again. The king then turned to the matter at hand. He reminded Ramlak and Madot to ensure the punctilious performance of their duties in securing the capital against unrest. Kawin was commanded to proceed that very day to Ayutthaya, attended by a company of Ramlak's guardsmen, to arrest the mutinous ringleaders, seize all other identifiable pillagers for corporal punishment, and ensure that the deputy governor be installed in a caretaker capacity to maintain law and order. Kawin was ordered to report back within four days, leaving his guardsmen behind to help the locals restore calm. With that final, subdued royal instruction, the audience ended. The silken draperies fronting the king's apartment were drawn shut, and the attending officials were ushered out of the audience chamber as the royal physicians bustled in.

Coup

Mobilization – With the abrupt conclusion of the royal audience, the vortex of events instantly speeded its dizzying whirl. Ramlak, Madot, and Kawin were escorted from Taksin's chambers directly to the Grand Palace Forecourt – the administrative quarter – where, in the ministerial pavilion, out of idle earshot, they conferred in guarded privacy on the precarious state of affairs.[44] It was agreed that, in view of the king's uncertain health, immediate action was called for. Kawin proposed that, in the absence of the Ministers of War and Interior (his patrons, the Chakri brothers), they should assume personal guardianship of their ailing sovereign. Without deep reflection on the many legal ramifications or practical implications of such an unauthorized initiative, they set as their primary task the doubling of all the capital's river patrols and dryland sentry postings, with Ramlak securing the upstream sector and Madot the downstream, while Kawin would ensure the readiness of all arms and munitions stockpiles. They agreed to meet again, upon Kawin's return from Ayutthaya some four days hence, to consider further steps.

Kawin sped off for Ayutthaya by longboat late that very afternoon, as directed, with his younger brother Kaew (his aide-de-camp) at his side and Colonel Rachasena (Ari, Ramlak's deputy officer) leading a company of royal guardsmen in their train. At Ayutthaya, the force disembarked to encamp at the old royal naval base along the Lopburi River, across from the devastated Grand Palace. The three commanders then crossed with a squadron of armed troops to survey the city's riot-torn market neighborhood, learned that the rioters had fled, and conferred with the municipal officials on plans to restore law and order. They incarcerated all malefactors they were able to identify and apprehend. Over the following three days, Kawin decided that his moment had arrived. He devised a scheme for the seizure of power centering on his manipulation of his malleable confederates Ramlak and Madot, management of the Thonburi situation, mobilization of his provincial allies in armed support, negotiation of Taksin's retirement into monastic convalescence, and ultimately his own assumption of the regency – each element of that strategy deeply flawed in its fevered conception. As the ancients have written, imprudent action is a fatal mischief that commanders often encounter in their insatiable appetite for honors and authority.[45]

Leaving Kaew and Ari to deal with the defused Ayutthaya situation, Kawin returned to Thonburi to find the city bustling with its accustomed vitality, seemingly unaware of its problematic governance. He proceeded straight to the Grand Palace to deliver his report but was informed by the gatekeepers that the king was indisposed and would receive him another day, that he should retire to his residence to prepare a written account. That snub fortified him in his intent. Passing Ramlak's riverside palace, Kawin noted the prince's state barge moored at his palace landing and decided to seek an interview straightaway. At that discussion he confided to Ramlak that he had uncovered many signs of unrest upcountry; as at Ayutthaya, many other provincial authorities had exploited their power to impose oppressive regimes. For the sake of the kingdom's integrity, he proposed that the king's three self-styled guardians reconstitute themselves as a Regency Council to ensure firm enforcement of the rule of law during the king's indisposition. He further intimated that, in the event that the king should soon succumb to his affliction – as seemed likely – Ramlak, as the most qualified candidate, would be called on to assume the throne. Intoxicated with those prospects (as expected), Ramlak swallowed Kawin's words without reservation. The two conspirators agreed to meet with Madot the next day to gain his assent to the Regency Council proposal – agreeing also not to mention, for the time being, the possibility of Ramlak's future enthronement.

Triumvirate – At their meeting the next morning, the three conspirators entered into a formal compact to form a triumvirate, with the intent of establishing a Regency Council upon the ailing king's prospective retirement from office. The pact rested on an uneasy alliance, with Kawin acting as a wily conciliator between his two fractious partners. Occupying equivalent, overlapping executive roles as directors of the Royal Guard and Palace Guard, Ramlak and Madot were an unmatched pair, the former consistently willful, the latter invariably cautious, persistently pulling in opposite directions, and requiring a restraining rein. Kawin indulged their disputatious inclinations while he whetted their expectations with fantasies that their gullible temperaments accepted without hesitation. Three days later they met again, and Kawin expanded on his plan. He affirmed that his brother Kaew was underway from Ayutthaya with a musket-bearing militia regiment to help ensure the capital's security during the king's convalescence. He further informed his colleagues (spuriously) that, with the Chakri brothers' assent, the governors of Suphanburi, Nakhon Sawan, and several neighboring provinces had promised armed assistance, if needed. Members of the Chinese merchant community, he suggested (also without foundation), had also indicated their endorsement.

At Kawin's behest, Kaew had cajoled some 400 of the detained Ayutthaya rioters, using the combined threats of continued confinement with promises of adventure and reward, to form a slipshod militia battalion. Their task, they were told, would be to aid Thonburi's Royal Guard in defending the interests of the ailing king against his adversaries. After only ten days of rudimentary training, they sailed off to Thonburi with the intent of augmenting the strength of Kawin's force. On March 10 they disembarked at the mouth of the Banglamphu Canal, directly upstream from the citadel. There they encamped at the vacant troop cantonment alongside Bunma's former Bang Lamphu residence now occupied by his younger brother La. Kaew conferred with Kawin and the next day rowed his men across the river and up the Bangkok Noi Canal to the royal boatyard, where they assembled a string of four war rafts, outfitted as floating gun batteries fashioned from hardwood timbers bound with stout cordage. In stealth, the bulk of the Royal Arsenal's stores of powder and shot were quietly ferried by night from the Grand Palace warehouses to the Royal Guard armory, situated on the opposing canal bank from the royal boatyard, leaving the Palace arsenal lacking. Batteries of field cannon and jingals plus a complementary supply of gunpowder and shot were then roped to Kaew's rafts to form a fleet of floating fortresses. The task was completed quickly but shoddily by inexperienced men, leaving questions as to the flotilla's seaworthiness. Nonetheless, it had been an impressive feat.

From the outset, Madot had harbored reservations concerning his membership in the triumvirate. His intent had been simply to support the king, but the conspirators' discussions had often veered from that prime purpose. The arrival of Kaew's militia, the transfer of munitions from the Royal Arsenal, and the rushed construction of a flotilla of fortified rafts stretched his suspicions to breaking point; his requests for explanation received no convincing response. In a quandary, he decided to confide all to the king. At a private hearing, Taksin heard him out with barely constrained rage, and after a lengthy pause to consider the matter, he responded with an extended harangue, to the effect that Madot had done well to serve the throne's security and discover his colleagues' duplicity. Taksin remarked further that, though ill, he had no thought of abdication. The balance of forces at Thonburi was temporarily in the conspirators' favor, though it had been reduced by Madot's reaffirmation of fealty. Furthermore, Duang, several days' march away, had already been requested to return to Thonburi. There was a good chance that his early arrival would right the situation with little effort. Meanwhile, Madot and his Palace Guard, though undermanned, should be able to hold off any threat posed by such a ramshackle fleet of floating gun batteries led by unworthy officers and manned by untrained marines. On March 13, Madot sent Kawin a brief note announcing his retraction from their understanding, with the simple explanation that he had no greater ambition than to serve his king.

Takeover – Kawin rallied quickly from the shock of Madot's disengagement (which he termed a betrayal), while Ramlak vacillated. To rekindle his co-conspirator's enthusiasm, Kawin played on the prince's vanity by regaling him with fantasies that the king was already preparing to abdicate, that the choice lay between a smooth transition of power and a chaos of contending power brokers, that the natural course of events ran via a regency to Ramlak's ascendancy to the throne as the senior of the few male survivors of Ayutthaya's royal family. He suggested that the Chakri brothers, with their well-known sympathy for the notion that Thonburi should rise as the new Ayutthaya, would surely support that dynastic succession. For good measure, he pointed out there was a chance that Choeng and his Mon militia could now be persuaded to affiliate with the Royal Guard in Thonburi's safekeeping. Seduced by Kawin's enticements, Ramlak succumbed, and the takeover plan continued to unfold.

As his first option, Kawin sought a private royal audience to assess the king's readiness to accept temporary retirement for convalescence under a caretaker government. As anticipated, that overture was brusquely refused. Without hesitation he turned to his second option, to force the issue through military mobilization. Although no great military strategist, Kawin had learned through his many years of active service the essential devices of a clever tactician. Ramlak readily agreed to his proposal for a two-pronged advance against the seat of power, by land and water. The Royal Guards regiments were mustered, arms were distributed, the officers were issued their orders, and all was prepared for action. The newly assembled gun-rafts were slipped into the waters of the Bangkok Noi Canal awaiting the boarding of troops and arms. To their officers, Ramlak and Kawin emphasized that they had no desire to precipitate death or destruction, but merely to provoke fright, flight, and forfeit to the requirements of the day. If called on to fire, the troops should be ordered to aim high to avoid bloodshed; if fired upon, however, aim true. All was readied on March 14.

In the still, pre-dawn moments of the next morning, Ramlak and Ari led their two Royal Guard regiments unopposed and unobstructed through the citadel's garden tracts, bypassing the ruling elite's long line of riverfront residences and retainers' hamlets behind. Their advance soon brought them to the Grand Palace Forecourt wall and its Chang Phoeak Gate. They aimed their grapeshot-loaded guns high to overreach the wall and pelt the Palace Guard cantonment within. A single cannon shot was fired, but no opposition appeared; the undermanned guards force was cowering within. Alarmed gardeners along Ramlak's line of march had forewarned Madot of the advance, and a courier had been rushed to his nearby village to rouse his men to his side. However, they amounted to only a battalion in strength, not near enough to withstand Ramlak's regiments, and in any case they arrived too late. Despite Madot's best efforts to rally his guardsmen, many fled. The northern palace wall and the precincts within were left virtually undefended.

Kawin's simultaneous downriver advance by gun-raft along the length of the citadel waterfront proved even more eventful. The rafts' rapid passage was maneuvered fore and aft by an assemblage of towlined longboats bearing musket-armed troops serving double duty as paddlers. An additional cordon of patrol boats was detached to hold the port under quarantine. All the riverport's trading junks were ordered to drop multiple anchors; all ships' officers and able-bodied seamen were ordered to disembark and remain ashore until further notice. The first of the four rafts was stationed at the mouth of the Mon Canal to intercept any possible opposition from upstream. A second was positioned to threaten the Grand Palace Wasukri Landing and Sao Thongchai Gate. The Bang Luang Canal was blocked by another gun-raft to contest the Grand Palace gun emplacements lining the waterfront alongside the Wichai Prasit Bastion and bottle up the Bang Luang Canal and its Cham naval garrison.

In the early morning sun, the last of the floating batteries, captained by Kawin's younger brother Kaew, was positioned downriver to threaten Santa Cruz.[46] He had been instructed to fire a barrage of light shot over the Portuguese settlement to panic the populace and draw to their side their kinsmen, the Portuguese guardsmen stationed as sentries, sharpshooters, and gunners along the nearby palace parapets. Kaew cried out the order to fire, and the raft's six cannon detonated with one accord in a thunderous discharge and massive recoil, the guns pulling at their lashings and tearing loose.

Panoramic river view of the Thonburi Grand Palace today, showing the Wichai Prasit Bastion (lacking its former fortress roof) at the center, flanked by the Bang Luang Canal confluence to the left and the Wasukri Landing to the right. (Shutterstock). The lines of guns that formerly ranged along the wall's embrasures and its riverfront and canalside base provided a formidable deterrent against naval incursion. It was among those cannon that King Taksin was executed in the early morning of the Chakri countercoup.

The raft surged akilter. Its cannon shifted on their wheeled carriages; several slipped overboard, snapping their tethers and loosening the lanyards binding the raft's log frame. Under the thrust of the heaving, grinding timbers, the crew tumbled into the now roiling waters, along with men from some of the accompanying longboats. Although all good swimmers, a number of the men were mangled between the rolling logs and sank screaming beneath the waves, others drowning entwined in the foundering cannons' netting. Kaew disappeared in the melee. His body was never recovered, presumably dragged to the riverbed with the sinking cannon – his brother not learning of his death until hours later. Leaderless, the damaged flotilla withdrew. Its mission, however, had been accomplished with the rush of horrified Portuguese guardsmen from the palace ramparts to the aid of their kin. With the abandonment of their posts, Madot was in that instant stripped of an essential component of his defending forces.

Confronted on two sides (land and river) by overwhelming force, while contending with the flight of the Palace Guard, Madot saw no way out. The belligerents were demanding that the gates be opened as a sign of surrender, or else they would blow them down. Threatened with unopposed bombardment, incapable of holding out against the concentrated assault with his remaining remnant of troops, Madot was forced to yield or suffer the threatened destruction of the Grand Palace and its occupants – the second time he had been forced into that position in two weeks. He sped to the king's side to explain the situation. Taksin heard, and with words that have gone unrecorded, accepted Madot's plea for capitulation.

Regency – Unopposed, Kawin seized command of the Grand Palace that day, March 15. He met with the king at dawn the next day. Facing a truculent Taksin and his dejected aides, Kawin pressed for the king's temporary relinquishment of the throne in favor of a Regency Council. The proposed council would consist of Ramlak, Kawin, and Madot – a surprising concession, given Madot's earlier defection from the triumvirate. Taksin conceded, with few reservations: he was guaranteed the safety of his family and allowed the assistance of his personal physician and monastic counselor Phra Prom

Reign Change 239

Map 14. The coup, Thonburi, March 15, 1782

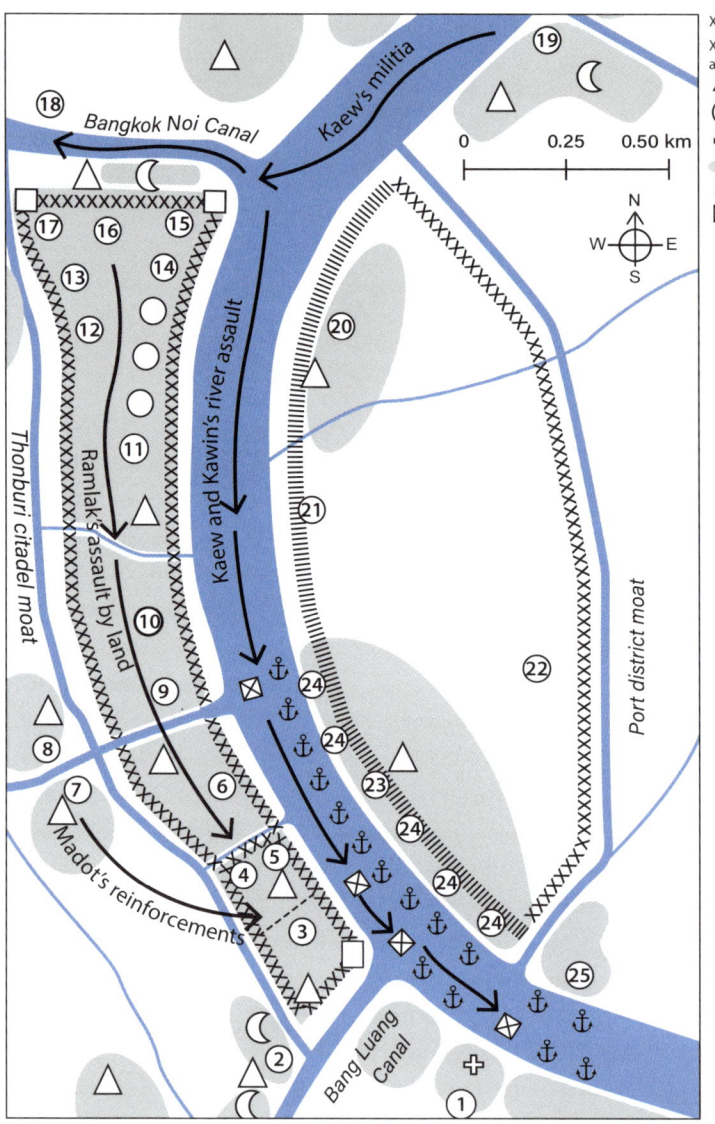

Right Bank
1. Santa Cruz
2. Cham naval garrison
3. Grand Palace audience hall
4. Royal arsenal
5. Palace guard
6. Prince Anurak Songkhram (Ramlak) palace
7. Colonel Ramanwong (Madot) residence
8. Colonel Cheng (Choeng) residence
9. Colonel Thamma Trailok (Bunrot) residence
10. General Chakri (Duang) residence
11. Colonel Suriya Aphai (Thong-in) residence
12. Cavalry stables
13. Elephant stables
14. Colonel Sankhaburi (Kawin) residence
15. Colonel Rachasena (Ari) residence
16. Powder magazine and arsenal
17. Royal guard cantonment
18. Naval boatyard

Left Bank
19. Bang Lamphu garrison (vacant)
20. General Surasi (Bunma) residence
21. Prince Inthara Phithak (Chui) palace
22. Taechiu Royal Guard cantonment (vacant)
23. Royal barge landing
24. Port docks and warehouses
25. Ban Yuan

Muni (Ngao) but was refused his repeated requests that he be consulted on all major policy decisions and that Bunrot, as Minister of the Palace, should be included in the Regency Council. The conditions of the regency were negotiated with studied formality. Taksin would enter seclusion within the Chapel Royal (Wat Noi) with his immediate ordination as a monk. His convalescence in monastic retreat would be tended by Ngao. The royal family and their retinue would continue to occupy the Inside under state security. The state administration would continue uninterrupted under Kawin's aegis as regent. The former tense relationship between the triumvirate partners was thereby revived. Having succeeded in orchestrating Taksin's retirement and arrogating to himself the regency, Kawin agreed that Madot would continue to serve as director of the severely depleted Palace Guard. A regiment of Ramlak's Royal Guard would be positioned along the palace walls and at dispersed sentry posts outside in support. Kawin's gun-rafts would be withdrawn, and the port reopened.

The city came to life without further incident, the riverside fresh food markets regained their bustling business, the daylong panoply of junk traffic returned to normal, the buzz of gossip could again be heard along the village lanes, much as if nothing of great import had occurred. Even Santa Cruz, so recently threatened with annihilation, regained its habitual calm with the village church bell chiming daily its call to morning Mass and evening Vespers. Within the palace, however, confusion reigned. The royal family and its flock of servants remained in protective custody, relegated to the Inside. Not even its kitchen scullions were permitted to attend to their daily food purchases at the neighboring canal's floating market; designated intermediaries were now assigned to trundle all provisions through the inner gates to prevent any direct outside contact. Kawin raided the royal treasury for bullion, ornaments and gemstones, gilded and beaten silver utensils, coins of all sorts, dyed and printed fabrics, and the like, for the regents' distribution as rewards to officers and troops, and bribes to other supporters of the triumvirate. Arrival of the expected provincial militias in support of the Regency Council's call to arms continued unanswered. The regency proceeded in a blur of impotent activity as Kawin struggled to find his footing in an unfamiliar role.

Countercoup

The waiting game – At Khorat and then at Saraburi, with Bunma in command of the Cambodian front, Duang had not been idle. His return to the warm embrace of Saraburi and Kham-waen had the additional advantage of placing him in strategic communication with the deteriorating situation at Thonburi. His brigades at Khorat, under Pin's command, were kept in fighting form with regular reconnoiters to ensure border security, domestic tranquility, and a regular flow of tax revenues into the state coffers, and trade profits into his. At Saraburi, a steady stream of officers from outlying provinces and envoys from neighboring principalities visited him to pay homage, negotiate agreements to mutual advantage, and request his advice and intervention on local matters. As his patronage network thrived, his reputation flourished.

Around the start of March, Bunnak and Pheng, two provincial officials who had joined the recent Ayutthaya uprising, managed to elude Kawin's searching troops in finding their way to Saraburi to plead their cause.[47] Duang had already heard rumors of the Ayutthaya disturbance and the equally troublesome Thonburi reaction, and he heard the two mutineers out with searching questions. Combined with information that he had been receiving from other sources, his suspicions of Kawin's conduct mounted. Within a day or so of the two Ayutthaya renegades' testimony, he dispatched couriers to all provinces to warn of Kawin's bogus blandishments. Much effort was spent collecting further intelligence on the evolving Thonburi situation. The true facts were assessed, and Duang started planning his countermove.

Bunrot – ostensibly on leave from his duties as Taksin's Minister of the Palace for a pilgrimage to the Shrine of the Buddha's Footprint – arrived at Saraburi around March 18 to inform Duang of the coup and related developments at Thonburi. He had succeeded in bypassing Ramlak's naval patrols with his household by proceeding up river by state barge, his ministerial pennants fluttering imperiously in the breeze. At Lopburi, he had entrusted his family and staff to the care of the provincial governor and had continued with a few aides directly to Saraburi. At an urgently arranged interview he narrated to Duang his insider's version of the events that had resulted in the installation of the newly created Regency Council and the king's ordination. He explained that, as instructed by Taksin, he had arranged for the king's and the royal family's comfort, tamped down all palace functions under his purview, and departed the next day. Duang's assessment, added to what he already knew, was that Kawin and his confederates had far overstepped their individual mandates. The state administration was faltering under their care, but the king and his household appeared to be in no imminent danger. He requested Bunrot to remain at his side for the time being, as he intended to seek his advice on the steps he himself had been contemplating.

Not a man to speak easily on matters of import, few of Duang's thoughts on the issues were recorded; his views can be construed only from a summary of his scattered comments, recorded in Bunrot's notes – that "Taksin could not last," that his reign was "failing along with his health," while "rats were gnawing at the door." He disparaged the conspirators as "no more than fireflies feuding with fire." Kawin, the primary instigator, had served as an opportune instrument in former years with his many intelligence reports on Thonburi's goings-on. That clandestine function, however, had apparently excited his frenzied imaginings to more grandiose prospects. His services had initially been courted by his betters with feigned amity, and he had taken the bait with "predatory greed." Duang had managed to install Kawin within the Grand Palace as director of the Royal Arsenal to serve as his covert agent, but his lackey had decided to be his own man, "an unreliable, unpredictable, clamorous knave." At each stage of his career – as gunnery officer, provincial governor, arsenal chief and secret agent, triumvirate member, Regency Council leader – "he had overreached himself." Duang opined that Kawin's actions, with Ramlak's willing collusion and Madot's reluctant complicity, had accelerated the regime's decline along a dangerous course. Their machinations required decisive response.

Duang's brooding reflections on the unfolding crisis coalesced that day, provoking a sudden end to his procrastination. With Bunrot at his side he formed his plan. Without hesitation, he ordered two of his finest regiments of battle-toughened infantry to prepare for action. A dispatch went out to Khorat instructing Colonel Kamhaeng Songkhram (Pin) to instantly send his deputy, Colonel Suriya Aphai (Thong-in) to Saraburi prepared for combat. Concurrently, he dispatched a coded message to Bunma – roving the Cambodian hinterlands in quest of remaining renegade bands – declaring his decision to act and requesting him to ensure that Chui and his Taechiu regiments remain bottled up at Battambang, out of harm's way. Throughout the following days, Bunrot remained at Duang's side as a counselor on the tactics required for the monarchy's restoration to its proper standing. Those days were spent in quiet conversation between the two men of refined intellect whose rich experience at many a council of state had given them deep understanding of the ways of their world.

Seizing the moment – Thong-in was Duang's nephew, the son of his elder sister Sa. Since the death of his father Sem during the fall of Ayutthaya, Thong-in had been privileged to gain Duang's favor as a surrogate son, battle-tested at his side on many a military expedition and clerking as his administrative apprentice during the calmer interludes. His posting as deputy governor at Khorat had demonstrated his uncle's confidence in his prospects. With the arrival of Duang's dispatch calling for his immediate presence, Thong-in rushed to his uncle's side, to be informed, to his delighted astonishment, that he was to lead a pair of elite regiments to confront the Thonburi crisis. His detailed instructions emphasized that he take an uncompromising line with the Regency Council. He should encamp his troops in the midst of the citadel as a show of force, a provocation to unsettle the insurrectionists (as they were now referred to). He was to meet with Kawin at the first opportunity to inform him of Duang's concerns for the kingdom's guardianship. Kawin's hospitable reception would surely mask unfriendly intentions.

A swarm of longboats carrying Thong-in and his lieutenants leading two regiments of battle-scarred veterans reached Thonburi the evening of March 25. They docked at his riverside family residence – directly upstream from Wat Bang Wa Yai, presided over by his mother Sa in his absence – and encamped in the gardens behind. While his troops set up their camp, Thong-in was greeted by his wives and children and then retired with his mother to regale one another with their views on the latest events. With his mother's wise advice, he devised his further action. At dawn the next morning a courier was sent to the palace to announce that Thong-in had arrived as Duang's emissary to establish rapport with the Regency Council. He requested an early meeting and was invited to present himself at the Sao Thongchai Gate at noon that very day.[48] In the evening hours following that meeting, Thong-in sent a dispatch to Saraburi that Ramlak and Kawin (Madot being absent) had received him with little ceremony, had informed him of the king's Wat Noi convalescence, had assured him of the capital's continued peace and prosperity, and had requested him to convey to Duang their invitation for his visit to allow consultations on the kingdom's future governance. During the course of their conversation, Kawin had broached the subject of Thong-in's troop encampment and had requested that, in compliance with established royal protocol, it be promptly relocated to an unoccupied area beyond the citadel wall and moat. Thong-in noted in his dispatch to Duang that, as instructed, he had ignored that demand, and its implicit threat.[49]

The following days grew increasingly tense as Ramlak repeated in ominous tones Kawin's demand for the removal of Thong-in's troop encampment. Thong-in conferred with his mother, and they agreed it expedient to request the support of the enigmatic Choeng (Colonel Cheng), who had for the past several years kept himself and his Mon followers aloof from Thonburi politics. It was known that Choeng was on friendly terms with Bunma, so Thong-in sought his aid through the intercession of Bunma's wife Rocha, at home directly across the river, within a short boat crossing.[50] Disguised as a common market-vendor, Rocha was paddled secretly up the Mon Canal to Choeng's Ban Ataran home, where she persuaded him to join the Chakri brothers' cause by supporting Thong-in in his moment of peril.[51] Choeng summoned his liegemen at Ko Kret[52] to rush to his side, and with the addition of that Mon militia Thong-in assured himself of sufficient firepower to resist with ease the Regency Council's threat.

At the close of that day, March 28, after three days of fruitless delay, the regents elected to expel forthwith Thong-in's encamped troops from the citadel. As the gardens were coming to life the next morning with gathering birdsong and crowing cocks, Ramlak and Ari led their two-regiment-strong Royal Guard the short distance from their cantonment to Thong-in's camp – and, unexpectedly, into direct confrontation with his battle-ready troops ranged in waiting ranks supported by batteries of field guns. The Royal Guard was well-versed in the protocol of stately processions but had received little training in battle maneuvers. A single accidental musket discharge magically transformed the intended démarche into a full-fledged firefight. The Guards encirclement was unprepared for the withering volleys of musket-balls and grapeshot poured out by Thong-in's massed men. Their line of march dissolved into broken ranks. The thatch roofs of nearby hamlets were set alight, and amid the shifting smoke and flame of the fast-spreading brushfire the frightened troops were pressed into full retreat. Their flight was hastened with the arrival of Choeng's Mon militia along their right flank. As they raced through the burning hamlets past the Royal Guard stables, Choeng and his attendants, skilled at elephantry, veered off to calm the tethered, trumpeting beasts and rode them off to battle, while other contingents rushed to free throngs of panic-stricken cavalry horses from their staked enclosures. Pursuit of the fleeing guardsmen continued inland, through the citadel wall's rear supply portals and across the moat into the outer garden tracts. At Wat Suttha the combatants came into close combat with spear and sword. Enveloped by the combined might of

Map 15. The countercoup, Thonburi, March 26–April 6, 1782

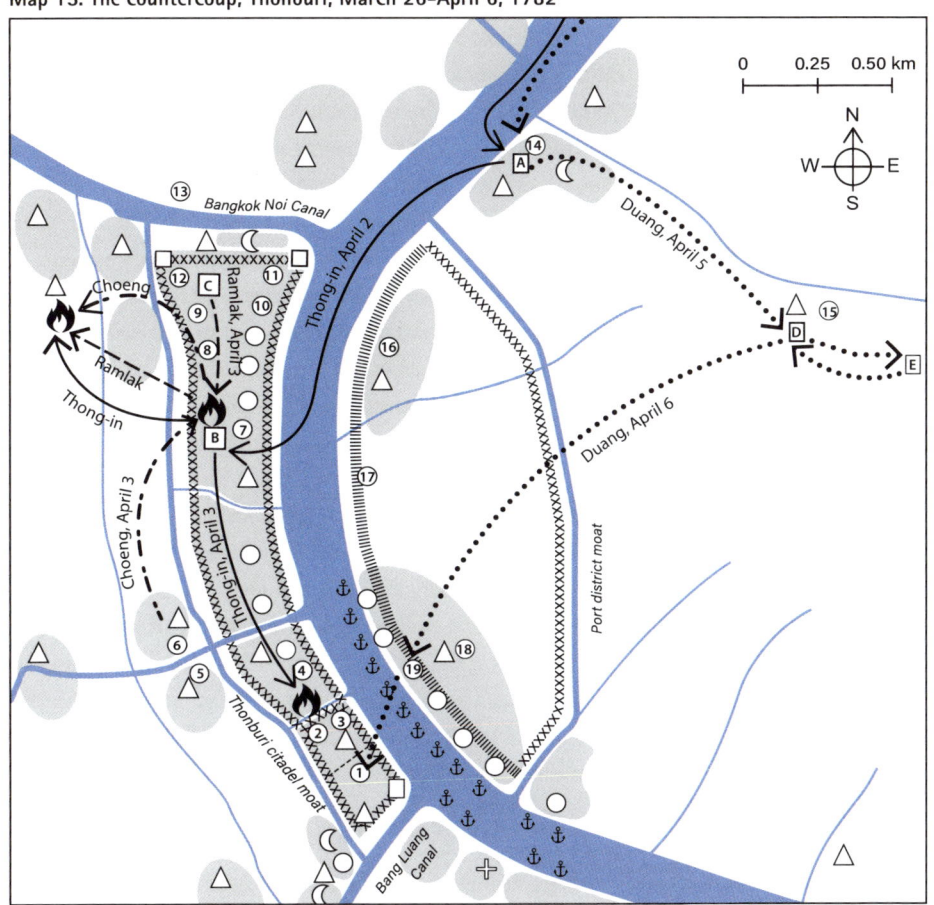

		Armed camps	Military movements
XXX	Thonburi citadel wall	A Bang Lamphu garrison	← Thong-in's assaults
XXX and IIII	Port district wall and stockade	B Thong-in's troop encampment	←— Ramlak's assault and retreat
△	Temples	C Royal Guard cantonment	←·— Choeng's assaults
☾	Mosques	D Duang's staff headquarters	←······ Duang's arrival and procession
✚	Church	E Duang's troop encampment	
	Densely populated areas		
⚓	Junk anchorages	**Right Bank sites**	11. Colonel Rachaseni (Ari) res.
🔥	Military engagements	1. Grand Palace audience hall	12. Powder magazine and arsenal
		2. Royal arsenal	13. Naval boatyard
		3. Palace Guard	
		4. Prince Ramlak's palace	**Left Bank sites**
		5. Colonel Ramanwong (Madot) res.	14. Bang Lamphu Prince Chakra Chesada (La) palace
		6. Colonel Cheng (Choeng) res.	15. Wat Sakae
		7. Colonel Suriya Aphai (Thong-in) res.	16. General Surasi (Bunma) res.
		8. Cavalry stables	17. Prince Inthara Phithak (Chui) palace
		9. Elephant stables	18. Wat Pho
		10. Colonel Sankhaburi (Kawin) res.	19. Royal barge landing

Reign Change 245

Thong-in's hardened veterans and Choeng's spirited militia, Ramlak's men suffered many casualties. Ramlak himself was finally forced to surrender or face extermination.

Leaving capture of the defeated forces in the hands of his lead regiment and Choeng's militia, Thong-in turned his second, disencumbered regiment in the opposite direction and raced toward the Grand Palace. At the palace wall he stepped forward – risking all against a deadly assassin's shot – and bellowed out that the Royal Guard had been defeated, and that the palace defenders were next. From atop the wall, Madot roared back that he and his troops were the king's men, not the regency's lackies. At the king's instruction he would refuse to set them against their compatriots in meaningless bloodlust. He proposed an honorable détente. Further words were exchanged, concluding with agreement that all hostilities would be concluded with the surrender of Madot – and also Kawin – to the besieging forces. It was Madot's second capitulation in a matter of two weeks, but through it he prevented a massacre, and retrieved his honor.

Coup de grâce – It can be conjectured, in hindsight, that Duang had for several years been tracing the troubles unfolding at Thonburi with growing trepidation and had come to envisage the broad contours of its resolution months in advance of the decisive moment. However, no battle plan survives first contact with the enemy. With that credo firmly in mind, he adjusted his strategy to conform to shifting circumstances, and so advised his aide Thong-in. Thong-in's compliance with his uncle's instructions, his initiative in seizing the day against Kawin, ended in triumph. The Palace Guard laid down their guns and were escorted into dignified detention. Kawin was captured and consigned to the privations of the municipal prison, along with Ramlak and Madot. The king, his family, and court were placed under protective custody, with every consideration for their care and comfort. For the following week, Thong-in and his battalions held the peace, in soldierly command of an expectant city awaiting the imminent arrival of Duang.

In spectacular procession, Duang glided down the river from Ayutthaya upon his ministerial barge accompanied by Bunrot's equally imposing vessel, surrounded by the lesser rivercraft of their staff officers and the many longboats carrying four paddling regiments of veteran warriors chanting their cadence to the complement of fife warble and drum pulse. At Ko Kret they disembarked amid the greetings of a joyful populace and the ceremonious reception of a throng of Thonburi dignitaries. Thong-in, Choeng, and La had been forewarned of Duang's imminent arrival a day before and had rushed upriver to greet him. They convened at Ko Kret in formal assembly, to be reminded by Duang of their common aim: the kingdom's continued peace and prosperity under a just and vigorous monarchy. To that end, they were apprised in broad terms of the next days' plans. In response, Duang received an enthusiastic acclamation of fealty. At the ensuing celebratory repast, Thong-in mustered the nerve, in the conviviality of the moment, to ask why his uncle had not sped directly to the citadel to take command in the first instant. In affectionate response, Duang smiled that he had had no wish to detract

General Chakri racing down the Chaophraya River to Thonburi to join the countercoup against Kawin. (No Na Paknam, *Murals Explained* (in Thai). Bangkok: Muang Boran, 1993, p. 90)

from his nephew's brilliant achievement. He then recalled, more seriously, his father's advice of many years before: "When savoring a bowl of rice porridge, a spoonful lifted gently from the rim will prove far preferable to one gobbled directly from the center."

The flotilla continued its stately journey down the great river later that day to disembark, as planned, at Bang Lamphu. The troops assembled at the riverside cantonment abutting Thonburi's old northern guardpost – recently occupied and then vacated as the base for Kaew's Ayutthaya militia – while Duang and his official party were hosted at La's neighboring residence. The regiments marched off to a secluded tract in Thonburi's eastern outskirts, where an encampment had been arranged for them awaiting further developments.[53] Thong-in had earlier that day consulted with Phra Phrom Muni (Ngao) to receive permission for Duang's overnight stay at the temple, a request that was graciously accepted. Ngao then accompanied Thong-in to the Chapel Royal (Wat Noi), where Ngao had been caring for the king in his monastic confinement. As instructed, Thong-in begged the king's pardon for the jeopardy in which he had been placed and sought his support for the armed reckoning presently underway. The king, however, refused to be beholden to a tyrant for his acts of tyranny, for it would be no more than usurpation for Duang, Thong-in's master, to govern the lives of those over whom he had no right to reign.[54] Taksin is said to have declared on that occasion: "I would rather die *by* Duang than *with* him."

Late that afternoon, Duang and his adjutants visited the eastern military encampment. There, he mounted a high-raised victory pavilion that had been quickly assembled to allow him to address his regiments in praise of their unflinching service, enthusiastic support, and unparalleled valor. He guaranteed them great reward on the morrow.[55] That evening, he entered upon a sleepless night of strenuous work at Wat Sakae.

Reign Change 247

With Bunrot and other aides at his side, he received a steady stream of nobles offering their services, issued orders to ensure firm control of the capital, and made detailed preparations for the next day's climactic proceedings. It was during those intense hours that he issued the orders laying the course of the following morning's royal accession and composed the series of edicts that would mark the start of his reign. Among the swarm of issues requiring urgent resolution, in consultation with his closest confidantes, were the logistics of the land and water processions from his Left Bank base to the Grand Palace; security arrangements at the Grand Palace in preparation for his arrival; arrangements for the investiture ritual; drafting of edicts proclaiming the new royal family and senior government appointments; and finally the most difficult task of all, issuance of decrees governing the execution of Taksin and others standing in his way. The many daunting, haunting decisions that he was compelled to make that night amid the torrent of administrative minutia led him to discredit the hoary adage that "arms and the law have each their own time."[56]

The final preparation for the next day's culmination was a solemn anointment at Duang's Wat Sakae headquarters.[57] Phra Maha Rachakhru (Sombat), dressed in his white devotional garb, carrying his gold-ornamented lustral conch in his formal role as a Brahmin priest, served as the chief officiant, followed by the chanting of Buddhist suttas by a line of fan-fronted, saffron-robed monks led by Phra Thamma Trailok (Si) of Wat Bang Wa Yai. Thereby, Duang, Siam's prospective king, was cleansed of all impurities in readiness for his coming ordination and enthronement rites. How far his own inclinations had led him thus to usurp sovereign power will forever remain a mystery.[58]

A *phlapphla* traditionally served as a grand podium from which a monarch or military commander could address his regiments in gathered assembly. At Ayutthaya's Grand Palace, the Chakkrawat Phaichayon Throne Hall, set upon the front palace wall overlooking the royal parade ground, had served that purpose. It served as the model for the victory pavilion from which Duang addressed his regiments at their Left Bank encampment preceding his seizure of the throne. Bangkok's present-day Phlapphla Chai District gained its name from the memory of that stirring event. (Shutterstock)

Epilogue

Editor's introduction

Diogo concludes his epic Chronicle of a tumultuous half-century of Siamese crises with a subdued recounting of General Chakri's (Duang's) nightlong vigil in preparation for the coming day's climax. Although Diogo's brief accompanying Testament touches on Duang's coronation as the founder of the Chakri Dynasty, and on aspects of its immediate aftermath, those later events were not his concern in writing the chronicle, nor did he live long enough to be able to gauge their impact. The relocation of the capital across the river from Thonburi to Bangkok, the unfolding of a new ruling dynasty, the implications for the kingdom's governance and the lives of its people – all that has been traced in later reign chronicles, supplemented by an endless litany of academic explorations.

In this epilogue, Claude and Cláudio, the translators of Diogo's manuscripts, round off his episodic tale with a brief recounting of the immediate aftermath – the reign change of April 6, 1782, the formation of a new governing elite, and the capital's transition from Thonburi to Rattanakosin. Their aim here is simply to link Diogo's narrative with the later, better understood course of events stretching through Duang's reign as King Ramathibodi (posthumously restyled as Phra Phutha Yodfa Chulalok, and later Rama I) and beyond through the subsequent Chakri Dynasty reigns that have continued uninterrupted to the present-day reign of King Maha Vajiralongkorn Phra Vajira klao chao yu hua (Rama X).

An ancient royal barge figurehead. (Author's photo). This salvaged 2.5-meter-tall hardwood carving of Garuda with Indra astride and a gunport beneath, stands on display at the Royal Barge Museum, Bangkok Noi Canal. (Author's photo) In centuries past it served as the figurehead for the Narai Song Suban Royal Barge, estimated to have been at least 45 meters long and propelled by 50 oarsmen and two steersmen. That vessel, long lost, is said to have carried General Chakri from Wat Pho across the river to the Thonburi Grand Palace on the morning of April 6, 1782, en route to his ascension to the throne of Siam. It would, however, have been exceedingly imprudent for Duang to have commandeered that preeminently royal conveyance while still a nobleman. There would have been many more discreet but scarcely less magnificent barges available to convey him on that climactic river crossing.

Translators' postscript

General Chakri's ascension to the throne – As best as can be reconstructed from the fragmentary records – and as Diogo recorded in his Testament based on personal observation – Duang was conveyed crossriver from Wat Pho to the Thonburi Grand Palace on a state barge at mid-morning, April 6, 1782. At the astrologically propitious moment, he disembarked for transfer to a regal palanquin that bore him in grand panoply through the Wasukri Gate to the Royal Audience Hall, where at the next auspicious moment he was consecrated in accordance with Brahmanical rites and then ascended the throne as King Ramathibodi, said to be the fifth king of Siam bearing that title. He is recorded as the thirty-sixth king of Siam (excluding Taksin) since Ayutthaya's founding by King Ramathibodi I (King Uthong) more than four centuries previously. He was posthumously retitled Phrabat Somdet Phra Phutha Yodfa Chulalok and then, more than a century later, additionally assigned the newly coined title of Rama I, the first of the ten successive sovereign "Ramas" of the Chakri Dynasty to the present day.

King Rama I the Great, an iconic image engraved on the back of a 500-baht banknote, issued June 6, 1996. (Shutterstock)

King Taksin's execution – So long as Taksin lived, he remained Siam's divine overlord (*devaraja*), consecrated in accord with Indic tradition as an avatar of the Brahman (Hindu) gods Vishnu and Indra. No king could legitimately assume the throne while his sacred predecessor still lived. Throughout the night's preparations for his ascension to the throne, Duang's preoccupation had been the validation of his own impending assumption of office. That concern impelled him to order Taksin's execution before his own enthronement. To confirm his claim that the Thonburi reign had been illegitimate, the death sentence was carried out by with his beheading by saber rather than in accord with the royal tradition of a bloodless blow to the neck by sandalwood club. Duang's enthronement thus recommenced the Ayutthaya dynastic succession, leaving Taksin's reign little more than an interregnum.

Taksin was compelled first to undergo formal separation from the monkhood, as the killing of a monk would have been an unthinkable sacrilege. The next morning, shortly after daybreak and hours before Duang's coronation, Taksin was taken under guard from the Chapel Royal to the Wichai Prasit Bastion, and there, at the rampart's base, among the gun batteries emblematic of his former military glories, he met his death. His corpse was conveyed up the Bang Luang Canal to Wat Intharam, well outside the capital bounds, for unceremonious burial in the temple's charnel ground.

With that cleansing of the political scene Duang, escorted on elephant-back by his marching regiments, proceeded from his Wat Sakae command post to Wat Pho and from there crossed the river by royal barge to take possession of the Grand Palace and ascend the vacant throne. Two years later, to placate continuing disquiet, Taksin's remains were exhumed and cremated with proper ceremony at Wat Intharam as a royal act of expiation, said to have been attended by a mass of dignitaries led by the new king and his viceroy. Taksin's crematory remains are said to have been enshrined in a monument that continues to grace the temple's forecourt to the present day.

Further executions – In the days following the reign change the books were cleared with the execution of some 40 royals and nobles who had led the opposition to the Chakri Revolution. An additional 80 or more additional supporters of Kawin's aborted takeover – later known as the Phraya San Rebellion – were beheaded over the following several weeks. Foremost among those executed were the insurrectionist triumvirate: Colonel San (Kawin), Prince Anurak Songkhram (Ramlak), and Colonel Ramanwong (Madot), along with a number of their senior aides, including Colonel Rachasena (Ari). Different grounds for execution were subsequently invoked against Colonel Phichai Dap Hak (Sanguan, known in later writings as Thong-in), who was foremost among those who suffered beheading for refusing to partake of the Water of Allegiance in fealty to the successor of their beloved king and commander. A month later, Taksin's senior son and would-be viceroy Prince Inthara Phithak (Chui) and his principal officers were executed at Prachin, where they had been conveyed from Battambang by the newly invested Prince Surasinghanat (Bunma, the new king's younger brother), ending the last hope for revival of the Thonburi Dynasty.

Expulsions – With the exception of Taksin's family and their personal attendants, all palace officials were dismissed from their posts and banished to settlements well beyond the city limits. Diogo's own exile to Rosario provides a vivid example. Among the other cases mentioned in the Chronicle and Testament is that of Lady Songkandan (Thong-mon), superintendent of the Inside and Taksin's former caregiver, who was relegated to the remote downriver settlement of Ban Tawai. The relocation of Thonburi's Taechiu merchant community to Sampheng is another. An exception to that rule of internal exile was Lieutenant Chinda (La), Diogo's former colleague in the Royal Secretariat, now elevated to Prince Chakra Chesada who, having injudiciously evinced his sentiments favoring the former regime, was not physically expelled but simply ostracized from the royal family's inner circle.

The former royal family – Taksin's two queens and many consorts and children were dispossessed of their royal ranks and emoluments but were allowed to remain in temporary residence within the Thonburi Grand Palace Inside with their personal service staff. Once the essential lineaments of the Bangkok Grand Palace had been

Table 7. Taksin family kinship links with the Chakri Dynasty

Taksin's offspring	Kinship links with the Chakri Dynasty
Amphawan	As a senior son of King Taksin, Amphawan remained closely associated with CF Kasat Anuchit (Men, son of Taksin and grandson of Rama I) and was executed with him in 1809, at the start of the Second Reign, on charges of conspiracy in the so-called CF Men Rebellion. Amphawan's eldest daughter, *Saeng*, was married to POC Phithak Thewet (Kunchon, son of Rama II). His fourth daughter, *Phoeng*, was married to POC Rachasiha Wikrom (Chumsai, son of Rama III).
Thasaphong	As Phra Phong Narin, Thasaphong served with his brother Thasaphai (Phra Inthara Aphai) during the Second Reign as a physician with the Ministry of the Capital. He married *Chap*, a daughter of *Kaew* (younger sister of Rama I's wife *Nak* [Queen Amarin]). His daughter *Sangiam* married Luang Rit, a son of Noi (CP Sutham Montri, Governor of Nakhon Si Thgannarat, "secret son" of *Prang* – see below). His daughter *Phlap* married POC Phumin Phakdi (Ladawan, son of Rama III) and bore three children: MC Saraphi, MC Ladawan, and MC Phoeak.
Sila	Sila rose to the rank and title of Phraya Prachachip during the Third Reign. His daughter, *Phlap*, married POC Kasat Sisakdidet (Phong Isaret, son of the Second Reign Viceroy and *Samliwan*, Sila's younger sister). She bore three children: MC Krachang, MC Chantri, and MC Saowarot.
Thasaphai	Thasaphai was titled Phra Inthara Aphai during the Second Reign and, with his brother Thasaphong (Phra Phong Narin), served in the Ministry of the Capital's physicians department. Found guilty of conducting an illicit affair with a consort of Rama II, he was executed. His orphaned daughter *Noi* was selected as a consort of CF Mongkut (later Rama IV) and bore his two eldest sons: POC Mahesuan (Nopawong, founder of the Nopawong lineage) and POC Wisanunat, (Supradit, founder of the Supradit lineage).
Samliwan	Samliwan was married to CF Senanurak (Chui, son of Rama I, later Second Reign Viceroy) and bore six children: MC Yai (died in childhood), *MC Prachumwong*, *MC Nadda, MC Khanitha,* MC Phong Isara (elevated to POC Kasat Sisakdidet, founder of the Isarasena lineage), and MC *Naroemon*. She was executed in 1809 on charges of collaboration in the CF Men Rebellion.

Naren Rachakuman	Titled Phra Naren Racha during the Second Reign, Naren Rachackuman served as a senior military officer against the Chao Anu rebellion in the Third Reign. His daughter *Phan* served as a consort of Rama IV and bore POC Thanom.
Panchapapi	Panchapapi was married to CF Isaranurak (son of Rama I's elder sister Sa) and bore five children: MC Yai, MC Klang, MC *Si-fa*, MC Sunthon, and MC *Rot-sukhon*.
Noi	Taksin's newly pregnant consort *Prang* was transferred to the custody of CP Sutham Montri (Phat), Viceroy of Nakhon Si Thammarat SK). Noi was thus spoken of from birth as Taksin's "secret son." He was appointed Governor of Nakhon Si Thammarat during the Second Reign with the title of CP Sutham Montri (the title formerly carried by his foster father). His daughter *Noi Yai* was accepted as a consort of Rama III; she bore POC Chaloemwong. Three other daughters became consorts of Rama IV. Of those, his daughter *Bua* bore POC Chaloem Laksanaloet, POC Sirithat Sangkat (founder of the Sirithat lineage), POC Orathai Thep-kanya, POC Maruphong Siriphat (founder of the Wathanawong lineage), and POC Damrongrit.
Madoea	A daughter of Taksin's senior son CF Inthara Phithak (Chiu), Madoea was married to POC Nara Thewet (Pan, son of Rama I's nephew and deputy Viceroy CF Anurak Thewet [Thong-in]).
Sali	A younger daughter of Taksin's senior son CF Inthara Phithak (Chiu), Sali was married to POC Seni-borirak (Taeng, younger son of Rama I's nephew and deputy Viceroy CF Anurak Thewet [Thong-in]).
Name unknown	A Taksin daughter, her name lost to history, was married to POC Sunthon Phubet (Roeang, a Chakri lineage adjunct [possibly a nephew of the family matriarch *Dao-roeang*] and First Reign intimate). Her daughter *Khiaw* married Prince Chesada Bodin (later Rama III) and bore two children, POC *Phanga* and POC Adun Laksana Sombat (Urai, founder of the Uraiphong lineage).

CF = chao fa (celestial prince/princess)
POC = phra ong chao (senior prince/princess)
MC = mom chao (junior prince/princess)
CP = chaophraya (minister)
Women's names are in italics.

laid out and its preliminary stockade erected, the entire assemblage was relocated along with their dismantled dwellings to an inconspicuous corner of the Inside of the new palace complex. Taksin's consorts were permitted to return to their parental families' homes accompanied by their personal attendants, and over the subsequent years the deaths of the remaining Taksin women and the departure of their children left their section of the Grand Palace Inside to wither gradually toward oblivion.

Of Taksin's more than 30 children, many survived his reign. Over the months and years following his execution, a number of his surviving sons entered government service, and some eventually attained prominent positions, while a number of his surviving daughters were married off into the Chakri Dynasty lineage. A number of their children, in turn, were absorbed into the Chakri lineage through further intermarriage, some founding memorable royal lineages. Others founded noble lineages that continue today. That continuing process of reignal coalescence progressively blurred the dynastic divide and dampened lingering factional rancor.

The new royal family – Among the first acts of Rama I as founder of the Chakri Dynasty (ignoring the titular anachronism) was his formal presentation of a gold-sheet certificate to each of his closest kin inscribed with their royal rank and title, confirming their exalted status as a member of the new royal family. Over the reign's course, the ablest of those family members came to be relied on by the king as his principal private confidantes and were called on to serve as his foremost royal household stewards, ministerial overseers, and military commanders.

Foremost among Rama I's kindred, his brother Bunma (formerly General Surasi, Minister of Interior) was elevated to Celestial Prince Surasinghanat, Prince of the Front Palace, the king's viceroy. Bunma's senior wife Rocha was accordingly elevated to Celestial Princess Siri Rochana. Bunma continued to serve as his brother's senior military commander and counselor; he was allotted administrative oversight over the northern provinces while the king dealt primarily with the realm's seaboard and southern reaches. Six of Bunma's 43 recorded children were born before the start of the First Reign. Two of them were executed and an additional three were banished in the wake of an aborted rebellion said to have been plotted in the wake of their father's death in 1803; their royal titles and accomplishments were subsequently expunged from the record. Only the eldest, Rocha's daughter Pikun-thong (Celestial Princess Si Sunthon), continued in good standing as guardian of Bunma's many younger children.

The king's two elder sisters Sa and Kaew were raised to Celestial Princesses Thep Sudawadi and Si Sudarak, respectively, and installed as joint supervisors of the Grand Palace administration; their total of nine children were incorporated into the royal family as a younger generation of Celestial Princes and Princesses. Sa's eldest son, Celestial Prince Anurak Thewet (Thong-in) rose to Prince of the Front Palace, the king's deputy viceroy. The king's younger half-sister Ku was raised to Celestial

Princess Narinthara Thewi, and her husband Muk joined her as Celestial Prince Narin Phithak. The king's younger half-brother La was designated Celestial Prince Chakra Chesada; La's later ostracism from the Chakri family's inner circle for his pro-Taksin views left the names and titles of his children unrecorded.

Rama I is recorded as having fathered a total of 42 children, all of whom were awarded royal rank. His senior wife Nak was mother of his first nine children; four of them, two sons and two daughters, survived into the First Reign. Her eldest son, Chim (Celestial Prince Isara Sunthon), was appointed his father's viceroy in 1806 and three years later succeeded him to the throne as Rama II, and the second, Chui (Celestial Prince Sen Anurak), was appointed viceroy to his brother Chim at the start of the Second Reign. Of the 32 children born after he became king, 11 sons lived to adulthood to rise to prominent positions as government overseers and form their own lineages, expanding the Chakri Dynasty through further generation: All that made for a tight inner circle that, complemented by adjunct role played by the leading children of Duang's brother Bunma and his two sisters Sa and Kaew, continued to dominate Siam's political scene for generations to come.

The new ministerial line-up – The reign change of 1782 saw a comprehensive turnover of senior government personnel. The clean slate allowed Rama I, in close collaboration with his brother and viceroy Bunma, to elevate a select group of family affiliates and trusted confidantes to the seniormost positions. Pli and Son, retainers and military officers under the Chakri brothers' command, were appointed the Ministers of War and Interior, respectively. Bunnak, a lifelong friend who had spent the Taksin years as warden of Duang's Thonburi estate and had married his sister-in-law Nuan, rose to Minister of the Capital and then Minister of War. Pin, whose elder brother Muk had married Duang's younger half-sister Khu, was installed as Minister of Lands. Hon, who had kept the Chakri brothers informed of developments at Thonburi during their years on military campaign and at Saraburi and Khorat, proved to be a brilliant Minister of Trade. The only minister continuing in office from the former reign was Bunrot, Minister of the Palace, who had deftly joined Duang's cause in the days leading to the reign change. In addition, the reinstatement of Phra Thamma Trailok (Si) as Siam's supreme patriarch with the new title of Phra Phonarat heralded a dramatic shift of the monastic order to a more conservative ecclesiastical stance.

As with many official appointments, ministerial titles were closely associated with the office and generally passed from one incumbent to the next, making it difficult to tell who was who, without the personal name being appended. Despite such complexities and confusions, the tight-knit bonds of the First Reign's ruling elite, their family connections, their close links with the ancestral Ayutthaya aristocracy, and their limited turnover are evident.

Table 8. Ministries and ministers of the First Bangkok Reign, 1782–1809

Ministry	Years in office	Ministers
War (*kalahom*)	1782 – 1787	Gen. Mahasena (Pli)
	1787 – 1805	Gen. Akhara Mahasena (Bunnak)
	1895 – 1809[1]	Gen. Aphai Phuthon (Pin)
Interior (*mahadthai*)	1782 – 1805	Gen. Ratana Phiphit (Son)
	1805 – 1809	Unknown
Trade (*phra khlang*)	1782 – 1785	Gen. Phra Khlang (Son)
	1780 – 1805	Gen. Phra Khlang (Hon)
	1805 – 1809[2]	Gen. Phra Khlang (Kun)
Capital (*moeang*)	1782 – 1785	Col. Yomarat (Thong-in)
	1785 – 1787	Col. Yomarat/later Gen. Akhara Mahasena (Bunnak)
	1787 – 1809	Col. Yomarat (Bunma)
Palace (*wang*)	1776[3] – 1785	Gen. Thammathikon (Bunrot)
	1785 – c.1804	Gen. Thammathikon (Thong-di)
	c.1804 – 1809	Gen. Thammathikon (Sot)
Lands (*na*)	1782 – 1805	Gen. Pholathep (Pin)
	1805 – 1810[1]	Gen. Pholathep (Bunnak Ban Maela)
Front Palace (*wang na*)	1782 – 1809	Unknown

1 Continued into the Second Reign
2 Transferred to Ministry of Interior at the start of the Second Reign
3 Carried over from the Thonburi reign

The founding of Rattanakosin – It appears that a proposal had been mooted in the later years of the Thonburi reign to move the royal redoubt to the Left Bank, but realization of that plan had to await the dynastic turnover of 1782 to reach fruition. Within the first two weeks of the start of the First Reign the decision to recenter the capital from the Right Bank to the Left had been confirmed with a survey of the new city site and the demarcation of its main features. The new, enlarged riparian capital of Rattanakosin, centered on the Left Bank, retained the Thonburi citadel as its Right Bank extension, but it quickly gained an independent identity. While the total area (Right and Left Banks) more than doubled Thonburi's former size to 4.6 square kilometers, the new Left Bank walled city alone covering fully four-fifths of that total. Yet, the greatly expanded size still left the kingdom's new capital only half as large as that of old Ayutthaya.

The new capital was laid out as an approximate, reduced-scale replica of its Ayutthaya prototype, turned 90 degrees on its axis to accommodate the river course. An elaborate inner citadel was designed for the aristocracy, with an outer precinct designated for the nobility, leaving the commons – other than small communities of artisans, servants, and retainers attached to individual elite households – relegated to the suburban periphery beyond the city's walled and moated bounds. The capital's basic parameters were quickly marked out. First, a city pillar was planted with appropriate Brahman ritual at the capital's precise center, guiding the geomantics of further work. Then, many months were spent draining, clearing, leveling, and raising the Left Bank's waterlogged terrain. A new city moat was excavated to define and defend the enlarged Left Bank bounds; a strong city wall was erected; the positions of the new royal palaces – the Grand Palace and Front Palace, and later the Rear Palace on the Right Bank – were determined; and the principal royal temples were rebuilt and renamed as Wat Phra Chetuphon (formerly Wat Photharam), Wat Mahathat (formerly Wat Salak), Wat Rakhang (formerly Wat Bang Wa Yai), and then Wat Saket (formerly Wat Sakae) and Wat Arun (formerly Wat Chaeng). Locations for the newly awarded princely palaces and noblemen's mansions were marked out. The thousands of Khmer, Lao, and other war captives conscripted to carry out the massive construction project were assigned settlement sites in the new city's sparsely populated outskirts, alongside the informal arrangement of commoner villages and garden smallholdings.

In miniature reflection of the kingdom's feudal configuration, the capital was laid out as a series of concentric zones of habitation radiating from the royal citadel in successively diminishing degrees of eminence: within, the aristocracy was surrounded by the nobility occupying adjoining sections of the walled city; without, along the urban periphery, settlements of lower social strata – freemen, war captives, and slaves of all ethnicities – abounded. Drawing on later studies of Bangkok's social history, a speculative accounting of Bangkok's ruling elite (aristocracy and nobility) as of the

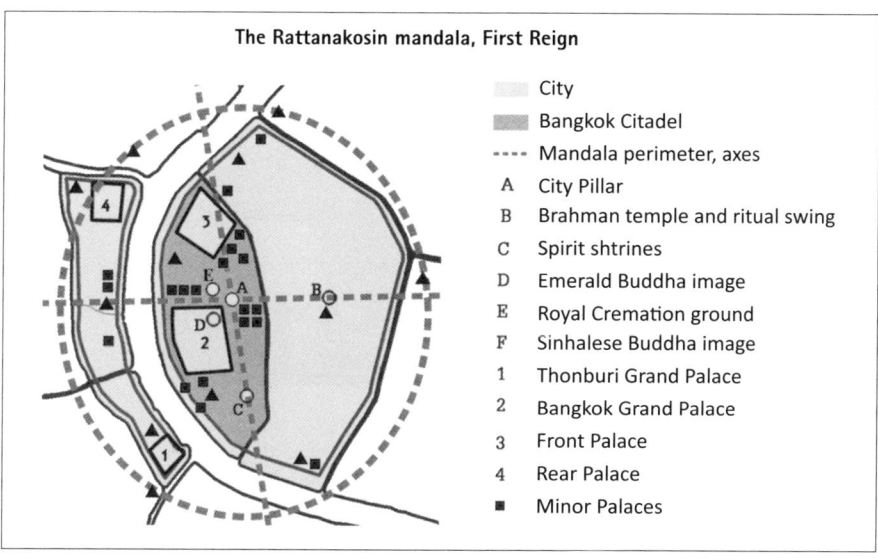

The Bangkok mandala, First Reign. Bangkok was purposely designed, as had been Ayutthaya before, in the form of a mandala (*monthon* in Thai), simulating the layout of Indra's celestial city, radiating symmetrically from the centrally positioned City Pillar (*lak moeang*), surrounded by the royal palaces, temples, and noblemen's mansions and encircled in turn by the city wall with its 16 bastions and circling moats, as the kingdom's spiritual, administrative, and economic center.

Epilogue 257

start of the First Reign came to no more than several thousand, occupying the walled city. At the same time, the capital's commoner population of Thai and diverse minority groups, came to perhaps 75,000. In all, the Bangkok conurbation at the start likely contained no more than a tenth as many people as Ayutthaya a generation previously.

Several years after the city's founding, a great celebration was organized to proclaim the completion of the fledgling capital's construction. Newly built Rattanakosin glittered under its heightened glory. The people rejoiced in frivolity as divers entertainments were staged and sweetmeats were distributed at public expense. Royal land and water processions were arranged, cannon fired their salutes, fireworks flared through the air, in the temples the monks chanted their prayers of praise. Within the Grand Palace, pipes trilled, horns and conchs blared, cymbals clashed, drums pounded. Atop the high-raised portico fronting the splendid Inthara Phisek Prasat Throne Hall (later renovated as the Dusit Maha Prasat Throne Hall), the recently crowned king, adorned in royal regalia, standing stiffly erect under the canopied spire of the Busabok Throne as sovereign of Siam, surrounded by his family, ministers, and masses of lesser officials prostrate in humble obeisance, could survey his realm with pride. Siam had broken from a half-century of dynastic turbulence. Under his reign, Duang swore to himself, Siam would continue to stride forward with confidence into a new era of peace and prosperity.

King Rama I presiding over a royal audience at the Bangkok Grand Palace. (Wikipedia Commons). This painting, formally titled "The coronation of King Taksin [at the Thonburi Grand Palace, 1768]," actually represents a different event presided over by a different king at another time and place. The architectural rendering shows the precise features of the Dusit Maha Prasat Throne Hall built 1806 within the Bangkok Grand Palace. It shows King Rama I (ascended the throne in 1782) standing triumphant in his *busabok* throne.

Translators' Coda

And there the matter rests, as this book presenting our edited English translations of Diogo's Chronicle and Testament nears completion.[1] We can finally lean back and reminisce a bit as we prepare for our Lisbon excursion to attend Leticia's wedding and reunite with João Ferreiro. Our promised inspection of Leticia's recently discovered sea chest with its "Menam Navigation Company" inscription poses, frankly, a less enticing prospect for us than she presumes, as we have completed our quest. The possibility of an exhaustive analysis of yet another pile of moldering Thai manuscripts from an earlier age promises little fresh excitement in the wake of our Diogo adventure. Strangely, our hesitancy in the presence of Leticia's enthusiasm places the shoe on the other foot. Letitia and João are now our supplicants, and we their anticipated benefactors. We come as their guests in their expectation of valuable help – Letitia in hope of unearthing a financial bonanza, and João seeking to save his soul. We stand ready to aid them both as best we can, but in both cases, we admit, our abilities are no more than those of amateurs. Our Lisbon reunion will, in any case, serve as a fitting capstone to our now-concluded decade-long quest.

As we depart on our journey back to the beginnings of this adventure, we cannot resist a brief meditation on Diogo's tale of his turbulent times. As the years between those remote events and the present accumulate, they have assumed an increasingly iconic place in Thai culture. Despite lingering ambiguities and uncertainties, the vision of that distant past has shaped itself into a cornerstone of modern Thailand's cultural heritage. Diogo contested many elements of that myth at the outset. He exemplifies the truth that great writers have "the power . . . to transcend the spirit of an age and provide for the critical reconstruction of reality."[2] With his dissident view, he composed a compelling narrative that he swore – on his life, in effect – to be a true retelling of the main events of his times. Who is to gainsay him?

Trapped between two worlds, he was struck by the universal human traits underlying the starkly different cultures of East and West. His tale of powerful personalities, brilliance and blunderings, courage and cowardice, loyalty, betrayal, and revenge, was composed, purposely or not, as an amalgam of those worlds' distinctly different literary traditions. As an heir to Western humanism as much as Eastern mysticism, he strove to illuminate the effects of individual temperaments on the course of great events. Each of the principal actors was revealed to have contributed to the intricate shadow play in which kings and princes and nobles strove with personal charisma and ruthless cunning to rise to supremacy through fear, patronage, reverence, and awe. Ultimately, as Diogo recounted, it was the leading characters' innate mix of virtues and vices (in the Western tradition), equivalent to their accumulated karmic merit (in the Eastern tradition), that shaped their lives and the course of their kingdom.

Diogo's Testament corroborates the authenticity of his authorship of his Chronicle and, in so doing, confirms its provenance in early nineteenth-century Bangkok. What remains open to debate is the legitimacy of his revisionist account. It is unlikely that fresh evidence will ever be uncovered to substantiate his interpretation of such controversial events as Prince Kung's and Queen Sangwan's adulterous affair, the poisoning of General Maha Noratha, the Cambodian escapades of Prince Sisang, the intrigues of Mac Thien-tu, the rupture in relations between Taksin and the Chakri brothers at the battle of Phitsanulok, or the injuring, torment, overthrow, and execution of King Taksin. Nor is it likely that any amount of historical detective work will ever turn up to corroborate Diogo's references to the historical ramifications of such tantalizing personal details as King Ekathat's sybaritic lifestyle, Prince Tui's sadism, Princess-Mother Thepamat's maternal influence, Kawin's venality, Madot's vacillation, King Taksin's "madness," or Duang's fusion of judicial restraint and militant ambition.

The ever-lengthening distance between those lives and the present is bound to relegate such uncertainties to endless debate. In the absence of perfect hindsight, "historians [will be] left forever chasing shadows, painfully aware of their inability ever to reconstruct a dead world in its completeness, however thorough or revealing their documentation."[3] Our modern translation of Diogo's long-lost writings has sought to bring texture and color to that shadow-world by filling in the lacunae with judicious evaluation. Diogo's Testament and Chronicle offer, in that spirit, a unique opportunity to reach across the twin chasms of historical time and cultural place.

The Siamese crown of state. (Courtesy of River Books)

Endnotes

Translators' Prologue

1. Leticia's affidavit has been appended to Diogo's Testament, appearing as a later chapter of the present volume.
2. Those reign chronicles were compiled by senior royal scribes in graceful chalk-white calligraphy on lengthy laced sheets of black-smeared palm-leaf paper folded in accordion fashion. Their texts are generally considered beyond reproach in their accounts of former reigns, reaching back centuries, and are stored with reverent care on reserved shelves in Thailand's national archives and leading university libraries. Many have been reprinted in locally published book versions (though most are long out of print).

    The "Thai chronicles" section of the Prologue bibliography appended to this volume lists the most accessible modern reprints relevant to the period dealt with by Diogo's Chronicle, most of them never translated into English.
3. The most authoritative of those redacted versions is the Phan Chanthanumat (Choem) *Royal Chronicle of the Thonburi Reign* of 1795 (Hanuman, 2008, pp. pp. 35-159), referred to by Diogo himself, in his Testament, as the motivating force behind the writing of his own, revisionist Chronicle.

    No copy survives of the original *Thonburi Chronicle* that Diogo had helped produce. It was apparently destroyed with the issuance of the redacted version of 1795 (the oldest extant recension). That version was not published for public consumption until well into the twentieth century, most notably as part of the comprehensive collection of chronicles assembled by Prince Damrong Rachanuphap (Damrong, 1969); a more accessible later reissuance is found in Hanuman, 2008, pp. 35-159. Several nineteenth-century chronicles focused on the Ayutthaya era and later periods (Bradley, 1863; Tri, 1964; Wongsa, 1973) appear to have relied on the Phan Chanthanumat manuscript in their compilations of the historical events.
4. The "Thai historiography" section of the Prologue bibliography appended to this volume contains a selection of that scholarly literature.
5. Wyatt, 1976, p. 120.
6. It was during that visit to Coimbra that Cláudio uncovered de Souza Pires' eighteenth-century Portuguese translation of Plutarch's *Parallel Lives* (Plutarch, 1748) in the city university's rare books collection. With patient search he identified a total of 123 Plutarch citations scattered through Diogo's texts, though he admits that he may have missed others.
7. See footnote 3.
8. Diogo lifted numerous Plutarch aphorisms, dictums, and musings from Luis de Souza Pires' *Plutarco, Vidas de alguns famosos gregos e romanos* (Plutarch, 1748). Where Plutarch referred to named individuals, Diogo simply substituted into the quoted lines the names of equivalent actors in his Chronicle. All the lines that Diogo drew from de Souza Pires' Portuguese version have been translated here based on A. H. Clough's 1859 English edition (Plutarch, 2001). We also found several apparent Diogo references to Machiavelli's *Prince* (here relying on Rebbhorn's 2003 translation), suggesting that there may well be other references to classical works that escaped our search.

Diogo's Testament

1. Plutarch, 2001, vol. 2, p. 139.
2. Sterne, 1967, p. 1. Diogo's quote is taken from the opening lines of a garbled Portuguese translation of *Tristram Shandy* dated 1795 (contained in the University of Coimbra's rare books collection), here restored to its original English rendering.
3. Ban Portuket, the core of Portuguese life at Ayutthaya, lined the Chaophraya River directly downstream from Ayutthaya's Hokkien junk anchorage. Its population is thought to have reached as many as 3,000 direct descendants of the original sixteenth-century Portuguese settlers during the decades leading to the capital's destruction. Many Ban Portuket residents were engaged in the capital's dual Hokkien and Taechiu port districts as tradespeople, interpreters, river pilots, and seamen, while others served the government in both military and civil capacities.
4. Ban Portuket had the dubious distinction of being the focus of three contending Catholic missionary orders: the Dominicans (stationed at St. Dominic's Church); Franciscans (St. Augustine's Church); and Jesuits (St. Paul's Church). Of those three churches, St. Paul's (affiliated with the Jesuits' larger, more centrally located St. Joseph's Church some six kilometers upriver) proved the least successful and was abandoned following Portugal's harassment of the Jesuit Order during the 1760s. Diogo was likely the last of the select few Ayutthaya-born students sent to Macau for higher studies.
5. St. Paul's College was built by the Jesuit Order in the early seventeenth century atop Macau's central hilltop as an adjunct to the Portuguese colonial outpost's renowned cathedral of the same name. After the 1759 Jesuit expulsion from Macau, the cathedral was assigned to Dominican administration, though a discreet Jesuit presence was retained at the

College to maintain the school's celebrated educational standards. It was under those regulated conditions that Diogo continued his studies and then taught there in a junior capacity to 1771. The Cathedral and College were both destroyed in a great fire in 1835, caused by the explosion of a gunpowder magazine located in the fort directly behind the cathedral. Only the cathedral's granite façade was left intact. It remains in place today as an iconic symbol of the old city's distinctly Portuguese Catholic cultural prominence.

6   As Portugal's prime minister from 1750 to 1777, Sebastião José de Carvalho e Melo, Marquis de Pombal, effected the Jesuits' expulsion from Portugal and much of its empire in 1759, on grounds of their political collusion with the French against Iberian interests worldwide. After his initial edict of 1759, followed by years of ecclesiastical turmoil, that proscription was rescinded in 1814. The continued clandestine presence of much of the Jesuit community at Macau – enabling Diogo's continued studies – was made possible by means of quiet local accommodations too devious to be recounted here.

7   Plutarch, 2001, vol. 1, p. 462.

8   This is the first of a number of references to the cascading sequence of events leading from 1767 to the reign change of 1782, witnessed personally by Diogo.

9   The refugee Portuguese-Siamese community was assigned the Santa Cruz site by the recently enthroned King Taksin. Its bounds intruded on the existing Kudi Chin waterfront, requiring the eviction of a line of Hokkien trading establishments with their docks, warehouses, and coolie lines, perhaps with the express intent of constraining the Hokkien junk anchorage in favor of Taksin's favored crossriver Taechiu port precinct. The longstanding rivalry between China's Hokkien and Taechiu speech groups is discussed in Chapter 5 of Diogo's Chronicle.

10 The new Grand Palace was established within the old Thonburi fort in late 1767. It was soon renovated in accordance with the classic architectural principles of Ayutthaya tradition to accommodate the physical facilities required by a fast-growing royal household and government apparatus. The Royal Secretariat was headquartered in the Royal Pages' pavilion in the palace forecourt. Portuguese personnel from Santa Cruz performed prominent functions as palace service staff: in addition to Diogo's appointment to the Royal Secretariat, Santa Cruz contingents manning the Royal Pages Corps and Palace Guard, and their senior officers serving under noble titles.

11 The Siamese *sampao* is a smaller, somewhat differently built, more maneuverable version of the Chinese sampan, but the better-known Chinese term will here be retained for convenience.

12 The miscellany of surviving royal records and reports in the National Archives dating from the Thonburi period may well include a number of documents inscribed by Diogo at the feet of King Taksin.

13 Here Diogo inadvertently confesses to his flawed grasp of Thai Buddhism as practiced in Siam (referring to it as a "theology"), as is repeated in his Chronicle's simplistic depictions of various Buddhist practices and beliefs.

14 The massive Phet Prakan Bastion stood as a key defensive position along the Ayutthaya city wall overlooking the Mae Bia Harbor, less than a kilometer upstream from Ban Portuket.

15 Diogo here refers to the *phra racha phongsawadan* tradition (see the Translation section of this book's Prologue) whereby each reign maintained a written record of its essential achievements. The Royal Secretariat was assigned that task as one of its most sacred duties. Over the centuries, the corpus of dynastic chronicles compiled from those records mounted to a massive collection, housed in the palace archives. The pillage and burning of Ayutthaya in 1767 destroyed that library, but replicas of some of its documents, each laboriously hand-copied by royal scribes, survived in provincial archives and were later reassembled.

16 The Translators' Postscript contained in this book's Epilogue refers to many of the post-coup events that Diogo alludes to here.

17 That formidably gunned fortification guarded the most prominent corner of the Thonburi Grand Palace wall, overlooking the river at its confluence with the Bang Luang Canal. It exhibited many of the characteristics of Ayutthaya's famed Phet Prakan Bastion and thus likely played for Diogo a particularly poignant role in coupling the grim soldierly deaths of his royal patron and his father.

18 Plutarch, 2001, vol. 1, p. 718.

19 Wat Bang Yi Roea Tai (later rebuilt as Wat Intharam) was located about two kilometers up the Bang Luang Canal from the Thonburi Grand Palace, well removed from the royal city. Taksin's corpse was exhumed there two years later, cremated in a grand ceremony, with the cremains interred in a small *chedi* fronting the temple's chapel.

20 Wat Sakae (Temple of the Breadfruit Tree) was a secluded Right Bank monastic meditation retreat bordering the swamp-lined Banglamphu Canal about 1.5 km inland from the riverside military cantonment at Bang Lamphu.

21 Other records suggest that that crucial rite of purification and mystical empowerment in preparation for higher office was conducted late the previous evening. It was later commemorated

in the temple's renaming as Wat Saket (Pali: *wat sra kesa*, Temple of the Anointment).

22 The Rosario settlement had been established only a few years previously by a disaffected faction of Santa Cruz villagers, apparently as a consequence of the unfamiliar liturgy, incongruous theology, and dissonant opinions introduced by the French Jesuit priests who had been assigned to replace the expelled Portuguese Dominican pastors. Rosario was eventually absorbed into the burgeoning Talat Noi extension of Sampheng, Bangkok's Chinatown, while managing to retain a whisper of its former Portuguese ambiance.

23 The Holy Rosary Church was rebuilt in the 1890s as a modern edifice today commonly known among locals as Wat Kalawa, a downtown Bangkok landmark serving a congregation of thousands.

24 Thonburi's new Left-Bank Taechiu junk anchorage soon came to be known as Sampheng, Bangkok's Chinatown.

25 That sanctuary survives today as the Lao Pun Thao Kong Shrine, commonly referred as Sanchao Kao (the Old Shrine), located at the river end of Sampheng's Rong Khom Lane.

26 The Hokkien-Taechiu rivalry as neighboring peoples and prefectures along the southeast Chinese littoral stretched far back in Chinese history, despite those two Chinese speech-groups' close cultural affinities. It carried over into Siam, where the Hokkien traders established an early residence as traders and court officials, with the more recently arrived and less affluent and less socially favored Taechiu being consigned to an inferior anchorage along Ayutthaya's port periphery. With the move to Thonburi, that distinction was reversed due to King Taksin's Taechiu ancestry, and it was reversed again with the Chakri coup due in part to the new dynasty's Hokkien ancestral roots.

27 Plutarch, 2001, vol. 1, p. 433.

28 La was a younger half-brother of Duang (General Chakri) and Bunma (General Surasi). During the last reign of the Ayutthaya era, their father, Thongdi (previously Captain Akson Sunthon), had been posted to Phitsanulok, apparently accompanied by one of his minor wives and their son La. Under the self-styled rule of the king of Phitsanulok in the tumultuous days following the fall of Ayutthaya, Thongdi was elevated by Phitsanulok's self-styled ruler to the august rank of General Chakri Ongkharak; he died soon thereafter, whether in battle or from an epidemic disease unknown. His cremains were carried back to Thonburi by La, who had providentially been reunited at Phitsanulok with his brother Bunma. Through Duang's and Bunma's sponsorship, La gained a posting in the Royal Secretariat – leading to his association with Diogo – and was eventually, upon Duang's elevation to the throne as Rama I, raised to royal rank.

29 Prince Chak's palace – the former residence of his brother Prince Surasinghanat (Bunma), situated alongside the military cantonment over which Bunma had been in command during the early years of the Thonburi reign – was located at Rattanakosin's northern tip, near the prominent Phra Sumen bastion. Only minor remnants of its former presence (a few small sections of the wall and the frame of an old gate) remain today.

30 That redacted document, inscribed in 1795, is known today as the Phan Chanthanumat (Choem) *Royal Chronicle of the Thonburi Reign* (Hanuman, 2008, pp. pp. 35-159), as referred to in the Prologue (footnote 3). Phan Chanthumant (Choem) is reported to have been a Fifth Reign palace clerk who was lucky enough to have stumbled upon that mysterious manuscript (now lost); he was not the author, as is often supposed.

31 As referred to in the Prologue, such textual revision or redaction of former reign chronicles was famously termed "cleansing" (*chamra*), a practice that provided ritual affirmation of the fresh start promised by each change of reign.

32 Were those papers perhaps among the manuscripts found by Leticia in Diogo's old sea chest, referred to in the Prologue?

33 The funerary rites attending the death of Prince Chak breached the convention that the cremation of senior members of the royal family take place a year or more after the dignitary's death, on the royal cremation ground fronting the Grand Palace or at some similarly exalted location within the city wall. In muted expiation of the injustice committed against him, Wat Choenglen was in a later reign rebuilt with royal sponsorship and provided the royal name of Wat Bophit Phimuk, "Temple of the Adjunct Prince."

34 To facilitate comprehension, we have perhaps exceeded Diogo's brief here with a simplified reworking of these several pages of his narrative as a straightforward listing of those key informants and their biographical particulars.

35 Nakhon Si Thammarat (or simply Nakhon) was a Siamese port situated far down the east coast of the Malay Peninsula. As the capital of a celebrated Southern province that had survived the Burmese invasion, it offered a prime refuge for Ayutthaya survivors.

36 The family lineage reconstructed by Thong-mon's present-day descendants record that she lived out her final years in the eastern crossriver suburbs of Ayutthaya. It is likely that she relocated there from Ban Tawai shortly after her interactions with Diogo, possibly around the start of the Second Reign.

37 Located in Upper Burma, along the Irrawaddy River about 110 kilometers upstream from Ava.

38 Plutarch, 2001, vol. 1, p. 695.
39 Voltaire, 1764, entry on "Limits of the Human Mind."
40 Gospel of John, *New Testament*, 19:30. These are the last words said to have been uttered by Jesus in his death agonies on the cross, perhaps the most enigmatic statement in all literary history. Diogo's use of those words as his final statement, after his consistent avoidance of theological metaphor throughout his Testament, may have been intended as an ironic capstone to his humanistic dissent from the Christian insistence that with death's departure, all is *not* finished.

Chapter 1 Death of a Dynasty

1 A *rai* equaled 1,600 square meters, or 0.4 acres; a typical holding thus covered only four acres or so.
2 That compound may originally have been laid out as a royal retreat during the previous reign of King Narai, with its defenses and the Banyong Ratanat Throne Hall being added by King Phetracha.
3 Plutarch, 2001, vol. 2, p. 446 (paraphrase).
4 Among the most recalcitrant nobles were the powerful governors of Suphanburi, Nakhon Chaisi, and Nakhon Sawan, who administered some of the most fertile rice tracts of the Central Plain. Those nobles and their heirs would prove, in later years, foremost among the kingdom's most fickle defenders against the Burmese foe.
5 The royal annals of Ayutthaya record recurrent instances of armed confrontation between contending aspirants to the throne, a tradition continued into Ayutthaya's final reigns and eventually carried over into the Thonburi period, as the later pages of *Diogo's Chronicle* confirm.
6 Ayutthaya's persistent trade surplus over the decades following the reopening of Amoy and Canton in 1727 was energized by massive Siamese rice exports to relieve recurrent Chinese famines and was marked by equivalent inflows of luxury goods and gold bullion.
7 Under Boromakot's successor, Ekathat, both the future kings Taksin and Rama I received their initial immersion in the workings of the royal bureaucracy as such outposted junior officers during the closing years of the Ayutthaya era.
8 Along with that post he was awarded the Front Palace, the viceroy's traditional residence and stronghold guarding the capital's vulnerable northeastern battlements, alongside the city's Front Moat linking the Lopburi and Pa Sak rivers.
9 Plutarch, 2001, vol. 2, pp. 540-541 (paraphrase).
10 The Thai-Western equivalencies implicit in those titles are identified in the Chronicle's introductory Technical Notes.
11 Neither this plan nor its negative reception is referred to in the "official" chronicles. That is unsurprising in view of the chronicles' selectively redacted, positive presentation of Boromakot's reign. Evidently, there was no wish in later reigns to highlight the king's waning power, as the intent was to hold him up as a model of righteous rule against the dismal example that followed him.
12 Political and personal tensions between king and viceroy, often through misunderstandings over their respective roles, posed a perennial problem in pre-modern Siam and, in fact, accounted for many of the internecine armed conflicts that punctuated the kingdom's history.
13 Those kings, reaching from King Asoka of India (Maurya empire, third century B.C.E.). and King Parakramabahu I (twelfth-century Sri Lanka) through King Luthai (fourteenth-century Sukhothai) and King Dhammacetiya (fifteenth-century Hongsawaddi), were renowned for practicing the ten virtues of enlightened sovereignty: moral conduct, generosity, liberality, honesty, mildness, moderation, equanimity, forbearance, patience, and tolerance.
14 Plutarch, 2001, vol. 1, p. 464 (paraphrase).
15 Commonly thought to have been a goiter, the king's affliction was more likely scrofula, a disease as ugly as its name. A chronic tubercular infection of the lymph nodes showing a tendency to hereditary transmission, its primary symptoms are a swelling of the neck, complicated by ulcerated lymph nodes, leading to draining fistulas, scarring, and general incapacity. It appears to have been a recurring, congenital affliction within the Ban Phlu Luang lineage, alluded to repeatedly in the royal chronicles. Interestingly, scrofula also plagued the successive kings and courts of Burma's contemporary Konbaung Dynasty.
16 The king's "goiter" and his efforts to hide it from public view were referred to by contemporary Dutch observers.
17 King Boromakot sired a total of 48 children. Of his 23 sons, more than half had been born before he ascended the throne, and eight had died in infancy, childhood, or youth. Of the 15 survivors, five were foremost in royal rank as celestial princes. The Queen of the Right had borne Prince Kung, the viceroy; the Queen of the Left was mother of Princes Ekathat and Dok-madoea, both later to ascend the throne; Sangwan, Queen of the Center and favorite during the king's advanced years, was mother of two princes and two princesses, none of whom had reached their maturity by the time of the king's death.
18 A number of those works have survived, and some continue to find a place today as standard grade school readings. His boat songs still feature in the repertoire of sailors' cadences intoned at royal barge processions.

19 It is probable that the *Ramakien* murals that today line the cloister walls of Wat Phra Kaew, the Bangkok Grand Palace's Chapel Royal, were inspired by memories of that vanished prototype.

20 A later version was compiled by the Department of Fine Arts on the basis of surviving fragments.

21 As subsequent chapters will note, a number of nobles who survived the fall of Ayutthaya to play leading roles in the Thonburi and early Bangkok periods had received their initial schooling in Ayutthaya's Royal Pages Corps.

22 To ease his connubial life, Kung acquired a number of other consorts. All told, his household is known to have contained at least 10 wives and lesser companions sharing a total of 12 children.

23 Kung's illness was reported by his enemies to have been a venereal disease, although it was more likely an outbreak of scrofula (shared with the king), which can vary in its symptoms to resemble second-stage syphilis.

24 The Ayutthaya chronicles, generally brief in their summation of Boromakot's reign, deal in considerable detail with many specifics of that palace scandal and its punishments.

25 Plutarch, 2001, vol 1, pp. 514-515 (paraphrase).

26 Under Ayutthaya's palatine law, execution was prescribed as the specific penalty for the offense of climbing over any inner palace wall.

27 Siamese law stipulated a variety of ordeals, the successful endurance of which, with the aid of deities, would prove the defendant's innocence. Among them were trial by: fire, walking barefoot through a 3-meter-long coal-fired pit; water, immersion in a three-meter-deep pond for a prescribed time; poison, withstanding the ill effects of a potentially lethal potion; molten metal, dipping a hand into a pot of boiling lead or tin without injury; and sacred oath-taking, requiring a seven-day period following the ritual devoid of the slightest misfortune.

28 The judicial solution was a nuanced balancing of the legal niceties. Caning with a sandalwood stave (or a bamboo rod for offenders of lesser stature) was a standard royal punishment for such offenses as insubordination, abuse of office, and dereliction of duty. For minor transgressions, 20 or 30 strokes of the cane was not an uncommon judgment. More heinous offenses short of treason merited up to 100 strokes, a sentence known to bring a healthy adult male to the brink of death. However, the penalty meted out to Kung far exceeded that limit; so many strokes could hardly have been intended as less than execution.

29 Plutarch, 2001, vol. 2, p. 422 (paraphrase).

30 Ibid., vol. 1, p. 325.

31 Ibid., vol. 2, pp. 565-566 (paraphrase).

32 The royal name "Uthumphon" was no more than an embellished, Sanskritized version of the unassuming personal name of "Dok-Madoea," both terms signifying the flower of the fig tree (referring elliptically to the Buddha's enlightenment). His brief reign prevented a full coronation ceremony (usually scheduled to occur a year or more after investiture and the cremation of the previous king), when his regal title would have been further elevated.

33 Plutarch., 2001, vol. 2, pp. 39, 591-592 (paraphrase).

34 Here Diogo draws on Machiavelli, 2003, p. 72.

35 Plutarch, 2001, vol. 2, p. 462.

36 Legal precedent specified that royal execution be restricted to a single powerful blow of a sandalwood club to the nape of the neck, in accordance with proscriptions against the spilling of royal blood.

37 Uthumphon's father, more than 50 years previously, had been ordained at that prestigious temple. A century later Wat Pradu was merged with the neighboring Wat Songtham and renamed Wat Pradu Songtham, the name by which it continues to be known to the present day.

38 It is likely that his affliction, like that of his father, King Boromakot, was scrofula. Use of the term "leper" here mistranslates a generic Thai term for "disease of festering lesions."

39 Plutarch, 2001, vol. 1, p. 520 (paraphrase). Ekathat's dental difficulty, and its remedy, was not uncommon in a society that favored the constant chewing of quids of areca nut flavored with slacked-lime paste bound in betel leaf.

40 A missive from Monsignor Brigot to the directors of the Société des Missions-Étrangères, dated January 10, 1758 (misdated 1756), mentions the king's ailment and its medical treatments (Launay, 1920, vol. 2, p. 207).

41 Here again Diogo appears to be referring to Machiavelli, 2003, pp. 71-73, and pp. 79-87.

42 Plutarch, 2001, vol. 2, pp. 350-351.

43 Ceilão, or Sereendip, was a contemporary rendering of Sri Lanka, later known as Ceylon. Khaek's further exploits in Sri Lanka are referred to in Chapter 4.

44 Plutarch, 2001, vol. 1, p. 57.

45 Ibid., p. 436 (paraphrase).

46 That figure is confirmed in the Christian missionaries' reports (Launay, 1920, vol. 3, pp. 140-141).

47 The remains of that second-tier palace wall were discovered in the 1990s during archaeological excavation of the palace's northern precincts.

48 Plutarch, 2001, vol. 2, p. 197 (paraphrase).

49 The Ayutthaya chronicles differ from Diogo's rendition, suggesting that Mang Rong's zealous artillerymen, in charging one of their largest cannon for his match to start their climactic bombardment, primed the charge for maximum effect, surpassing the gun's capacity; the instant the fuse burned

50 The Burmese chronicles hold that King Alaungpaya retreated from Ayutthaya because of a fever (not an injury caused by a burst cannon) and died on 11 May 1760 near Thaton, on the Andaman coast, after his litter had crossed the Tenasserim divide into Burma.
51 It is suggested in the Ayutthaya chronicles (that Ekathat on that occasion displayed great hostility toward Uthumphon by receiving him with his unsheathed sword resting across his knees, a gesture brimming with malice, leading Uthumphon to believe that he had come into his brother's royal disfavor. That anecdote exemplifies the chronicles' consistent efforts to paint Ekathat as malicious rather than simply deficient.
52 The Five Negations of Buddhism are: not to take life, not to steal, not to lie, not to engage in sexual misconduct, and not to partake of intoxicating substances.
53 With characteristic foresight, Uthumphon, a year prior to the 1767 Burmese sack of Ayutthaya, had the image plaster-covered, painted with black lacquer, pasted with gold leaf, and moved to an upcountry temple. In 1950 such an image was discovered, with a corner of its plaster coating flaked off and its long-hidden golden visage gleaming beneath, at Wat Pa Yao, Sao Hai District, Saraburi Province. Today, with all its former plaster coating removed, the restored image is enshrined in a commemorative pavilion. Whether it is actually the original Trailoka Pathimakon image remains to be certified.
54 Plutarch, 2001, vol. 2, p. 251.
55 Ibid, vol. 1, p. 131.
56 This summary of the dynasty's end foreshadows the more detailed description of the fall of Ayutthaya presented in Chapter 2.
57 Plutarch, vol. 2, pp. 476-477.
58 Ibid., vol. 1, p. 708.
59 Ibid, vol. 2, p. 408 (paraphrase).

Chapter 2 Burmese Ramayana
1 Myo Myint, 2010, p. 314.
2 Symes, 1800, pp. 177-178.
3 Diogo refers to Burma's Konbaung Dynasty kings Alaungpaya (Emerald Buddha, r.1752-1760) and his successor/son, Hsinbyushin (Lord of the White Elephant, r.1763-1776), respectively, by their military names of Mang Rong and Mang Ra ("*mang*" meaning "commanding general"), and for consistency and convenience that usage is retained here.
4 Plutarch, 2001, vol. 1, p. 87 (paraphrase).
5 Burmese sources state that Mang Ra was born in 1736, received his early military training under his father's personal guidance, rose to become king at the relatively young age of 27, and was 31 at the time of his generals' conquest of Ayutthaya.
6 Plutarch, 2001, vol. 2, p. 472. With their imperial power based on a powerful military, the Konbaung dynasts were also preoccupied with the need to keep their restless troops and ambitious commanders engaged far from home. Thus, Mang Ra undoubtedly found his Siamese campaigns a welcome diversion from never-absent fears of disaffection and mutiny.
7 Ibid., p. 485.
8 The most difficult of those dispersed adventures was along the northern front. Burma's efforts to extend its political sway into the Yunnan borderlands prompted a series of four Chinese invasions between 1765 and 1769, each of which was defeated at great cost. Its rushed withdrawal from Siam to bolster the northern front weeks after its April 1767 conquest of Ayutthaya demonstrates the fragility of that empire-building strategy. Mang Ra had overreached; fighting simultaneous wars across diverse fronts had stretched his resources beyond his capacity.
9 Diogo's reference to Mang Ra's two generals as Hanuman and Thosakan is not mentioned in any other contemporary source. It stands as Diogo's evocative contribution to an understanding of their contrasting personalities and the dynamics of their interaction. Following Diogo's usage, presumably based on de Costa's reminiscences, the two generals will be further referred to here by those memorable bynames.
10 Mang Ra's metaphor was imperfect. Unlike the contesting armies of Hanuman and Thosakan in the *Ramayana*, Generals Maha Noratha (Hanuman) and Sihabodi (Thosakan) served a single master, Mang Ra (who coordinated their invasion to achieve a single objective, the conquest of Ayutthaya.
11 Plutarch, 2001, vol. 2, p. 591 (paraphrase).
12 Ibid., vol. 1, p. 266 (paraphrase).
13 Ibid., p. 493.
14 Ibid., p. 525 (paraphrase).
15 Ibid., p. 599.
16 Ibid., p. 282 (paraphrase).
17 Ibid., p. 670.
18 Mang Ra's intent was never realized, given the political preoccupations fueled by the unanticipated advance of Chinese armies across Burma's northern reaches in early 1767 and the several years of warfare that followed. That new warfront absorbed the bulk of his energies and compounded his progressive decline under the ravages of virulent scrofula.
19 Plutarch, 2001, vol. 1, p. 238 (paraphrase).
20 That military firepower ranged from wheeled

cannon, lighter field carronades, and mortars to hand-held flintlocks, accompanied by massive stores of cart-borne powder and shot.

21 Reading the writing on the wall, the Dutch, the last Western resident presence at Ayutthaya, abandoned their riverside "factory" (business premises) in December 1765 and fled by ship to Batavia.

22 The Golden Mount (phukhao thong), a colossus visible from afar, held great symbolic significance for the Burmese, commemorating their earlier suzerainty over Siam. It had apparently been built by them in 1569 in celebration of the reduction of Ayutthaya to (temporary) vassalage after a war between Burma's King Bayinnaung and Siam's King Maha Chakraphat.

23 Plutarch, 2001, vol. 1, p. 246.

24 One of those officials, Colonel Wachira Prakan (Sin, the putative governor of Kamphaeng Phet, known in later years as Colonel Taksin in memory of his former posting as commander of the border outpost of Tak) survived the fall of Ayutthaya to become the future sovereign of Siam.

25 Battle in the mired wetlands during the rainy season invariably favored defense over offense. Rapid marches across the sodden fields left the attackers weakened by the time they entered combat. The defending forces, ensconced within their redoubts awaiting the onslaught, could choose to fight from behind their ramparts or send forward commando units into the open field at a moment's notice.

26 Along the northern side of the city, the Golden Mount (phukhao thong) and the royal elephant stockade (paniat luang) were designated as markers for the installation of a series of evenly spaced Burmese forward positions.

27 We have taken the editorial liberty of rearranging Diogo's sequence of those events in keeping with the dating cited in the Burmese chronicles (Pe Maung Tin and Luce, 1923). As a side note, it appears from those battle sitings that the Pho Sam Ton River was at that time the main channel of the Lopburi River.

28 Neither Diogo (in this chronicle) nor the Burmese chronicles provide any estimates of relative force strength or casualties in that series of battles. One obscure Burmese source suggests, however, that for one of these battles the Siamese mobilized 50,000 troops versus only 20,000 Burmese.

29 In the customary manner of the dynastic chronicles, the loss of military leaders was consistently written out of history. Through Diogo we learn a bit more about this failed commander than was the usual practice.

30 The combat description may well have come straight from Diogo's confidante, António da Costa, who apparently served as a rearguard officer at that notable engagement.

31 Plutarch, 2001, vol. 1, p. 448 (paraphrase).

32 Ibid., p. 566-567 (paraphrase).

33 The Burmese camp positions and names are recorded in Soe, 2011, p. 115.

34 Those outposts were apparently manned by troops rotated out of the artillerymen's cantonment and arsenal housed within the Front Palace, which had been left vacant but for its caretakers since the death of the former viceroy, Prince Thamma Thibet (Kung, died 1755).

35 Among those isolated fortified positions was Wat Pa Kaew (today Wat Yai Chai Monkhon, located about two kilometers east of the city moat), from which Colonel Taksin and his troops were forced to retreat to Wat Phichai (located along the outer bank of the Pa Sak River stretch of the city moat) and then, cut off from further retreat – bereft of support from his own commanders – and threatened with annihilation, were compelled to take flight eastward toward Prachin and then onward to Siam's Eastern Seaboard provinces.

36 Plutarch, 2001, vol. 1, p. 631 (paraphrase).

37 Ibid., p. 493 (paraphrase).

38 Ibid., p. 493.

39 Ibid., p. 314 (paraphrase).

40 Ibid., vol. 2, pp. 466-467 (paraphrase).

41 Ibid., p. 153 (paraphrase).

42 If not poison, the cause of death may have been what today we call typhoid or amebiasis – though not cholera, which did not arrive on the scene until some four decades later.

43 Plutarch, 2001, vol. 2, p. 403.

44 The city's 12 watergates, each set upon soaring pilings resting within the city wall, were built of massive timbers that required giant winches plied by teams of experienced workmen to raise themgate panels above the waterline by pulleyed cables to allow the passage of authorized rivercraft into the city's grid of transport canals.,

45 Plutarch, 2001, vol. 2, p. 283 (paraphrase).

46 The Forward Moat (khoe na, connecting the Lopburi and Pasak Rivers past the Front Palace) and Head Wier (hua ro, blocking the flow of the Lopburi River into the moat) were among Ayutthaya's most eulogized defensive attributes. The weir was famed for its timbered elephant causeway, which had formerly carried many a royal procession to crossriver temples and the nearby royal elephant stockade. Under the concentrated assault of a year's unrelenting siege, however, both the weir and its causeway had proved faulty, and both had been dismantled to increase the moat's defensive attributes. They were never rebuilt, and the waterflow pattern around the city was in consequence permanently disrupted.

47 Several Burmese accounts place this event a day later.

48 In his Testament, Diogo eulogizes his father's death as one of Ayutthaya's staunch Portuguese defenders commanding the Diamond Bastion in that engagement.
49 Plutarch, 2001, vol. 1, p. 421 (paraphrase).
50 Ibid., p. 619 (paraphrase).
51 Ibid., vol. 2, p. 276 (paraphrase).
52 That number accounted for a tenth or less of the former population of the city and its immediate environs.
53 Diogo contradicts that Burmese report in the preceding chapter, which asserts, as do the Ayutthaya chronicles, that King Ekathat fled the burning city and survived in hiding for some 10 days before succumbing to the effects of abandonment, privation, exhaustion, and terror.
54 Plutarch, 2001, vol. 2, p. 101 (paraphrase).
55 Diogo extracted this passage from the reminiscences of Phra Phonarat (abbot of Bangkok's Wat Pho after the 1782 coup), who had composed them several years after the fall of Ayutthaya, while memories were still fresh. Phra Wanarat's lament was later incorporated into a manuscript issued for the landmark 1788 Great Council of the Siamese Buddhist monastic order (Phonarat, 1923, pp. 409-410; translation drawn from Wyatt, 1982, p. 30).
56 Much of the captured gold was used to gild the spire of Yangon's Shwe Dagon Pagoda.
57 The Burmese chronicles state, however, that both armies marched from Siam on May 30, 1767. The northern trek reached Ava in July/August 1767; the arrival date and destination of the other army are not mentioned.
58 A grand performance of the *Ramayana* was staged again in 1783 for King Bodawpaya (fourth son of King Mang Rong, r.1781-1819) to celebrate the founding of the new capital of Amarapura. The event was deemed sufficiently important to receive mention in the Konbaung dynastic annals. In 1789 Bodawpaya established a royal commission to translate the entire epic as well as other Thai literary classics into Burmese. *Ramayana* performances in Burmese thereafter served as a powerful vehicle for the Burmanization of the kingdom's ethnically diverse population.
59 He reappears in 1765-1766 as General Sihabodi (no longer carrying the sobriquet of Thosakan) at the Phitsanulok campaign (see chapter 6).
60 In the Yodaya Bazaar, the old Siamese quarter of Mandalay (the modern successor-city to Ava), there still stands a shrine dedicated to Rama, erected by descendants of the Ayutthaya royal dance troupe that had introduced their art form at the court of Mang Ra.
61 Travelers' reports claim that he lived on at Sagaing in melancholy exile for 28 years, until his death in 1795. His passing was commemorated at the new capital of Amarapura the following year with a royal cremation sponsored by King Bodawpaya (Mang Ra's successor) and attended by a large assembly, including the entire Siamese community. Burmese sources confirm that the cremation took place in 1796 at the Linzingon burial ground alongside Wat Kyauktawgyi, overlooking Amarapura's Taungthaman Lake. The remains of a large stupa stand there today to mark the spot.
62 Plutarch, 2001, vol. 1, p. 499 (paraphrase).

Chapter 3 Upstart Regime

1 A perplexing omission at this point is any detailed account of Taksin's heroic escape from beleaguered Ayutthaya to the Southeastern Gulf littoral. However, Diogo describes the famed flight of Taksin and his comrades to Prachin and then the Gulf coast, followed by their climactic takeover of Chanthabun, in Chapter 5.
2 Diogo provides little information on Taksin's origins; only later sources have unearthed what are believed to be the basic facts (many in dispute). In summary, he was the son of an Ayutthaya-based Taechiu émigré merchant, Hai-hong sae Tae (or Zheng Yong), and a Mon mother, Nok-iang. His father plied the Gulf's coastal shipping lanes as a junk trader who had managed to secure a minor government post at Ayutthaya as the gambling tax farmer for Rayong (situated along Siam's Eastern Seaboard not far from Chanthabun). Taksin's mother, distantly related to Phetburi's governor (Roeang), joined her husband at Ayutthaya, where they prospered under the patronage of General Chakri (Mut), Ayutthaya's penultimate Minister of Interior, which ensured their son's admission to the Royal Pages Corps. Hai-hong was lost at sea while on a trading voyage some years before the Burmese invasion of 1765; Nok-iang survived the fall of Ayutthaya in the relative safety of her provincial home and was reunited with Taksin at Thonburi during the first year of his reign. Sin, in the meanwhile, completed his military training in 1764, was assigned command of a troop cantonment at the border outpost of Tak (and thus his sobriquet Taksin), and was recalled to Ayutthaya in 1765 to join in the capital's defense, after which his career advanced rapidly.
3 Plutarch, 2001, vol. 1, pp. 99-100.
4 Ibid., vol. 2, p. 236 (paraphrase).
5 Ibid., vol. 1, p. 162.
6 Ibid., vol. 2, p. 462 (paraphrase).
7 Ibid., p. 495 (paraphrase).
8 Sanguan's military designation as a non-commissioned army officer was *asa* (volunteer), which typically referred to recruited inductees (as distinct from conscripts).

9. Plutarch, 2001, vol. 2, p. 485.
10. Phichai survives today as the southernmost district of Uttaradit Province, abutting Phitsanulok.
11. The term dap hak (broken swords) referred to Sanguan's military valor, commemorated in the shattering of both his swords, which he brandished in battle in the traditional Siamese two-handed fighting style.
12. The Water of Allegiance was a sacred potion, reputed to spell the death of whosoever should dare swear false fealty to the king. All senior nobles participated in that solemn royal ritual at the feet of the king at the reign change and annually thereafter (formerly during the New Year's festivities in April). As referred to in the Epilogue, Sanguan, as all other provincial chiefs, was called to Thonburi to drink the Water of Allegiance following the reign change of 1782. At that event he refused to renounce his fealty to his former liege lord Taksin in favor of the new king and was trundled off to his execution.
13. One *chang* = 80-baht weight (1 baht = 15.244 grams). The market value of 320 *chang* of pure gold as of mid-2022 was the equivalent of $2.2 million, affording a rough measure of its worth by eighteenth-century standards.
14. Mut was succeeded as Minister of War by Duang (see below), who was appointed at the lesser rank and title of Colonel Chakri (later raised to general).
15. The reason for that subtle change remains unknown. Succeeding generations of Mut's lineage continued to carry the title of Racha-bangsan far into the Bangkok period.
16. An obscure figure scarcely mentioned in contemporary accounts, Li-ang *sae* Tang (Chen in Mandarin pronunciation) is referred to in later sources by a variety of names, including Tran Lien, Chen Lian, Liang, and Chiam, and by various titles that conflate him with other personalities.
17. Thonburi's indenture system, adapting a system earlier introduced at Canton by the city's famed merchants' guilds, offered indigent Chinese peasants multi-year work contracts, including free or low-cost passage to Siam, with the prospect of securing an independent economic future in a resurgent Siam. To support that scheme, a secure remittance procedure – in effect, a simple international banking arrangement – was devised by Thonburi's junk traders in coordination with their China-based affiliates, to enable the immigrant workers to send periodic remittances to their families over the years of their overseas sojourn.
18. The eminent title of Chodoek Rachasethi (Illustrious King's Merchant) had been conferred on the chief of Siam's Hokkien community since far back in the Ayutthaya period. Taksin's revival of that title for Li-Ang came as a singular honor.
19. Among the Mon nobility, Mapu held the traditional chief's rank of "*saming*," equivalent of the Thai "*phraya*," translated here as "colonel."
20. Though Duang's personal name is in later sources recorded as Thongduang, Diogo's abbreviated form, apparently based on contemporary usage, is here retained for convenience.
21. Thongdi was descended from a distinguished Mon-Thai lineage dating from the early seventeenth century, served as a mid-level official with the Ministry of Interior under King Boromakot and thereafter. Several years before the fall of Ayutthaya he was posted to the northern capital of Phitsanulok. Following the fall of Ayutthaya, he was raised by the self-styled, short-lived ruler of that briefly independent principality to the commanding rank of Phitsanulok's General Chakri Ongkharak. He died in late 1767 or early 1768, during the turmoil attending the stillborn Phitsanulok kingdom's collapse.

Dao-roeang had been brought up in a prosperous home situated alongside her father's business premises in the city's bustling Hokkien market quarter, near the Mae Bia Harbor. She perished during the Burmese conquest, as did her eldest son Narong, leaving her younger two sons Duang and Bunma and two daughters Sa and Kaew, plus Thong-di's several children by minor wives, as the family's surviving generation.
22. Plutarch, 2001, vol. 2, p. 270.
23. Ibid., p. 236.
24. Ibid., p. 541 (paraphrase).
25. Ibid., vol. 1, p. 608.
26. Ibid., p. 393 (paraphrase).
27. Diogo's narrative is disentangled here with the insertion of subheads and rearrangement of some of the sentences to allow for its division into the three respective subsections of royalty, nobility, and clergy, clarifying his intent without distortion of the whole.
28. Thong-mon, the most important of Nok-iang's retainers and a senior Thonburi palace official, later served as one of Diogo's principal confidantes in the preparation of his Chronicle. Her particulars are recited in his Testament.
29. With the eventuality of Chui's elevation to viceroy evidently in mind, Taksin laid out the site of his future palace in the gardens lining the Left Bank across the river from Wat Bang Wa Yai (later Wat Rakhang). That possibility was erased with Chui's execution soon after the 1782 coup and incorporation of that site into the Bangkok Grand Palace.
30. Nakhon here refers to the old Ayutthaya dependency of Nakhon Si Thammarat (often referred to by Western seafarers as Ligor), abutting the sultanates of the Malay Peninsula. Following the 1767 catastrophe, Nakhon's ruler, Nu, had renounced

Nakhon's tributary status. Taksin's 1769-1770 Southern campaign reduced Nakhon to a Siamese province. Nu was deposed and carried off as hostage to Thonburi, where he negotiated his release and reinstallation as Nakhon's governor, and presented his daughters as consorts in token of his fealty.

31 The Ayutthaya refugee royals included children and grandchildren of six Ayutthaya kings, ranging in rank from celestial prince/princess (*chao fa*) to lesser prince/princess (*phra ong chao*), to adjunct prince/princess (*mom chao*). Taksin referred indulgently to the men of that group of Ayutthaya royals as his fictive nephews (*lan*).

32 Use of the term "ministry" here in specification of the generic Thai term "*krom*" is a modern (Western) bureaucratic approximation of what was in effect a cluster of senior feudal offices with particularly lofty status and broad power delegated in a diffuse range of executive functions under the king's direct aegis.

33 Diogo's Testament refers to his presence at those councils of state as "an invisible observer" in his capacity as a royal scribe.

34 For purposes of simplicity, we refer here to the Buddhist monkhood (Sangha), as well as the Brahmin priesthood, as clergy and clerics despite the general Western restriction of those terms to the Christians faiths.

35 In presenting that selective interpretation of Siamese Buddhism and its monastic brotherhood, Diogo's words reflect his eighteenth-century humanist leanings, honed by his years of Jesuit affiliation in Portuguese Macao.

36 Six temples were newly built and 15 more were restored in the Thonburi area over the course of Taksin's reign. At least nine of those projects were royally sponsored and became known as royal temples, among them Wat Bang Yi Roea Noea (later Wat Racha Khroe), Wat Bang Yi Roea Tai (Wat Intharam), Wat Tai Talat (Wat Molilok), Wat Chaeng (Wat Arun), Wat Pho (Wat Phra Chetupon), Wat Hong (Wat Hong Ratanaram), and Wat Bang Wa Yai (Wat Rakhang), the last serving as the seat of Siam's supreme patriarch.

37 That pernicious Burmese practice favored burning the soles of their captive clerics' feet (avoiding the sacrilegious spilling of blood) as a means of extracting information.

38 Di's tenure as Supreme Patriarch, as well as his title, was expunged from the ecclesiastical records of Thonburi/Bangkok; the official sequence of Siam's post-Ayutthaya monastic heads has ever since started with his successor, Si.

39 Among the fellow monks accompanying Si to Thonburi was Ngao (Phra Phrom Muni), his former deputy abbot at Wat Phanan Choeng, who was installed at Thonburi as abbot of Wat Sakae. There, he later served as one of the Diogo's principal informants in the compilation of this Chronicle, as recounted in Diogo's Testament.

40 The further adventures of Phra Thamma Trailok (Sa, 1769-1781) at Wat Bang Wa Yai (later Wat Rakhang) are referred to in Chapter 7 (Reign Change) and the Epilogue.

41 Those facilities were later relocated crossriver to the shore of Thonburi's emerging Left-Bank Taechiu riverport.

42 The Department of Pundits had traditionally been administered by Brahmin priests who served as ritual experts on royal ceremonies such as the coronation, the swearing of allegiance, royal processions, royal cremations, astrological reckonings, and the like. The few surviving court Brahmins recreated that role at Thonburi with all the esoteric lore that they could recall.

43 Though the proffered plan was never executed, the city pillar was eventually erected. Like such spirit shrines throughout the Tai/Thai world, it was believed to house the capital's protective deity (the pillar, according to Brahman lore, representing a *Shivalinga*). No remains of the Thonburi pillar survive. The original pillar may have been transplanted in 1782 to stand alongside the newly implanted Bangkok city pillar. The Bangkok city pillar shrine today still boasts two pillars, the shorter one said to be the older, Thonburi version standing alongside its dominant successor.

44 On the Left Bank, across from the Bangkok Yai Canal confluence, the crumbled remains of the old abandoned Wichayan Fort were dismantled, and its remaining brick foundations were rafted across the river to contribute to the upgrading of the Thonburi fortifications into King Taksin's Grand Palace. Further barge-loads of bricks were provided by the Mon brickworks situated along Thonburi's Mon Canbal.

45 It appears that within several years of the start of the Thonburi period the stretch of the Bangkok Yai Canal reaching inland from the Grand Palace toward the Dan Canal came to be known as the Bang Kha Luang Canal (Royal Retainers' Canal), referring to the many nobles' estates and retainers' villages lining its shores. That name was soon shortened, for convenience, to the Bang Luang Canal (Royal Canal).

46 A shadow of that outer Thonburi demarcation remains visible along the course of today's Isaraphap Road.

47 Diogo revisits that economic crisis in Chapter 5.

48 It did not take many years for the refugee communities to adapt to the cultivation of the lower delta's traditional agrarian specialties of fruit orcharding

and market gardening, which provided a profitable smallholder trade.
49 That long-lost riverside settlement of conscripted rice cultivators was marked by a village temple, Wat Klang Na (Temple Amidst the Paddy Fields), which survives to the present day as Wat Chana Songkhram.
50 Further discussed in Chapter 4.
51 The confidential information concerning Taksin's ill-fated shipboard injury, his subsequent suffering, the relapse of his malady during the Phitsanulok campaign of 1776, and his later physical decline was apparently provided to Diogo by the Venerable Phra Phrom Muni (Ngao), abbot of Wat Saket, who utilizing his herbalist skills treated the king at Thonburi throughout his years-long lingering affliction (discussed in Chapter 7).
52 The circumstances are summarized in the Editor's Introduction to Chapter 4.
53 This is one of several quotes contained in the Doigo manuscript that we are certain derives from Plutarch (with the terms "Tak" and "Chinese merchant" substituted for ancient originals), but we have so far been unable to trace it to the source.
54 Although left unmentioned by Diogo, the redacted chronicles later reported that, after Taksin's safe return to Thonburi, Duang and Bunma were both tried and found guilty of infraction of a royal command (the order to assault Udong and restore it to tributary status) and were subjected to the relatively light punishment of 30 lashes of the cane.
55 That further resolution is briefly referred to in the closing paragraphs of this chapter and further in Chapter 5.
56 More fully examined in Chapter 5.

Chapter 4 Royal Scoundrels
1 Plutarch, 2001, vol. 1, p. 52.
2 No reference to those two Khmer princesses and their Ayutthaya connections appears in the Ayutthaya chronicles, nor in the Cambodian royal annals; it was a line of descent so convoluted that it was never clearly recorded. Diogo's information here is evidently based on information known to his confidantes Lady Songkandan and Phra Phrom Muni.
3 A similar case occurred during the first Chakri reign (1782-1809) with the Bangkok exile of Siam's nominee for the Cambodian throne, Prince Eng, along with his mother and three sisters (Princesses Men, Ee, and Phao). The Siamese viceroy, Prince Surasinghanat (Bunma), took the entire exiled Cambodian royal household under his patronage. He then accepted Eng's three sisters as his concubines and fathered by them four daughters.
4 Although Western kinship relations would consider the two pairs of brothers as cousins, the Thai vernacular referred to them as elder and younger brothers; they are referred to thus by Diogo.
5 His personal name, Khaek, has been said to suggest a person of swarthy complexion, as those of Khmer ancestry are often considered, by Siam's standards.
6 The highest royal spousal rank of queen was reserved for Siamese princesses; Khaek's mother, Chaem, as a Khmer princess (the daughter of a deposed, exiled king), was assigned the lesser rank of first-class concubine. That placed Khaek, despite his primacy in age, in a lower princely echelon than Kung, son of Boromakot's Queen of the Right, and Ekathat and Dok-madoea, sons of the Queen of the Left.
7 Plutarch, 2001, vol. 1, p. 148 (paraphrase).
8 It was a near-universal practice in pre-modern Siam for Buddhist boys at the age of puberty to be ordained as monastic novices and take temporary residence at a local temple. Some chose to continue in the monkhood as a lifelong calling following their full-fledged ordination at age 20. Khaek turned to that expedient several times over the course of his notorious career as an escape from the predicaments into which he repeatedly stumbled.
9 Such omens were not unknown. Legend has it that a similar prophesy was uttered some years later regarding Sin (better known then as Colonel Taksin) and Duang (General Chakri), both of whom eventually rose to the Siamese throne as King Taksin of Thonburi and King Rama I of Bangkok.
10 The devolution of viceregal command over Siam's various administrative regions was formalized more than a century later, during the fifth Chakri reign, with the title of Superintendent Commissioner and the designation of a number of senior princes to that position (after the proscription against princes serving in regular civil service positions had been lifted).
11 The Cambodian capital, initially at Angkor (Angkor Thom), was relocated downriver, southeastward, successively to Lovec (1505), then Udong (1618), and lastly Phnom Penh (officially 1865) in a continuing effort to distance the Khmer state from Siamese meddling.
12 Ha Tien was a prosperous principality and junk port situated near the eastern limit of the Gulf of Siam at the boundary between the Cambodian and Vietnamese spheres of influence It was in the eighteenth century a dependency of the Vietnamese at Hué. In specifying Sisang as Ayutthaya's envoy to that distant outpost, Diogo may have been giving him undue credit, as no other source, including the Vietnamese annals, mentions him in that capacity. Any ties that Sisang may have cultivated with Ha Tien were more likely of a private nature building on his mercantile activities at Udong.
13 Cambodia's Cham minority comprised remnants of

the ancient kingdom of Champa, formerly centered in present-day south-central Vietnam, most of its surviving populace today settled along the lower Mekong drainage basin in southeastern Cambodia and southern Vietnam, with an important extension in Battambang Province, west of Udong. Well before the eighteenth century the Cham people had converted from their ancestral Brahmanism to Islam in apparent deep-seated resistance to Khmer Buddhist cultural assimilation. Although the Cham interacted civilly with the Khmer majority, their ancestry as war captives and their entrenched resistance to Buddhist conversion relegated them to subordinate status within the Cambodian state.

14 The disastrous conclusion to Sisang's political adventure may well have contributed to the Cham community's further political marginalization in later Khmer history.
15 Plutarch, 2001, vol. 1, pp. 753 (paraphrase).
16 Ibid., vol. 2, p. 607 (paraphrase).
17 His personal name, Tui, was a pejorative vernacular homophone for water buffalo, meaning fool or blockhead. It is likely for that reason that the dynastic genealogies refer to him instead as Chui.
18 Plutarch, 2001, vol. 1, pp. 8-9, 597, and 611-612 paraphrase).
19 Ibid. vol. 2, p. 612.
20 Ibid., vol. 1, p. 443 (paraphrase).
21 Ibid., vol. 2, p. 201 (paraphrase).
22 The great Indian Ocean island of Lanka (today Sri Lanka), was at that time governed by the kingdom of Kandy. Close relations had historically been maintained between Kandy and Ayutthaya in recognition of their shared veneration of the Buddha, his teachings, and his monastic lineage.
23 Plutarch, vol. 1, vol. 1, p. 147.
24 Ibid., vol. 2, p. 14.
25 According to Ayutthaya's resident Catholic missionaries at the time, "The court of Ayutthaya, irritated by [Khaek's] audacity [in offering his services,] sent some detachments against him" (Pallegoix, 2000, p. 376).
26 Ibid., vol. 2, p. 424 (paraphrase).
27 Ibid., vol. 1, p. 45 (paraphrase).
28 Ibid., vol. 2, p. 588 (paraphrase).
29 Ngoen's execution was designed in accordance with an incident recounted in the *Chula Paduma Jataka* (Jataka no. 193).
30 Ibid., p. 655 (paraphrase).
31 Khaek's selection of Phimai, about 60 kilometers east of Khorat, as the capital of his renegade kingdom was no random act. It was a highly symbolic decision, evoking the grandeur of his Thai-Khmer lineage. Phimai had for some eight centuries stood as a prime stopover for pilgrims, traders, royal excursions, and military marches along the 300-kilometer-long Royal Road (*thanon dharmasala*, initiated by Angkor's King Jayavarman V in the late tenth century and finished by his successor, King Suriyavarman I, decades later) reaching westward from Angkor. Its main shrine was built of white sandstone 28 meters tall in cruciform design, with an assemblage of surrounding structures of pink sandstone and laterite.
32 Plutarch, 2001, vol. 2, p. 467 (paraphrase).
33 Spiritual validation of the new regime was as essential to that decision as its military considerations. Phimai's selection as the new state's ceremonial center was on those grounds a judicious choice. Its legendary past and magnificent monuments placed Khaek's lot firmly in the Khmer cultural camp, linking him to the bulk of the Khorat Plateau's Khmer populace, as his Siamese royal credentials alone would never have allowed.
34 Nothing further is reported here or in any other source on the particulars of Khaek's takeover of power and installation at Phimai
35 Plutarch, 2001, vol. 1, p. 708.
36 An earlier near encounter between Khaek and Taksin, during the latter's January 1767 flight from Ayutthaya to the Eastern Seaboard, is left unmentioned. It seems inconceivable that their forces would not have engaged in conflict as Taksin passed by Prachin. From that experience, each retained a view of the other as a deserter from the Siamese cause. The haste with which Thonburi's campaign against Phimai was mounted the following year may have owed much to that earlier encounter.
37 Plutarch, 2001, vol. 1, p. 504 (paraphrase).
38 Ibid., p. 469 (paraphrase).
39 Not that much convincing was needed – Thien-tu bore a longstanding grudge against Taksin from earlier humiliations. It had been Thien-tu's junks that had been commandeered by Taksin in 1767 carrying armed troops en route to Thonburi (as referred to in Chapter 3 of this Chronicle).
40 Plutarch, 2001, vol. 1, p. 523.
41 Taksin was at that time (July 1769-February 1770) leading an expedition against Nakhon Si Thammarat, far south, along the Malay Peninsula.
42 Plutarch, 2001, vol. 1, p. 546 (paraphrase).

Chapter 5 Warlords of the South Seas

1 Later chronicles intimate that Taksin was appointed commander of the Tak garrison not long after 1760, the year he reached age 26. Several years later he was promoted to Colonel Phraya Wachira Prakan, governor of the larger neighboring province of Kamphaeng Phet (though, even if true, he apparently never took up that assignment).
2 Plutarch, 2001, vol. 2, pp. 10 and 137 (paraphrase).
3 Ibid., vol. 1, p. 236 (paraphrase).

4. Ibid., vol. 2, p. 541 (paraphrase).
5. Ibid., p. 11 (paraphrase).
6. This is the first of many references to the eastern Gulf's escalating hostilities between the Cantonese/Hokkien alliance and the Taechiu interlopers, which in due course cascaded into open warfare between Siam and Ha Tien.
7. A revelatory observation in the official Ayutthaya chronicles states: "All the Thai and Chinese . . . in the villages and in the forests of every vicinity around the provincial municipalities [of the Eastern Seaboard] led their followers . . . in great numbers to submit to [Taksin]. . . . His fighting forces accordingly increased abundantly" (Cushman, 2000, pp. 528-529).
8. Thien-tu succeeded his father, Cuu *sae* Mac, in 1735. As a Ming partisan, Cuu *sae* Mac (1655-1735) had fled Kwangtung for the South Seas in the late 1600s to escape certain death under charges of insurrection and piracy. He had found sanctuary at the court of Cambodia, where he was offered opportunities as a tax farmer at Banteay Meas. Over the ensuing decades he built a robust commercial presence, raising his base at Ha Tien from an anonymous fishing village to a fledgling junk port. In 1709, as Cambodia slipped into political turmoil, he transferred his allegiance to Quang-nam, with its capital at Hué. Under Hué's protection he developed Ha Tien into a full-fledged port of call linking the lower Mekong Delta's agrarian hinterlands and their rich surplus of rice and associated exportable commodities with the junk carrying trade. His son Thien-tu continued that policy.
9. Plutarch, 2001, vol. 1, p. 462 (paraphrase).
10. The vast body of water today known as the South China Sea was in Diogo's day referred to simply as the South Sea, or Seas (*nan yang* in Chinese).
11. Diogo's manuscript was here found to be badly bleached with damp and the mildew of age. In replacement of the largely illegible narrative, several pages have been condensed into the following translated summary statements, which we believe convey the essence of the original narrative.
12. Quang-nam (later known as Annam), with its capital at Hué, dominated southern Vietnam.
13. The Cambodian annals, with typical exaggeration, reported a 15,000-man, 400-ship force.
14. The Vietnamese annals suggest that the reinforcements sent from Saigon to Ha Tien's aid by both sea and land never arrived. Apparently, the relieving forces were delayed by typhoon rains.
15. Plutarch, 2001, vol. 1, p. 395 (paraphrase).
16. Ibid., vol. 2, p. 129 (paraphrase).
17. Portions of Ha Tien's masonry city wall, forming a 500x200-meter rectangle some four meters high set well back from the unfortified waterfront, were later restored. Portions were still in place as late as the 1960s.
18. Plutarch, 2001, vol. 2, p. 129 (paraphrase).
19. This section elaborates Diogo's Chapter 3 discussion of Taksin's continuing struggle to reconstruct Thonburi, with a discussion of his policy resorting to his Taechiu retainers as an essential rice supply source, which grew into a driving force behind the Ha Tien showdown.
20. Plutarch, 2001, vol. 1, p. 336 (paraphrase).
21. The Taechiu Prefecture had long been an impoverished area replete with landless peasants in search of work as itinerant labor. It was a continuing source of mercenary fighters arising out of local conflicts between clans and classes. Indeed, the area later became well known for the martial traditions, devolving into piracy, that served as an economic mainstay for its poor.
22. Plutarch, 2001, vol. 1, p. 161 (paraphrase).
23. Vietnam found withdrawal from the Cambodian front timely in view of the emerging domestic crisis posed by the Tayson rebellion (1773-1802). Similarly, Thonburi was motivated to defuse the Cambodian conflict as it turned its energies to countering a resurgent Burmese threat in the north as well as a brutal Burmese suppression of the endemic Mon insurgency in the west.
24. Prince Tong (titled King Narai Racha) should not be confused with Prince Ton (the recently deposed King Outey Racha).
25. In recognition of that appointment, he received the Siamese title of Colonel Rachasethi Yuan ("Yuan" meaning "Vietnamese"), distinguishing him from Li-ang who had received the parallel (but more powerful) title of Colonel Rachasethi.
26. The detail with which Diogo reports the proceedings of Thien-tu's Thonburi visit suggest that he may well have been present on that occasion as a royal scribe, or possibly even as a Cantonese-Thai interpreter at the royal audience and banquet and the ensuing private discussions.
27. Plutarch, 2001, vol. 2, p. 163 (paraphrase).
28. Ibid., vol. 1, pp. 469 (paraphrase).
29. It is generally believed today that the name of the Tien Landing (*tha tien*), a line of docks along the river behind Wat Pho, some 50-100 meters distant from Thien-tu's former residence, derives from the place-name "Ha Tien." However, the term actually dates from the Fourth Reign (1851-1868), long after Thien-tu's residence had disappeared, when a major fire cleared ("*tien*") the riverfront docks and dwellings and opened the area to comprehensive redevelopment.
30. Ban Yuan lay along the outer bank of the Ong Ang Canal, which was expanded during the First Reign to become the lower stretch of the new city

Endnotes 273

moat. "Ban Yuan" can be translated as "Vietnamese Village." Although labeled Vietnamese, Ban Yuan's refugee population was in fact largely of Cantonese ethnic background, as Ha Tien had been a Cantonese commercial outpost. In later years it merged with the neighboring Ban Mon and today is generally included under that encapsulating name.
31. That bell remains on display today in the old throne hall of the partially preserved Thonburi Grand Palace.
32. The Daoist deity Ma Cho, alternatively transliterated as Mazu (also appropriated as the name of Macau), was otherwise known as Tian Fa (Heavenly Mother), or in Thai, Mae Thabthim (Ruby Mother) for her red robes. In the twentieth century, Ma Cho came to be increasingly conflated in the minds of many Bangkok devotees with Kwan Im (or Kwan Yin), the Mahayana Buddhist Goddess of Mercy, as evidenced by the later replacement of Kwan Im for Ma Cho as the presiding image in the Ban Mo Shrine, along Foeang Nakhon Road (formerly Ban Mo Road), marking the approximate center of the former Cantonese/Vietnamese settlement.
33. With the later decline of the Ha Tien émigré presence, Wat Kham Lo was abandoned during the Third Reign, but it was reestablished in the Fourth Reign during a new Chinese influx and then renamed Wat Thipawari following its renovation at the close of the Fifth Reign. It remains today, with the present facilities dating from 1951, when the former rotted, fire-prone wooden structures were rebuilt with brick and mortar.
34. That temple was eventually relocated downriver to Sampheng, where it was renamed Wat Mongkhon Samakom.
35. The Daoist deity Pun Thao Kong, often displayed together with his wife, Pun Thao Ma, is revered in Taechiu lore – and more widely throughout southeastern China –, holding a place equivalent to the occult site guardians of Thai tradition.
36. When, following Taksin's overthrow, Thonburi's Taechiu community was evicted downstream, the main Pun Thao Kong shrine was dismantled and then rebuilt on the Sampheng waterfront, where it still stands today, tellingly called the Old Shrine. In 1822, after a devastating fire had ravaged Sampheng, Thien-tu's Kwan U image was judged an inauspicious presence and was therefore transferred to an old Hokkian shrine (today known as the Bu Sia Bia Shrine) located across the river at Kudi Chin.
37. Nothing further is said by Diogo of the Hokkien community, possibly because it played no significant role in subsequent events at Thonburi. Many of Ayutthaya's Hokkien merchants had fled in 1766-1767 to safe havens in Siam's southern provinces, where they maintained branch offices overseeing their lucrative birds' nest and tin concessions. The lesser number who risked staying on at Thonburi made it a practice to maintain a low profile under Taksin, until the local Hokkien-Taechiu balance of power was reversed with the Chakri coup of 1782.
38. It has been suggested that Hok-chu had procured Duang's approval with generous contributions to the reserves that the Chakri brothers had been accumulating to further their political ambitions.
39. Diogo was apparently unaware that Prince Nguyen Anh had recently been crowned at Hué as Emperor Gia Long, founder of the Nguyen Dynasty.
40. Plutarch, 2001, vol. 2, p. 245 (paraphrase).
41. Although Mu was an upstart, he aspired to royalty. It has been conjectured that his title as "*fa*" may have served as an abbreviation for "*chao fa*," inferring royal status, while "*thalaha*" may have been a variant on "*kalahom*," referring to his role as Minister of War (in a kingdom so desperately short of leadership that royals took on the functions of nobles, and vice versa).
42. The bloodbath of death sentences imposed on Thien-tu and his sons and retainers was later referred to by the Chakri faction as contributing evidence of Taksin's alleged insanity, but the entire process had been carried out in an orderly fashion in conformity with legal precedent. The Law on Crimes against the State was contained in the Three Seals Code (an exhaustive compilation of Ayutthaya's accumulated laws), copies of which had survived the burning of the former capital.
43. Plutarch, 2001, vol. 1, p. 516 (paraphrase).
44. Machiavelli, 2003, p. 39.

Chapter 6 Turning Point

1. "Yuan" here, in reference to the Lan Na Tai, not to be confused with the homophone used in reference to the people of Vietnam.
2. Asae Wunki (Athi Wongyi in Burmese), also known as Maha Thiha Thura (an honorific approximating "Great Warrior Brave as a Lion"), occupied one of the highest positions in the militarist Burmese nobility. "Asae" referred to his senior military rank, "Wunki" signified his ministerial title (equivalent to Siam's Minister of War – *kalahom*). Though of Mon pedigree, he was closely associated with the Burmese royal family (his daughter was married to Prince Singu, Mang Ra's son and heir presumptive). His instrumental role in the repulsion of several Chinese invasions into northern Burma led to his designation as commanding general in the 1775-1776 Siamese campaign against Siam.
3. This was the first of a number of Western-dated references entered directly into Diogo's Portuguese text (unlike other chapters, in which we have inserted Western dates equivalent to the Thai dates on which Diogo generally relied). Apparently, da

Costa had kept a diary into which he entered his daily observances using the Gregorian calendar, with which he was more comfortable than the Burmese lunar dating system to which he was persistently subjected. The written reminiscences that he submitted to Diogo for the present chapter must have contained those dates as his timeline.

4   Whether this General Sihabodi was the same commander as Thosakan, who had led the Burmese conquest of Ayutthaya less than a decade previously (see Chapter 2), is unclear.

5   Taksin received those seasoned fighters as a welcome addition to Siam's depleted manpower base. Their chief, Saming Choei (Choeng or Cheng in Thai) was awarded the equivalent Siamese title of Colonel Cheng as a commander of the Mon militias defending Siam's western uplands. (See Chapter 7)

6   These details apparently record da Costa's personal experience as a prisoner of war assigned to the training of those Burmese infantry corps.

7   Pak Praek later grew into the provincial hub of Kanchanaburi.

8   An additional reason for Taksin's rushed march to Ratburi was the news that his mother had recently been taken seriously ill there during a stopover en route to her Phetburi home. She died at Ratburi soon after his arrival. His grief, compounded by the ceremonies associated with her funerary rites, diverted him from close attention to the mounting Burmese threat, and much of the generalship during what came to be known as the siege of Bang Kaew thus devolved on his deputies Duang and Bunma.

9   Here again da Costa appears to be speaking from his personal experience, as the Burmese army's training sergeants were assigned the additional responsibility of ensuring the troops' compliance with regulations.

10 Brigand bands of unsupervised Burmese troops were left free to torment the local population. Asae Wunki evidently faced great difficulty in dealing with deficiencies in the lower ranks of his field command structure. His recruitment of such war captives as da Costa into the officer corps and their assignment to deal with that issue is suggestive of his officer staffing problems. Repeatedly, da Costa refers to what was evidently his troubled experience in dealing with malingerers, recalcitrants, and deserters within the infantry. The course of the war reflects that Burmese leadership deficit.

11 This paragraph and several that follow, providing detailed information on events at Phitsanulok and the role played by Duang and Bunma during the Burmese siege, diverge from the general tenor of this chapter. They were evidently inserted into the text based on information provided by Prince Chakra Chesada (La), who as referred to in Diogo's Testament, had intimate knowledge of Phitsanulok affairs.

12 Again, an insertion evidently provided by Prince Chakra Chesada (La).

13 The additional guardpost at Bang Phayom, upriver from the city, lay beyond the contested supply route and thus has received little notice.

14 Especially popular in Taksin's emphasis on mobile warfare, jingals (miniature field guns) were more economical than conventional cannon in both the weight of their shot and the quantity of gunpowder required, and capable of being conveyed in a sling between a pair of artillerymen and fired in the open field, or even from the backs of elephants.

15 An extraordinary incident is claimed to have occurred at around this time. The commanders of the two contending forces are said to have met on horseback at the center of the cleared field of combat. There, the 73-year-old Asae Wunki offered his 30-year-old adversary, General Chakri (Duang), his congratulations for having risen to such prominent military rank so quickly. A later Burmese account of the meeting has him remarking "You have the bearing of a king. Perhaps you will be king one day" (Phayre, 1883, pp. 207-208), insinuating that Asae Wunki had the intent of fomenting a rivalrous tension between Taksin and his senior general. The later Siamese chronicles record that Taksin subsequently conferred on Duang the extraordinary title of General Maha Kasatsoek (Great King of Battle), though Diogo makes no mention of either the incident or the title.

    The entire episode, both the battlefield parley and the titular award to which it is said to refer, is possibly apocryphal, devised in the post-Thonburi years to glorify the new dynasty (and later picked up by British colonial historians). Would the famously cautious Duang have chanced such a battlefield encounter, however carefully orchestrated, where a sharpshooter's musket ball (range 300 meters or more) posed an ever-present threat? Furthermore, under the laws of both Siam and Burma, such a battleground meeting would have constituted a treasonous breach of protocol. The tale may well have been conjured up from the many chivalrous mid-combat encounters contained in the *Romance of the Three Kingdoms*, a Chinese epic that was translated into Thai during the First Reign and gained great popularity among the Bangkok reading public.

16 The annual holy day marking the Great Assembly of Buddha's Disciples, the first full moon of the third lunar month.

17 That may well be the moment that da Costa elected to escape his long Burmese captivity into Siamese sanctuary (see Diogo's comment on da Costa's escape in the Testament), which would explain

Taksin's discovery of Asae Wunki's actions and its military implications "a day later."

The details that follow apparently came from information supplied to Diogo by Prince Chakra Chesada (La).

18 What is not mentioned in all this is Taksin's personal difficulties following the Pak Phing disaster. Chapter 7 refers to the reactivation during that frenzied time of the injury that the king had suffered in a storm at sea. It appears that he was evacuated to the newly established Royal Guard camp at Pichit for recouperation and then barged downriver to Thonburi for more effective medical attention. From that date, he played no further active role in military command, marking the start of his reign's decline.

19 It may be inferred, as contended in the "Editor's introduction" to this chapter, that Diogo composed this section based on information provided by Prince Chakra Chesada (La).

20 Plutarch, 2001, vol. 2, p. 308.

21 Ibid., p. 476.

22 Wat Yai, formally known as Wat Mahathat, was left in ruins by the invading Burmese forces, its sanctuaries stripped of their treasure and its Buddha images desecrated in the enemy's search for plunder. Under royal sponsorship, the temple was thoroughly renovated and renamed Wat Phra Si Ratana Mahathat in later reigns, with its Phra Phutha Chinarat image being fully restored and covered with a thick gilding..

23 By that time, both da Costa and La had made their separate escapes to Thonburi. Diogo thus lacked any first-hand information from his principal informants on the subsequent course of battlefield events. The remainder of the present chapter consists of little more than an unadorned summary of the war's unwinding.

24 Plutarch, 2001, vol. 2, p. 213.

25 Ibid., p. 485.

26 As the father-in-law of Burma's king-designatee, Asae Wunki had a major stake in the succession. He rushed back from the Phitsanulok campaign to participate in the reign change, with high expectations. However, he had overreached. Within a year he was ousted from office into forced retirement.

27 In consequence, the reputations of Duang and Bunma did not suffer, and the later cleansing of the record managed to polish their celebrity with a heroic patina.

28 According to the redacted Thonburi chronicle, Taksin departed for Thonburi by rapid royal rivercraft repeatedly, in great secrecy, during the period April-June 1776. Those frequent absences from the battlefront were considered essential to deal with a diversity of pressing domestic issues: preparations for the funeral of Princess-Mother Thepamat, negotiations with his ministers and provincial governors on issues of military mobilization and acquisition of supplies, installation of officials into senior posts vacated upon the deaths of incumbents, arrangements for the dispatch of monks to the war zone to aid in reviving the religion. It may be inferred from Diogo's narrative that they were also necessitated by Taksin's deteriorating health.

29 In late 1776, however, Bunma rushed north to Chiangmai to join his Lan Na confederates in countering a renewed assault from Burma's Chiangsaen base. His solidarity with the Lan Na cause and symbolic position of being Siam's man in the North was affirmed through his marriage to Rocha, a younger sister of Prince Kawila. As his senior wife, she took on the prestigious role of managing his household affairs at Thonburi.

30 French missionary priests wandering Siam in the war's aftermath wrote in their dispatches that conditions in the Central Plains provinces had returned to normal by 1790; there was no longer any threat of Burmese incursion, and the food situation had been restored.

Chapter 7 Reign Change

1 Plutarch, 2001, vol. 1, p. 329 (paraphrase).

2 Ibid., vol. 2, p. 405 (paraphrase).

3 Ibid., vol. 1, p. 328 (paraphrase).

4 Taksin's symptoms resembled those that modern medicine associates with sepsis, bacterial infection spreading through the bloodstream, often from an erupting cyst (sometimes long benign), leading to severe damage to major organs, which can be fatal. The principal symptoms, short of a confirmatory microscopic blood examination, are an increased respiratory rate, low blood pressure, and often an altered mental state, including confusion, volatile emotions, and distorted judgment.

5 Diogo apparently received this information from Lady Songkandan (Thong-mon) who, as directress of the Grand Palace Inside (the women's quarter), is said by Diogo to have aided in the king's convalescence, and also from Phra Phrom Muni (Ngao), abbot of Wat Sakae, who, also according to Diogo, assisted the king's physicians in the application of herbal elixirs to his injured leg.

6 From this point on, Diogo takes to referring to them as the Chakri brothers.

7 Royal cremations were invariably staged a year or more after the person's death, with the corpse being preserved through the year-long waiting period nested in a golden urn displayed for veneration under a multitiered royal parasol, raised in prominent display upon a dais within an audience hall in the Grand Palace.

8 Diogo's information here apparently stems from his

personal recollections of attendance at those sessions as a court scribe, observing the proceedings as unobtrusively as a fly on the wall, or a gecko from the rafters.

9. The citadels of Vientiane (a francophone rendering of Wiang Chan, anciently known as Si Satana Khanahut) and Champasak (originally known as Bassac, not to be confused with Cambodia's neighboring Bassac region), as well as Luang Prabang (formerly known as Chiang Thong) further north, each commanded an upriver stretch of the mighty Mekong River. From those administrative centers radiated their three eponymous feudal states, carved out of the ancient inland kingdom of Lan Chang over the decades following its political disintegration during the late seventeenth century. Downriver from those Lao states, the declining power of neighboring Cambodia opened to both Vientiane and Champasak new opportunities to extend their sway across the lawless Khorat Plateau.

10. Formerly known as Angkor Thom, later as Siemreap.

11. Later estimates suggest that more than 10,000 Lao war captives were carried off from the Vientiane kingdom, with the largest share being settled at Saraburi and perhaps 2,000 being sent on to Thonburi.

12. To allay those concerns, the Phra Bang Buddha image was returned to Vientiane a year later in the care of Prince Nanthasen. It was returned to Bangkok following the Siamese conquest of Vientiane in 1827 and then returned to Chiang Thong (and hence that city's modern name of Luang Prabang) during the Fourth Reign.

13. Prominently absent from the Lao royal hostage contingent was King Siri Bunsan (the captive prices' father), who had managed to escape into the eastern hills and Vietnamese sanctuary. He was later pardoned by Taksin and allowed to return as vassal king (r.1781-1782), to be succeeded, in turn, by each of his sons Nanthasen, Inthawong, and Anuwong.

14. Those two settlements came to be known, in due course, as Wang Lao and Bang Khun Phrom.

15. Plutarch, vol. 2, p. 660 (paraphrase).

16. Ibid.., vol. 1, p. 664.

17. Ibid., vol. 2, p. 660 (paraphrase).

18. Chapter 4, table 4 "Cambodia's royal succession, 18th century," summarizes the essential details of the exceptionally complex Cambodian reign sequence.

19. With that cryptic sentence Diogo may have meant to suggest, retrospectively, that the Chakri brothers had reached the conclusion (as of mid-1781) that Taksin's time on the throne was nearing its end and had decided to distance themselves for the portending crisis.

20. For instance, a Jesuit priest reported to his Paris-based superiors in early 1782, after a brief tour at Thonburi: "For some years, the King of Siam has tremendously vexed his subjects and the foreigners who dwelt in or came to trade in his kingdom…. This past year the vexations caused by this King, more than half-mad, have become more frequent and more cruel than previously. He has had imprisoned, tortured, and flogged, according to his caprice, his wife, his son's faction – even the heir-presumptive, and his high officials" (Launay, 1920, vol. 2, p. 309).

21. Plutarch, 2001, vol. 2, p. 336.

22. Earlobe-clipping was a special punishment that went beyond temporary pain and permanent disfigurement to the symbolism of a shortened lifespan, as it was commonly believed that the length of one's earlobes predicted life expectancy, associated with the dangling earlobes attributed to the Buddha and prominent on all his images.

23. The ferocity with which Siam's eighteenth-century military commanders regularly applied justice corresponded closely to the prevalence of infractions against the rules of military conduct both within the officer corps and among the ranks. Taksin's conduct in that regard was by no means exceptional.

24. Plutarch, 2001, vol. 2, pp. 261.

25. Machiavelli, 2003, p. 72.

26. In the Buddhist canon, a "stream enterer" or "stream winner" (Pali: *sotāpanna*; Thai: "*sodaban*") is a person who has attained a degree of understanding that indicates an intuitive grasp of the Buddha's doctrine –metaphorically, one who has set himself/herself on the path to enlightenment (Pali: *bodhi*).

27. That procrustean decision was reversed a year later, following the Chakri coup, with the ouster of Choen and the reinstatement of Si as Supreme Patriarch with the title of Phra Phonarat.

28. Diogo's admission that he remained ill-informed of the obscure circumstances of this case is reflected in later studies, which present sharply differing interpretations of its causes and consequences.

29. Plutarch, 2001, vol. 1, p. 159 (paraphrase).

30. Ibid., vol. 2, pp. 293-294.

31. Choeng, as hereditary chief of Ataran (a Mon insurgent hotbed stretching up the Aratan River from Martaban to the Three Pagodas Pass) claimed affiliation with the former ruling dynasty of Hongsawaddy (the former Mon kingdom centered on the Irrawaddy Delta, more anciently known as Ramanya Desa, which had been systematically absorbed into the Burmese empire) and therefore insisted that he be accorded deference. The unresolved squabbling over that demand likely contributed to his decision in March 1782 to confront Madot and the Palace Guard in the dynastic crisis that ended the Taksin reign.

32. Plutarch, vol. 1, p. 437.

33. Ibid., p. 327 (paraphrase).

34. Ibid.

35 Ibid., p. 393.
36 Ibid., vol. 2, p. 557 (paraphrase).
37 A district of Chainat Province, not to be confused with the Northern province of Sawangkhaburi.
38 Plutarch, 2001, vol. 1, p. 454 (paraphrase).
39 That assignment placed Kawin in control of Thonburi's stocks of military ordnance and bladed weapons, most of which were amassed in the storehouses lining the Grand Palace Forecourt wall, with the powder magazine and munitions depot located for security and safety alongside the Royal Guard cantonment at the far end of the citadel. All that weaponry was required to be inventoried, maintained in good order, dispersed, and repossessed under Kawin's command – the commons, and even troopers, being prohibited from unauthorized possession of firearms and other military-grade weaponry – placing him in a unique position of control over the capital's defenses.
40 Plutarch, vol.1, p. 454 (paraphrase).
41 Ibid., vol. 2, p. 283 (paraphrase).
42 The detail with which Diogo presents the particulars of this meeting leaves little doubt that he was in attendance, performing his usual scribe's duties as a silent observer.
43 A *chang* was a monetary measure equal to an 80 *baht* weight, or 1,200 grams of silver. Tek-ki's 500-*chang* fee would have amounted to about US$475,000 at 2023 prices, hinting at the magnitude of the buried treasure that his scavengers were expecting to recover.
44 That information, and much of what follows, was apparently contained in the conspirators' statements extracted (under compulsions best left unspecified) during their later interrogations, presumably made available to Diogo by Prince Chakra Chesada (La).
45 Plutarch, 2001, vol. 1, p. 353 (paraphrase).
46 Diogo, resident at Santa Cruz (*Ban Portuket*) at the time, must have been present at those events. That presumably accounts for his detailed description of the disaster, and his participation in his community's humiliation, left unmentioned in his Testament.
47 Both those defectors to Duang's camp continued in his service. Bunnak eventually rose to his office, attaining the post of Minister of Lands late in the First Reign and known to history as Bunnak Ban Maela to distinguish him from Duang's close associate Bunnak, progenitor of the Bunnag lineage.
48 The absence of detail concerning that meeting and the brevity of Diogo's reportage on subsequent palace doings suggest that he was not present on those occasions, likely because his secretarial functions had been dispensed with under the new administration. Perhaps Kawin had little stomach for preserving a near-verbatim transcript of his troubled incumbency.
49 A copy of that dispatch, or a summary version contained in other records, was evidently included among the documents later provided to Diogo by Prince Chakra Chesada (La).
50 Rocha was approached as Bunma's surrogate, as he was off fighting in Cambodia. As noted in Chapter 6, Bunma had years before married Rocha, a sister of Prince Kawila of Lampang, and brought her back to Thonburi. There, he had installed her as his senior wife at his new ministerial mansion (later expanded into Bangkok's Front Palace) alongside Wat Salak (later Wat Mahathat), directly across the river from Thong-in's Thonburi citadel residence.
51 Choeng's decision to assist Thong-in may not have been difficult for him, as he was on good terms with the Chakri brothers and, flattered by their request for his aid, was well aware of the humiliation that the Kawin-Ramlak-Madot triumvirate had recently wreaked on his benefactor King Taksin, and had long been at odds with Madot.
52 Ko Kret was a Mon refugee settlement an hour's passage upstream from Thonburi.
53 The scrubland that had been cleared to encamp Duang's troops later came to be known as Thung Phlaphlachai (Field of the Victory Rostrum) in commemoration of Duang's stirring address to his troops preceding their procession to the Wat Pho royal boat landing the next morning.
54 Plutarch, 2001, vol. 2, p. 313 (paraphrase).
55 That "victory pavilion" (*phlapphla*) was ascended by Duang again early the next morning to rally his troops for the coming procession to Wat Pho and the crossriver barge ride that would take him to the Thonburi Grand Palace and a new future. cf. fig. 49 caption.
56 Ibid., p. 223.
57 In commemoration of that consequential lustration rite (Pali: *sa kesa*), Wat Sakae was later renamed Wat Saket (from the Thai: *sa*, "wash" and Pali: *kesa*, "the hair of the head").
58 Plutarch, 2001, vol. 1, p. 286 (paraphrase).
    Diogo's Chronicle ends here, looking ahead the next day, marking the execution of King Taksin start and the installation of a new dynasty. The Epilogue that follows this chapter provides a summary of the key events beyond Diogo's telling through the initial days, months, and years of Duang's reign as King Rama I of the Chakri dynasty. Diogo's Testament, viewing subsequent events from a more personal perspective, carries his tale forward into the early decades of Duang's reign as Rama I.

Bibliography

General sources (a personal selection)

Aung-Thwin, Michael and Maitrii (2012). *A History of Myanmar since Ancient Times*. London: Reaktion Books.

Baker, Chris, and Pasuk Phongpaichit (2022). *A History of Thailand*. 4th ed., Cambridge, UK: Cambridge University Press.

Chandler, David P. (2000). *A History of Cambodia*. 3rd ed., Chiangmai: Silkworm Books.

Charney, Michael W. (2004). *Southeast Asian Warfare, 1300-1900*. Leiden, Netherlands: Brill.

Charnwit Kasetasiri (1982). *Phama: prawatisat lae kanmoeang* [Burma: History and Politics]. Bangkok: Social Sciences and Humanities Textbook Foundation.

Chatthip Nartsupha (1999). *The Thai Village Economy in the Past*. Chris Baker and Pasuk Phongpaichit, trans. Chiangmai: Silkworm Books.

Chula Chakrabongse, Prince (2020). *Lords of Life: A History of the Kings of Thailand*. 60th anniversary ed. Bangkok: River Books

Englehart, Neil A. (2001). *Culture and Power in Traditional Siamese Government*. Ithaca, NY: Cornell University Southeast Asia Program.

LeBar, Frank M., et al. (1964). *Ethnic Groups of Mainland Southeast Asia*. New Haven, Conn.: Human Resources Asia Files Press.

Lieberman, Victor B. (2003). *Strange Parallels: Southeast Asia in Global Context, c 800-1830*. 2 vols. Cambridge: Cambridge University Press.

Machiavelli, Nicolò (2003), *The Prince and Other Writings*. Wayne A Rebhorn, trans. New York: Barnes and Noble Classics.

Nidhi Eoseewong (1995), *Krung taek Phrachao Tak lae prawastisat Thai* [The destroyed capital, King Tak and Thai History]. Bangkok: Matichon.

Nidhi Eoseewong (2019). *Wang phaendin: prawatisat priyabthiyap "krung taek"* [Interregna in Comparison: Ineffectual Adjustment to Changes among Three Southeast Asian Kingdoms]. Bangkok: Toyota Thailand Foundation and Social Sciences and Humanities Textbook Foundation.

Pallegoix, Mgr. Jean-Baptiste (2000). *Description of the Thai Kingdom of Siam: Thailand under King Mongkut*. Walter J. Tips, trans. Bangkok: White Lotus.

Plutarch, Lucius Mestrius (2001). *Plutarch's Lives*. 2 vols. A. H. Clough, trans. and ed. New York: Random House, Modern Library Edition.

Sarasin Viraphol (1977). *Tribute and Profit: Sino-Siamese Trade, 1652-1853*. Cambridge, MA.: Harvard University Press (Council on East Asian Studies).

Tambiah, Stanley J. (1976). *World Conqueror and World Renouncer: A Study of Buddhism and Polity in Thailand against a Historical Background*.Cambridge: Cambridge University Press.

Terwiel, Bareend Jan (2006). *Thailand's Political History: From the Fall of Ayutthaya to Recent Times*. Bangkok: River Books.

Thaw Kaung, U (2010). Aspects of Myanmar History and Culture. Yangon: Gangaw Myaing.

Wyatt, David. K. (1984). *Thailand: A Short History*. London: Yale University Press.

Prologue
a. The Translators' quest

Boxer, C. R. (1969). *The Portuguese Seaborne Empire 1415-1835*. New York: Alfred A. Knopf.

Cornwel-Smith, Philip (2020). *Very Bangkok: In the City of the Senses*. Bangkok: River Books.

Pinheiro, Magda (2018). *Lisbon: A Biography*. Mario Pereira, trans. Amherst, MA: Tagus Press.

Plutarch, Lucius Mestrius (1748). *Plutarco, Vidas de alguns famosos gregos e romanos* [Plutarch,

Lives of Some Famous Greeks and Romans]. Luis de Souza Pires, trans. Lisbon.

Saramago, José (1998). *The History of the Siege of Lisbon*. Giovanni Pontiero, trans. New York: Harcourt Books.

Wank-Nolasco Lamas, Rosmarie (1999). *History of Macau*. 2nd ed. Macau: Institute of Tourism Education.

b. Thai chronicles relevant to the late Ayutthaya and Thonburi periods (English-language translations referred to where available)

Anon. (2010). "*Prachum khamhaikan krung si Ayutthaya ruam 3 roeang*" [Collected Testimonies of the City of Ayutthaya, 3 Combined Tracts]. Bangkok: Saengdao.

Bradley, Dan Beach, ed. (1863). *Phra racha phongsawadan krung thonburi phaendin somdet phra boromarat thi 4 (somdet phrachao taksin maharat) chabap phim khong mo bradli* [Royal Chronicle of Thonburi, Reign of King Boromarat 4 (His Majesty King Taksin the Great), Dr. Bradley Edition]. Thonburi: Bradley Printer.

Cushman, Richard D., compiler and trans. (2000). *The Royal Chronicles of Ayutthaya*. David K. Wyatt, ed. of the trans. Bangkok: Siam Society.

Damrong Rachanuphap, Prince, ed. (1969). *Prachum phongsawadan* [Collected Chronicles]. 57 vols., Bangkok: Khurusapha.

Hanuman Kamathan, et al., eds. (2008). *Phra racha phongsawadan krung thonburi . . .* [The Royal Chronicles of Thonburi . . .]. Bangkok: Si Panya.

Phonarat, Somdet Phra (1923). *Sangkhitiyawong: Phongsawadan roeang sanghayana phra tham winai* [Lineage of the Sangha: Chronicle of the Great Councils on the Monastic Brotherhood's Doctrine and Discipline)] Bangkok: Mahamakut Press.

Thipakorawong, Chaophraya (1978). *The Dynastic Chronicles, Bangkok Era, The First Reign*. Thadeus and Chadin Flood, trans. and ed. Tokyo: Centre for East Asian Cultural Studies.

Tri Amaayakun, ed. (1964). *Phra racha phongsawadan krung siam chak tonchabap thi pen sombat khong British Museum krung London* [The Royal Chronicle of Siam: British Museum Edition]. Bangkok.

Wongsa Thirat-sanit, Prince (1973). *Phra racha phongsawadan chabap phra rachahat lekha* [The Royal Chronicles: Royal Autograph Edition]. Rama IV, ed. Bangkok: Khlang Withaya.

c. Thai historiography

Charnvit Kasetsiri (2020). "Thai Historiography," in Pavin Chachavalpongpun, ed., *Routledge Handbook of Contemporary Thailand*. New York: Routledge, pp. 26-35.

Ivarsson, Søren (1995). "The Study of the Traiphum Phra Ruang: Some Considerations," in Manas Chitakasem, ed., *Thai Literary Traditions*. Bangkok: Chulalongkorn University Press, pp. 56-86.

Jory, Patrick (2011). "Thai Historical Writing," in *The Oxford History of Historical Writing: Volume 5: Historical Writing Since 1945*. Oxford: Oxford University Press, pp. 536-558.

Lagirarde, François (2015). "Historiography: Thailand," in Jonathan A. Silk, ed., *Brill's Encyclopedia of Buddhism*. vol. 1, Leiden: Brill, pp. 792-799.

Manas Chitrakasem (ed.) (1995). *Thai Literary Traditions*. Bangkok: Chulalongkorn University Press.

Nidhi Eoseewong (2005). "The History of Bangkok in the Chronicles of Ayutthaya," in *Pen and Sail: Literature and History in Early Bangkok*. Chris Baker and Ben Anderson, et al., trans. Chiangmai: Silkworm Books, pp. 289-341.

Wyatt, David K. (1976). "Chronicle Traditions in Thai Historiography," in C. D. Cowan and O. W. Wolters, eds., *Southeast Asian History and Historiography*. Ithaca, NY: Cornell University Press, pp. 107-122.

Diogo's Testament

Basto da Silva, Beatriz (1995-1997). *Cronologia da História de Macau*. 4 vols. Macau: Direcção dos Serviços de Educação e Juventude.

Bidya Sriwattanasarn (1998). "*Chumchon chaw portuket nai samai krung ayutthayapho. pho. so. 2059-2310*" [The Portuguese Community During the Ayutthaya Period, 1516-1767]. Ph.D. thesis. Bangkok: Chulalongkorn University.

Boxer, C. R. (1969). *The Portuguese Seaborne Empire 1415-1835*. New York: Alfred A. Knopf.

Smithies, Michael, ed. (2011). *Five Hundred Years of Thai-Portuguese Relations: A Festschrift*. Bangkok: Siam Society.

Tang, Kaijian (2015). *Setting off from Macau: Essays in Jesuit History During the Ming and Qing Dynasties*. Leiden: Brill.

Van Roy, Edward (2017). *Siamese Melting Pot: Ethnic Groups in the Making of Bangkok*. Singapore: Institute for Southeast Asian Studies.

Voltaire, François-Marie de (1764). *Dictionnaire philosophique* Project Gutenberg (http.s:www.gutenberg,org).

Diogo's Chronicle – *Chapter 1*

Baker, Chris, and Pasuk Phongpaichit (2017). *A History of Ayutthaya: Siam in the Early Modern World*. Cambridge: Cambridge University Press.

Baker, Chris (2013). "The Grand Palace in the *Description of Ayutthaya*: Translation and Commentary," *Journal of the Siam Society*, vol. 101, pp. 69-112.

Baker, Chris, and Pasuk Phongpaichit. trans. and eds. (2016). *The Palace Law of Ayutthaya and the Thammasat: Law and Kingship in Siam*. Ithaca, NY: Southeast Asia Program Publications, Cornell University.

Boran Rachathanin, Phraya (Phon Dechakhup) (1969). "*Wa duai phaen-thi krung si ayutthaya*" [Commentary on the Plan of Ayutthaya], in Damrong Rachanuphap, Prince, ed., *Prachum phongsawadan* [Collected Chronicles]. Bangkok: Khurusapha, vol. 37, pp. 139-211.

Busakorn Lailert (1972). "The Ban Phlu Luang Dynasty 1688-1767: A Study of the Thai Monarchy During the Closing Years of the Ayuthya Period," Ph.D. dissertation, University of London.

Chitrasing Piyachat (2008). *Kabot krung si ayutthaya*. [Rebellions at the Capital of Ayutthaya]. Bangkok: Yip Si Group

Ekarong Phanuphong (2002). *Sek nai rachasamnak*. [Sex in the Royal Court]. Bangkok: Siam Inter Books.

Manop Thawruansakun (2005). *Khunnang ayutthaya* [Noblemen of Ayutthaya]. Bangkok: Thammasat University Book Center.

Wales, H. G. Quaritch (1931). *Siamese State Ceremonies: Their History and Function*. London: Bernard Quaritch.

Diogo's Chronicle – *Chapter 2*

Baker, Chris, and Pasuk Phongpaichit (2017). *A History of Ayutthaya: Siam in the Early Modern World*. Cambridge: Cambridge University Press.

Damrong Rajanubhab, Prince (2001). *The Chronicle of Our Wars with the Burmese: Hostilities between Siamese and Burmese when Ayutthaya was the Capital of Siam*. trans. Phra Phraison Salarak, Thien Subindu [U Aung Thien]; ed. and intro. Chris Baker. Bangkok: White Lotus.

Goss, Frederick B. (2008). "'*Anucha*': The Younger Brother in *Ramakien* and Thai Historical Narratives," *Rian Thai: International Journal of Thai Studies*, vol. 1, no. 1, pp. 26-51.

Launay, Adrien, ed. (1920). *Histoire de la Mission de Siam 1662-1811*. 2 vols., Paris: P. Téqui.

Lieberman, Victor B. (1984). *Burmese Administrative Cycles – Anarchy and Conquest, c.1580-1760*. Princeton, NJ: Princeton University Press.

Lieberman, Victor B. (1996). "Political Consolidation under the Early Konbaung Dynasty, 1752-1820," *Journal of Asian History*, vol. 30, no. 2, pp. 152-168.

Myo Myint (2010). *Collected Essays on Myanmar History and Culture*. Yangon.

Pe Maung Tin and G.H. Luce, trans. (1923). *The Glass Palace Chronicle of the Kings of Burma*. 2 vols. Oxford: Oxford University Press.

Pramin Khroeathong (2015). *SHUTDOWN krung si* [SHUTDOWN of the Ayutthaya Capital]. Bangkok: Silpa Wathanatham.

Singer, Noel F. (1989). "The *Ramayana* at the Burmese Court," *Arts of Asia*, vol. 19, no. 6, pp. 90-103.

Soe Thuzar Myint (2011). *The Portrayal of the Battle of Ayutthaya in Myanmar Literature*. Bangkok: Institute of Asian Studies, Chulalongkorn University.

Symes, Michael (1800). *An Account of an Embassy to the Kingdom of Ava*, London.

Thaw Kaung, U (2002). "The *Ramayana* Drama in Myanmar," *Journal of the Siam Society*, vol. 90, parts 1 and 2, pp. 137-148.

Wyatt, David K. (1982). "The 'Subtle Revolution' of King Rama I of Siam," in David K. Wyatt and Alexander Woodside, eds., *Moral Order and the Question of Change*. New Haven, CT: Yale Southeast Asian Studies, pp. 9-52.

Diogo's Chronicle – *Chapter 3*

Anutra Hongsuwan and Worawut Semangoen (2000). *Somdet phrachao Taksin maharat* [King Taksin the Great]. Bangkok: Foundation for the Preservation of the Ancient Structures in the Former Grand Palace.

Breazeale, Kennon (1999). "Thai Maritime Trade and the Ministry Responsible," in Kennon Breazeale, ed., *From Japan to Arabia: Ayutthaya's Maritime Relations with Asia*. Bangkok. Foundation for the Promotion of Social Sciences and Humanities, pp.1-54.

Chanya Prachitromran (1994). *Somdet phrachao taksin maharat* [King Taksin the Great]. Bangkok: Chulalongkorn University Press.

Ishii, Yoneo (1986). *Sangha, State and Society: Thai Buddhism in History*. Honolulu: University of Hawaii Press.

Nidhi Eoseewong (1996). *Kanmoeang thai samai phrachao krung thonburi* [Thai Politics in the Time of the King of Thonburi]. Bangkok. Silpa Wathanatham.

Nidhi Eoseewong (2005). "The History of Bangkok in the Chronicles of Ayutthaya," in *Pen and Sail: Literature and History in Early Bangkok*. (Chris Baker and Ben Anderson, et al., trans. Chiangmai: Silkworm Books, pp. 289-341.

No Na Paknam (1993). *Chitrakam lao roeang: somdet phrachao taksin maharat phra phu ku chat na thong phra chao krung thonburi moeang boran* [Murals explained: King Taksin the Great, the King of Thonburi]. Bangkok: Muang Boran.

Suchaw Phloychum, ed. (1998). *Phra kiantikhun somset phra aryawongsayan somset phra sangkharat (si) wat rakhang kositaram* [In Honor of His Excellency Phra Ariyawongsayan, the Supreme Patriarch (Si), Wat Rakhang Khositaram]. Bangkok: Mahamakut Rachawithayalai.

Wyatt, David K. (1986). "Family Politics in Seventeenth- and Eighteenth-Century Siam," in Robert J. Bickner, et al., *Papers from a Conference on Thai Studies in Honor of William J. Gedney*. Ann Arbor, MI.: Center for South and Southeast Asian Studies, University of Michigan, pp. 257-265.

Diogo's Chronicle – *Chapter 4*

Adisorn Muakpimai (1995). "Chantaburi: A Gateway for the Coastal Trade of Ayudhya in the Eighteenth Century," in Kajit Jittasevi, ed., *Ayudhya and Asia: Proceedings for the International Workshop, 18-20 Dec. 1995*. Bangkok: Thammasat University, pp. 163-179.

Chandler, David P. (1973). "Cambodia Before the French: Politics in a Tributary Kingdom, 1794–1848," Ph.D. dissertation. University of Michigan.

Chandler, David P. (1996). *Facing the Cambodian Past: Selected Essays 1971–1994*. Chiangmai: Silkworm Books.

Manich Jumsai (2001). *History of Thailand and Cambodia*. 7th ed. Bangkok: Chalermnit.

Dewaraja, L. S. (1972). *The Kandyan Kingdom of Sri Lanka, 1707-1782*. Colombo: Lake House Investments.

Gerini, G. E. (1895). "Trial by Ordeal in Siam and the Siamese Law of Ordeals," *Asiatic Quarterly Review*, vol. 9, pp. 415-424 (April) and vol. 10, 156-175 (July).

Piyanart Bunnag (2000). "Religious Contacts between Sri Lanka and Thailand from the Pre-Colonial Period to the Colonial Period," *Asian Review 1999-2000*, vol. 13, pp. 12-35.

Srisak Vallibhotama (2002). *Ariyatham fang thale tawan ok* [Civilization Along the Eastern Seaboard]. Bangkok: Matichon.

Sumait Suchintranond (1999). "Mergui and Tenasserim as Leading Port Cities in the Context of Autonomous History," in Kenneth Breazeale, ed., *From Japan to Arabia: Ayutthaya's Maritime Relations with Asia*. Bangkok: Foundation for the Promotion of Social Sciences and Humanities Textbooks Project, pp. 104-118.

Diogo's Chronicle – *Chapter 5*

Antony, Robert J. (2003). *Like Froth Floating on the Sea: The World of Pirates and Seafarers in Late Imperial South China*. Berkeley: University of California, Institute of East Asian Studies.

Chang Ian-chiu (1991), "*Kan ophayop ma prathet thai khong chaw chianghai*" [The Migration of the Chianghai People to Thailand], in *Chaw chin taechiu nai prathet thai lae nai pumisamnao doem thi chaosan . . . (2310-2393)* [*The Taechiu Chinese in Thailand and in Their Former Homeland in Chaosan: The First Period, the Port of Changlin (1767-1850)*], Supang Chanthawanit, ed.. Bangkok: Institute of Asian Studies, Chulalongkorn University, pp. 27-35.

Cooke, Nola, and Li Tana, eds. (2004). *Water Frontier: Commerce and the Chinese in the Lower Mekong Region, 1750-1880*. Lanham, MD.: Rowman & Littlefield.

Chen, Chingho A. (1977). "Mac Thien Tu and Phraya Taksin: A Survey on Their Political Stand, Conflicts and Background," *Proceedings of the Seventh Conference of the International Association of Historians of Asia*, vol. 2, Bangkok, pp. 1534-1575.

Lapian, Adrian Bernard (1995). "Eighteenth-Century Power Politics in the South China Sea," in Kajit Jittasevi, ed., *Ayudhya and Asia: Proceedings for the International Workshop, 18-20 Dec. 1995*. Bangkok: Thammasat University, pp. 36-42.

Sakurai, Yumio, and Takako Kitagawa (1999). "Hatien or Banteay Meas in the Time of the Fall of Ayutthaya," in Kennon Breazeale, ed., *From Japan to Arabia: Ayutthaya's Maritime Relations with Asia*. Bangkok: Foundation for the Promotion of Social Sciences and Humanities Project, pp. 150-237.

Sellers, Nicholas (1983). *The Princes of Ha-Tien (1682-1867)*. Brussels: Thanh-Long.

Wanwipa Burutratanaphan (1991). "*Chaw chin taechiu nai sapap sangkhom thai samai thonburi lae rattanakosin ton ton*" [The Standing of the Taechiu Chinese in Thai Society in the Thonburi and Early Rattanakosin Periods], in *Chaw chin taechiu nai prathet thai lae nai pumisamnao doem thi chaosan . . . (2310-2393)* [The Taechiu Chinese in Thailand and in Their Former Chaosan Homeland . . . (1767-1850*)*], Supang Chanthawanit, ed. Bangkok: Institute of Asian Studies, Chulalongkorn University, pp. 88-113.

Diogo's Chronicle – *Chapter 6*

Chanya Prachitromran (1994). "*Asaewunki lom moeang phitsanulok*" [Asae Wunki Besieges Phitsanulok], in Chanya Prachitromran, ed., *Somdet phrachao taksin maharat* [King Taksin the Great]. Bangkok: Chulalongkorn University Press, pp. 157-205.

Macauley, Melissa (2021). *Distant Shores: Colonial Encounters on China's Maritime Frontier*. Princeton, NJ: Princeton University Press.

Phayre, Arthur P., Sir (1883 [1967 reprint]). *History of Burma*. 2nd ed. London: Susil Gupta.

Sarassawadee Ongsakul (2005). *History of Lan Na*. Chitraporn Tanranatanbakul, trans. Chiangmai: Silkworm Books.

South, Ashley (2003). *Mon Nationalism and Civil War in Burma: The Golden Sheldrake*. London: Routledge Curzon.

Yingcong Dai (2004). "A Disguised Defeat: The Myanmar Campaign of the Qing Dynasty," *Modern Asian Studies*, vol. 38, no. 1, pp. 145-189.

Diogo's Chronicle – *Chapter 7*

Banchoet Inthuchanthayong, ed. (1978). "Chaochom waen" [Royal Consort Waen], in Banchoet Inthuchanthayong, ed., *Phongsawadan krasip* [The Whispered Chronicles]. Bangkok: Praphansasan, pp. 128-134.

Butt, John W. (19778), "Thai Kingship and Religious Reforms (18th-19th Centuries)," in Bardwell Smith, ed., *Religion and Legitimation of Power in Thailand, Laos and Burma*. Chambersburg, PA: Anima Books, pp. 34-51.

Gesick, Lorraine (1983). "The Rise and Fall of King Taksin: A Drama of Buddhist Kingship," in Lorraine Gesick, ed., *Centers, Symbols, and Hierarchies: Essays on the Classical States of Southeast Asia*. New Haven.: Yale University Southeast Asia Studies, pp. 87-105.

Manich Jumsai (2000). *History of Laos*. 4th ed., Bangkok: Chalermnit.

Mayoury and Pheuiphanh Ngaosyvathn (1998). *Paths of Conflagration: Fifty Years of Diplomacy and Warfare in Laos, Thailand, and Vietnam, 1778-1828*. Ithaca, NY: Cornell University, Southeast Asia Program.

Pakon Kittitharo, Phra Maha, et al., eds. (2021?). *Wat Saket Rachaworawihan*. Bangkok.

Puangthong R. Pawakapan (2018). "Warfare and Depopulation of the Trans-Mekong Basin and the Revival of Siam's Economy," in Michael W. Charney and Kathryn Wellen, eds., *Warring Societies of Pre-Colonial Southeast Asia: Local Cultures of Conflict within a Regional Context*. Copenhagen: Nordic Institute of Asian Studies, pp. 21-46.

Pramin Khroeathong (2010). *Chamlae phaen yoet krung thonburi* [Dissection of the Plan to Seize Thonburi]. Bangkok: Matichon.

Pramin Khroeathong, ed., (2012). *Prisana phrachao taksin maharat* [The Riddle of King Taksin the Great]. Bangkok: Matichon.

Wyatt, David K. (1963). "Siam and Laos 1767-1827," *Journal of Southeast Asian History*, vol. 4, no.2, pp. 13-32.

Wyatt, David K. (1968). "Family Politics in Nineteenth-Century Thailand," *Journal of Southeast Asian History*, vol. 9, no.2, pp. 107-130.

Epilogue

Braudel, Fernand (1980). "The History of Civilizations: The Past Explains the Present," in Sarah Mathews, trans., *Fernand Braudel: On History*. Chicago: University of Chicago Press, pp. 177-218

Gaddis, John Lewis, 2002. *The Landscape of History: How Historians Map the Past*. New York: Oxford University Press.

Polhemus, Robert M., and Roger B. Henkle, eds. (1994). *Critical Reconstructions: The Relationships of Fiction and Life*. Stanford, CA: Stanford University Press

Schama, Simon (1991). *Dead Certainties (Unwarranted Speculations)*. New York: Vintage Books.

List of Maps

Map 1. The Ayutthaya Grand Palace and its royal environs, pre-1767 (p.65)

Map 2. The Burmese Advance on Ayutthaya, 1766 (p.94)

Map 3. The siege of Ayutthaya, late 1766 (p.97)

Map 4. The climactic assault on Ayutthaya, April 7, 1767 (p.103)

Map 5. Thonburi revival, c. 1776 (p.131)

Map 6. Reintegration of Siam under the Thonburi regime, 1768-1771 (p.135)

Map 7. The travels of Prince Thep Phiphit (Khaek), 1760-1768 (p.154)

Map 8. The travels of Prince Thip Phiphat (Sisang) and Prince Tui, 1759-1769 (p.155)

Map 9. Ha Tien and its neighborhood, 1771 (p.175)

Map 10. The Thai conquest of Ha Tien, 1771 (p.176)

Map 11. The Burmese campaign of 1775-1776 (p.198)

Map 12. The Phitsanulok theater of action, February-March, 1776 (p.202)

Map 13. The escape from Phitsanulok, March 15, 1776 (p.210)

Map 14. The coup, Thonburi, March 15, 1782 (p.240)

Map 15. The countercoup, Thonburi, March 26-April 6, 1782 (p.245)

List of Tables

Table 1. The Ban Phlu Luang Dynasty (principal personae), 1688-1767 (p.64)

Table 2. The Thonburi royal family (p.123)

Table 3. Ministries and ministers of the Thonburi reign, 1768-1782 (p.126)

Table 4. Cambodia's dynastic succession, 18th century (p.144)

Table 5. Major Siamese military campaigns and principal engagements, 1767-1782 (p.207)

Table 6. The Vientiane royal succession, 18th- early-19th centuries (p.223)

Table 7. Taksin family kinship links with the Chakri Dynasty (p.252-253)

Table 8. Ministries and ministers of the First Bangkok Reign, 1782-1809 (p.256)

Acknowledgements

I have been privileged to have received, through the various stages of this project's progress, the warm friendship and sound advice of John Loftus, Simon Landy, Chris Baker, Michael Montesano, Chalong Soontravanich, Thanapol Limapichat, and Kantasilo Bhiku. For their generous assistance in the preparation of the book's graphics and for software support, I thank Khanh Vu and Parker Van Roy, Ty Van Roy, Ronny Saulon, and Thanaroj Vanasrisawad. To attempt a listing of the many other Thai scholars whose brains I have picked along the way poses a challenge beyond my capacity. Let me simply thank them here collectively. It has been a pleasure to collaborate with my intrepid editor and publisher Narisa Chakrabongse and her staff in their fine physical production of this book. Lastly, but ever firstly, my thoughts lie with my dear wife Amporn and our children Jantra, Dan, and Ben and their spouses, and our grandchildren, all of whom in their inimitable ways have sustained me over the course of this lengthy project.

None of the above should be held accountable for any errors of fact or unwarranted opinion that may have crept into these pages. In my capacity as trustee of the translators, the late Claude Williams and Cláudio da Ceira, on whose behalf I have had the privilege of editing this work and bringing it into print, I can attest that we three retain sole responsibility for the contents of this book.

The mural of Wat Saket, within which Diogo's image appears (see the front cover illustration), portrays the tumultuous onslaught of the armies of Mara seeking to disrupt the meditations of the Buddha seated beneath the Bodhi tree.